FORGED BY A GOD.   FORETOLD BY A WIZARD.   FOUND BY A TEEN.

THE SWORD
AND THE
SOPHOMORE

AMERICAN MARTYR TRILOGY

B.P. SWEANY

Copyright © 2024 by B.P. Sweany

3WS Books, an imprint of Th3rd World Studios, Inc.
All rights reserved. Published by Th3rd World Studios, Inc. Publishers since 2007.
Th3rd World, Th3rd World Studios, and associated logos are trademarks
and/or registered trademarks of Th3rd World Studios, Inc.

Th3rd World Studios
12823 Pintail Drive
Ocean City MD 21842
www.th3rdworld.com

Ordering Information:
Quantity sales. Special discounts are available on quantity purchases by corporations, associations, and others. For details, contact the publisher at the address above.
Orders by U.S. trade bookstores and wholesalers.
Please contact- sales@th3rdworld.com.

Book Design by Brian Robertson
Illustration by Victor Maristane

Sweany, B.P.
The Sword and the Sophomore/B.P. Sweany. – 1st ed.
p. cm. – American Martyr Trilogy series; bk. 1)

Library of Congress Cataloging-In-Publication Data available upon request

ISBN: 978-1-956694-14-7

Printed in Canada
July 2024

10 9 8 7 6 5 4 3 2 1

First Edition

To Robin and Sophie,
without whom Rosemary would not exist.

The moon shall beest from wh're
the flote engluts the fallen son.
The lust b'rne tide, thy shalt subside,
the course of Avalon run.
H'r f'rtile song ne'er ov'r long
shalt play then play nay m're.
By thine blade, the bed is made.
The kingdom at thine doth'r.

—"Lust boren profecie," *Anonymous* [ca. 490 A.D.]

How, how can it be
That a love, carved out of caring
Fashioned by fate, could suffer so hard
From the games played much too often?
But making mistakes was a part of life's imperfections
Born of the years.
Was it so wrong to be human after all?

—Level 42, "Something About You" (1985)

CHAPTER

1

Sixteen years ago, give or take a millennium.

She stumbles outside the building made of reflective glass and red stone, the contractions noticeably ripping through her body. Two steps. Three steps. She loses her footing again, reaching for the wall beside the doors that slide open and closed of their own accord. She catches herself before she falls, but just barely.

I hide behind a tree as her water breaks. The people in aqua-blue vestments come to her aid, unfurling around her beneath the portico that reads *South Entrance Hospital Pavilion.*

The baby is coming early.

When the soon-to-be mother is asked her name, the reply catches in her throat. She groans once, twice. "Jennifer," she says. When asked the name of the baby's father, she answers, "My husband's name is Alan."

Neither "Jennifer" nor "Alan" are their given Christian names, but I will maintain this ruse on their behalf.

I saw Alan earlier that morning. He and Jennifer were standing outside as I walked by their house. Alan told Jennifer he was taking "a day trip sailing on the Chesapeake Bay" with some "friends from the pub." Jennifer nodded, saying something in reply that I couldn't hear from a distance.

Whilst observing them these last few weeks, I'd pieced together that they arrived in this place, in this time, roughly seven months ago. Right after Alan and Jennifer discovered she was pregnant and their world turned upside down. Neither of them carried around those personal communication devices people called "cell phones." Jennifer walked to the hospital because, I assumed, she could not yet afford a low-slung metal carriage.

Alan never had the time nor the inclination to sail when I knew him, but the water had always been his escape. Not so long ago, it was Jennifer's escape as well. When her husband was away, she would often rendezvous with Alan at his lake cabin, far from prying eyes. Even when Jennifer couldn't make it to the lake, a passageway beneath the stone bridge near her home allowed for many stolen moonlit kisses.

Jennifer loved Alan, and Alan loved Jennifer. They thought they could carry on with their illicit affair indefinitely, but theirs was the worst-kept secret in the kingdom. They were always being watched.

It seemed the water was no longer a shared experience for Alan and Jennifer. Nothing in their life seemed shared, really. The conversation I witnessed this morning was the same exchange they had every morning these last two weeks: Alan lamenting his commitments, Jennifer silently suffering from loneliness. It was as if she could not summon the courage to impose on him after he'd already sacrificed so much for her. His best friend, his kingdom. All of it gone. Even in the short time I'd been here watching them, I saw how that sacrifice weighed on Alan, in the way he withdrew from Jennifer's touch at times. I'd catch a wistful glint in his smoky blue eyes when he thought no one was looking. His eyes to the east. Always to the east.

This is not to suggest that Alan and Jennifer are alone in this world. The other person in their lives is a man, or a boy, depending on your perspective. Jennifer is still young, nineteen. Alan is in his thirties. Emrys Balin, that is what people call him here at least, appears to be somewhere in between the two in age.

It is Emrys who is waiting for Jennifer at the hospital.

I walk carefully behind a large man as I follow Jennifer into the hospital, using his girth to shield me from view. I sit on the opposite side of the room of the sick people, slumped in a chair, my face buried in a thin book of pictures that I grab off a nearby table. I'm still within earshot of Jennifer and Emrys, but barely. I peer over my book. An individual wearing the customary aqua-blue vestments taps her fingers on a board of individual lettered cubes while looking at a bright rectangle of illuminated words and asks Jennifer questions. Jennifer refers to Emrys as a "close family friend."

After a few more questions, Jennifer is surrounded by several more people in aqua-blue. The one giving the orders is distinguished by a long white coat. She is the one they call "doctor." I hear someone call her, "Dr. Mirren." They take Jennifer into the delivery room. Emrys does not follow her. He stands watching as Jennifer is wheeled away on a bed, then turns in my direction.

I lean in close to the large man to shield me from view. The man looks at me, fidgets uncomfortably. I know that Emrys will eventually sense my presence, but I am not ready for our reunion. Not yet.

The delivery was quick. Mother and child are resting now, attended to by a midwife. I hide in the small basin room attached to their larger room; the door cracked open enough for me to hear their conversation. The midwife just asked Jennifer about her English accent. I suspect the magical herbs they gave her during the procedure are doing the talking, as Jennifer is now presenting an inspired, albeit completely imagined, biography. She was a member of the British Archery Team before a surprise pregnancy derailed her Olympic ambitions, forcing her to move to the States with her fiancé. Her competency with a bow and arrow makes this lie believable. Jennifer is skilled with a lot of weapons—swords, axes, slings, bo staffs. Her father taught her how to use them, famously bragging to his friends on more than one occasion, "My daughter will grow up to be more prince than princess."

Jennifer had a beautiful baby girl, as Emrys and I knew she would. She named her daughter "Arlynn Rosemary." The name carries sentimental value that is obvious to me, although not to most. "Rosemary" is a version of Jennifer's original middle name, *Rosmarinus*. "Arlynn" is a combination of her two husband's names, Arthur and Alan. Arthur was Jennifer's first husband and Alan's best friend. Arthur didn't want to have any more kids after his son was born. He didn't mean to hurt Jennifer by neglecting to tell her about the bastard he had with another woman—just as Jennifer didn't mean to fall in love with Arthur's best friend.

Jennifer and Rosemary have fallen fast asleep after another successful feeding. The nurse retrieves Rosemary, tucks her into her crib, and exits the room.

I squint as I open the door and enter Jennifer's room. My eyes have not adjusted to these hard artificial lights, preferring the muted glow of a thick-wicked candle. If Jennifer wakes, she might recognize me; there is only so much that can be concealed by a white doctor's coat, bright lights, and a pair of eyeglasses. Then again, maybe Jennifer would not recognize me. We were always more acquaintances than friends. We never frequented the same gatherings, Jennifer being mortal and me being—well, not.

Ancient words come to me in an almost conversational flurry. The great secret of magic is that it is not unnatural; you are merely asking the world a different question and getting a different answer. I stand over Rosemary's crib, on the side opposite Jennifer's bed. Arms raised over Rosemary's sleeping form, I start to sway and chant. I hope I have enough left in me to cast this spell correctly. If someone had walked in at that moment, they might dismiss the vague buzzing sound as one of those flickering lights in the ceiling. That is, assuming they don't notice the tiny swaddled bundle in the crib glowing like a giant ember.

I open my eyes at his touch.

"Hello, Fay," the warm, familiar voice says. Too warm. Too familiar. Emrys Balin cradles my head in his lap.

Fay. Emrys is the only one who has ever called me that. It is a childhood nickname. A nickname given back when all I ever wished was that Emrys look at me the way he looks at my sister, Vivian. "I wondered when you and I would be reunited."

Emrys brushes my hair back from my brow. He is dressed plainly, in blue pants and a shirt rolled at the sleeves. His eyes travel down to the small brass placard on my white coat. "Dr. Mirren?"

"She's not using it right now," I say.

"I can see that," Emrys affirms. "Should I be worried?"

"The doctor is fine. It will be dismissed as a mere fainting spell."

"Looks like she isn't the only one fainting around here."

His comment was probably sincere, not that it matters. If there is one thing on this earth by which I cannot abide, it is a man's pity. "Spare me your condescension disguised as concern. I am still far more powerful than—"

"How many spells, Fay?"

"What do you mean?"

"How many did you do?"

I inhale a deep breath, then exhale. "Two."

"You shouldn't have done that to yourself. A cloaking spell? Really?"

"Never mind the cloaking spell," I say. "It was the temporal displacement spell to transport me here that about did me in. I've been here following you, Jennifer, and Alan for weeks, and I'm still not what I would call dependable on my feet."

"Oh, my dearest Fay…"

The look on his face confuses me. Concern? Remorse? Affection? Have we been apart so long that I can no longer read his emotions? "I am struggling, Emrys, to recall a time when I ever qualified as 'dearest' in your universe."

"Temporal displacement spells are dangerous, especially when they go horribly wrong."

"You should know," I counter.

Emrys ignores me. "And to throw on top of that a cloaking spell?"

"What else would you have me do?" Swatting away Emrys's hand, I sit up defiantly. "A cloaking spell will hide Rosemary's powers. You of all people should know he will not stop until he finds her. There's no telling what might eventually come after her—incubi, succubi. Those wretched demon scouts would have been already tracking Rosemary by her smell. She has a unique signature. You know this. The cloaking spell will mask that signature while limiting her powers."

Emrys has yet to break eye contact. He points back to himself and shrugs. "I'm the magician here. I should be the one lying in *your* lap right now."

"You should be so lucky." I hate it when Emrys does this, the flirting. To Emrys, it's innocent—the stroking of my hair, the staring.

To me it, it is everything. Or at least, it used to be everything.

"I still have a trick or two up my sleeve." Emrys's assertion sounds more like a hopeful guess than a boast.

"By the looks of things, two tricks might be pushing it." I reach up and rub his peach-fuzzed face. Seeing him here now, looking so young, brings back the old feelings. "Is it really you?"

He smiles while squeezing my hand. "I ask myself that same question every day I look in the mirror, expecting the man I was and seeing this boy's face staring back at me."

I try in vain to ignore the pang of want at seeing Emrys, who I once adored as an aged man many years my senior, now younger and even more attractive. "Oh, Mer—"

"Please," he interrupts, helping me to my feet. "It's Emrys here."

"Of course it is," I say. "My apologies."

"Took me a couple hundred years to get used to it. I'll cut you some slack for not nailing it on the first try."

"Cut me some slack? Nailing it?" They are sayings with which I am unfamiliar.

"Never mind," Emrys says. "It's good to see you, Fay."

I ignore the sentiment, reminding myself that I did not embark upon this quest to see Emrys. "When did you know?"

"That Jennifer was pregnant?"

I nod.

"The day I sent her away. How about you?"

"Soon thereafter," I say. "It has taken me this whole time to track you down."

"So you have been in Maryland how long?"

"As I said, a few weeks."

Emrys cocks his head. "And you waited until now to show yourself?"

"I had to be sure of your…" I trail off, the Fates whispering in my ear.

"My what?" Emrys asks, as if telling the Fates to mind their own house.

"Intentions," I answer.

Emrys presses on. "Does anyone else know you're here?"

"You think I'd go to the trouble of nearly killing myself traversing space and time, casting these soul-sucking spells, just to let myself be followed?"

"'Soul sucking.' You know that's what you've done, right? The cloaking spell gives the baby—gives Rosemary—a part of your soul to hide her identity. You're basically mortal now, even if you still retain a trace of your immortality. You might be long-lived, but you can die from injury or disease a lot more easily. And temporal displacement spells will diminish your powers for centuries. Believe me, I know. Is that what you want?"

"Please, Emrys." I exhale dismissively. "I have lived a thousand lifetimes and grow bored with the tedium. Perhaps knowing my life has limitations will make it more meaningful. And besides, contrary to your earlier sentiment, you're not the only magician here. If they come for Rosemary, they'll be looking for a donkey or a horse—but all that they will find is a mule."

"So, she's safe?"

And there's the Emrys I was once so accustomed to: feigning concern before obliviously segueing to the next girl in the room. "Our mutual enemy will not be able to find her, if that's what you are asking. Rosemary will still be of course enhanced as a child—a little stronger, a little faster. A cloaking spell can only do so much to diminish the magic inside this little girl. But to borrow a phrase from this world I have recently learned, she will 'remain off the grid' as long as no one fully activates her gift."

"Her *gift*?" The Emrys I knew had always been good at disguising most emotions, but this younger version of his self cannot contain his resentment. "I believe the word you're looking for is *curse*."

I place my hand on his shoulder. "*The moon shall beest from wh're the flote engluts the fallen son...*"

"You don't need to recite the prophecy to me." Emrys scolds. "Was I not the one who the goddess Arianrhod came to in a dream? Was I not the one who first sacrificed nearly all my powers to save Jennifer and Alan, to ultimately keep Rosemary away from, away from...*him*?"

"Then you of all people cannot deny the prophecy," I said.

"Sure, I can."

I reach for his hand. "I know you are well-intentioned, Emrys, but I think you might be too close to this. Rosemary cannot hide forever. At some point, she *will* need these powers, and the training that comes with them. Just think what would happen if *he* found her before she was capable of fighting him off."

"So eventually Rosemary will be a lot stronger and a lot faster?"

"All that and more."

"Well, she's going to need all that and more."

"I trust you to put her on the correct path, Emrys, to be her mentor and her—"

"Bestie?"

"Her what?" I ask.

"Bestie," Emrys says. "It is short for 'best friend.' Another word for it is 'BFF,' which stands for 'best friends forever.'"

"May I make an observation, Emrys?"

He bows slightly. "By all means."

"Twenty-first century vernacular fits you like an ill-fitting codpiece."

"Don't I know it?" Emrys smiles. "So what's left for you to do here?"

"Between finding you and cloaking Rosemary, I fear I am stranded for the foreseeable future. I guess I am what you call a tourist now. What can you tell me about this place called Mexico?"

Emrys shakes his head, smiling.

I bow again, stepping well back from the crib. "*Hwyl fawr, Myrddin.*"

It has most likely been centuries since anyone has spoken to Emrys in his native Welsh. He nods in appreciation of the gesture. "*Hwyl fawr, Muri-gena.*"

I kick off my white shoes. While comfortable, they are ghastly looking, also borrowed from Dr. Mirren. I focus on my body's movements more this time around, lifting onto my toes and spinning like a top until my scrubs and lab coat become a blur of blue-white light. I can feel my body starting to fall away, like a waterspout receding into a spring.

"Until we meet again," I whisper. I am disappearing into the ether, saying goodbye one more time to my dear Emrys. Leaving him to turn the page with a disinterested father, a weary mother, a newborn baby, and a pair of ugly hospital shoes.

"Uh, Fay?"

I open my eyes. "Why am I still here?"

"I told you those spells would tap you out," Emrys boasts. He reaches down into his pocket. "Allow me to help."

"Absolutely not," I snap, grabbing him by the wrist. "I do not need you to cast an enchantment on my behalf with whatever talisman or bauble lies hidden in your pocket."

Emrys wrenches his hand free from mine, retrieving his cell phone from his pocket. "I was just going to call you a cab."

"What is *a cab*?" I ask.

"It is a mode of transportation," Emrys answers.

"So this cab would convey me to Mexico?"

"Not technically. The cab will take you to a place where they have large vessels that will then fly you to Mexico."

"I am flying?" This was a welcome, unexpected surprise. "So I am to be escorted by this cab to a den of benevolent dragons?"

Emrys laughed. "I guess you could call an airport that."

CHAPTER

2

"Here you go, Dad," I said, handing him his satchel as he was halfway out the door. Tucked inside the satchel's front pocket was a toasted bagel with cream cheese. Mom made him one every morning, wrapping it in a napkin with a message scribbled on the front. Today the message read, *Have a great day, hon. Love, J.*

My father is classically handsome. Blue eyes, square-jawed, his thick hair never more than four weeks removed from a fresh cut. From as early as I could remember, women have acted weird around him, blushing and stumbling over their words. That only started bothering me when I entered high school and noticed even teenage girls blushing and stumbling.

Mom and I are less enamored by him. We have our reasons.

There were days I wondered what Dad did with all of Mom's notes. Today was not one of those days. I ran upstairs, skipping every other step. I poked my head into the master bathroom. "Hey, Mom."

My mother stood in front of the bathroom mirror, her face framed by a chest-length mass of brown curls. "Your father leave already?" she asked.

"Yeah." I nodded, wanting to tell her Dad had said something like, "Thanks for the bagel," or "Give your mother a kiss for me." But he never did.

Mom stared into the mirror, twirling a few wisps of hair around her right index finger. Dad may be classically handsome, but Mom is stunning. Her beauty is nearly as effortless as her confidence. Rather than battle the Maryland humidity with gallons of leave-in conditioner and a flat iron, she wears her hair back all the way from Memorial Day through Labor Day. She throws some soap and water on her face, maybe a little powder or moisturizer, and then walks out the door. That's it.

Unlike mine, her skin is unblemished, the color of Snickerdoodle cookie dough. Her mother, a grandmother long dead who I never met named Cynthia but pronounced "SEEN-cha," was from Portugal. She's the only relative either of my parents ever speak of. Neither have siblings, Dad's parents died when he was young, and Mom's father ran out on Grandma "SEEN-cha" after she was born. Mom told me not to worry about a little acne, because the darker oily skin on her side of the family didn't scar or wrinkle with age. "You'll look beautiful forever," she routinely assures me.

Beautiful forever? Moms are required to say these kinds of things to their daughters. My style tended to waver between trying too hard and not trying hard enough. I liked both dresses and yoga pants, but little in between.

After Benz broke up with me, the not-trying-hard-enough days tended to outnumber the trying-too-hard ones. Like Mom, I've become accustomed to pulling my hair back in a ponytail. Unlike Mom, I come off as more sloppy than carefree. People looked at Mom's unkempt look and said, "Jennifer, I just have to know, who does your hair?" People looked at me and asked, "Is everything okay, Rosemary?"

It didn't help that my hair couldn't make up its mind. In the winter months, I looked like my mother, hair straightened and the color of Maryland mud. By summer's end, my hair turned straw-gold and frizzy. More like my father's hair, but not quite.

"Rosemary?" Mom asked.

I was staring at her. "What?"

"Why are you just standing there?'

"Have you seen my favorite jeans?"

Mom looked at me curiously. It was a Monday after all, and I was already dressed in my school uniform. "Jeans?"

"Thinking about going to the movies after school with Joslin," I clarified.

"Have you tried your hamper?"

"My hamper?"

"Yes, Rosemary."

"My laundry hamper in my room?"

Mom cocked her head sideways, smirking. "You actually know what a laundry hamper is? That comes as a bit of a surprise to me."

I smirked right back at her. "You're funny, Mom."

"Funny nothing," she replied. "I counted four wet towels on your floor yesterday."

I had little leverage with my mother at this point. My bedroom smelled like dirty feet. "Make it six as of about twenty minutes ago."

Mom chuckled in spite of herself. "Rosemary, if you put your favorite jeans in the hamper, then that's probably where they still are."

"You mean you haven't done *any* of my laundry since last week?"

"I get confused in my old age. Are we talking about your normal laundry hamper, or the one equipped with a teleportation device that magically transports it to the laundry room without you moving it?"

"If only it were that easy," I said.

Mom was right of course. My laundry hamper was a problem. Never less than overflowing, its lid stood perpetually half-open in my closet, like a snake trying to choke down an animal twice its size.

Mom winked at me. "Rest assured that your tragic incapacity to do laundry is well-documented."

"Sorry, Mom, but not all of us have made a pact with the Devil that grants us the mystical power to fold a fitted sheet into a perfect square."

"Rosemary, you washed reds and whites together, in hot water."

"It was one load of whites. I was like twelve years old."

"Fifteen," Mom said. "You did it just last year. Ruined my favorite white sports bra."

"Yeah, but I got a free pink sports bra out of the deal."

My mother and her sports bras stood out in Severna Park, Maryland, a town halfway between Baltimore and Annapolis that was equal parts blue collar and blueblood. For her part, Mom was equal parts good mom and badass. While most of the moms relied on trainers, plastic surgeons, and Keto-friendly meal plans, Mom stayed in shape by hiking for hours at a time in the woods behind our house. We lived just north of Cypress Creek, along which Mom had built herself this wild obstacle course over the years with a moat, rope bridges, swinging vines, and a climbing wall.

Badass or not, Mom never asked me to work out with her because she knew she couldn't keep up with me. No one could keep up with me if I didn't want them to.

I tell myself it's just basic human physiology. I was a competitive gymnast when I was little, and in terms of strength-to-weight ratio, pre-teen girl gymnasts are proportionately the strongest athletes on the planet. I was the perfect storm of desire and athleticism. That plus I was old for my grade. Mom held me back in kindergarten. Last spring, I turned sixteen when most freshman were turning fifteen. I might be the only licensed driver in the entire American Martyr sophomore class.

The thing is though, I never really lost that edge. Even after my classmates caught up with me visibly, I was still faster and stronger than everyone. I continued to pull my punches—not running as fast as I knew I could run, not hitting the bullseye in archery class when I could hit it every time, not doing more push-ups and pull-ups than anyone, girl or boy, at American Martyr Preparatory School.

Who was I kidding? Mom could keep up with me. I just didn't work out with her because of the snakes.

Mom claimed she almost died from a snake bite as a child, which is why I was deathly afraid of them and why Mom never ventured into the woods without her trusty dandelion weeder—a three-foot-long wooden rod ending in a forked metal blade. After her workouts, Mom obsessively prowls the undergrowth, decapitating Copperheads and Timber rattlers with extreme prejudice. Like I said, badass. Not all snakes had reason to fear my mother, and she was careful to teach me which ones were non-venomous, like the Red Bellied water snakes and the Northern water snakes found along the creek beds, or the Black rat snakes and Eastern garter snakes in our garden. It wasn't a big garden—tomatoes and cucumbers, some herbs, the stuff that was easiest to grow—but the snakes seemed to like it.

Living close to the creek, we drop traps stuffed with chicken necks into the water and pull out blue crabs as big as our dinner plates. Mom and I paddle our canoe into the Magothy River and spend our summer days tanning on Manhattan Beach. Autumn has us picking apples from the abandoned creekside orchard for Mom's pies and our neighbor Hector's apple-infused moonshine. Come winter, the creek freezes over just enough to dare Hector, drunk on moonshine, to run across. He falls through the ice almost every time.

The day before had been a good Sunday at the beach. Unseasonably warm. Felt more like mid-summer than early fall. It hadn't rained in weeks, so the winding ribbon of brackish water connecting the North Cypress Branch stream bed to Cypress Creek had dried up into a green-brown wisp. Mom and I walked the canoe for the length of the stream bed, and then once we paddled out into the main Cypress Creek channel and into the Magothy, we ran into a bit of chop. But we managed.

Benz and I broke up a little less than three weeks ago. Mom kept trying to talk about it with me, but I shut her down. She always took advantage of these opportunities when we were stranded alone to try to gain intel on my personal life—like on drives to the doctor's office or the all-too-frequent occasions that Dad worked late and missed dinner. We would've stayed out even longer, but a security guard for the Manhattan Beach Homeowners Association kicked us off the beach. "Private property!" he shouted at us. "You can't just paddle up here like you own the place." Mom flipped him off as we paddled away.

Mom and I have always been "chuckaboos," a term we Bansons use to describe good friends. But lately, telling her everything about everybody had become just too weird for me. It was as if we both just woke up one day and chose to be occasional strangers to one another. Much of the time it was harmless—an inappropriate comment here or there that would be met with an eye roll. Other times it was not so harmless, like when the neighborhood wives invited her over for Bunco night. My life became theirs—that story I told Mom in confidence about my latest drama with Benz dropped casually in between rolls of Bunco dice. There were many things I would call my life, but "casual" wasn't one of them.

Kind of like right now.

"I'm thinking about getting a tattoo like yours," Mom said.

I had a rose vine tattooed on my right forearm the day after Benz broke up with me. An Annapolis tattoo parlor by the Naval Academy never checked IDs to see if you were eighteen. Two red roses bloomed about halfway between my wrist and elbow, nestled among a dark green tangle of leaves and thorns. The tattoo was above-average in size—something a little more substantial than your basic "spring break mistake" a tequila-fueled sorority girl gets stamped on her ankle. But I reassured my mother by saying it wasn't noticeable if I was wearing a long-sleeved shirt.

A tattoo was reasonably on-brand for me, boyfriend or no boyfriend. I defied authority with a semi-casual regularity. Just enough to notice, but not enough to get me into any kind of real trouble. I rotated my arm as I looked in Mom's bathroom mirror, the vanity lights picking up the red of the rose's petals. "Are you mocking me?" I asked.

"Mocking you?" Mom said. "I'm supporting you, Rosemary. You have a tattoo, now I'll get one. Screw Ebenezer!"

"Literally nobody calls him that, Mom." Still admiring my ink in the mirror, I yanked a black corded hairband off my opposite wrist. I pulled and tucked my hair into a loose bun, wrapping the hairband three times around its base. "I've heard a few of his teammates call him Coker, but that's about it."

My ex-boyfriend's name is Benz Cooke. Ebenezer is an old family name. Benz's dad, also an Ebenezer, goes by Eben.

Mom wasn't giving up. "What can I do to help get you out of this funk?"

"Who's in a funk?" I countered. "How about we just forget about Benz? I'm fine, and I sure as hell don't need you to permanently engrave something in your skin all in the name of mother-daughter solidarity."

"Maybe Benz just had cold feet?" Mom speculated.

Mom saw me at my worst after Benz broke up with me. I cried myself to sleep for several nights. You would think this memory would override her memory of Benz's habitual smile—his "gigglemug" as Mom and I call it—his way of comfortably talking to everyone, even grownups. But she didn't know the truth about Benz, about us. She didn't know I was no longer a virgin.

"Cold feet?" I said. "It's not like Benz left me at the altar. I was dumped by my high school boyfriend. It happens to a lot of girls. We get over it and move on."

If I said it enough times, maybe I would start believing it. But for now, the only person I needed to convince was my mother. The last thing she needed to know was that my heart was broken.

Broken was maybe a bit of an exaggeration. But a battered heart? Most certainly. Less certain was Mom's role in mending it. Welcome to bunco night, Jennifer. Shut up and roll the dice.

CHAPTER

3

"I think we can all agree that the theme for this year's Fall Fling should be, 'Too Much Fun in the Two-One World.'"

Student body president Avery DeVincent looked at us, her council, as she shuffled her papers. The boys fidgeted impatiently in their American Martyr Preparatory School standard-issue red polos and khaki pants, looking at the clock waiting for it to ring. I sat calmly with the female faction, all of us in matching white short-sleeve button downs and red-and-gray plaid skirts. An open box of bagels dotted the center of the round table.

Fall Fling was American Martyr's version of homecoming, a weeklong festival leading up to a Saturday dance the weekend before Thanksgiving. Homecomings had been sparsely attended for years, so the student council came up with the idea to push the party into November and cash in on the holiday season.

Avery DeVincent and I used to be friends when we were little kids. She was two years older than me, but we'd been gymnastics teammates from Pre-team all the way up to Level 9. I still do gymnastics whenever I can, but Avery quit the sport after she grew six inches her seventh grade year. All the girls in the gym made fun of Avery for about a month, which was basically how long it took for them to notice all the boys staring at her. I wasn't one of those who made fun of her, although she assumed I was. Once Avery decided she didn't like you, it was hard to get out of her doghouse.

Avery's crusade this morning was the music for Fall Fling. She'd become inexplicably obsessed with the new R&B trio Angels of Maybe and was intent on ramming their summer hit "Too Much Fun in the Two-One World" down our throats.

It was time to put another coat of paint on that doghouse.

"And by 'we can all agree,' you mean this is your unilateral decision?" I challenged.

Avery pretended to be surprised by my dissension. "And just what would you suggest for the theme, Rosemary?"

Planning Fall Fling was new to me, but talking music meant Avery was on my turf—or more accurately, my mother's turf. My childhood was filled with eighties and nineties alternative music. There was a song for every occasion.

"What would I suggest for the theme?" I pondered. "Probably something other than an overplayed techno rip-off of The Smithereens's 'Too Much Passion.'"

I was one of the sophomore reps, currently serving my second year in student government. My term in office has had its highs and lows. As a freshman, I convinced the school to replace the plastic straws in the cafeteria with paper straws—a less-than-popular choice, given the tendency of paper straws to dissolve into mush the moment they get wet. While I wasn't much of a joiner, still feeling my way around the cliques and clubs of American Martyr, I enjoyed student council. More to the point, I enjoyed one-upping Avery. I had my reasons for disliking her.

"The Smithereens?" Avery asked.

"They're a band from the nineties."

"I've never heard of them."

"Your loss."

The plum-haired girl beside me laughed. Avery glared at her. "Do you have something to add to this discussion, Joslin?"

Joslin Kelly reached down to the plate in front of her. She smiled, raising the sesame seed-covered ring of dough to eye level. "I'm just here for the free bagels, Madame President."

Joslin and I have been best friends for going on eight years, ever since she moved to Severna Park in the middle of elementary school. That was when she first dyed her hair purple, the color it has been ever since. Sorry, *plum*. Joslin insists her hair is plum-colored. She gets annoyed when people say it's purple.

"How about 'Wonderful Tonight?'" I asked.

"What?" Avery said.

"That's my suggestion: Eric Clapton's 'Wonderful Tonight.'"

A collective "*Awwwwww!*" filled the room.

I guess we could chalk one up to Team Dork. "Wonderful Tonight" beat out "Too Much Fun in the Two-One World" by a vote of seven to one.

My mother taught me never to underestimate the nostalgic, irresistible pull of classic rock. No one in student council probably knew Eric Clapton beyond "Wonderful Tonight" and a few chords of the acoustic version of "Layla," but that was enough.

On her way out the door, Avery said to the freshman and sophomore officers, "Enjoy Fall Fling, underclassmen, because come May, I'm going to throw the biggest Angels of Maybe-themed senior prom American Martyr Prep has ever seen, and there's nothing you can do about it." We all looked at one another, an unspoken acknowledgment between us that we would somehow manage to get over it.

My locker was just across the hall from the student council room. Joslin stood in front of it, waiting for me. Avery walked by us. With a flip of her hair, she headed in the direction of the senior hallway.

"Nice work in there," Joslin said.

Opening my locker, I nodded at the back of Avery's head as she walked away. "Her Royal Highness might disagree with you."

"It isn't that bad, you know," Joslin said.

"What isn't that bad?" I asked. "The way Avery treats everybody?"

"No, the song. 'Too Much Fun in the Two-One World.' It's really quite catchy. *Too much fun in the two-one world, the eighties can't handle these two-one girls. Leave the nineties for your daddy and your mo', cuz there ain't no place better than the twenty double-oh.* It's an anthem to the twenty-first century."

My eye roll was immediate and sincere. "Yeah. I know what the song means. And it's still terrible."

"Your opinion," Joslin countered.

"You're better than that music, Joslin. They call themselves Angels of Maybe."

"So?"

"So? Consent is kind of a big deal, especially in the 2020s. I wouldn't think you'd let something like that slide."

Joslin shrugged. "What are you talking about?"

"Angels of *Maybe*. That means they never say 'no,' to boys, in bed."

"I see it as just the opposite. They're telling us that not only does 'no' mean 'no,' but 'maybe' means 'no.' Only 'yes' means 'yes.'"

I slammed my locker door shut. "You're seriously off your game today. I would argue that 'maybe' is closer to 'yes' than 'no,' and that the band's willful ambiguity sets feminism back a hundred years."

"And I would argue that *maybe* I'm just distracted because my best friend ignored me all weekend," Joslin replied. "Where were you? Texted you a bunch of times."

"I know. Sorry about that. Wasn't up for much of anything. I was just hanging with my mom. Kind of felt under the weather."

"I have some green tea and honey in a thermos in my locker. It's still warm."

Joslin believed green tea mixed with a teaspoon of honey cured everything from a cold to HPV. "Thanks, but no thanks," I said. "I'll be fine."

"Under the weather, huh?" Joslin eyed me skeptically. "It's Benz, isn't it?"

I looked around to make sure nobody was listening. The lump lodged firmly in my throat, I leaned in like I had a secret to share. "I just can't stop thinking about the way we broke up. I can't get that night out of my head."

She squeezed my shoulder, nodding. "You shared something intimate and instead of bringing you closer, it drove you apart. You're not the first couple to go through that, and you won't be the last."

Joslin was an expert at disarming me. She had a way of straight talking without ever judging. I didn't know what it was: her voice, her smile, the recognition that whatever I told her in confidence never went beyond us. People thought I was the cool one in our friendship, but I'd never be as cool as Joslin. The lump in my throat verged on real tears.

Joslin noticed. "I'm sorry, Rosemary. I don't know what to say except, love freaking sucks."

I sniffed, wiping my nose, the sadness already dissipating. "It sure does."

Convinced I was reassured, Joslin waved her thumb over her shoulder. "Walk you to class?"

"I'm good." I said, starting to lean in the opposite direction.

"Don't do it," Joslin said.

"Do what?"

"You're following Avery to Benz's locker."

There really was no mystery as to why Avery annoyed me. Word spread quickly, as word tended to do at American Martyr. Avery and Benz were an item. The two most popular seniors at American Martyr, if not the two most beautiful humans in Severna Park. Given their shared circle of friends and social status, they just made sense together. Benz and I never made sense, no matter how much he claimed to like my confidence or that I was "different." I was not the other woman; I was the other *girl*—a child by comparison. Avery was way out of my league. I was jealous of her. Jealous of *them*.

"I'm not following anybody," I said dismissively.

"What are you going to do, start a fight?"

"Maybe."

Joslin shook her head from side to side as she turned her back to me. "Well, I'm not going to be your accomplice."

"I don't need an accomplice."

"Fine," Joslin said.

"Fine," I shot right back.

Everyone was already in class, so Avery and I had the hallway to ourselves. I rounded the corner just as she walked away from Benz's locker. She didn't see me, but someone else did.

I recognized him immediately. He'd introduced himself to me back in August at student orientation. I was one of the student council members who volunteered to give school tours, and by that I mean Avery wrote my name on the sign-up sheet. His name is Emrys. He's a foreign exchange student from who knows where. Scotland maybe? He kept interrupting me during the tour of the weight room with oddly specific questions about what kind of workouts I liked to do. He seemed to be always lurking around and randomly showing up wherever I happened to be. His general oddness was tough to navigate, but I just figured he was lonely, so I cut him some slack.

"Is there a problem, Emrys?" I asked.

"N-no, no problem at all," he stuttered, spinning on his heels and fleeing the scene like he'd been caught doing something he shouldn't have been doing.

Benz's locker was about halfway down the hall. I'd decorated it weeks ago for a football game. The faint white chalk paint outline of GOOD LUCK, BENZ bracketed in hearts and smiley faces was still visible. I reached for his lock, spinning the dial to the right, to the left, and to the right once more. I knew the combination by heart.

The inside of Benz's locker read like a collage of our relationship. His letter jacket hung on a hook, my lipstick still visible on the collar. He said I did that on purpose, to mark my territory. He was right. The word "Rosemary" was etched in my handwriting on the fore-edge of a solitary geometry textbook—the last of Benz's classes not to go fully online. Multiple pictures of me, of us, were plastered on the inside of his locker door. Benz was a bit old school. If his other classes offered physical text books, he'd probably buy them. He preferred photos, *physical* photos, over pictures on a phone or an Instagram story. A printout of a first-date selfie, taken after I'd made the mistake of letting Mom cut my hair. Me sitting on his lap on the dock behind his house. A black and white close-up of me sleeping.

This was still the locker of a boyfriend, not an ex-boyfriend. It made me sad. So sad that I almost failed to notice the plastic bag tucked in Benz's letter jacket pocket.

I took the bag from Benz's pocket. They were brownies loaded with chocolate chips, Benz's favorite. Massaging the bag with my hand, I could tell they'd been baked that morning and quickly thrown in the bag because the chocolate chips had melted and smeared everywhere. There was a note inside, neatly folded in half, inscribed with hand-drawn hearts that bled through the paper from the moisture inside the bag. I grabbed the note, unfolding it with a mixture of anxiety and curiosity.

Eight words. That's all she wrote to him. But that's all she had to write to him.

Surprise! For after the game, superstar...Love, Avery.

Love. Avery.

Benz had ripped out my heart. The least I could do was rip up his new girlfriend's love letter.

"Rosemary Banson," the woman's voice said on the other side of the locker door. "Just *what* do you think you're doing?"

"Littering?" I crouched down and started to pick up my trash. With each successive scrap of paper, I counted off inside my head, *he loves me, he loves me not.*

"I see that," Ms. Vandergriff said, offering her scooped hand.

I handed her the Avery confetti, trying to ignore the fact I ended on a *he loves me not.* I stuffed the brownies into my pocket while simultaneously shutting Benz's locker door. "Sorry, Ms. Vandergriff. I was just getting some of my things out of my boyfriend's locker. Well, *ex*-boyfriend. Hence the getting some of my things."

Ms. Vandergriff's gaze was measured, more sympathetic than judgmental, which was probably why she was a guidance counselor and not a teacher. She hooked my arm in hers. "Let's take a walk, shall we?"

The black and white analog clock on Ms. Vandergriff's office wall punctuated the silence, each tick of the second hand drawing me closer to either punishment or reprieve.

"We have to stop meeting like this," I said.

"This isn't a joke, Rosemary. It's only October, and half your teachers are telling me you're already skipping class."

"Half my teachers?" I leaned back in my chair, defiant for no reason. "More like two of my teachers."

"More like your Honors Pre-calculus and AP U.S. History teachers."

"So what."

"I'm trying to be your friend here, Rosemary." Ms. Vandergriff stood behind her desk, hovering. She opened my file and started reading some of my progress reports aloud. "Too smart for her own good. Often tries to get by on charm and humor when only hard work will do. Somehow manages to always earn good grades while never arriving to class on time...ever."

"Guilty on all counts," I affirmed. "I pride myself on straddling the line between academic excellence and juvenile delinquency."

Ms. Vandergriff switched gears, ignoring my flippancy. "How are your mom and dad?"

"Same as always," I answered.

"Is that a good thing?"

"For them it is, I guess."

"What's that supposed to mean?"

This was where I should have told Ms. Vandergriff that my parents had become strangers to one another. My father was a workaholic, and it was ripping my family apart. Why did I so immediately recognize my heart was broken after Benz dumped me? Because the look staring back at me in the mirror was the same one on my mother's face. That look she'd get every morning Dad walked out the door to work without saying, *I love you, Jennifer.*

I wanted to say all these things and more. But instead, all I could muster was, "They got their routine. Seems to work for them."

Shaking her head, Ms. Vandergriff circled around her desk until she stood directly in front of me. It was her favorite spot for a face-to-face chat—right next to her student, leaning against the edge of her desk, with her elbows slightly bent and bracing herself with her hands. She still had that bronzed look of a summer spent sunbathing with cheap erotica novels and even cheaper white wine. This was more than just an educated guess on my part. I called her Katie outside the office. We both belonged to the Severn River Swim Club. She never tried too hard to hide the shirtless cowboys on the covers of her romance paperbacks, or the empty travel bottles of white wine sticking out of her beach bag.

"Can we talk frankly, Rosemary?"

"Always," I assured her.

Ms. Vandergriff raised her right hand to her chest, balling it up to a fist. She rotated her fist in two clockwise motions.

She was signing to me. An inside joke between us since Ms.

24

Vandergriff convinced me to take the course as an elective my freshman year. It was either that or Intro to Jewelry.

"You're sorry?" I said. "What are you apologizing for?"

"For whatever, or should I say *whoever*, is hurting you."

"Look, Ms. Vandergriff, I'm totally fine. Benz and I—"

"*Ex*-boyfriend, huh?"

"Yeah, we broke up."

"I can see why you might be a little distracted. He seems like such a sweet kid."

"Yeah, he's quite the charmer. Can we just get this over with? I assume you didn't bring me in here to talk about my boy trouble."

"I just thought you might need someone to talk to."

"Well, you're mistaken."

"Rosemary," she said in her best soothing tone. "If you wish to get into a good college, Honors Pre-calc and AP U.S. History are the types of classes you can't just coast through."

"Then change my schedule so these classes don't come before and after lunch period."

"The last thing you need is a three-hour lunch."

Folding my arms, I shook my head. "Oh, please. So I take long lunches. Who am I hurting? Half the girls in this school don't even eat lunch."

Ms. Vandergriff leaned back against the edge of the desk, shadowing me with folded arms of her own. "You know, Rosemary, for being a self-professed feminist, your quips and barbs about your fellow female classmates can be quite regressive."

"Is that your roundabout way of saying I'm mean? I'm not mean. People like me."

"Yeah, but do *you* like yourself?"

"Um, I'm a teenage girl," I said, shrugging. "Not liking myself is kind of part of the job description."

Ms. Vandergriff tilted her head to the side, shaking her finger in the air. "A bit harsh and again, regressive." She started back around her desk, but stopped suddenly, sniffing the air. "Rosemary?"

"Yes, Ms. Vandergriff?"

She nodded at the plastic bag poking out of my pocket. "Do I smell brownies?"

I extracted the plastic bag from my pocket. "Well, yeah."

"Chocolate chips baked in?"

"Pretty sure." I felt a little bit like Robin Hood. At this point, my only choice was to carry the theft to its natural conclusion and redistribute the wealth. "You want one?"

"If you're offering." Ms. Vandergriff grabbed a brownie out of the bag, a childlike eagerness in her eyes. She took a bite, but her look wasn't what I expected, more puzzlement than satisfaction.

"Something wrong with your bone box, Ms. Vandergriff?"

She tried to clear her throat, holding her hand over her mouth as she chewed—that thing older women always do in public, as if they're embarrassed for the world to know that they eat. "My what?"

"Your bone box," I said, tapping my mouth with my finger. "It's one of many 'Jenniferisms' I get from my mother. Your mouth is your 'bone box,' although I don't use that one in everyday conversation because nobody seems to know what I'm talking about. Your friends are 'chuckaboos,' smiles are called 'gigglemugs,' and Banson women are never, ever depressed. We just 'get the morbs.' It's stupid, but funny."

Ms. Vandergriff wasn't laughing. She swallowed and tapped her throat. Dipping her chin, she winced, like she was struggling with the bite.

"Are you choking?" I asked.

Mrs. Vandergriff shook her head. She snatched the brownies out of my hand, staring accusingly at the bag and then at me.

Oh my God, I thought, *Avery's brownies are poisoned.* "Do they have nuts in them? Are you allergic to nuts?"

Mrs. Vandergriff shook her head again, coughing to clear her throat. "No allergies. I'll be fine. But the brownies. They taste—"

"They taste bad, don't they?" My reaction was almost too immediate, too eager. Mere seconds after realizing my guidance counselor was neither choking to death nor about to go into anaphylactic shock, I was concerned only with confirmation that Avery was a terrible baker.

"It's not that the brownies taste bad, Rosemary," Ms. Vandergriff said. "It's that they taste like marijuana."

And at that moment I pictured Avery somewhere laughing manically, the Angels of Maybe debut album playing in her earbuds.

CHAPTER

4

Lying in my bed at home, I stared at the ceiling. A Bob Marley "One Love" tapestry hung above my bed. Bob peered just over my right shoulder, refusing to make eye contact, like any man with intimacy issues. Given that he had something like fourteen children by nine different women, I assumed the "one" love thing was a metaphor.

Level 42's *World Machine* album spun on my cassette deck, part of a vintage stereo console I got off eBay for fifty bucks. I bought the stereo after I found a milk crate of Mom's cassettes in the attic, a hodge-podge of eighties and nineties alternative music. Mom being British, she was partial to British New Wave, especially Depeche Mode, The Cure, and Duran Duran. My preferences trended Brit as well, but a little more obscure toward bands like Level 42, Haircut 100, and The Church. Okay, The Church was technically Australian, but close enough.

Mom pressed "Stop" on the cassette player in my bedroom. She'd been quiet the entire drive home from the police station. She was ever quieter now, as she had snuck into my room unnoticed.

"Hey, I was listening to that."

She had little patience for my attitude. I feared it was lecture time. "Sit up," she insisted.

Like many high school days, I wished today had never happened. Ms. Vandergriff was required to report me to Headmaster Benedict, who in turn was required to call the authorities and my parents. My guidance counselor seemed to regret her decision almost immediately, especially when the police officers arrived. My headmaster? Not so much.

Monsignor Julius Benedict enjoyed making an example out of me. American Martyr was an elite Catholic prep school loaded with silver-spooners and overachievers who didn't have much respect for the good monsignor. For the most part, we all called him "Father Jules," rarely called him "Monsignor," and never called him "Headmaster." The school board's disciplinary committee was weak and toothless in Father Jules's mind. About the worst punishment he was ever authorized to impose was when he turned off all the Coke machines in the student commons for a month after someone kept pulling the fire alarm.

Father Jules was the one who tried to mandate separate boys' and girls' trophies for Field Day after I swept all the events in the third grade. His administrative career seemed to progress lockstep with mine. He was principal at St. John Neumann the day I showed up for kindergarten all the way through my eighth grade year, and then the diocese promoted him to Headmaster of American Martyr when I was a freshman. Every year along the way, Father Jules seemed to find a reason to punish me. Granted, sometimes I made it really easy for him to find a reason: locking a mean substitute teacher in a utility closet in the fourth grade; kiss and tag games I organized before sixth grade cotillion class; sneaking away from my eighth grade D.C. field trip to meet a boy I met at summer camp at a Washington Nationals baseball game. I was, to put it mildly, a tad precocious.

"Sit up, Rosemary," Mom repeated. "Please."

I spun my feet around until I was perched on the side of the bed, my hands at my sides. Mom sat down next to me. The antique wrought iron bed responded to our movements with its usual chorus of springy squawks. Needless to say, Benz and I could never get away with anything on that bed.

Other than harassing me, most of the time it seemed like Father Jules's only job was marching menacingly up and down the hallway in his long, flowing black cassock. The Catholic priesthood had largely dispensed with this monkish look well over a century ago, going with the far more practical jacket and pants combination. But not Father Jules. His goal was always to instill fear more than respect, and he rarely had a chance like my arrest to flex his muscles. Father Jules never stopped smiling as they handcuffed me in his office. When the police asked if there was a back way out of the school to avoid any potential commotion, he insisted they escort me through the student commons area. They didn't even let me change into my favorite pair of jeans. The last person I saw as they walked me out the door on my way to jail was Benz.

"Look, Mom, I know what you're going to ask me."

The bed squawked, magnifying Mom's annoyance. "Do you?"

Today would probably qualify as real trouble, although as a first-time offender I got off easy. Mom and Dad showed up to the police station with one of Dad's attorney friends, a gentle-voiced bearded man named Daniel Schuetz who wore a sport coat with elbow patches and insisted I call him "Daniel" instead of "Mr. Schuetz." Words were exchanged with the prosecutor, a woman named Dorothy who Daniel called "Dot." Daniel smiled when he liked what Dot said, scratched his beard when he disagreed with her. In the end, they granted me something called a pretrial diversion. No jail time, no court appearance. Just a small fine, followed by probation and restitution.

"The brownies weren't mine," I said. "I didn't eat or smoke anything. I've never eaten or smoked anything."

Mom shook her head, unconvinced. "How naïve do you think I am?"

"Not very."

"Exactly."

"Which is why I'm telling you the truth."

"Rosemary, come on."

"You want me to pee in a cup? Because I'll pee in a cup."

"I don't need you to pee in a cup."

"What *do* you need, Mom?"

"I know it hasn't been easy, with your father putting in so many hours at the Naval Academy."

"I have a father?"

"*Rosemary*," Mom scolded.

"Are you talking about that strange man who showed up with Daniel to bust me out of jail then went right back to his office for the rest of the night?"

Dad had been angling for a big promotion in the history department at the Naval Academy for the better part of my teenage years. Mom kept reassuring me that once he was offered Department Chair, things were going to slow down. I had little confidence in this happening. Dad chose work over us a long time ago.

Mom ignored my snide comments. "And I know I'm overbearing, and that I stick my nose in where I shouldn't, and that I try too hard to be your friend."

"Mom, you might find this hard to believe, but this isn't about you." I sprang up from the bed and walked across the room, anything to distance myself from the conversation.

Mom stood, closing the gap between us on nimble feet. She grabbed me by the side of my arms. "It's about *us*, Rosemary. We're a team, aren't we?"

I tried not to make eye contact. "I guess."

"You guess?"

"You can choose your friends," I said, "but you can't choose your parents."

"Gee, Rosemary, that's comforting." Mom released me, retreating to a neutral corner. There weren't a whole lot of neutral corners left in our house, but I felt like no matter what, Mom would always be on my side. She didn't deserve this from me. I was taking my resentment of Dad out on her.

"I don't mean that in a bad way. I mean, of course we're a team. You're my mom. I love you."

Mom seemed to accept my contrition as genuine. She edged back toward me, into the center of my bedroom. "And I love you too, Rosemary, but I can't just overlook the drug thing."

"I told you, they weren't my pot brownies. I've never smoked, vaped, inhaled or eaten any weed of any kind. I don't even know what being stoned feels like. Is it nice? Is it better than being drunk? Have you done it?"

"Now you're deflecting."

"I take that as a 'yes'?"

"My answer is immaterial to your mistake," Mom said. "You talk to Benz lately?"

Mom's deflection game was more on point than mine. She had managed to somehow segue in mid-deflection to asking about my ex-boyfriend. "Uh, can we maybe go back to talking about marijuana?"

She shrugged. "Just curious."

"Benz and I are done. Why would you even ask me about him? What happened to 'Screw Benz'? What happened to wanting to be my tattoo sister?"

I tried not to snap at her. Mom was still on my team, not Benz's. Sometimes she just couldn't help herself, and I was okay with that because here's the thing: Mom was more than just a helpless romantic. She loved being in love, but she also loved watching other people feel love, responding to affection. This compulsion unfortunately manifested itself in her being flirtatious, almost out of habit. Sometimes she flirted to attract Dad's attention, but other times she flirted to secure that bright-eyed appreciative smile from a stranger that she couldn't induce in her husband. Her act was convincing— the forced laughter, the presumptuous touching, the cursory "Have you lost weight, Bob?" when in fact our next-door neighbor's waist was just as thick and his hair just as thin as ever. Dad largely ignored her in these moments. He ignored her in most moments.

"Rosemary, I'm sor—"

I reached for my mother's hand. "Don't, Mom."

"Don't what?"

"You don't need to apologize to me." I took Mom's hand in mine. Her hands were the only indicator of her age. Wrinkled at the knuckles, her fingertips calloused. They were working hands, digging in the dirt hands, a mother's hands. "You are an amazing woman, and Dad notices."

Mom flipped her hand in mine, our palms meeting. She squeezed my hand reassuringly, a gigglemug streaking across her face. "You're a terrible liar, Rosemary, but thanks anyway."

CHAPTER

5

"Keep your hands off him," I muttered under my breath. "Those are my shoulder pads!"

Joslin shook her head. "This is embarrassing."

"No one forced you to come with me."

"Someone had to save you."

"From what?" I asked.

"Yourself."

We were hiding under the bleachers watching the football team practice. It was their usual non-contact Thursday run-through before tomorrow night's game—helmets and shoulder pads with shorts. Benz had just come off the field for a water break. Avery bounced right over to him in her cheerleading outfit, her short skirt sprouting almost impossibly toned legs.

Avery handed Benz a water bottle. He nodded, leaned in and said something to her. She smiled. She reached up and tugged at his jersey sleeve, which had gotten caught under one of his shoulder pads. I saw him mouth the words "thank you" as he handed the water bottle back to her. Their hands touched. Avery bounced away, backwards this time so she could maintain eye contact. She held her extended pinkie and index fingers to the side of her head while mouthing "call me" back to him. That was when I lost it.

"God dang it!" I shouted, throwing my fist in the air. The

wooden bleacher above me splintered as my hand punched a hole clean through.

Joslin stared at me. "What has Jennifer been feeding you?"

"Bleacher must have been rotted," I observed. "I probably just saved someone's life."

I said this casually, hoping Joslin would just nod in agreement and move the conversation along. My mother wasn't feeding me anything special, but the evidence that I was special—gifted, exceptional, talented, whatever you wanted to call it—was certainly there from our childhoods.

My best friend shook her head. "Do we really need to rehash this every time you exhibit some random act of freakish athleticism?"

"No, but you seem to insist upon rehashing it, so…"

"Third grade, St. John Neumann Field Day," Joslin recited. "Fastest grades one through four fifty-yard dash, girl or boy. Fastest grades one through four hundred-yard dash, girl or boy. Most push-ups and pull-ups grades one through four, girl or boy. How many pull-ups did you end up doing that day—thirty-seven or something crazy like that?"

I actually did forty-seven pull-ups, and I only stopped because I was bored. The second place finisher, a boy twice my size, did twenty pull-ups. In the hundred-yard dash, my bandana fell off my head, I broke stride to catch it, and still beat the fastest fourth grade boy by a nose. After I kept winning, the principal at St. John Neumann tried to insist that Field Day organizers separate the events into boys' and girls' categories, but they didn't have enough trophies.

There was more than just third grade Field Day, if I was being honest. For sure I was fast and strong, but I was a quick healer too. I'd bleed and bruise up like any kid, but my recoveries were always quicker than they should have been. A doctor would tell me, "Stay off that bad ankle for the next three or four days, Rosemary," and I was fine by the next morning. Seasonal flus that would gut my entire school barely gave me a runny nose. But Joslin almost never dwelled on these moments. She treated my physical quirks like a pimple in the middle of my forehead or a bad outfit choice; they were things I'd deal with, and her two cents would do more to annoy me than make them go away. She was my best friend. My chuckaboo of chuckaboos. The person who would defend me to her dying breath when I said things like, "I'm not really feeling Jesus today" or "*Grease 2* is better than the original."

"Don't be so modest," Joslin said. "God knows where in that hundred and nothing pound body you store all that muscle."

While an acknowledgment was unusual for Joslin, I appreciated her effort enough to string her along. "I also had a good workout in the gym today and am just feeling a little amped up."

"Some workout," Joslin acknowledged again. "But speaking of the gym, I ran into the fencing team today. They asked if I was joining you for gymnastics tonight, which is funny, because I thought we had movie night plans."

The fencing coaches lorded over the gym at night and seemed to know my workout schedule better than I did. "Oh crap, I forgot to tell you. I'm sorry, Joslin. With everything that's been going on with my new career as a drug dealer, I just needed to blow off some steam and clear my head."

I thought my sarcasm would land, but it did not. Joslin didn't laugh. She barely even cracked a smile. "So, raincheck, *again?*"

"Look, I'm really sorry," I answered. Lately, my rainchecks with Joslin had been piling up. Being boy crazy gave me tunnel vision, and weeks after our breakup I was still in the middle of a massive Benz hangover. I knew that, and so did Joslin.

"You know, Rosemary, even without the boyfriend dragging you down, you still manage to be an extremely unreliable best friend."

"Thanks," I said.

"You're welcome," Joslin replied.

"Okay, fine. You win."

"What do I win?" Joslin asked.

"Your raincheck. What are you doing for Fall Fling?"

Joslin shrugged her shoulders. "Nothing."

"You're going to make me ask, aren't you?"

She nodded. "Yep."

I grabbed her hand in mine, holding it to my heart while trying not to laugh. "Joslin, my dearest chuckaboo, who puts up with my crap spectacularly and with endless patience, will you be my date to Fall Fling?"

Joslin shrugged, her head bobbing like she was thinking it over. "Sure, I got nothing better to do."

This was usually when Joslin would try to sneak a look at my injury, and I'd pretend I didn't notice. But she was looking past me, back over my shoulder to the darkened corner of the bleachers.

"What are you looking at, girlfriend?"

"Over there." Joslin nodded as she leaned in toward me, whispering. "The skinny kid with the bushy brown hair watching us under the bleachers."

"That's Emrys," I said.

Joslin was more curious about his sudden appearance than I was. "Who?"

"Emrys Balin," I clarified. "He's a foreign exchange student."

"From where?"

I shrugged. "I want to say Scotland. Does that sound right?"

"If I knew, I wouldn't be asking you," Joslin replied. "Should we be concerned?"

"Concerned?"

Joslin nodded.

"He does kind of give off that stalker vibe, doesn't he?"

I said this without really meaning it. Emrys gave off a vibe for sure, but it wasn't necessarily off-putting. It was interesting—weird but in a good way. To quote Michelle Pfeiffer from *Grease 2*, "Not *weird* weird, but, like, exciting weird."

CHAPTER
6

My first tumbling pass was simple but strenuous: a few roundoff back handsprings and side aerials. Once my adrenaline was flowing, I worked my way to some more aggressive combinations.

Gymnastics has always been my escape. I don't have a specialty. Vault, uneven bars, balance beam, floor: all of them come easily to me. I had the scores and the skills to qualify for the U.S. National Team, or to at least be competitive at the Elite level. Coaches knocked on our door, literally, but Mom always turned them away. She said it was because she wanted me to have a normal life.

Last spring, the local club disbanded their gymnastics program to concentrate on competitive cheerleading. Cheering as a sport does not appeal to me in the least; I'm more of a solo artist than a team player. So I relegated my tumbling to the occasional after-school workout, just to clear my head and refocus. Last month, the fencing team agreed to lend me a mat while they practiced. They practiced late nights, so we had the whole gym to ourselves. I don't know why, but the tinny cling-clang of their foils and the shuffling of their feet helped me concentrate.

The fencing team's practice mat is nothing more than a four-inch pad of foam rubber, which doesn't give the spring of a conventional gymnastics floor. Even so, I felt like cranking up my last pass tonight. I did a roundoff back handspring, then a whip into a full. I took a couple steps on the landing, but I felt good about the routine in general.

"Going to have to deduct three-tenths on that landing, but solid otherwise."

Emrys Balin stood in front of me.

"Hello, Emrys," I said.

"Working up a sweat?" he asked.

"Trying to."

Emrys reached down for my towel on the mat, balled it up, and threw it at me. "Is this where you come after detention every night?"

While Dot and the Circuit Court for Anne Arundel County let me off with a slap on the wrist, Father Jules predictably felt less charitable and handed me a month of detention. Emrys was on the back-end of a slightly more severe sentence—a week of in-school suspension followed by a month of detention. He'd been busted using the Gaming Club as a front for a Dungeon & Dragons gambling ring.

"Is this where I come after detention?" I repeated back to him. Closing my eyes, towel in hand, I wiped down my face from my forehead to my chin. I opened my eyes, a part of me hoping Emrys had walked away, but he was still standing there. "I feel like you might already know that answer."

"Just curious," Emrys assured me.

"Was that what you were doing under the bleachers, just being curious?"

"I don't know what you're—"

"Joslin and I saw you spying on us, Emrys."

He shook his head. "I wasn't spying."

"Then what do you call it?"

"Observing," Emrys said. "You were the one spying, on Benz and Avery."

And now I was busted. Moving on. "Anybody ever call you Emmy?"

"No, why?"

"No reason," I said. So much for disarming him with an endearing nickname.

"Emmy is a stupid name," Emrys replied, as if he was answering my thoughts.

His tone suggested I had insulted him. This conversation was going off the rails quickly. "Look, I'm just trying to strike up a conversation. You don't have to bite my head off just because I asked if you had a nickname."

"My mother picked my name out."

That explained his tone. "Yeah, I totally understand that. My mom is pushing forty and my dad is in his fifties, so they grew up in the 1980s and nineties too. No doubt in my mind that they thought about naming me something ridiculous like Summer or Skylar."

"You're saying my name is ridiculous?"

"I've heard worse." I had made fun of his name, again. Only this time, I sensed he was in on the joke, aware that I tended to be more accidentally stupid than purposely insulting.

"If you must know, Emrys Balin is an old family name."

"Scottish?" I asked.

"Welsh," Emrys replied.

I toweled the sweat that continued to drip down my face. "Close enough."

"Is calling someone from Maine 'a New Yorker' close enough?"

"Is it?"

"The distance from the northernmost New York border to the southernmost Maine border is about four-hundred miles, which is roughly the same as the distance from the northernmost Welsh border to the southern border of Scotland."

"Learn something new every day I guess," I said.

"Hey, can you two turn down the dork speak?"

There were only the four of us in the gymnasium now. Richard Alexander, the guy who just called us dorks, removed his helmet first. He flashed me an insincere grin. The other fencer, Levi Lampton, removed his helmet as well. Levi did a couple hands-free hair flips with his head until his hair was just above his eyes. They're both good-looking, but in a weirdly generic, symmetrical way. Definitely not Benz hot.

Richard and Levi whispered to one another and started laughing. Their dual laughs sounded conspiratorial. They were college kids, student coaches on loan from the Johns Hopkins University fencing team. On campus for less than two weeks, they had already acquired a reputation for being, well, college kids. American Martyr boys tried hard to avoid them, while the girls of American Martyr had developed a sudden interest in fencing.

"Calm down, *Dick*," I said.

"My name is 'Richard,' 'Coach Alexander' to you."

"You're not my coach, and we're not hurting anyone, *Richard*. If Emrys wants to talk to me about geography, mind your own business."

Richard exhaled a *harrumph*, resuming his fencing exercises with Levi. Emrys nudged me. "I can stick up for myself. And you realize that they're calling us both dorks."

I threw the towel at him. "I think the words you're looking for are, 'Thank you, Rosemary.'"

Emrys dropped the towel and stared at me. I tried not to let it bother me, but it did. It was close to being that wanting, needy teenage boy look—that deliberate look when the hormones low-jacked their brains—but maybe I was misreading his signals.

"Want to go grab a bite to eat?" Emrys asked.

Okay, maybe I wasn't misreading his signals.

"I don't know, Emrys. It's getting kind of late."

"Message received."

"Message? *What* message?"

"Hey you two," Levi said. "Get a room."

"Me and Geography Boy?" I countered offhand. "Please don't give his Welsh wiener any ideas."

I regretted saying it immediately. It was smarmy and cruel. What was worse, I could see the pleasure derived from what I had just said on the faces of Richard and Levi. And now they were laughing at Emrys. I didn't want to be in their club. I was *not* in their club.

"Em-Emrys," I stammered. "I'm sorry."

"No, you're not," he said.

"No, you're not," Richard echoed.

"They're right," Levi added. "You're just mean."

"Dick and Levi," I growled, "shut up or I'll shut you up."

Richard and Levi retreated from the gym after my threat. I didn't know why I cared so much about the fact I hurt Emrys. I barely knew him, but there was some sort of connection between us. I couldn't put my finger on it. There was a comfort level developing, as if I'd known him for a lot longer than a few weeks. After a minute or so of sullen silence, I tried to salvage whatever this connection was.

"It's nothing personal against you, Emrys," I said. "You know that, right?"

"I realize this fact, Rosemary," Emrys said. "That's what makes you so disappointing."

There was an uncomfortable intimacy to his words. He didn't have to be so condescending, even if I did talk about his Welsh wiener. I could feel the attitude boiling back up inside me. "Hold on a second, where do you get off telling me that I'm disappointing? You don't even know me."

"Oh, I know you, Rosemary."

"No, you don't. You better watch yourself, Emrys."

"Or what?" he said, almost eagerly. "What will you do to me? We're on a wrestling mat. Come on, let's see you in action!"

"See me in action?" At this point, I couldn't tell if he was flirting with me or mocking me, and I was bothered by either proposition. "I would stop talking if I were you. I'm stronger than I look."

Emrys smirked. "I think I'll be okay. You are, after all, just a gir—"

And with that, Emrys's nose joined the wooden bleacher on my list of "Things I Punched Today."

CHAPTER

7

"To what do I owe the pleasure of this visit?" Benz asked sheepishly.

Joslin tried to talk me out of waiting for him after tonight's game. I think she was more just annoyed that I was her ride home and she had to wait in the car. Mom and Dad had gifted me the old Subaru Outback when the odometer hit 200,000 miles. They pay for my car insurance and oil changes, Joslin pays for my gas. It's a pretty sweet setup.

Even after everything that had happened between us, I still loved watching Benz play football on a Friday night. He first asked me out after a game last year. I was a freshman fan girl, and he was this untouchable, godlike junior. Too nervous, I turned him down the first time. What was I supposed to do? Tell him, "I'd love to go out with you, Benz. But only if you autograph your picture I keep under my pillow and give me some honest feedback on my statistical analysis of your American Martyr football career that I've maintained in this fully annotated spiral notebook." No. Way.

Benz didn't give up though. The second time he asked me out was after one of my last-ever gymnastics meets. I'd crushed the competition. And anyone who knows me will tell you I'm so hopped up on adrenaline after a meet that I'd be confident enough to ask Timothée Chalamet out on a date. We were together for ten perfect months—well, ten months minus the last few days of our relationship and the breakup aftermath, which I spent alternating between sobbing into a pillow and eating my weight in salted caramel ice cream.

I stood opposite the football locker room in an orange, knee-length rain jacket as my ex-boyfriend walked out. Just seeing him made the hairs on my arms and on the back of my neck stand on end. I hid my arms behind me, trying to ignore the goose bumps.

God, Benz is gorgeous. He just looks more…I don't know… *finished* than a lot of the dough-faced teenage boys at American Martyr. His thick, wavy hair, the color of worn leather. Those ridiculously long, almost feminine eyelashes that flutter over piercing hazel eyes.

"Have you been waiting out here for me this whole time, Rosemary?"

"For you?" I said. "Please. I just wanted to tell Andrew 'good catch.'"

Andrew Sparks was Benz's best friend. He caught the game-winning touchdown pass, but what I purposely neglected to acknowledge was that Benz was the one who threw him the ball. It was a perfect pass, although Benz had a bad game overall, especially by his lofty standards. He was a perfectionist in public—playing and winning at sports, making eye contact and greeting my father with a firm handshake, holding my hand in the school hallway when other boyfriends barely noticed their girlfriends. It was the quieter, more intimate moments he struggled with.

Benz smiled, seeing right through me. "Andrew already left."

"Oh," I said, trying to avoid eye contact. If he started batting those eyelashes at me, I was done. "You had a good game too."

"No, I didn't."

"No, you didn't."

"Thanks for noticing."

"Karma sucks."

"Karma? What's that supposed to mean?"

"Really, Benz?" I sneered.

"You haven't given me much of a chance to…" He trailed off, like he was distracted.

"To do what?"

"To just talk to you," Benz finished. "I've tried, but you've shut me completely out of your life."

Benz and I never knew one another before we started dating. Our first exchange of more than a dozen words was literally on the car ride to our first date. We went to a movie, and three hours later he asked if I wanted to be his girlfriend. It wasn't until we broke up that I realized in our rush to be a couple we never learned how to be friends.

I was, at times, obsessed with Benz. But I couldn't even tell you his favorite color or the name of his grandmother. We were good at being dramatic, but terrible at being boring. A knockdown, drag-out shouting match in the student commons? Sign us up. Skipping class to make out in his car in the school parking lot? Too many times to count. But watching TV with his parents? Eating lunch, just the two of us, with nothing going on? Hard pass. I think that was part of our problem.

"Can you now?" Benz asked.

"Can I *what* now?"

"I don't know, talk. How've you been?"

"Good."

"Well, you look great."

"Yeah, I bet I do." It rained the whole game. I ran my fingers through my hair, pretending I didn't like the attention. "Hair sopping wet and matted against my head. Pretty freaking sexy."

"No one pulls off soaking wet like you. And the tattoo really adds to the look."

I hadn't noticed the right sleeve of my rain jacket pushed up. I pulled down the sleeve, still avoiding eye contact. "I bet you say that to all the girls."

"Just the one with the tattoo." Benz grabbed my hand. "You have a date to Fall Fling?"

I had agreed to go with Joslin, but Benz didn't know that. I didn't know why his name popped into my head, but it did.

I pulled my hand away. "Emrys Balin asked me."

"The foreign exchange student from Scotland?" Benz asked.

"Wales."

"Whatever. Did you say yes?"

"None of your business, jackass."

"Hey, now…" Benz grabbed my elbow, squeezing it. "Play nice, Rosemary."

I wrenched my arm away again from his unsolicited touch. "Nice? Is that what we're doing now? Playing nice?"

"You tell me," Benz said. "I'm not the one waiting outside the football locker room looking like a sad puppy."

"You're a jerk." I shoved my hand in my pocket, retrieving what I came here to give him. "And I believe this is yours."

Benz looked at his class ring in my palm. "You don't have to give this back. Just hold on to it, for safekeeping." He acted as if he was going to grab the ring but squeezed my hand instead.

We stood for a moment, hand in hand, staring into each other's eyes. I thought back to last year, and how I got the morbs after the gymnastics club disbanded. Maybe that was why I let things move so fast with Benz. When I was with him, he made me feel special again. He put me back on that podium.

I forced the ring into his hand. He stared at it, then at me, then at the ring again. Shaking his head, Benz stuffed the ring in his pocket. It was almost as if he was having the harder time accepting this breakup, and it was his stupid idea. Like I said, we were good at being dramatic.

"You're insulting my intelligence with this act, Benz. I still haven't gotten past you stonewalling me in the student commons."

"Stonewalling you?"

"When the police took me out in handcuffs. You were the last one I saw."

"I know, Rosemary. I felt terrible."

"If you felt so terrible, then why didn't you—"

"Why didn't I *what*?"

"Come after me! Students were laughing as they took me out."

"I'm sorry people laughed at you, Rosemary. You know I'd never do that."

"Never?"

"Never."

"What about the time we went swimming in our underwear off your back dock, and you hid my clothes?"

"That wasn't laughing," Benz said. "That was flirting."

"I don't believe you."

"Rosemary, you were wearing a bra and lace panties. While I have many adjectives for your half-naked body, 'funny' is not one of them."

"Are you flirting with me now?" I poked him in the ribs. Crap, I really sucked at not being his girlfriend.

Benz flashed me a dimple-framed gigglemug. "Maybe."

I poked him in the ribs again. My poking became tickling. "That's what I thought."

"Rosemary, stop!" Benz's cheeks reddened.

"You're cute when you're embarrassed," I said. My cheeks hurt from smiling. Had I been smiling that whole time? I had missed Benz's flirting. I'd missed everything about him.

"Hello?" Benz waved his hand in front of my face. "You still with us?"

"What?"

"You zoned out there for a second."

I needed to collect myself. I was flustered. I was an idiot. *Get it together, Rosemary. Change the subject.* "What about Avery?"

"What about her?"

"You two an item?"

"There's nothing going on between us."

"Sneaking drugs and a love letter into your letter jacket seems like something to me."

"Her older sister came home for the weekend from college in Massachusetts with a bag of weed and an edibles recipe book. Avery wanted to surprise me. My bumps and bruises on the football field were starting to pile up, and she said it was good for pain management. And what's this about a love letter?"

Apparently, Avery hadn't told Benz about the letter. Interesting, but not interesting enough for me to keep her secret. "The note Avery included with the brownies. It was very sweet." I batted my eyelashes. "*Surprise! For after the game, superstar... Love, Avery.*"

"That's just a figure of speech, Rosemary."

"What? Superstar?"

"Love," Benz said. "Come on. There's no love there. Mutual

affection as friends? Maybe, but nothing serious. Nothing real. Not what you and I share."

"What we share?" I pondered. "Present tense?"

"I don't just stop feeling, Rosemary. Especially when it comes to you."

Benz didn't know how to turn off the charm, ever. "Don't change the subject."

"What did you do with the letter?" Benz asked.

"I ripped it up, of course." The conversation had become more snapping at each other than talking. Again, we both gravitated toward the drama of the moment.

"You have to believe me, Rosemary. I never knew anything about the weed until after you were dragged out of school."

"Then how did you connect the dots that it was Avery who put the brownies there?"

"Avery told me, right when it happened."

"She told you the truth?"

"How else would I know about her sister? Avery is not the terrible person you think she is, Rosemary. You know it's not her fault that you were arrested, right?"

"Word of advice, ex-boyfriend: If you want to get back on my good side, stop sticking up for Avery. *She* stuffed the brownies in *your* letter jacket."

"And *you* stole the brownies from *my* locker."

I poked him in the chest as I enunciated my words. "And *you*... dumped *me*...the day after you took my...the day after we had sex!"

I sounded old-fashioned, almost framing my virginity in the context of being "taken," as I was a more than willing participant, but the last thing he deserved at the moment was my forgiveness. Benz had been doing well there for a few precious minutes—flirting with me, more or less absolving himself of the edibles incident and its aftermath. I was even willing to ignore his lame defense of Avery. It was inevitable that we circled back to our last night together. Back to snapping instead of talking.

"About that..." Benz said.

"Yes, about that," I responded. "No, wait, you know what? I don't want to hear an explanation. I've moved on."

"You have?"

"Yes."

"And you're sure you want to move on?"

"Double yes."

"Damnit, Rosemary, just listen to me!" Benz blurted out, "I love you!"

His words took me back to that night. I told Mom and Dad that I was staying at Joslin's house. Benz's parents were gone for the weekend. We drank some of his parents' wine and danced. We did it in his parents' bed. It was over in a matter of minutes. I assumed I did it right. Benz smiled, I think. Afterwards, we both rolled away from each other, and I pretended to fall asleep. He drove me to Joslin's in the morning and didn't kiss me goodbye. We watched Season 4, Episode 9 of *One Tree Hill* for about the billionth time. Joslin didn't ask me any questions, even after I cried a little too hard when Lucas said to Peyton, "It's you…When all my dreams come true, the one I want next to me. It's you. It's you, Peyton."

I shoved Benz away from me. He stumbled back a few steps, not anticipating the force. "You think smelling good and telling me you love me makes everything better?"

Benz rubbed his chest. He sat on the ground, his back against the lockers. "You think I smell good?"

"Don't try and change the subject," I said, sitting down next to him. "Was it me? Was I that bad?"

"What? Bad?" Benz grabbed my hand. "God no, Rosemary. You were…you were everything."

I placed my hand over his. "Sleeping with someone is a big deal for me."

"It's a big deal for me too."

"You have a funny way of showing it."

"I'm sorry, Rosemary."

"I want you to not have a reason to be sorry, Benz. I want you to go back in time, let me fall asleep in your arms, and give me a damn kiss goodbye!"

"I can't change the past." Benz's tone seemed more regretful than remorseful. I liked that he wanted a do-over, but I would've liked it more if he sounded like he couldn't live without one.

"You can't change the past," I echoed him, "and I can't get over it."

After we had sex, Benz and I went on a couple sad dates. I told him at the end of our last date that I wanted to work things out. We'd tried to talk for what seemed like hours but might have only been twenty minutes, until finally, he just kissed me on the forehead and said he wanted to take some time for himself. He told me, "I need some time to breathe, Rosemary."

Some time to breathe? Yeah, just a little tip for guys who want to let a girl down easy: Don't tell her she's suffocating you.

After Benz turned the corner out of my neighborhood, I threw up in my driveway. Mom heard me crying when she pulled in and found me balled up on our front porch swing with vomit on my shirt.

"So you don't want to get back together?" Benz asked.

"Look…" I trailed off, trying not to notice that I was still holding his hand. "Can we talk about this when we're both a little more clearheaded—when you're not coming off a big game and I'm not standing here soaked to the bone with wet socks?"

"You hate wet socks."

The water seeped out of my shoes as I stomped my foot for emphasis. "I know I do!"

Benz smiled. "If I can get you to a strongly implied 'maybe' while wearing wet socks, the sky is the limit."

I tried not to smile back at him as the blood rushed to my face. I did want to be Benz's girlfriend again, but just not yet.

CHAPTER

8

"Seriously, Crash?" I said, snow shovel in hand. "I just cleaned your stall a half hour ago."

When I was given a shortlist of restitution options last month, the Boys and Girls Club over on Meade Village Circle seemed like the easy choice. That assignment lasted all of two days, after which time they apparently realized that playing foosball with pre-teens for three hours a night wasn't exactly restitution. I was reassigned to custodial duty at Laurel Park, the horse track south of Columbia.

My four weeks of work at the Laurel Park stables had comprised mostly weekends, with the occasional weekday if I was dismissed from detention early. It kept me busy at a time when, even six weeks post-breakup, I still thought a lot about Benz. A place that smelled of manure seemed like an appropriate metaphor for my boyfriend blues, and I was beginning to understand why the Circuit Court of Anne Arundel County deemed this job punishment.

They didn't let me near the racing thoroughbreds. I was tasked with cleaning the pony stables. The ponies are the companion horses to the racers, the horses with lesser pedigrees or disappointing results on the track that have been relegated to helping train the bluebloods. Sweet and generally mild-mannered, companion ponies are the horses you see on television escorting the contenders between the stables and the starting gate.

Note the "generally" qualifier. One horse in particular lives to torment me. The only gray in the barn, Gatecrasher, or just "Crash," earned his name from his tendency to refuse to leave the starting gate. His warmups were legendary around the paddock. Trainers called him "Bid fast," in reference to arguably the fastest gray thoroughbred of all time, Spectacular Bid. But put him on a track with a dozen other horses, and he's like, "Nah." Crash is loud and obnoxious, and he poops more than any other creature on earth.

As I tried to navigate Crash's latest mess, he head-butted me in the chest. It was a playful nudge, not hard enough to knock me down, but I tripped over my own feet and fell down regardless.

"Son of a…"

He neighed almost gleefully. As mischievous as he was, Crash liked me. Begrudgingly, I had to admit I liked him too. In my two weeks at the stables, I'd never seen him let anyone near him, but he let me brush his coat every night and hand-feed him.

"You have a way with Gatecrasher, Rosemary. He's usually a handful."

Emrys Balin walked up to me. As he approached, I slid to the other side of Crash's head, creating some separation between us. "What are you doing here?" I asked.

"I could ask the same thing of you: popular high school girl, hiding out with a bunch of horses on a Saturday night. I sent you a couple texts. Tried to call, but I guess either your phone was dead or turned off."

Or I was ignoring you, I wanted to say, but I bit my tongue.

"It took me straight to voicemail," Emrys continued. "I finally just called your mom. She told me you were here. How long you think you'll stick around at this job?"

"Until coming home smelling like wet straw and horse manure just isn't worth it. How do you know my mom anyway?"

"Who said I knew your mom?"

"You obviously have her cellphone number."

"That's because she posted an ad on the online school bulletin board offering private archery lessons."

"Well of course she did."

Emrys grabbed a handful of alfalfa. He reached up to Crash, who ate from his hand without hesitation.

"Impressive," I observed.

"You're not the only horse whisperer," Emrys said.

I pointed to his face. "I was talking about your nose. You can't even tell I punched you. Sorry about that."

Emrys raised his hands. "Nonsense. I had it coming. I was presumptuous and cruel."

"And misogynistic."

"Yes," Emrys affirmed. "That too. My point being, I should be the one who's apologizing to you."

"For what? Hurting my hand with your face?"

"No, Rosemary. For hurting you with the most vicious weapon a teenager has at his disposal—his words."

"Yeah," I replied. "I still feel like you got the shorter end of the stick on that one. Just let me do the right thing here and apologize."

"Fine," Emrys acknowledged. "I accept your apology."

"Good, but you still haven't answered my question. What are you doing here?"

"I just figured, since I was taking you to Fall Fling, that you might want to fill me in on the details."

"Oh," I said. "You heard about that."

"The whole school did. I guess I was the last to know, unless perhaps you proposed to me after you punched me in the face while I was briefly catatonic."

"I thought you said that the most vicious weapon a teenager has at his disposal is his words?"

"If I'm being honest, my words rank a distant second to your right cross." He offered me a brown paper bag. "You hungry?"

"Starving," I said.

"Do you like peaches?"

"I like them very much, especially when the peach trucks come up from Georgia in July. But October peaches?"

"Yeah, I realize they're scarcely in season."

Emrys handed me the bag, which I tore open. The crumpled, brown sack contained a half-dozen peaches. Famished, I pulled out the ripest one and consumed a third of it in one big bite. They weren't bad for October.

Streams of sweet syrup dripped down my chin. I wiped the juice off my mouth. "Don't feel like you have to take me to Fall Fling."

"What kind of gentleman would I be if I stood you up?"

Handing me a napkin, Emrys bowed. It was a gesture that from your average sixteen-year-old should have been awkward, but his bow was tight and polished. "Lady Banson, would you honor me with the pleasure of your company at the American Martyr Fall Fling?"

My curtsey was not nearly as precise. My old jeans and even older pair of Converse didn't do much to add to the picture, but I managed. "Sir Balin, I would find that most agreeable." Nobody was there to witness this spectacle, thank God.

"Where is everybody?" Emrys asked.

I rolled the brown paper bag shut. "It's this dead most of the time. With race season winding down, I only see a handful of trainers and jockeys around."

"Take the rest of the peaches home with you," Emrys insisted. "Just don't keep them in that bag too long. They'll be soft in no time."

"Yes, I realize that, Emrys. I have in fact eaten peaches before today."

"Just trying to be helpful."

"Then grab a rake."

Emrys and I finished Crash's stall with a layer of fresh straw. Crash tapped his front right hoof as Emrys stroked his nape. "You're welcome," Emrys replied.

I shook my head with a chuckle. "Whatever."

"You don't think Crash is appreciative?"

"I think he's a horse." I started to exit the stall behind Emrys. Crash followed me, again nudging me playfully against his stall door. "Easy, you big lug."

The gray snorted, stomping his right hoof again. I stepped outside the stall, shut the door behind me. "What is it, buddy?"

Crash reared up. He shook his head, neighed twice. The first neigh was low and short, the second higher-pitched and more drawn out.

"Something has him spooked," Emrys said, looking from side to side.

"I don't think so," I said, latching the stall door behind me. I reached for a handful of alfalfa. "He's just tired of that awful vitamin feed the vet makes him eat." I held the alfalfa under the horse's nose. "Here you go, boy."

Crash refused the offering. He reared again, this time more aggressively, kicking the stall door.

"Hey now," I said, growing concerned. "Calm down."

"You really need to listen to Crash," Emrys cautioned. "He's trying to tell us something."

The clip-clop of horseshoes interrupted us. A black horse, bigger than Crash, trotted leisurely into the barn, a jockey sitting astride.

"Crash acting up?" The jockey dismounted. His patterned, multi-colored racing silks gave him the look of a court jester. He hung his bridle over an empty stall door across from Crash, but didn't remove his helmet.

"Nothing we can't handle, sir," I said, trying to stay composed and not to be a typical awkward teenager around strangers.

He extended his hand to me. "I don't believe we've met, young lady. My name is Roland Wilamuck."

"Hello, Mr. Wilamuck," I said, shaking his hand.

"Please, call me Rolo," he said. "You say 'Mr. Wilamuck,' and I look to see if my dad has entered the room."

"If you say so, Mister...uh, I mean, Rolo. My name is Rosemary."

Rolo had the prototype jockey physique. He was shorter than me, five feet with his riding boots on, if that. "Rosemary?" he said, removing his helmet finally. "That's a beautiful name."

"You think?" I asked.

"You don't like it?"

"Sometimes it just sounds a little too...oh, I don't know..."

"Old?"

"I was going to say 'floral,' but thanks for putting that in my head now."

"It was a compliment."

"If you say so, Rolo."

He released my hand, turning to Emrys with a smile as he nodded back at me. "Looks like management hired a real spitfire with this one."

"Management?" Emrys gave the jockey a half-gigglemug at best. He didn't like the guy, I could just tell. "I'm sorry, *Rolo*, do we know each other? I come around these barns to see the horses quite often, and I don't remember seeing you."

"You come around these barns *often?*" I interjected.

He winked at me, again skirting that uncomfortable line between friendly and flirtatious. "Of course."

I grabbed the reins of the black horse. Raven is his name—after the Edgar Allan Poe poem, not Baltimore's professional football team, which is also named after the poem. "Emrys has a point, Rolo. Are you new here? And why are you running horses so late?"

"Flew in from Santa Anita earlier this week," he answered. "I think my body is still on Pacific time."

"Raven looks tired," I said, leading the horse to a trough of water. "Was it necessary to work him so hard?"

"He's just a little out of shape is all." Rolo nodded at the bucket of alfalfa. "Maybe if you eased up on the treats."

"Maybe if you didn't run him like he was in the Preakness," I countered. As was the case in most situations in which people poked me, I poked back.

"Rosemary, that's enough," Emrys cautioned.

"It certainly is," Rolo said, eyes narrowing.

The jockey started to approach me when Emrys raised his voice. "Uh, Rolo?"

"What?"

"Just curious."

"Yes?"

Emrys pointed at Raven's left stirrup. Now that the horse was standing in the full light of the barn's interior, a wet red stain was visible. "What's that?"

"No big deal," Rolo said. He reached down to a rip in his pants along the outside of his left thigh. "Clumsy horse just brushed the inside rail. We both were cut up a bit."

"Interesting." Emrys walked over to Raven. He rubbed his right middle and index fingers across the stirrup and lifted his fingers to his nose.

"Not really," Rolo said, standing almost nose to nose with

Emrys—well, technically nose to Emrys's chin. He refused to back away as Emrys grabbed the stirrups.

"Oh, I find it very interesting." Emrys said, smelling the stirrups directly now.

I chimed in. "Why do you say that?"

Emrys looked at me, then at the jockey. He dropped Crash's stirrups. "Because this blood smells a lot like it came from an incubus."

I couldn't possibly have heard that correctly. "An incu*what?*"

My question was left unanswered. The jockey shouted, "*En garde!*" In a frenzied blur of motion, he produced a small sword from a scabbard hidden in his non-ripped pants leg while at the same time knocking Emrys to the ground. He straddled him, pressing his sword underneath Emrys's chin. I stood frozen.

"Relax, Rolo," Emrys said, hands raised. "I mean you no harm."

"What do you know of me?" he asked.

"I know that Wilamuck is not a name from this world. It's a name from your world, a name from *our* world."

"Our world?" the jockey asked. "Impossible."

"I know that you are an incubus," Emrys said.

"An incubus?" he pressed. "As if you, a mere boy, can even comprehend what that is."

"You are a demon who preys upon women, often sexually, and often while they're sleeping." Emrys glanced at me, as if he were explaining this for my benefit more than the jockey's. "The Wilamuck, or should I say *Vellamus* incubi bloodline has a particularly long and notorious history."

"A demon?" I blurted out. "Who does *what?*"

"Bite your tongue, trollop," the jockey, or whatever the hell he was, said. He returned his attention to Emrys. "I don't have time for the incessant drivel of teenagers. Who are you, boy?"

Emrys smiled. "Oh, surely you have figured it out by now."

Rolo pushed the edge of the blade harder against Emrys's throat, drawing blood. "I'm losing patience."

"Just as you are not what you seem, I am not what I seem," Emrys answered. "Does the name 'Emrys' not sound familiar to you?"

"If it did, I suspect I would not be preparing to slice your throat."

"Emrys is a Welsh name meaning 'immortal.' My full given

Welsh name is 'Myrddin Emrys.'"

"What?" Rolo removed his sword from Emrys's chin. He stood up, offering his hand to Emrys. "Forgive me. I did not know."

Emrys accepted Rolo's assistance as he stood. "Honest mistake."

"Hold on a second." I waved my arms wildly, as if I could somehow just fan the crazy out of the room. "What in the hell is going on here?"

Rolo nodded at me, then at Emrys. "So I take it we're both here for the same thing?"

Emrys looked at me deliberately while brushing himself off. "I'm here to take the girl to our master. I doubt he'd be too happy if he heard you'd decided to pleasure yourself before you handed her off."

"Wait...*what?*" I screamed, squeezing both shock and anguish into two syllables.

Rolo approached me, sword still in hand, his gait slow and deliberate, like he was savoring what he was about to do. Emrys stood just behind him.

"Please, Emrys," I said. I wanted to cry. Was this really happening? "Help me."

Emrys stepped a few paces back.

"Please," I said again. Emrys turned his back to us, as if he couldn't bear to watch.

Rolo laughed. "It would seem Myrddin doesn't have the stomach for this. He is familiar with the old ways, but apparently not that *familiar.*"

A bolt of lightning flashed outside, followed by a clap of thunder. Rolo jumped, startled.

"You'd be surprised," Emrys said. He faced us now, holding a sword aloft.

The sword was extraordinary. It seemed to radiate more than reflect light. A silver blade sprouting from an ornate crossguard and a leather-wrapped hilt reminiscent of snake scales. Three golden crowns set against a silver-rimmed disc of blue formed the pommel.

"No!" the jockey said. As fast as he had previously disabled Emrys, he leapt to his horse. Raven galloped past us in the direction of the indoor riding arena.

"*Dedimus potestatem!*" Emrys shouted, thrusting his sword higher into the air. The blade began to shine even brighter. Lightning flashed again, thunder shook the room, and my head started to spin.

I closed my eyes…

More lightning and thunder…

Images of warriors, dead and dying…

Familiar faces…

My face…

I was suddenly hyper-aware of everything around me. The bright lights. The overwhelming noise and humanity. I could hear rats scurrying down alleys, panhandlers shaking cups of coins. And the smells. God, the smells. Not just rotting fish and horse manure; the blue crab carcasses and oyster shells in the dumpster behind the raw bar across the street. The permanent layer of cigarette smoke on the ceiling and walls of the Laurel clubhouse. The urine on the floor of the men's restroom. The nervous sweat of an incubus.

Focus, Rosemary. Focus.

The spinning stopped. The lights dimmed. I peeled back the sounds layer by layer. I suppressed the fetid stench and thought only of the moment.

And then I opened my eyes.

I was riding Crash bareback. And we were galloping, chasing Raven along the front stretch of Laurel Park and into turn one. And Emrys's sword was in my hand.

"Stay away from me," Rolo warned over his shoulder.

"What?" I said, my brain still not completely caught up.

"I said, stay away from me, wench!"

His insult snapped me out of it. "Wench?" I said. "Most guys wait until at least the end of the date before calling me that. You and I haven't even ordered dessert yet."

"Don't let him get away!" Emrys shouted. Wait a second. How did he make his voice carry like that from so far away? I took quick inventory of my surroundings as we rounded turn two down the backstretch.

What the hell is happening to me? Why was I taking inventory of my surroundings? Why was I chasing a sword-wielding jockey, on a horse, with a sword in my hand? And since when did I know how to ride a horse? It was like my body and brain were on autopilot.

Crash matched Raven stride for stride, then started to overtake him midway down the back stretch. I was nearly even with the horse and his rider.

"Rosemary, watch out!"

I'd made the mistake of approaching Rolo at his sword side. His backswing was aimed right at my throat. I leaned back in my saddle, my head nearly touching Crash's hindquarters. Just as his sword flew by my face, I delivered a palm strike to his elbow, breaking his sword arm nearly in half. Rolo dropped his weapon just past turn three, shrieking in pain. Dazed, he let up as Raven slowed down the short chute between turns three and four, but quickly recovered.

As we came out of turn four heading down the home stretch, I didn't care what happened to Rolo anymore; it was Raven I was worried about. I leapt from Crash onto the backend of the massive black horse's saddle. Crash steered himself clear as I grabbed Rolo's right hand, twisting his broken arm while pulling back on Raven's reins in an attempt to slow the horse. He again cried out from the pain, but still managed to elbow me underneath the ribs with his good arm. He paused for a second, which gave me a moment to gasp for air, then backhanded my face with his fist, bloodying my nose and knocking me off the end of the saddle.

I bounced on Raven's hindquarters, barely holding on. Still, I had an idea. I could do this if I timed it just right. A one-handed roundoff from Rolo's shoulder into a back handspring full-twisting layout off the horse's neck.

I leapt to my feet, sword arm at the ready. Rolo attempted to throw another elbow, but all he found was air as I jumped over him, my free hand using his shoulder for leverage on my roundoff.

Just like on a gymnastics springboard, I let instinct take over.

Emrys's sword swinging free in my right arm, I sprung off Raven's neck, jumping and twisting, tugging hard on Raven's reins at the same time. A whirling flurry of steel and flesh, my sword sliced cleanly under Rolo's chin. I turned Raven just enough to pivot me toward the inside guardrail, where I landed on my feet.

Don't mean to brag, but I stuck the landing. Sweat and blood ran down my face. Short of breath—although not nearly as spent as I should have been—I crouched on the guardrail. Sword raised in my right hand, Raven's reins in my left, I stood eye-to-eye with Rolo.

Raven dug in his hooves, stopping just before the guardrail. Blood flowed freely from the slit in Rolo's throat, but amazingly, he was still seated in his saddle, *and he was smiling*.

Rolo raised his one good arm, the blood from my nose still fresh and dripping down his fingers, and saluted me casually. The last thing I remembered before passing out was the jockey falling off his horse.

Rolo lay on the ground, his head swiveled awkwardly over to his far shoulder, nearly severed from his neck.

CHAPTER
9

Joslin slid into the passenger seat of my Subaru Outback. "You look like crap, girlfriend," she observed astutely.

Pushing my sunglasses up the bridge of my nose, I glanced down at my wrinkled hand-me-down dress. "Thanks for noticing."

How much did I sleep last night? I was clueless. I was clueless about a lot of things. I remembered Emrys showing up to the barn, eating peaches with him, being asked out to Fall Fling, absentmindedly forgetting that I'd already promised Joslin, and then cleaning the stables. But everything beyond that seemed like a dream—an intense dream, but a dream nonetheless. It had to be. Otherwise, how did I end up back home, safe beneath the shifty yet familiar scrutiny of Bob Marley? Safe in my small, comfortable home. Safe in my small, comfortable life.

"When did you get back last night?" Joslin asked.

"I don't know, midnight maybe?" The "maybe" gave me plausible deniability, although I could still be telling the truth. It felt more comfortable than denying it.

"Can't bother to return a text or two?"

"Or ten," I replied.

"So your phone *was* on?"

"Sorry," I said. "I was brain-dead by the time I clocked out at the stables. Wasn't much for socializing at that point."

As far as our parents were concerned, Joslin and I were currently attending Sunday morning mass. What they didn't know was that we attended "McMass." It was our weekly ritual, aided by the fact that my mom preferred Saturday evening mass, Dad spent most weekends working, and Joslin's parents, though officially Catholic, had started going to the Episcopal church over in Columbia ever since they brought in a woman priest. Joslin picked me up around 8:15 a.m. We popped into the St. John Neumann Basilica during the entrance procession of the 8:30 mass, just to verify who the presiding priest was. Once that was confirmed, we grabbed a church bulletin and headed over to the McDonald's off Route 2 for an hour. Some people consumed consecrated hosts on Sundays. Joslin and I preferred hash browns.

We stood at the McDonald's counter. Joslin looked at me, money in hand. "Your usual?"

I shook my head. "Give me two large Egg McMuffin meals."

"Gluttony. How retro of you."

We sat down at a table, me with my two McMuffins, two hash browns, and two large orange juices, Joslin with her usual hash brown, side of ketchup, and small cup of black coffee. She sipped her coffee, watching me drink my orange juice. "You going to take off your sunglasses?"

"Nope."

"You hungover or something?"

"Nope." I pushed one of the cups of orange juice toward her, trying to change the subject. "Here, have one."

"My body can't handle that much sugar, especially in the morning." Joslin said.

"Excuse me, ladies."

Emrys stood in front of us in a blue blazer and khaki pants. The jacket framed a yellow polo shirt, more brunch than churchgoing. His hair was slicked back. He reeked of aftershave—funny, given his baby face I was almost certain had never seen a beard. But the application of cheap cologne was purposeful, trying but failing to mask another odor.

On cue, Joslin looked over Emrys's shoulder while waving her hand in front of her nose. "Did a freaking horse trot in here when I wasn't looking? The whole place suddenly smells like manure."

Horse manure.

"Where did you come from?" I swallowed hard, wondering if I was somehow still in that dream.

"Nice shades, Rosemary."

"Stink you very much," I said, addressing the elephant—I mean, the horse in the room.

Joslin pointed to both of us. "Are you two like friends now?"

"Yes," Emrys answered.

"No," I refuted.

Emrys extended his hand to Joslin. "Emrys Balin."

"Joslin Kelly," she said, shaking Emrys's hand. "I love the accent. Welsh?"

"Right you are, Joslin. You might be the first person who ever guessed correctly on the first try."

"I have an ear for accents," she said, her cheeks turning pink.

For Christ's sake. Was my best friend...*blushing*?

"I love your hair, by the way," Emrys continued. "Plum is a great color on you."

Joslin eyed me, smirking with relish. "Yes, *plum* is a great color on me. Thanks for noticing."

"And Joslin is such a cool name. It's English, you know."

There was no denying the blushing now; Joslin's cheeks were as red as her side of ketchup. "Don't tell my very Irish father that."

"It means, *Little Goth*." Emrys smiled, his eyes almost twinkling.

Joslin smiled back. "If you say so."

Emrys brought his free hand over the top of their handshake, squeezing affectionately. "I know we just met, Joslin, but can I ask a favor of you?"

I'd underestimated Emrys, big time. I didn't know if he had what I'd call charisma or charm, but there was certainly something there. "What kind of favor?" she asked.

"May I steal Rosemary away for a little while? There's something we need to go over, for a school project."

Joslin paused, like she needed to think about it for a second. Some best friend. *Hello*, strange boy wanted to steal me away, and all she could muster was indifference?

"Oh, I don't know," Joslin said.

That was more like it.

"Just promise to bring her home before dinner."

Freaking perfect.

CHAPTER

10

"I don't appreciate you barging in on me and my chuckaboo like that."

"Your chuckaboo?"

"My best fr—"

"Yes, I know what that word means," Emrys said, cutting me off at the exact moment he cut off a car trying to merge into our lane.

"You do?" I asked. "I thought it was a word my mom just invented."

"It's British slang," Emrys clarified. "More specifically, it's Victorian Age slang. Which is what makes it so funny hearing you say it in your decidedly American accent."

After we dropped Joslin off at her house, Emrys insisted on taking the wheel. As my Subaru crossed the South River into Edgewater down Route 2 and Emrys cut off another car, I realized he was a terrible driver.

"Can you please be aware of other people on the road?" I asked. "You've about wrecked my car twice. Where are we going anyway?"

"Someplace safe," Emrys answered.

I rolled down my window. "Other than the possible risk of dying in a mangled car wreck, I wasn't aware I was in danger."

"So in your mind, last night didn't happen? It was all some sort of…"

I nodded. "Out of body experience? Astral projection? Whatever you want to call it. Yes, that's the story I've been going with all morning."

What did Emrys know? Maybe last night *didn't* happen. Maybe it was just one of my crazy dreams, the super-lucid kind I have when I take Melatonin. Last week I dreamt Benz and I got married. It was a large, expensive wedding. Level 42 showed up to play the entrance hymn, their 1985 hit "Something About You," which reached #7 on the Billboard Hot 100. Avery passed out the programs, and I caught her crossing out my name with a pen and writing in hers. Benz turned into a brownie just as he was about to say his vows, so I ate him.

"Last night?" I reacted defiantly. "I don't know what you're talking about."

"You didn't decapitate an incubus with a sword?"

"I don't even know what an incubus is."

"Rolo Wilamuck was an incubus, more specifically a demon who—"

I raised my hand. "I'm going to stop you right there, Emrys. Deep down you seem like a nice boy, but I think you've spent a little too much time living in that Dungeons & Dragons fantasy world of yours."

"More time than you know."

"Keep saying stuff like that, and people are going to think you're crazy."

"The 'crazy' part I will definitely concede," he affirmed. "You would be too if you lived on this earth for 2,000 years."

"2,000 years?" I exclaimed. "Cut the crap, Emrys."

"I know this is a lot to take in, Rosemary."

"I'm not taking it in. I'm ignoring it."

A row of magnolia trees whizzed by as we hit the roundabout in Lothian and headed south on Solomons Island Road. Emrys slowed to let an emergency vehicle pull into the fire station and continued this pace as we passed Lothian Elementary and Southern Middle School.

"School's not in session," I said. "How about we get to where we're going a little faster?"

Emrys ignored me, waving at the police office directing traffic for Sunday services at St. James' Episcopal. "I was hoping I could ease you into the situation. That's why I egged you on in the gym the other day. It was a controlled environment, a safe space in which I thought that maybe your *abilities* could just manifest themselves."

"My abilities?" I asked. "W-what do you know about...*my abilities?*"

I mumbled my words, catching my breath as my heart pounded. Emrys was still closer to a stranger than an acquaintance, no matter what happened last night. His presumption was unnerving. He knew something, maybe everything about me.

Emrys timed the stoplight at Bay Front Road perfectly, motoring on through. "I came to the horse stables to prepare you, to explain why you are the way you are. But then the incubus showed up, and things just spun out of control. I had to improvise."

"That's what you call last night? Improvising?"

My first out-loud acknowledgment that last night actually happened earned an eyebrow raise from Emrys. "Well, yes."

"Improvising is using a flat iron to iron a shirt collar or spraying tights with hairspray to avoid runs. Improvising is not possessing me and forcing me to kill a guy."

"I didn't possess you, Rosemary. Last night was all you."

"What about the light show, you standing there with that sword and crawling into my head?"

"I was just doing my job."

"*What* job?"

"Think back to the horse stables. Do you remember what happened?"

"Before or after I chopped off a guy's head?"

"Before."

"We were cleaning up horse poop, Rolo the sex demon horse jockey attacked me, called you Meerdin or something, and then things went off the rails," I said.

"Let's start there," Emrys insisted. "*Myrddin* is my birth name, Myrddin Emrys. I was born in Wales."

"Yeah, you're a Welsh exchange student," I affirmed. "I think we both remember the time I was a bitch to you, thanks for reminding me. That still doesn't explain how the incubus recognized you, why the incubus was there in the first place, or how it's possible for an incubus to even exist outside of a fairytale."

"We actually might run into a few faeries if we're not careful."

I waved him off. "Whatever. Back to your name."

"Translated from Welsh into English, the long-form version of my name is actually Merlinus Ambrosius. But most people know me best as…"

"Ambrose?"

"No."

"I was kidding."

"This isn't a joke."

"Not a joke? You're claiming to be Merlin." My day had officially progressed from unbelievable to certifiable. "As in *the* Merlin?"

"*The* Merlin?" Emrys shrugged. "I don't know about that. Merlinus was actually a somewhat common name back in my day. In fact, I knew a Merlinus in a neighboring kingdom who went by the name 'Merl.'"

"Was Merl mentor to a boy king? The all-powerful wizard of Arthurian legend? Star of page, stage, screen, and bad nineties television CGI?"

"Nineties CGI was quite wretched, wasn't it?"

"*Hercules* blows," I confirmed. "But that BBC Merlin series in the early 2000s isn't so bad, and *Xena* is freaking awesome."

"I would actually agree on all three of those assessments, Rosemary. What I would not agree on is your depiction of me as all-powerful. A wizard with prodigious skills, yes. Arthur's mentor, of course. Mage, sorcerer, enchanter, Welsh foreign exchange student— whatever you prefer."

The roadside magnolias transitioned to oaks and hickories, the occasional lingering chestnut still holding on against the blight that had wiped out all of its brothers. As we crossed over from Anne Arundel County to Calvert County, a palpable sense of calm descended upon Emrys. It was hard to explain how I knew, but this was home for him.

"Ha!" I did not share in that sense of calm. I was almost manic. "Whatever I prefer, whatever I prefer. What I would prefer is for you to be…"

My tongue caught in my throat. My manic state gave way to confusion. If there were right words for this moment, I didn't have them.

"You'd prefer me to be what, Rosemary?"

"*Sixteen!*" It was all I could think to say. I could not accept what Emrys was telling me. It was ridiculous. He was just a boy. Or else, I was just as insane as he was.

"One of the unusual manifestations of my powers is that I am slowly aging *backwards* in time."

"Well, of course you are."

"I'm being very serious, Rosemary. I was an old man sometime in the fourth or fifth century, depending on which calendar you use, and now I'm slowly but surely aging toward infancy. But even that's an oversimplification of things."

I stepped back, motioning my upturned right hand from Emrys's head to his feet like I was just now seeing who he was for the first time, like my Intro to Biology teacher, Mr. Hughes, showing our class the parts of a human skeleton. "That's what you call all of this? Overly simplified?"

"I'm not so much aging backwards, as I am aging backwards through time. My tomorrow is yesterday. I was born in the future and will die in the past."

"That makes no sense whatsoever."

"That's magic for you."

"Do you know what's happening tomorrow?" I asked.

"Tomorrow as in twenty-four hours from now, or tomorrow as in the future in general?"

"Either, both, I don't know."

"I can see into the future," Emrys clarified. "But only in riddles and flashes."

"Riddles and flashes?"

"Visions and dreams actually, in which Druidic gods speak to me."

I pointed at Emrys, nodding. "Druidic gods. Super. And yet you remember yesterday even though in your timeline it supposedly hasn't happened yet?"

"Yes."

"You remember me decapitating an incubus last night?"

"I can see how this might confuse you."

"It confuses me because it's insane."

"The problem is you think of time as a straight line. Your perception begins at A, and ends at Z."

"Yeah, Emrys, people in the non-crazy world call that physics."

"Think of time more as a sphere than a straight line, everything existing and flowing into itself all at once. How we choose to physically appear at any point in that sphere is immaterial."

We made the turn where Route 2 merged with Route 4, one of the major arteries for the ever-expanding caravan of commuters fleeing the high taxes and high crime of the Beltway for the lower taxes and lower literacy rates of southern Maryland.

"My head hurts," I said. "Let's stick to the basics. You're aging backward through time, but for reasons you can't explain beyond some kooky 'time is a sphere' theory, you're still aware of your past."

"Correct," Emrys said. "Another thing to note is that I am aging very slowly. To the untrained eye, I might not appear to age at all over a period of twenty or even thirty years. But there will come a time, many years from now, when I will be awake in the womb with all my memories, and I will be fully conscious in that split-second before my brainwaves cease."

"And how can you know that will happen?"

"Because it has already happened. It is a memory of the future. My death is my birth and my birth is my death."

"Thanks for clearing that up, Benjamin Button."

"So you've seen the movie, huh?"

"It has Brad Pitt in it," I said. "You can safely assume I've watched any movie that has Brad Pitt in it."

"Even *The Dark Side of the Sun*?"

"I own a DVD copy of *The Dark Side of the Sun*, although I no longer possess a working DVD player."

"I'm assuming then that you know *Benjamin Button*, the movie, is based on a book by F. Scott Fitzgerald?"

"Well..." I didn't feel the slightest need to impress Emrys at this point, so I didn't even try to lie. "I do now."

Emrys rolled his eyes. "Rosemary."

"What could the book tell me that the movie doesn't? If I wanted to learn more about New Orleans, I'd go to Mardi Gras."

"Well, for one thing, the movie was set in New Orleans, but the book was actually set in Baltimore."

"Fine," I said. "If I wanted to learn more about Baltimore, I'd… wait a minute."

Emrys tilted his head, pointing at me. "I can see those gears spinning in that brain of yours. I'll give you a second or two to figure it out."

"*The Curious Case of Benjamin Button* took place in Baltimore. You're Benjamin Button!"

"Sort of," Emrys replied. "I'm more just someone who ran into F. Scott Fitzgerald in a bar and shared one too many whiskeys and one too many stories."

"When was that?" I pressed.

"1917, or thereabouts."

"1917?"

"Or thereabouts."

Flora retreated from the road as we plunged deeper into Calvert County. Groves of trees and fields of detasseled corn gave way to bowling alleys, tire shops, liquor stores, a happening Applebee's for a Sunday, and the requisite Dollar General.

I hoped our drive was nearing its end. This extended back and forth was more just a drawn-out deflection on my part. It was easier to pepper him with questions than to stop and think about the gravity of Emrys's litany of revelations. "So how fast are you de-aging? Does it take you ten years to look a year younger? Twenty years?"

"Tough to guess."

"Where do I fit in all of this?"

"Also difficult to speculate."

"Then let me make it easier for you to speculate. I will concede that you're the real, goddamn, living and breathing Merlin. Okay? Now, how does my unique athletic prowess fit in with you being Merlin? What could they possibly have in common? What does this have to do with the incubus I *fucking killed* last night? And why in the hell is this all happening now?"

"That's a lot of questions," Emrys said. "And a lot of profanity."

"The moment required profanity," I replied. "Being a lady is my mom's department."

"It is?" the wizard asked.

It took everything in me not to reach over and wrench the steering wheel from Emrys's grasp. Apparently I had the strength to do it. "What's that supposed to mean?

"Nothing." Emrys brushed off my agitation. "Just trying to keep it light."

"I'm done with light. Be specific. Give me my backstory."

"You were born with special powers."

"Powers?" I wondered aloud.

"Gifts, abilities, attributes, whatever you want to call them. Shortly after your birth, the sorceress Morgan le Fay visited you in the hospital and cast a cloaking spell that would diminish these powers, hide them from people who might seek to exploit them. I have been charged with watching over you."

"Powers?" I repeated.

Emrys started counting them off one by one on his hands. "Enhanced strength, speed, stamina, the total package. Surely, you've noticed."

Random moments popped into my head. St. John Neumann Field Day. The forty-seven pull-ups. Father Jules throwing a fit about having trophies for the loser boys. The bleacher I tore through with my bare hands without a scratch. How I run only at night so people can't see me reeling off five-minute miles while hardly breaking a sweat.

"Okay, so maybe I've been a little more athletic than most kids my age, but that doesn't prove anything."

"After Morgan le Fay cloaked you as an infant, these powers remained largely dormant inside you—until yesterday, when I activated them."

At this point, I was just along for the ride. "The lightning, and the sword trick?"

Emrys nodded. "Yes, Rosemary, the lightning and the sword trick. This is something I did not want to do, at least not yet. These powers mark you. You're like a neon sign for mystical creatures."

"But if my powers are what give me away, and you hadn't activated them yet, how did Rolo find us? And how many mystical creatures disguised as humans are just walking around out there waiting to kill me?"

"Not as many as you'd think, at least not for now."

I ran my fingers through my hair, leaned back into my seat. "That's reassuring."

"Because of their unique *tendencies*, an incubus is a little different than your average mystical creature."

"By 'tendencies,' you mean the whole sexually preying on sleeping women thing?"

Emrys seemed at a loss for words. I think my abruptness startled him. As we neared the town of Prince Frederick, he waved at the old couple sitting outside an old pop-up camper with a sign promising "Greg & Vicky's Fresh Blue Crabs to Go!" Presumably, these two were Greg and Vicky.

"So you *do* remember what an incubus is?" Emrys asked.

"I wish I didn't, but yes, I remember. What makes an incubus so different from your average mystical creature?"

"Incubi have the capacity to act as diviners for other magical beings."

"Diviners?"

"Detectives, intermediaries. You know, like the guys in those old period films who walk around with dowsing sticks waiting for them to point the way to water."

"A dowsing stick? You mean a divining rod?"

"Yeah, divining rods, diviners. That's what I said. Think of an incubus as a divining rod. Only instead of detecting water, he can detect changes in people's emotional and physical states."

"How does that work?"

"Hmm…" Emrys pondered his answer. "When girls reach a certain age, they go through *changes* that uniquely define them as, uh, women. While Morgan la Fay's cloaking spell was technically intact until I activated your powers last night, I suspect the enchantment started weakening the moment you had your first, you know, period."

Dear God in Heaven, was I really having the menstruation conversation with Emrys Balin? "What in the hell does that have to do with anything?"

"Teenagers go through profound changes during puberty, Rosemary…"

Apparently, I was having the menstruation conversation with Emrys Balin.

"Hormones stimulate libido and the growth, function, and transformation of the brain, bones, muscle, blood, skin, hair, breasts, and sex organs. The person you became as a teenager is fundamentally different than the person you were as an infant. The cloaking enchantment Fay put on you as a baby is, for all intents and purposes, short circuiting because you're not the person it cloaked."

"So hormones are like a vaccine against magic?"

Emrys nodded. "In a way, yes. But it's still unusual for Fay's magic to break down that quickly. There had to have been an inciting factor. Something that caused a hormonal imbalance. Have you been sick lately?"

"Does being sick of your bullshit count?"

Emrys refused to acknowledge my superlative, albeit profane wit. "A sharp rise in your pheromone levels maybe?"

I could feel my cheeks turning red. Now was not the time for an image of Benz Cooke shirtless to pop into my head, and yet there it was. "Next subject, Emrys."

He pressed on obliviously. "Think back over the last few weeks, Rosemary. Was there any particular instance you can point to when you felt stimulated or might have experienced a heightened feeling of passion?"

A particular instance? When I was in Benz's arms, when I was not in his arms and wishing I was, the dozen times a day I walked by Benz in the hallway and my heart skipped a beat. At this point, I was an all-day pulsating pheromone covered in a thin veneer of flesh. If an incubus was looking for me, he was going to find me.

"I said, *next subject!*"

For being 2,000 years old, Emrys was profoundly clueless. But clueless was better than nothing, and I needed his help. Something had changed inside me. I had tried to deny it, but it had been there since last night. It felt like I was intoxicated, but in the best way possible. Like I just chased a bowl of chocolate-covered espresso beans with a gallon of Red Bull. So much energy. So much strength. So much power. I just needed to be pointed in the right direction.

CHAPTER

11

It felt like we were lost. A paved road gave way to a dirt road just east of Prince Frederick.

"Where are we going?" I asked.

Emrys nodded in a vaguely southern direction. "My house of course."

"I thought your house was in Eastport. Don't you live with a host family?"

Emrys nodded. "I have a house in Eastport. A friend in town poses as my host father."

"A friend?"

"Atli Saevarsson, the owner of Volumes & Vinyls. Good guy."

"The record store guy with the cotton-white beard and slicked-back ponytail who looks like a cross between a Nordic god and a librarian and always smells like cigarettes?"

"That is a strikingly detailed description of Atli," Emrys said.

"Atli is a striking Swede."

"He's from Iceland actually. Likes reading novels in German. He's lived here for a while."

"Define 'a while.'"

"He's been pretending to be my father on an as-needed basis since the sixties."

I rolled my eyes. "Of course he has. So where do you and your sometimes fake dad call home?"

"About 200 acres down along the Western Shore."

"200 acres? Get out of town!"

"That's what I'm trying to do." Emrys smiled.

"But how could you afford—"

"Really, Rosemary? You have to ask? Think about interest compounding annually, and now think about it doing that for 2,000 years."

"Valid point," I said. "But still, 200 acres? That isn't exactly lying low."

"I bought it during the big real estate panic and have managed to keep my owning interest a secret by hiding behind various dummy organizations: non-profits, land trusts, conservation easements."

"The real estate panic of 2008?"

"More like 1797 actually."

"Come on, Emrys. Be straight with me."

"I feel like that's what we're doing here."

"Why here? Why *me*?"

"What?"

"You've told me I have superpowers, and that part is pretty cool. You've told me you're this old wizard, sent to watch over me, who's trapped in a teenage boy's body, and that last part is pretty freaking weird. I want to believe you, and I'm chalking up my lack of genuine internal conflict to the fact I'm just a fabulously adjusted teenager. But you haven't answered the most basic question: Why did Morgan le Fay waltz into *my* delivery room sixteen years ago? What makes me so special that you'd chase me through time just to relive high school? And what's so great about Maryland?"

"That's three questions." Emrys observed.

"Stop deflecting," I said.

"I'm not deflecting, Rosemary. Everything will be revealed. It's just not my place to reveal…well, everything."

As we passed through the town of Prince Frederick, I fought the compulsion to punch Emrys in the face again. Instead, I took a deep breath, and thought back to a simpler time. A time when my father pretended to care.

"What are you thinking about Rosemary?" Emrys interjected.

"My dad used to take me fishing down here," I said.

"Your father, he's a professor at the Naval Academy, right? And he still finds time to take you fishing? That's nice of him."

"*Nice* of him?" I scoffed. "He's a dad, Emrys. Showing up is literally the least he can do, and he rarely does that."

"What do you mean? He works hard, puts food on your table."

"Puts food on our table? You make it sound like Dad is some kind of manly hunter slaying wild beasts in the night. He's a paper pusher. The extent to which he 'puts food on our table' can be measured in his Naval Academy salary that's auto-deposited into our family's checking account once every two weeks. Mom buys the food, Mom makes the food, Dad eats the leftovers because he never bothers to show up for dinner."

"Rosemary, I'm sorry. I…I-I didn't…

I raised my hand, quietly accepting his apology. Emrys slouched in his seat. I wanted to cut him some slack. To say he was raised in a different time was an understatement.

"You had no way of knowing," I said. My tone was measuredly reassuring only to the extent he deserved it. "Like I said, Dad *used to* take me fishing. He had a doctor friend who ran a charter fishing business out of Flag Harbor. Our fishing days are behind us though. Dad's on the shortlist for Chairman of the History Department at the Academy. He's been working long hours, day and night. Doesn't have much time for his daughter, or his wife."

"Again, I'm sorry," Emrys said. "That's so unfortunate. I bet Jennifer is a great woman."

"You don't even know her."

"I know she managed to raise you for sixteen years without going nuts. That's saying something."

"What the fuck, Emrys?"

"Oh crap, you're swearing again. Did I say something wrong?"

"You sure did, Captain Sexistpants. One, it's the twenty-first century, not the sixth century. It's not my mother's exclusive job to raise me. The two immutable facts of my teenage years are this: She'd done the best she could, and Dad has failed to carry his weight. And two, you might look sixteen, but that doesn't entitle you to act sixteen and talk to a young woman like that, with your backhanded compliment like some Vineyard Vines-wearing high school jabroni."

The jabroni comment was probably over the top, but it accomplished its goal: It shut Emrys up. I took a page from Depeche Mode and enjoyed the silence.

"Home sweet home," Emrys said. He slammed on the brakes, taking a sharp turn onto a gravel road lined with honeysuckle.

"How about a little more heads up next time?" I asked.

Emrys eased the Subaru up to a tall, ivy-covered iron gate. He moved the gearshift into the park position. "Can I say something, without you ripping my head off?"

"I'm good at that, you know."

"Rosemary, please."

"Sorry," I said. "That was just too easy. Please continue."

"Thank you." Emrys exhaled, like he had been practicing this speech in his head for quite some time. "I am not your father, and I am not your mother. What I am is your friend. I'm also an old guy who's worked hard to change his old ways of thinking. When I make a mistake, that doesn't give you free license to come after me like I'm the manifestation of every bad man you've ever met. Respect goes both ways."

Damnit. The one-two metaphorical punch: sensitivity *and* empathy. Score one point for the wizard. "My bad," I said.

"Really?" Emrys countered.

"We're friends now, just as you said." I reached over with my left hand, gave his right knee a quick tap. "And you're here, which is something the men in my life generally suck at."

We exited the Subaru. I took a moment to admire the gate—a patchwork of peeling black paint and rust, flanked by two massive columns of stacked fieldstone overgrown with vegetation.

"You need to get a landscaper down here and cut back all this crap."

"Tell me about it," Emrys replied. "It's called kudzu. It was introduced from Japan into the United States at the Japanese pavilion in the 1876 Centennial Exposition in Philadelphia. It's invasive obviously, growing at a rate of about a foot per day, or as much as sixty feet per season."

"Good to know," I said without meaning it. I didn't want to encourage him. The fount of useless information in his head was likely too staggering for me to even comprehend. He was the greatest *Jeopardy!* champion no one would ever know.

Emrys waved his hand. "*Aperta*," he commanded, and the gates swung open.

"Can I ask you a favor, Emrys?"

He nodded. "Anything, Rosemary."

"Can you maybe slowly work your hocus pocus into my everyday life?"

"I thought you were a fabulously adjusted teenager?"

"Yes, I take most things in stride. And yes, tumbling off a moving horse while chopping a sex demon's head off makes for a great icebreaker in the magic department. But can we sometimes just not do magic?"

"Of course," Emrys replied. "But that wasn't magic."

"It wasn't?"

"No," he assured me. "This place is crawling with security cameras. Installed them a few years back. That was just some basic facial and voice recognition software. I busted out the Latin to make you think I was using the Force or something."

Sensitivity, empathy, *and* a Star Wars reference? Emrys was definitely growing on me.

We navigated a narrow gravel road for about a quarter mile until the road opened up to a grass clearing. A bare-timbered cabin, its foundation made of the same fieldstone that graced the entrance, sat on a gently rolling hill overlooking the clearing, which was lined on both sides by trees and divided in half by a creek that emptied into the Chesapeake Bay. A collection of rundown outbuildings dotted the property, with the exception of a red barn on the edge of the tree line that looked relatively new.

"It's beautiful out here," I said as I stepped out of the car.

Emrys nodded at the winding tendril of brackish water two knolls over. "Parker's Creek is one of the few unspoiled tributaries in the continental United States."

"You mean before you built a house here and spoiled it?"

"My property notwithstanding, this area remains one of the least disturbed watersheds on Maryland's Western Shore. You were talking about fishing with your dad."

"Not this again."

"These waters have great brown trout fishing."

"*Brown* trout?"

"They're actually indigenous to Europe. My father was a fisherman, and my mother always made brown trout when I was growing up. The Welsh call it *sewin*. Great eating fish. All it needs is a little olive oil, salt, and pepper. I like adding chili powder, but my mother's secret ingredient was sage. The smell of trout sizzling over an open fire always reminds me of home. I miss it."

"Home," I pondered. It was hard for me to imagine Emrys now as anything but the duplicitous enigma he had become. A part of me didn't trust him. But when he talked like this, I could almost pretend he was that awkward foreign exchange student again, or just a boy who missed eating dinner with his mom and dad.

"I can see why you like it out here," I said.

"You can?"

"I figure a guy who's been tooling around America since forever can't find a whole lot of things humanity hasn't managed to screw up."

"Is that what you think, Rosemary? That I've been in America this whole time?"

"I just assumed that—"

"Gods, no!" Emrys refuted. "I'd have gone stir crazy. I traveled back and forth between England and the New World for years. Served in the British Royal Navy for a bit. Even did a couple years at a Catholic seminary back in the early sixties."

"A Catholic seminary? I didn't figure you to be the religious type."

"You'd be surprised. I find comfort in many religious teachings—Judaism, Islam, Buddhism, Taoism. I once spent five years at a Tibetan monastery in total silence."

"You not talking? Now that's a miracle. So, what's the verdict?"

"Verdict?"

"On Christianity."

"There's no verdict, Rosemary. If religion could be answered with a simple 'yes' or 'no,' it would be called science. All I will say is that Christianity is less miraculous than believers want it to be but truer than skeptics will ever give it credit for."

"So you believe?"

"Do you?"

"Mental note: Never engage in a religious discussion with a wizard."

Emrys grinned. "My travels aside, I really wish I'd spent more time down here. It's been a working farm for most of the years I've owned it. I paid people to work the land until the turn of the twentieth century, when I grew weary of hiding my…*condition*. The cabin is a converted hundred-year-old granary. I hope you learn to love it as much as I do."

I knew this was the type of situation that was supposed to raise all kinds of red flags with teenage girls. A guy I barely know drives me nearly two hours from home and is talking about keeping me on his farm. But all I could do was laugh.

"*Learn to love it?* You act like we're staying here forever."

"We are."

Okay, the laugh was now a little nervous, bordering on incredulous. "I came today for some answers, not to be kidnapped."

"I'm not kidnapping you, Rosemary. You have school tomorrow. You're free to go at any time. Call your parents and check in with them right now, for all I care."

"That won't be necessary," I said. "I'm just glad we cleared that up."

"So now that you know I'm not abducting you, let me just say this was a place I hope you learn to appreciate and visit often."

"You should have led with that line. I mean, this place is beautiful and all, but a girl like me is not wired for the Western Shore."

Maryland is the only state that borders the Chesapeake Bay on both sides. If you are looking at a map, the Western Shore is on your left and the Eastern Shore is on your right. The Eastern Shore is James Michener country—summer homes of the D.C. elite rubbing elbows with working fishing towns. The Western Shore is Tom Clancy country; it's a little different.

"How is one *wired* for the Western Shore?" Emrys asked.

"You know better than I do," I said. "Farmers, factory workers, bikers, Civil War reenactors who think the wrong side won and now wear poorly fitting red baseball caps while hoping for a rematch."

"Accurate," Emrys affirmed. "We'll go back into town later this evening. I'm not kidnapping you. I'm training you."

"Training me?"

Emrys nodded. "Yes."

This was news to me. "To do what?"

"Fight."

"Who?" I asked.

"Not sure exactly."

"This whole vague, ambiguous routine you're doing makes me want to fight *you*."

"I wouldn't recommend that," Emrys said.

My eyes popped open. "Oh, really?"

"Yes, Rosemary," he answered. "Really."

"I tagged you pretty easily last week."

"Because I let you."

It sounded more like a challenge than a warning. "Relax, Emrys, I'm not going to—"

I gave him my best right hook in mid-sentence, just to catch him off guard. I was fast—really fast. I didn't need to cheat, but I did. My fist bore down on his right cheekbone. This wasn't going to end well.

Suddenly, I was face-down on the ground. Emrys sat on top of me, his forearm pushing against the back of my neck while his free hand twisted my arm behind me like a human pretzel.

"That all you have for me?" Emrys asked casually.

"Uh, what just happened?" I asked.

Emrys rolled off of me. He stood up, brushing the dirt off his knees, and offered me his hand. "Your brain got in the way. My job is to make sure it doesn't."

"I can get up on my own." I scowled, more embarrassed than angry. Taking inventory of my current state, I noticed my dress was soiled, my left knee scuffed and bleeding.

"Let's grab some lunch," Emrys said. "Maybe we can find some club soda for your dress and clean up that knee of yours."

"I just had two breakfasts an hour ago."

"Then let's grab some coffee."

"How about some ice-cold ginger beer? You shouldn't be drinking coffee at your age. It will stunt your growth."

He smiled and winked at me. "The road to salvation is paved with sarcasm, Rosemary."

I sat on Emrys's back porch sipping a glass of iced ginger beer as he dabbed my knee with an alcohol swab. I winced out of habit, but it didn't sting in the slightest. Even before my newfound powers, nothing much ever hurt me, at least in the physical sense. I executed a gymnastics routine, started a race, climbed a rope, lifted a weight, started a fight thinking no one could beat me. I would end this day knowing no one can beat me. Except maybe Emrys, when he cheated.

Why couldn't I have this kind of confidence with Benz? Was I bulletproof? Doubtful. But I could take a punch. Why couldn't I take heartbreak as easily as I could take a punch?

"You're still not training me," I said a little too defiantly, still thinking about my inadequacy when it came to Benz. "You know that, right?"

"So my demonstration meant nothing to you?" Emrys asked.

"It convinced me you're even more out there than I thought. It's one thing to be lectured by a lunatic, but quite another to be trained and stuck on an old farm in the middle of nowhere.

"To say that I will be training you might be an overstatement. It's more like I'm focusing you."

"They have pills for that, you know."

"You now have a variety of fighting aptitudes, both armed and unarmed, built into your muscle memory. You can do almost anything, from fencing to Israeli tactical knife fighting, from karate to Scandinavian folk wrestling."

"You mean I can do all that crazy stuff my mom does?"

"Jennifer?" Emrys paused. He seemed surprised, but he was hard to read sometimes, certainly harder to read than Benz. "What can your mother do?"

"She's just your basic snake-killing, obstacle course-running ass kicker. Not that it matters, as my skills didn't seem to help me just now when you had me eating dirt."

"Having the knowledge and being able to apply that knowledge are two entirely different things," Emrys said. "There's no substitute for real-world scenarios. I'm actually nowhere near as fast as you, but a little focus and discipline can make all the difference."

"If you say so," I countered skeptically.

Emrys backed away from me, stepping off the porch. He opened his right hand, his palm facing up. "*Apparentis*," he said. A staff crowned with a small yellowish gemstone appeared in his hand. He began spinning it around his body and under his arms, his movements tight and choreographed. It reminded me of the Marine Corps whenever they performed their rifle routine on the Naval Academy grounds.

"Great, so you can spin a baton." I stood and reached for the staff, pretending to be unimpressed. "What's your staff made out of anyway, a unicorn's horn?"

"A unicorn horn?" Emrys said. "Yeah, good luck catching one of those elusive beasts, let alone getting anywhere near one of their horns."

"Is that a challenge?"

Emrys ignored me. "If you must know, it is a narwhal tusk."

I let go of the staff. "Well, that's cruel."

"Trust me," Emrys said. "He didn't need it anymore."

Emrys escorted me away from his house, across the clearing to the red barn. The barn stood over three stories tall, red horizontal siding trimmed in white. Two sliding doors hung in the center of the barn on stainless steel tracks. The hayloft doors were closed tight several feet above the sliding doors, while a vintage gooseneck barn light hung above the loft doors, just below the widow's peak.

Emrys raised his staff again. The yellow gemstone started glowing. "*Aperta*," he ordered, and the barn doors slid open.

"Facial and voice recognition software?" I asked.

"Nope," Emrys answered. "Magic."

The place smelled of straw and cedar, and horse stables lined the west wall. We walked under the hayloft to the center of the barn.

"Is that what I think it is?" I said, pointing. An elevated square platform trimmed in black ropes rose from the middle of the floor.

"If you think it's a boxing ring," Emrys replied, "then yes."

It was then I noticed the weapons of every shape and size hanging on the wall opposite the stables. Old weapons interspersed with new. Spears and compound bows, maces and boxing gloves.

I was trading old awards for new awards. The St. John Neumann Field Day trophy case replaced by a literal arsenal. I giggled at the juxtaposition of it all, and not just because I love the word "juxtaposition."

"Is this all for me?" I asked.

"More or less," Emrys answered. "Been collecting them for years. But while we're on the subject of stretching your imagination, do you remember that weapon you used last night?"

"The sword? Yeah, I remember it."

"You take Latin in school, I assume."

"Of course."

"Do you know the Latin word for 'sword'?"

I nodded.

"Well?" Emrys asked.

"Well *what?*"

"What is it?"

"Now that you're putting me on the spot, I forget."

"It's *gladio.*"

"*Gladio?*" I asked. "That doesn't sound—"

My words were interrupted by a bright flash of light. I closed my eyes.

When I opened my eyes, a sword was in my right hand.

"That's better," Emrys observed.

I stared at the sword in disbelief. "How did you do that? *How did I do that?*"

Emrys ran his fingers along the flat side of the double-edged blade. "A sword isn't the most discrete of weapons. I cast a spell of portability on it."

"A spell of portability?" I asked.

"That's not what it's really called, but for our purposes that's what it does. You can now summon and dismiss this sword at will. The spell essentially creates an extra-dimensional storage locker for your weapon."

I smirked, spinning the sword by its handle. "Get out of here!"

"Don't believe me? Try it. Do you know the Latin word for 'disappear'?"

"I don't think so."

"It's *evanescet.*"

"Okay then." I stood, shoulders squared and feet planted, just in case I needed to brace myself. "*Evanescet.*"

The sword disappeared.

"*Gladio!*" I commanded, and the sword promptly reappeared. "*Evanescet... Gladio... Evanescet... Gladio.*"

Emrys raised his hands, looking to ratchet down my enthusiasm. "Okay, Rosemary, I think you got it. But there is one important restriction on the portability spell."

The asterisk. There's always an asterisk. "Which is?"

"You must remain in contact with the sword. If you're disarmed or throw your weapon at someone, you can't transport it back to your hand by making it dematerialize where you left it and then have it magically rematerialize back in your hand. It always defaults to re-appearing in your right hand, your sword hand. But you need to be touching it with some body part, any body part, to make it disappear."

"Noted," I said. In a shape loosely resembling a cross superimposed on a windmill, I did four diagonal cuts with my sword, two verticals, two horizontals, and one straight stab. "How'd that look?"

"That was your basic nine-cut practice exercise," Emrys observed. "One of many exercises I would suggest for conditioning attack movement muscles."

"If you say so," I replied. "But what do I have to worry about with this piece of hardware in my hand?"

Emrys shook his head. "That sentiment was expressed by literally everyone before you who has possessed that piece of hardware."

"Everyone before me?"

"The three crowns in the pommel. You know what they signify?"

"Not a clue," I said.

"The House of Pendragon. The Coat of Arms of King Arthur. Three golden crowns on a field of azure representing the three realms of Britain—England, Scotland, and Wales."

"This isn't just any sword, is it?"

My wizard bestie crossed his arms. "I think you know the answer."

"Yeah, but I want to hear you say it."

Emrys bowed, his arms still crossed. "You, Rosemary Arlynn Banson, are Excalibur's keeper."

The midday sun shined through the open door in the barn. I held the silver, practically translucent blade in the light, watching it reflect the colors of the rainbow. *Excalibur's keeper.* Me? The girl who loses her iPhone when she goes to bed at night and then ends up searching for it using the flashlight…on her iPhone?

"But why?" I asked.

"I dodged that question earlier, didn't I?"

"You dodged multiple questions, but I can repeat them. You are, after all, pretty freaking old."

"Go for it." Emrys caught my punchline and threw it right back at me. "But I'm pretty freaking old, so please, talk slowly."

"Why did Morgan le Fay waltz into my delivery room sixteen years ago? What makes me so special that you'd chase me through time just to relive high school? And what's so great about Maryland?"

"Fay was protecting you." Emrys nodded at my sword. "For reasons we can get into later, you're Excalibur's rightful owner, your social life at American Martyr is a bit of a train wreck right now and an extra friend in your corner wouldn't hurt, and Maryland is a bit of a nexus for things that go bump in the night and softshell crab sandwiches."

"*Evanescet!*" Excalibur disappeared. I raised my hands to my hips, balling them both into fists while tapping my foot. "Well, that answer was wildly vague, judgmental, and punctuated by unnecessary culinary sarcasm."

Emrys bowed. "I learned from the master."

That made me smile. "And don't you forget it."

"I've given you a lot of information to process in one day."

I pointed at him accusingly. "But what you haven't given me are stakes."

"Are you hungry?"

"Not *steaks*, you idiot. *Stakes*! What's missing from this entire day is a reason for me following you out here. A reason to stay.

No moment where you grabbed my hand and said, 'Whether you trust me or not, you have nothing to lose.' I just went along with everything, no questions asked, didn't bother to call my parents, Joslin, or even my study group."

"Study group?" Emrys asked.

"Honors Pre-calc midterm."

"Still got a C-?"

"Might be pushing a D at this rate."

"Yikes." Emrys reached for my hand, much like he had done in McDonald's with Joslin, only instead of a headshake he slid his hand palm up beneath mine. Did my breakfast with Joslin really only happen this morning? It seemed like days, weeks had passed, and yet if I thought about it, I could still taste McMuffins and hash browns in my mouth. Emrys brought his free hand over the top of our clutched embrace.

"I *want* you to trust me," Emrys said, squeezing my hand hard but not really. "You *do* have something to lose. Today was about more than just showing you my war room and formally introducing you to Excalibur. It was about opening a door to a world you won't understand at first, but will hopefully learn to appreciate, to forgive, and to love. My training will save your life, Rosemary Arlynn Banson. It will save the lives of your parents, the lives of your friends, and ultimately save the world."

This time, I brought my one free hand over. Looking Emrys in the eyes, I gently rapped his knuckles with my fingers. "You should've led with that line instead of the out-of-season peaches, but at least I have one less thing to worry about."

Emrys released my hand. He took a couple steps back, befuddled. "Why do you say that?"

"Telling me the fate of the world rests on my shoulders really takes the pressure off me acing that Pre-Calc midterm."

CHAPTER

12

"It's a triple full. It's not rocket science, Joslin."

"You just make sure your layout is high enough, Rosemary."

"It *will* be high enough if you set it high enough."

A gymnast's greatest nemesis is not her weight, her nerves, the judges, or even her opponents. It is her leotard. The key to being a great gymnast is not connecting your skills, nailing your landing, or staying on that stupid balance beam. It's seeing how long you can resist the urge to fix your wedgie. Some never adapt; they're a constant flurry of fidgeting and pulling. Others are so oblivious to their bare butt bouncing around that they're practically strippers. I was always somewhere in between. I made eye contact with the judges, smiled, and then found a quiet corner of the gymnasium to dig my way out of trouble.

Tonight, I didn't care. I was too tired to care. Emrys eventually drove me home, just as he promised he would. We started our training in earnest. Even with my "enhancements," my right arm was sore from casting a fishing rod for three hours a night—an exercise Emrys added this week to condition my muscle memory for my new sword. On top of which, I forgot to pack my sweatpants, so the fencing team was going to get a show.

My new sword. Holy crap. Here I am acting like I just received the next-generation iPhone for my birthday, not the most famous sword in the history of ever.

I didn't really need a spotter, but I asked Joslin to be one anyway. I felt guilty. With everything that had been going on, I had been blowing her off the last few days and missed our Sunday morning McMass run. Mom asked me to pick up a few bags of Halloween candy for the trick or treaters later in the week, so I invited Joslin along. We stopped in the candy store at the Annapolis Mall on our way to the gym. I could tell she wasn't particularly keen on being at the school gym on a Sunday night. That made two of us.

"You're going to break your neck," Joslin said.

"Only if you suck at spotting me," I clarified.

"Hitting for the other team now, Rosemary?" Levi shouted across the gym.

Just my luck, Richard and Levi were in the building. The gym was dimly lit, the tradeoff for Sunday mat time being that the school didn't spring for the electricity. I had heard the boys clinging and clanging for about an hour. I could smell them from here. Maybe it was my heightened nose latching on to every little sensory nugget, but I could swear their sweat smelled good, like honey. I didn't tell them that.

"Lesbian humor," I shouted back. "How original of you, Levi." I looked to Joslin for her usual affirmation. She stared blankly into space.

"Joslin?"

"What?" she said.

"Something on your mind?"

"I thought we agreed that we were going to be each other's dates to Fall Fling."

"We did."

"And your boyfriend is fine with that?"

"My boyfriend?"

"That's what I said."

"Look, I know people saw Benz and me outside the football locker room last week after the game. But nothing happened."

"I'm not talking about Benz," Joslin said. "I'm talking about Emrys."

"Oh, that."

"Yeah, *that*. I don't know what's worse—you ditching me again, or the fact you're taking my Emrys to Fall Fling."

"*Your* Emrys? Since when?"

"Since McDonald's," Joslin replied. "Come on, you had to have noticed the connection. He was practically undressing me with his eyes."

Emrys had confessed to putting "a harmless enchantment spell" on Joslin that morning at McDonald's, just so she'd be more agreeable to him taking me away from her. After lecturing him about the rules of consent in the twenty-first century, he promised to never do it again. But that didn't matter tonight. Spell or no spell, best friends weren't supposed do this to one another. I'd made a commitment to her, and I had broken it.

Then again, circumstances had changed. Compartmentalizing my guilt wasn't a luxury; it was a necessity. I'm not a parent casually telling their child Santa is real or that the family dog has gone to a farm. I'm saving my best friend's life with my deceit. Keeping the mystical creatures focused on yours truly. I fought the urge to tell Joslin my secret on a daily basis, but she couldn't know. As long as our friendship could be measured in *One Tree Hill* binges, a pint of salted caramel ice cream, and a dry shoulder to cry on, Joslin was safe.

"You two need to just make out and get it over with," Richard said. He and Levi stood at the edge of the mat, arms folded, fencing bags at their feet.

I looked in the direction of their pretty, honey-smelling faces. "Mind your own business, guys."

Richard smiled at me, his expression more menacing than smarmy now. "The name is *Coach* Alexander, and you are my business, apprentice of Myrddin."

"Oh no," I said. This couldn't be happening. Not now. Not with Joslin here.

She looked at me quizzically. "Apprentice of *who*?"

"Nighty night," Levi said. He threw two small, marble-like spheres at our feet that exploded to dust on impact.

The dust rose to our noses. Joslin stumbled, coughing as I covered my nose and mouth with the crook of my arm. In the split second after Joslin's eyes rolled back into her head and before she hit the floor, I caught her. Kneeling beside her, I placed my index and middle fingers on her neck to the side of her windpipe. She was just unconscious, her pulse still strong. I was disoriented, but still upright.

"We would've taken care of you earlier," Levi said, "but that meddlesome wizard was always around. It's a rather aggressive sedative, but completely harmless. We're bounty hunters, not murderers."

Richard raised his finger, tilting his head toward his partner.

"Fine, Richard," Levi acknowledged. "If the money is right, yes, we are technically sometimes murderers. But in this instance, the gas was just supposed to knock you both out. Don't worry, Rosemary, all we really want is you. If you make nice, we'll leave Joslin here, and when she wakes up, the last thing she'll remember is you being a bad friend."

Fantastic. Levi wasn't just a bounty hunter, but an insightful one. The total package.

I stood, fists clenched but knees wobbling. Whatever was in those spheres packed a punch, but I couldn't let them know that. "You better hope she's okay," I said, "because it will take a lot more than magic dust to stop me from kicking both your butts."

"Richard," Levi said, turning to his teammate. He spun his foil in his hand and reached for his fencing bag at his feet. "Under the circumstances, I find foils a bit too civilized, don't you?"

"But of course," Richard said, having already dropped his foil. He crouched down, rifling through his bag, looking for something. "You see, Rosemary, fencing is comprised of three disciplines: the foil, which Levi and I were just using, the épée, and the saber. The foil is slender and needle-like, the épée a little heavier, the saber the biggest and deadliest of the three."

"Let me guess," I said. "You're going with sabers."

They raised their blades in unison. "Indeed."

"Cute swords." I clenched my fist as I brought my right arm down to my side. "*Gladio!*"

I tripped as Excalibur appeared in my hand, somewhat mitigating the intimidation factor of my gesture.

"Dizzy, Rosemary?" Richard said, apparently unimpressed by the sword.

"*Rosemary?*" My name sounded strange coming out of my mouth, like someone else was saying it. The sedative was starting to kick in. My fine motor skills seemed reasonably intact, but my tongue was numb, and it felt like I had pudding in my brain.

I didn't like my odds. I needed to distract them. Hopefully, what I lacked in sword-fighting technique I made up for in sarcasm. "So I guess we've established that you're both in on the conspiracy to turn my life into a teen slasher movie?"

"I'm actually partial to coming-of-age films with an underlying social message," Richard said, his smile hovering just over the cutting edge of his saber. "They're just a tad more believable. How about you, Levi?"

"Me?" Levi said, pointing at himself. "I would have to go the completely opposite direction. I like young adult fantasies in which the fantasy elements exist as metaphors for real-life teenage problems."

"How ironic of you, brother," Richard remarked.

Their back and forth gave me time to look around the gym and assess my options. The exit doors were close enough to reach, but that would have left my best friend a vulnerable, unconscious pincushion. Richard and Levi said they weren't interested in killing Joslin, but taking this fight away from her was still my first priority. The ceiling maybe? Yes. It was worth a shot.

"Shall we begin?" Levi asked.

"Anything that will make you two shut up works for me," I said.

They both rushed at me. I grabbed Excalibur with two hands. Lifting it over my head, I threw it end over end at Richard and Levi.

They dodged the throw easily, stepping aside as the sword spun directly between them. "You missed."

I leapt straight in the air. My fingers caught one of the gymnasium rafters, but barely. I made my way across the room, then dropped back to the floor. I turned, facing my adversaries from the other side of the gym, Excalibur in my hand.

What Richard and Levi didn't realize was that my acrobat routine was a distraction. All I did was follow the path of my sword, land on the other side of the gymnasium floor, and then conveniently retrieve Excalibur from the foam-core poster behind me on the gymnasium wall. Life-size pictures of the American Martyr senior cheerleaders lined the wall. Excalibur had plunged through the cheer captain's poster in the middle, through the cinder block wall, and embedded itself halfway down the blade in the middle of Avery's face. Oops.

"Surely you can do better than that," I chided. "I expected a lot more of a fight from idiot frat boys like you."

Richard and Levi responded to my taunting in kind. They ran like gazelles, covering the gym floor in only a few strides. They were not human; I knew that much now. They surrounded me, sabers raised.

"More incubi, I assume?" I said.

"The incubus you faced before was not that much of a warrior," Richard replied. "The one you called Wilamuck was an average swordsman, an even worse horseman, and a poor overall fighter, all of which I realize in hindsight is woefully obvious, given that you still have all your limbs attached."

"Can't say the same for ole' Rolo," I said, trying to keep them talking. "Color me unimpressed. If you've seen one incubus, you've seen them all."

"Dear child," Richard said. "Levi and I are not incubi."

Richard and Levi closed their eyes. A shadow seemed to fall over them. Their hair and skin turned white. Goosebumps raised on my arms. The temperature in the gymnasium dropped. I could see my breath.

They opened their eyes, four black almonds staring not at me, but through me.

"Okay, I'm at a loss," I said. "What are you? Albinos with an attitude?"

"We are faerie," Richard said. "Older than the oceans, wiser than the wind, fair of face though dark of heart. You'll not find it so easy to defeat—"

Richard's mouth was half-open when he was stabbed from behind, a sword poking through his chest. He looked down at the blade in disbelief, his face a twisted smile as he dropped his saber. Slowly, he slid off the blade, face planting on the gymnasium floor.

Richard was dead.

A familiar, sweater-vested man stepped over Richard's body. My father wiped the blood off his blade with the monogrammed pocket square my mom had given him on their ten-year anniversary.

"*Dad?*" I asked in disbelief.

"That's the thing about faeries," he said. "They never shut up."

"Brother, I shall avenge you!" Levi screeched. He hurled himself at my father, who was caught off guard by the faerie's ferocity. Dad was slow to defend himself. Levi raised his saber for a killing blow, but then stumbled backward, his head wrenching back as if someone had just punched him in the face. That was when I saw the long-handled dandelion cutter embedded in his forehead. Levi fell to the ground, his black faerie blood splashing on my mother's camouflage cargo pants.

Mom approached Levi's corpse. She paused to admire her handiwork, then pulled the long-handled dandelion cutter out of his frontal lobe. She casually wiped her bloodied weed whacker turned weapon on the sole of her left hiking boot. "There will be no avenging tonight, faerie."

"*Mom?*"

If I was being honest, killing things is kind of in my mom's wheelhouse. She was less of a surprise than Dad, but not by much. Whereas Dad was dressed for a day in the office, Mom looked like Marion from *Raiders of the Lost Ark*: the button-down long-sleeved khaki shirt rolled at the sleeves, the sweat-soaked bandana knotted around her neck, the camo cargos and hiking boots.

"Getting a little rusty, husband?" Mom asked, looking up at Dad.

Dad wiped the nervous sweat off his brow. "That's what I have you here for, wife."

Mom squeezed the back of Dad's arm, giving an affirming rub for good measure.

I didn't know what was grossing me out more: the faeries bleeding out on the American Martyr gymnasium floor, or the fact that my parents were flirting.

"Ahem," I said.

"Oh, hello dear," Mom said, turning to me.

Dad's sword was a beautiful blade—double-edged like Excalibur, but closer to white than silver, with a golden grip ending in a dragon's head. "So, Rosemary," Dad said, "tell us about this boy who's taking you to Fall Fling."

Of course the guy with the longsword would ask me that question. Segues were so overrated. "Excuse me?" I said.

"I think we can stop kidding one another at this point," Mom said. "Wouldn't you agree, Emrys?"

He seemed to appear out of nowhere. A random shadow slinking out of the corner of the gym and taking form in the blink of an eye.

"*Emrys?*" This was my new thing apparently. Repeating names dumbfounded as people jumped from the shadows.

He nodded at me. "Hi, Rosemary."

I turned back to my mother. "You mean, you know about *him*, about *me?*"

She looked away from Emrys and straight at me. "Your father and I have dedicated our lives to protecting you."

"Got to say I'm a little over being told how I need protecting. I think I can manage all on my own." I pointed to the two fresh corpses on the ground. "Not to mention, you two seemed to have gone a little overboard on the protection front tonight."

"Please, Rosemary." Dad raised his hand. "When Emrys told us your secret was revealed, we thought about coming to you right away."

"Why didn't you?"

"Maybe we were just being naïve, your mother and me. Maybe we thought we could live out the rest of our days in peace and quiet, tucked happily away in this small town, with Merlin watching over us."

"If Merlin is supposed to be watching over you, why was he hiding just now and letting you two fight Richard and Levi?" I asked.

"Because I like to make a dramatic entrance?" Emrys mused.

"Shut up," I said, looking at Dad while pointing at Emrys. "Wait a second. Why are we all just casually calling Emrys 'Merlin'?" Are my parents part of this mass delusion too?

Mom jumped back into the conversation. "It's no delusion, Rosemary."

"I don't know about that," I said. "We all have to be pretty delusional at this point to buy into whatever *this* is."

"Rosemary," Emrys interjected. "I know this is a lot to take in. Let me try to simplify this a bit—in fact, why don't I start with your parents? Your mother's name, Jennifer. Does that name strike you as unusual?"

I shook my head. "No."

"You're right, it probably wouldn't. As popular as it is now, however, 'Jennifer' is a thoroughly modern name that only came into widespread use in the twentieth century."

"Yeah, so?"

"So, it's actually a Cornish adaptation of a much older name."

I could not believe where this was going. "*How much older*, Emrys?"

"In the Irish tongue, it was pronounced *Findabair*. In Welsh, *Gwenhwyfar*. But the original English derivation of Jennifer is—"

"Let me guess," I said, feigning a bow that morphed into a goofy head bob. "Guinevere?"

Mom curtsied in her cargo pants and hiking boots. "Guinevere Rosmarinus Pendragon, former Queen of the Realm, at your service."

"And I suppose Dad is King Arthur?"

"Hardly," Dad scoffed. He dropped his left hand, gripping the bejeweled gold sheath fastened at his waist, and returned his sword to its housing. "I am as my name suggests, as your name suggests. I am—"

"Wait," I interrupted. "Before you finish. Say it like Mom did. With the genuflecting and everything. Really sell it to me."

Dad narrowed his eyes disapprovingly, but played along anyway, although he bowed instead of genuflecting.

"I am Banson, the heir of Benwick, son of King Ban. Where once stood the hand of King Arthur now stands your father. I am Sir Lancelot du Lac."

His revelation carried its own air of hallowed reverence, and I did my best to respond to the moment the only way I knew how.

"Good lord, Dad."

CHAPTER

13

Emrys dipped a bite of waffle and fried chicken in the maple syrup pooling on his plate. "There's nothing a plate of chicken and waffles can't solve," he said, stuffing the bite in his mouth.

"Oh, I can think of a few things," I retorted.

I was barely starting to warm up to the idea of Emrys being Merlin. Now, I was supposed to believe that I was the daughter of Guinevere and Lancelot? My life had become a run-on sentence of ridiculousness, the world I thought I knew an afterthought. It was scary.

My plate of bacon and eggs sat untouched on the table. "Rosemary, dear, you need to eat," Mom noted. "You have to keep up your strength."

"Why?"

"For *various* reasons," Dad added.

I folded my arms, leaned back in my chair. "Consider me officially on a hunger strike until I have some answers."

Emrys took charge of Richard and Levi. After he stashed them in his trunk, I asked him what he was going to do with their bodies. He said, "Same thing I did with Rolo Wilamuck's headless corpse. The farm has a big incinerator." So that's freaking gross.

Joslin woke up right before we left the gym. We told her she had a fainting spell, and she bought it. I thought the dead faerie blood on Mom's and Dad's clothes would be the harder sell, but it was black and smelled like honey, so dark chocolate was believable. After dropping Joslin off at her house, we went home for a change of clothes—Mom and Dad to change into something not stained by "dark chocolate," me to slip out of my leotard—then headed over to Chick & Ruth's Delly for a late-night meal.

Chick & Ruth's was a legendary diner in downtown Annapolis. Mom, Dad, Emrys, and I sat at a four-top table in the back corner. We were the only ones in the restaurant save for the third-shift waitress. Mom ordered the Western omelet. Dad wanted pancakes, but Mom said, "You're obviously going to have to order something with onions in it," kissed him on the lips, and then winked at him. After all these years of watching them fall out of love and praying they figured things out, I was not prepared for them to suddenly be a functional, let alone publicly affectionate couple.

Dad just kept smiling at Mom, like he'd found a long-lost Christmas present hidden in the attic. For reasons that were now obvious, Mom and Dad had very few photographs from before I was born. The only frame of reference I had for what Dad might have looked like as Lancelot was an old ID card I found tucked away in his sock drawer. Guessing Emrys had acquired it for Dad after he popped fresh out of the time machine, temporal portal, wormhole— whatever BS name Emrys was calling it. In the picture, Dad had yet to cut his hair short, his thick mop a perfect complement to those earnest blue eyes, the color of a spring sky. Why he had chosen to cut his hair off, I would never understand.

Holy crap. Was I starting to believe in all this? Was I starting to believe in *them*?

Mom wiped the omelet remnants off her mouth. "Where do you want us to begin?" she asked.

"Apparently about 1500 years ago," I said.

Mom opened her mouth to speak. Emrys cut her off. "I can handle this, Jennifer."

"Hold that thought," I instructed, flagging down the waitress. "Ma'am, some more coffee please." And a shovel while you're at it, I thought to say, because it was about to get deep in here.

"Coffee will stunt your growth," Emrys chided.

"Nope, not now," I said, just as Emrys started to smile. "The next joke out of you gets a fist out of me."

"It will all make sense very soon, Rosemary," Dad said.

The waitress poured me a fresh cup of coffee. I was normally an orange juice kind of gal, but today qualified as a black coffee day. The coffee was acidic on my tongue, scalding my throat on the way down. The pain was a needed distraction.

"Somehow, Dad, I doubt you and Mom are going to clarify much of anything for me. So, your parents dying when you were young, Mom's dad running out on his family, Grandma 'SEEN-cha': all lies?"

"'SEEN-cha' was indeed my mother, Rosemary," Mom interjected. "You still have her skin, and you would've loved her."

"And the Victorian slang?" I replied. "*Chuckaboo, gigglemug, bone box.* That's all just a bunch of gibberish?"

Mom shrugged with a self-congratulatory smile that appeared more mug than giggle. "I happen to like that gibberish. It reminds us where we come from."

"But you were born 1400 years before the Victorian Age."

Mom refused to relent. "I don't see why that makes any diff—"

"Enough." I bowed my hand with my head raised. "Care to bail them out of this conversation, Emrys?"

The boy wizard tried to balance an overloaded bite of chicken and waffles on his fork, then he pointed the fork at me. "Our story begins with—"

"You can skip ahead," I said. "I've seen enough of the movies, read the books." Arthur pulls the sword out of the stone, becomes ruler of Camelot, falls in love with Guinevere, makes her his queen, becomes pals with Lancelot, then catches Mom and Dad rolling around in the sheets. What's next?"

"Your abridgement does your parents a disservice, Rosemary" Emrys said.

I glanced at Mom and Dad. "It'll do for now, *Merlin.*"

As was the case in most situations in which people poked him, Emrys poked back. "No, it won't do. We owe you a full account of events, but Jennifer and Alan are your parents, and you still owe them your respect as their daughter. Arthur, your mother, your father, Merlin: We were all different people back then, each of us broken in fundamental ways that prevented us from having healthy relationships and making good decisions."

Emrys was right of course. They had dropped a lot on me, but my attitude wasn't helping. Sixteen years ago, Mom and Dad were young and in love. Only nineteen then, Mom was very young. People young and in love do stupid things. It didn't earn them my forgiveness, but it probably deserved at least a cordial chat over chicken and waffles.

"Whatever," I said. It was as close to an apology that I'd be giving my parents for the foreseeable future. "Continue."

"Very well," Emrys acknowledged. "The stories told through the ages always of course speak of your parents' relationship, but they neglect to mention a child. They neglect to mention *you,* Rosemary. Guinevere had suspected she was pregnant for several weeks. When the goddess Arianrhod came to me in a dream and confirmed her pregnancy to me, I told Guinevere I knew her secret."

"Arian *who?*" I asked.

"Arianrhod. She's the Druidic goddess of fertility, among other things. I was one of the chosen few to whom she entrusted *Lust boren profecie.*" Emrys said.

"The Lust Borne Prophecy?" I translated.

Emrys nodded.

"Lay it on me," I said.

With Emrys sitting beside her at the table, Mom extended her arm in front of the boy wizard, like that thing moms do while driving with their kids in the passenger seat when they slam on their brakes. I doubted even my mom's muscular arm could prevent this wreck from happening.

"I got this," Mom said. "The original proto-Germanic and later Latin version of the prophecy are barely decipherable, and even the Old English translation is a bit clunky. I for one like the newer, more modern English version of the prophecy. It retains the prophecy's meaning, meter, and lyricism while not—"

"Just spit it out, Mom!" I shouted, banging my fist on the table. Our waitress was on a break, so we had the diner mostly to ourselves. But the fry cook standing at the grill heard me. He turned to see what the commotion was about.

"All good here," Dad said, raising his hand. The cook returned to his grill.

Jennifer's eyes darted up and to the right, like she didn't quite remember the words. But then, she remembered. The poem rolled off her tongue, like a prayer. Or a warning.

> *"The moon shall be from whence*
> *the sea consumes the fallen son.*
> *The lust borne tide, thy will subside,*
> *the course of Avalon run.*
> *Her fertile song naught overlong*
> *shall play then play no more.*
> *By the blade, the bed is made.*
> *The kingdom at your door."*

I sat there for a moment, not knowing what else to say. My parents and Emrys just stared at me, waiting for a response. Cold bacon and eggs suddenly sounded good. I stabbed my two over-easy eggs with a fork. Rather than eat the lacerated eggs right away, I dipped a slice of bacon in the yolk and shoved the bite in my mouth.

Mom, Dad, and Emrys afforded me a few more blissfully quiet bites of bacon and eggs. I finished things off with a swig of coffee. Raising my hand to my face, I cleared my throat. I dabbed my mouth with a napkin, then ran my tongue across my teeth. "That prophecy is about me, isn't it?"

The Three Musketeers nodded in unison.

"Well…" I said, navigating the profanity in my head for that one word to give this moment a proportionate response. "Bullocks."

CHAPTER
14

"Bullocks, huh?" Emrys mused.

"Would you have preferred something a little more offensive?" I asked.

"Bullocks is plenty offensive. You know it means 'balls,' right?"

"I've heard Mom and Dad say it around the house. I thought it was just another word for bullshit."

"A word you're obviously comfortable using," Emrys noted. "But that's not what it means."

I smacked Emrys on the knee. "I think I like your definition better."

The morning was cold, the air tinged with that perpetual fall smell of burning leaves. The pink hues of twilight gave way to the oranges of sunrise. After breakfast, I told Mom and Dad to go home and not talk to me for the next hundred years or so. Emrys and I walked the two blocks down to City Dock. We sat on the stone bench next to the Kunta Kinte-Alex Haley Memorial overlooking Annapolis Harbor.

"So, this Lust Borne Prophecy," I said. "Care to elaborate?"

"Arthur's father was the passionate but equally headstrong King Uther Pendragon," Emrys replied.

"Wait, you're just starting—from the beginning? No ambiguous half-truths or annoying riddles? No needlessly elaborate setup ending with a 'gotcha' cliffhanger?"

"Uther..." Emrys sighed, ignoring me. "Never was there a king more passionate—nor more lustful and single-minded. He ordered me to disguise him as the Duke of Cornwall so he could share a bed with the Duke's wife, Igraine. The Duke of Cornwall and Igraine also happened to be the parents of Morgause. The price of Uther's lust was a child, Arthur. I took Arthur from Igraine and had him raised secretly by a trusted friend, Sir Ector, alongside his stepbrother, Kay, until such time when Arthur happened upon the Sword in the Stone and pulled the sword out. Arthur became king by divine right, slept with his half-sister Morgause, who had disguised herself as Guinevere so that she might conceive a son to become heir to Arthur's throne. That son's name was Mordred. It is Mordred who—"

"On second thought, let me stop you right there," I interrupted. "Like I said back at the diner, I've seen plenty of the movies, read some of the books. We don't need to rehash the origin story, and I'd especially like to stop thinking about Arthur sleeping with his sister, and having a kid with her. Gross!"

"Half-sister," Emrys corrected me with a nod and a pointed index finger.

"As if that makes it okay."

"We really should talk about Mordred. The prophecy says that—" Emrys began.

"Can we maybe back things up a bit, before we dive right into the prophecy?"

"Ask me anything, and I'll answer," Emrys boasted. "At this point, that's the least we owe you."

I appreciated how he said "we," not letting Mom and Dad off the hook. "I have one main question, but in three parts: How did you, Mom and Dad, and Excalibur get to twenty-first century Maryland?"

"Are you sure you're ready for those answers?"

"Emrys," I replied. "I've been ready for these answers since the day I went from crying over boys to chopping their heads off."

"Point taken," Emrys said with a knowing smirk. I liked these moments, when we were on the same wavelength, as peers more so than teacher and pupil. When he was more Emrys than Merlin.

"When I found out your mother was pregnant," Emrys began, "I swore I'd never let her child be born and raised in Camelot. Not under the same roof as Morgause. So, I performed a temporal displacement spell that transported you and your parents through time, far away from Camelot."

The math wasn't adding up in my head. "And then you did what exactly? Hung out? Waited for Arthur, Morgause, and their toothless, banjo-playing son to die, and then just loitered around the planet for 1500 years?"

"That's not a very nice thing to say about Mordred, Rosemary. You're marginalizing a person you don't even know."

"I know his dad is also his uncle, and that's not great genetic odds. You were the one who said we should talk about Mordred. Be honest. What are his teeth like? I bet they're terrible, aren't they?"

Emrys ignored me. "We're getting way off topic. You were asking me what I did. I drugged King Arthur, stole Excalibur, and followed your parents through the temporal displacement portal. Only I ended up in the 1600s and your parents ended up in the 2000s. I've only been 'loitering around the planet' for a little over 400 years. In linear years, I'm actually closer to 1000 than 2000 in age."

Emrys was attempting to be sarcastic, but I didn't care. "So you, Morgan le Fay, Mom and Dad, and Excalibur, didn't travel through time together?"

Emrys nodded. "That's what I'm telling you, Rosemary. I sent your parents ahead of me when we were fleeing Camelot, and then I followed shortly thereafter with Excalibur. While the temporal spell pointed us all to the same place, it did not send us all to the same time. The spell was calibrated to the exact moment each of us entered the portal. I couldn't have been any more than a few minutes behind your parents, which somehow translated to being 400 years ahead of them on the other side of the portal."

"It's like Mom and Dad took a left turn and ended up in the twenty-first century, while you took a right turn and ended up in the seventeenth century."

"Yes." Emrys offered a half-shrug, as if he was appreciative of my attempt to reason out the unreasonable. "A simple but accurate analogy."

"How did Fay get here?" I asked.

"She arrived here under her own power."

"What does her own power consist of?"

"A better grasp of temporal spells, for one," Emrys answered. "Fay arrived about a month before you were born, to observe your parents."

"So, Mom, Dad, and Fay take the people mover to the twenty-first century. What the hell were you doing for 400 years?"

"Making history," Emrys boasted. "I found a job straight away as chief steward to George Calvert, the first Baron of Baltimore. We traveled from England to the New World, and under the orders of Queen Consort Henrietta Maria founded a new colony on the Newfoundland peninsula, which we named Avalon. The name was my idea, and the colony was a colossal failure."

"Because it was in Canada and North Face jackets hadn't been invented yet?"

"She'll be here all week, ladies and gentlemen," Emrys said.

I shook my head, grinning. "I can't always be pretty, but I can always be funny."

Emrys continued. "I stayed on as master of the house for Lord Baltimore's second son, Leonard Calvert, the first colonial governor of the Province of Maryland."

"And I suppose you had a hand in naming Maryland after Henrietta Maria as well?"

"That I did," Emrys affirmed. "And I dutifully served Governor Calvert for twenty years, until the jokes about me getting younger with age turned to accusations of heresy and witchcraft."

"And Excalibur?" I asked.

"I gave it to Lord Baltimore as a gift, who in turn gave it to his son. Excalibur hung over the fireplace in the Calvert home for decades, until I stole it again right after they fired me."

"So, you've kept Excalibur all this time?"

"I misplaced it once or twice."

"Misplaced it?" I chuckled in spite of myself. "How does one misplace Excalibur once or twice?

He shrugged. "The important thing is I got it back."

"Did you get it back for me?"

"For you, for your family."

"Speaking of family, when Mom and Dad arrived, you and Excalibur were waiting for them at the airport with your little 'Banson' sign, and basically have spent the last seventeen years getting them acclimated to the twenty-first century?"

Emrys nodded. "Pretty much."

"But why the doom and gloom with this Lust Borne Tide business? We're here now, some 1500 years removed from Camelot. Aside from an incubus and a couple faeries, what do we have to worry about? I just assume the occasional mystical creature is going to come knocking on our door because—*hello*—you're Merlin. But what are the stakes, really? Are there any? You said yourself that you and Mom were the only ones who knew she was pregnant, that you were the only one to whom a fertility goddess entrusted the secret of the Lust Borne Prophecy."

Emrys shook his head. "You're choosing to hear things I did not say."

"And you're choosing to lie to me!" I replied forcefully.

"I told you only that Guinevere had just discovered she was pregnant when the goddess Arianrhod came to me in a dream. I confided in Morgan la Fay, and your mother of course. Who's to say when and how Lancelot found out, who else he or your mother or Fay told, or what spies Morgause had slinking around Camelot? And I told you I was *one of* the chosen few to whom the Druidic fertility goddess entrusted the Lust Borne Prophecy, not the only one. Arianrhod appeared to someone else in a dream, which is why we left in such a hurry, why I bungled the temporal displacement spell."

I knew it before he said it. Maybe I had known it this whole time. In hindsight, it would explain the incubus and the faeries, how they toyed with me, and their reluctance to strike a killing blow. All three of them—Rolo, Richard, and Levi—could just as well have pulled out a gun and shot me dead.

"She came to Arthur."

"Yes, Rosemary," Emrys confirmed. "She came to Arthur."

We topped off our to-go cups of Chick & Ruth's coffee with free refills from a street vendor. As we waited for our drinks to cool, I tried to mimic my mother's overly dramatic reading back in the diner, but it came out more like an off-key nursery rhyme or terrible free-style rap:

> *"The moon shall be from whence*
> *the sea consumes the fallen son.*
> *The lust borne tide, thy will subside,*
> *the course of Avalon run.*
> *Her fertile song naught overlong*
> *shall play then play no more.*
> *By the blade, the bed is made.*
> *The kingdom at your door."*

"I see you've already committed the prophecy to memory," Emrys said.

I flexed my bicep while pointing at my head. "Brain and brawn: the total package."

Emrys didn't laugh. "First, let's look at the beginning of the prophecy:

> *"The moon shall be from whence*
> *the sea consumes the fallen son.*
> *The lust borne tide, thy will subside,*
> *the course of Avalon run."*

"That's the part I understand," I said. "At least the first two lines."

Emrys nodded. "I assumed you would understand. Just as I assume you want to dazzle me right now with your powers of deduction."

"If you insist," I replied. "It's just basic word play. The prophecy manages to hide its clues in plain sight by making the definitions of two words, 'moon,' and 'son,' completely fluid. You'd think that 'the sea consumes its fallen son' has to do with someone's son drowning. But 'son' is spelled S-O-N to throw you off, at least at first. If you spell 'son' S-U-N, then the sea consuming the fallen sun is just a sunset, which brings us back to the moon in the first line. The sun and moon are the siblings of the sky, therefore the moon symbolizes a daughter, and the definition of S-O-N comes back into play. But the kicker is that the moon, a.k.a. the daughter, comes from where the sun sets. When viewed from England, the sun sets far to the west, which means the daughter will be born in…"

"Yes. Rosemary?" Emrys prodded.

"Holy hell." I shook my head. I had those first two lines nailed practically the moment I first heard them, but saying them out loud made them seem all the more absurd and unbelievable. "It means the daughter in the prophecy will be born in America. It means that sometime around the late fifth century, a Druidic goddess spoke to you in your dreams, and predicted my birth over 1500 years in the future in a country that was roughly 1200 years from even existing."

Emrys clapped. "Well done. You're a quick study."

I didn't reply, my tongue feeling like it was swelling in my mouth. Rubbing the nape of my neck, I thought, *This is real.*

"Rosemary?"

I sat there in silence. I brought my hand from my neck around to my mouth and exhaled, my shoulders slumping in resignation.

"Rosemar—"

"Well done?" I interrupted tersely. "That's all you have to say? Lord only knows what the rest of the prophecy means."

Emrys raised his hand. "I can't vouch for the Lord, but I know what the rest of the prophecy means."

I let Emrys endure a few minutes of uncomfortable silence. When he asked if I wanted some more coffee, I nodded. When he brought back a fresh cup from the street vendor, I told him I changed my mind.

"Any more fool's errands you want to send me on before I sit down, Rosemary?"

"If the shoe fits," I replied.

"Where were we?"

I held up three fingers. "Line three."

"Right." Emrys nodded. "Lines three through six are actually the easiest lines to decipher. They're so obvious you might think they mean something else, but they're also the lines that really ground the prophecy in hope. On the one hand, they connect the ambiguity of lines one and two with the prophecy's ominous last two lines. But on the other, they promise not even halfway into the prophecy a happy ending, or at least a normal ending."

"The world's first-ever spoiler alert?" I asked.

"I guess you could call it that," Emrys answered. "Take lines three and four: *The lust borne tide, thy will subside, the course of Avalon run.* There's your happy ending. The lust borne tide will subside. It will come to an end. The curse will be lifted, and eventually Camelot, like so many great cities before and after it, will just be forgotten."

"Just to be clear, we're calling the Lust Borne Prophecy a 'curse' now?"

"The Prophecy of the Lust Borne has always been more accurately thought of as a curse—one passed down through the Pendragon royal line that began with Uther's seduction of Igraine."

"*Gladio!*" I commanded, summoning Excalibur to my sword arm. "This sword, these powers...They don't strike me as much of a curse."

"The curse is not necessarily in how the Lust Borne Tide manifests itself in you. In fact, all of its inheritors have been blessed with tremendous strength, speed, endurance, longevity."

"Blessed with these attributes, but from what I gather, lacking in ethics, morals, and basic restraint when it comes to the bedroom?"

"Is that at a swipe at your parents?"

"No," I said, "but it can be."

By the way he bit his lip, I could tell Emrys wanted to take their side. *Know your audience, wizard.* Choose a side and move on.

"Instead of your powers being a manifestation of the curse," Emrys continued, "the curse derives from the root cause of those manifestations."

"In plain English, please," I instructed.

"The curse holds that a Pendragon can conceive of only one child, and only through ill intent, which is explained in lines five and six: *Her fertile song naught overlong shall play then play no more.*"

"So... I'm Rosemary the Incubus Slayer because I'm a lust child as opposed to a love child, and I'm destined to have no more than one kid, and only if it's conceived with a dude to whom I have zero emotional attachments?"

Emrys nodded. "That about sums it up."

"That's not the worst curse, as far as curses go."

"If you will allow me to explain in more detail, Uther's only child was Arthur, conceived while Uther was disguised as Igraine's husband. Arthur's only child was—"

"So now we can talk about Mordred?" I wasn't in the mood for asking if I could cut in anymore.

"Yes," Emrys affirmed. "Now we can talk about Mordred. He was conceived as Arthur's only child when Arthur's half-sister Morgause shared his bed disguised as Guinevere."

"Yeah, you said that part already. So, Mordred is part of the prophecy."

Emrys nodded. "As are you."

"How do you figure?"

"It would appear that Guinevere, as Arthur's wife, somehow inherited the curse. She conceived you in lust, with Lancelot."

"So technically, I'm not a Pendragon. I'm more Lust Borne Adjacent."

"Wishful thinking at this point. It's called the Lust Borne Prophecy after all, not the Blood Borne Prophecy. You were conceived with bad intentions, and you are Guin—Jennifer's only child. If you can point me to another sixteen-year-old girl who can heal broken bones in a matter of days, I'd be happy to reconsider. Otherwise, I'd say you're definitely the next heir in the Lust Borne line."

"Bad intentions? Lust?" I scoffed. "Mom and Dad were in love when they conceived me."

"Perhaps," Emrys said. "But the fact is you were conceived in adultery. The curse is fickle. Sometimes it chooses an heir based solely on the intent of the lovers; if one is not in love with the other, even if they are married, the terms of the Lust Prophecy is fulfilled. Other times, the curse is very by the book. Marriage is marriage. Sex outside of marriage is lust. The end."

"I take back what I said earlier," I replied. "The curse sucks. Although, that healing broken bones thing might come in handy.

Emrys sipped on his coffee in deference to my disgust. He cleared his throat. "You being Lust Borne explains a lot actually."

"Says you."

"Jennifer was told by her midwife at a young age that she could not bear children. Legend holds that your mother was barren, like *every* legend. No notable post-Arthurian fable in the history of the written word has ever so much as pondered the existence of a child by Guinevere. Furthermore, any story involving Arthur's illegitimate children, with the exception of one Sir Walter Scott poem, 'The Bridal of Triermain, tells of him having only sons. It's impossible to deny that you're special. It's as if the history books and fairy tales have conspired to keep your identity secret. That's why Morgan le Fay traveled to the future to cloak you. That's why your parents and I traveled to the future to protect you."

"From who?" I asked. Christ almighty, why did *every* answer they give me come with another question?

"You almost got this," Emrys said. "What are the last two lines?"

"*By the blade, the bed is made. The kingdom at your door.* You said these are the ominous lines in the prophecy. They don't scare me. I'm special, remember?"

"Well, they should scare you. You've asked me, what are the stakes? *Those* are the stakes, Rosemary. Think about the Pendragon family tree. Of the people mentioned as heirs to the Lust Borne curse, what element is missing?"

"Table manners?" I said sarcastically. "Birth control?"

"You think you're joking, but your second guess isn't too far off. *Kids.* The line of the Lust Borne is missing kids. This is the part I'm glad your parents aren't here to piece together with us."

"What are we piecing together, Emrys?"

"The most popular legends tell us that Arthur and Mordred died on the battlefield by each other's hand. Some legends say Mordred ruled by Arthur's side. I wouldn't know because Mordred was a toddler when I left Camelot. What I do know is that when I left Camelot, Arthur and Morgause were peacefully co-existing. My guess is starting around sixteen or seventeen, Morgause started playing matchmaker and discovered that the Prince was apparently shooting blanks. And the thing is, if you read the old scrolls, there is in fact mention of Mordred's possible impotence, but then there is nothing."

I leered at Emrys. "Nothing?"

"Nothing," Emrys echoed. "There are five notable Arthurian entities that vanish from history at roughly the same time: Merlin, Morgan le Fay, Guinevere, Lancelot, and Excalibur. Mordred disappears sixteen years later. He's about four years your senior, which means he left Camelot when he was nineteen or twenty."

"I apparently don't know how time travel works then," I said.

"What's to know?" Emrys asked.

"Where were they?" I asked.

"Who?"

"Mom and Dad," I said. "If they're not with you, and not set to arrive in Maryland for another 400 years, where are they?"

"They're in the temporal waiting room, what modern physicists would call the space-time continuum. Remember what I told you before, about time being more like a sphere than a straight line, everything existing and flowing into itself all at—"

"Oh shut up, Emrys," I scoffed. "So you're kicking it in the 1600s, Mom and Dad are stuck in the space-time continuum until the 2000s roll around. What are you doing in the meantime? And don't start in with that making history crap again."

"I was waiting for them to get here."

"How did you know you'd eventually find them?"

"Magician's intuition."

Emrys was testing my patience. "And in all these centuries, nobody notices you just vanishing from history?"

"You'd be surprised. 1,500 years dulls the memory. Speaking as someone who's been an eye-witness to the slow walk of time, days blur into months, months blurs into years, years into centuries. In hindsight, we believe our most endearing legends have simply always been around. It seems preposterous to think that the Santa Claus we all know as the immortal Father Christmas in the red and white suit was invented by a Coca-Cola marketing team in the 1930s. But if you were to place the late fifth century A.D. under a microscope, looking only in that small window of those sixteen or so years, you'd notice that the stories about Merlin, Morgan le Fay, Guinevere, Lancelot, Excalibur, and Mordred just stopped being told for a little while. Then, beginning in the eleventh century, medieval writers like Geoffrey of Monmouth and Chrétien de Troyes brought them back in the fold, turning history into myth and myth into history."

I felt like Emrys was drifting into riddle territory again, stringing me along. "Speak plainly and boldly, wizard."

"The fifth and sixth centuries were not a great time to be a woman. Why do you think we left? The blade in the prophecy is clearly in reference to *the* blade, the Sword of Power, Excalibur. Reading the last two lines within the full context of the prophecy, it tells us that Excalibur will travel through time, which it has, and that the son will travel through time to share a bed with the daughter. Mordred is here, in the twenty-first century, and he isn't sterile. He can have a child, but only if it's conceived through ill intent—"

"No way!" I yelped in horror. "No *way*! Gross! That's so gross!"

"Well, yes."

"Sexual assault of your stepsister at sword point would certainly qualify as ill intent."

"Really, Rosemary? Do you always have to be so glib about everything?"

"Glib? Is that what I'm being?" I stood up, needing to put some distance between me and this conversation. But I couldn't. No way in hell. That's exactly what guys like Mordred want in these situations: girls who run away and hide instead of stand and fight. I turned to face Emrys.

Emrys knew he was in trouble. I'd punched him in the face for far less. "I'm sorry. Maybe 'glib' was the wrong word."

"You're damn straight it was the wrong word," I said, pointing at him. "You just dropped a prophecy on me that's every girl's nightmare and every crusty old, limp-dicked misogynist's wet dream: a sexual encounter that requires a woman's womb, but not her consent."

"Please forgive me," Emrys implored. "I can't possibly know what it's like to be in your shoes."

"In *any* woman's shoes," I added. "Ever."

"That too. I just…"

"You just *what?*" I snapped.

"I-I can't bear to even think about it," he stuttered. "I won't…"

"Won't what? Spit it out, wizard!"

"I won't let him hurt you, Rosemary. I'd die before I let anything happen to you."

I could see the pain in his eyes. Was I was being too hard on him? Probably. As my adrenaline started to subside, I gained clarity. Emrys took being my protector seriously. He always had, even as the reality started to set in that I was probably better equipped to protect him. He wasn't stringing me along with riddles. He was just trying to shield me from the truth.

Oh my God. I knew the truth, and it was awful.

"Please, Emrys. Just say it. I'm a Banson. I can take it."

Emrys shook his head. "These prophecies can sometimes be purposely ambiguous and misleading."

I shook my head. "Don't coddle me, Emrys. There's no ambiguity here, and you know it. Lines three and four give us hope, just as you said. They promise us not that the Lust Borne Tide will endure, but that it will end somehow."

"A prophecy is a guess, Rosemary, not a promise."

I poked him in the chest. "I said *don't* coddle me. The promise comes immediately after the prophecy tells us in lines one and two that it would be a good idea if the moon and the son hooked up."

"*Hooked up*, Rosemary?" Emrys folded his arms, a gesture that couldn't make up its mind between defensive and confused.

"There's only one way the curse can end, and that's if the current male and female heirs of the Lust Borne Tide have a child, together. But to say the curse ends is a lie, at least for Mordred and me. While the kids we have together are no longer cursed, that doesn't end *our* curse."

"You're reading too much into this."

"Stop it, Emrys."

"But maybe—"

"Maybe nothing!" I shouted, cutting him off. "If Mordred is shooting blanks without me, am I shooting blanks without him? The prophecy says we can conceive children together, but can we ever conceive children with anyone else? Can I ever fall in love, get married, and have kids if and when I want to, and not when some stupid prophecy tells me to?"

Emrys unfolded his arms, bowing his head. His reaction said what his words could not: I wasn't reading too much into this. For the rest of my natural life, I could only have Mordred's children.

"Well..." I pondered. "Ain't that a kick in the uterus?"

"I don't know what to say, Rosemary."

"Yeah, I kind of picked up on that."

Emrys raised his head. "I've been fooling myself this whole time. Mordred is coming, I don't know if we'll ever be ready for him, and even if we are, I don't know if I can promise you will ever live a normal life."

CHAPTER

15

"How are you doing?" Emrys asked.

"All things considered," I said, "somewhere between awful and terrible."

"Maybe look at tonight as a needed distraction."

I shrugged. "Yeah, maybe."

"She is something else, isn't she?"

My Fall Fling date cast a side glance to the American Martyr gymnasium floor. Joslin whirled about the crowd to the latest Taylor Swift hit, dancing with herself. Oh to be Joslin, flailing around with those spaghetti arms and that fearless gigglemug. I stopped watching her; Emrys did not.

Emrys was good at being a teenager, almost too good. He was as complicit as my parents in the mess my life had become, if not more so, but there was something about his youth that disarmed me. I could be in study hall with "Emrys" at three o'clock, do three hours of fencing and mixed martial arts training with "Merlin" at eight o'clock, and by the next morning be chatting with "Emrys" in homeroom about Joslin having a crush on him. He had become one of my best friends despite himself, and with that friendship came his baggage of half-truths I was willing to accept as good intentions.

I had forgiven him in the week since he turned my world upside down over a plate of chicken and waffles, because really, what choice did I have? Everything he was doing was to protect me. Yes, the revelation that we were most likely ill-equipped to actually defeat Mordred and that I might be infertile for the rest of my life if I tried to conceive with anyone but Mordred the Wonder Schlong was a bit of a downer. But what's high school without a few dazzling moments of disappointment?

Speaking of distracting myself with high school drama, something had to be done about Joslin's crush. Her affection was at least genuine now, having progressed from Emrys's enchantment to an intense curiosity. I told myself there was no way Emrys reciprocated her feelings, but lately, what did I know about anything? He *couldn't* reciprocate her feelings. Could he? Was he an old man in the body of a teenage boy with a crush on a teenage girl, or was he a real teenage boy just surrendering to his youth? It was a fine line between odd and *ewww*. I wanted to tell Joslin that it was gross, but could I tell her without revealing—well, everything?

Emrys was still staring at her. "Take a picture," I said. "It'll last longer."

We had picked an inconspicuous location away from the dance floor, a row of folding chairs just behind the DJ where no one would notice us. My snide cliché snapped Emrys out of his Joslin trance. He turned his attention to me, finally. "Are you okay, Rosemary?"

It was the most rhetorical of rhetorical questions. So absurd that it deserved an equally rhetorical answer. "Why wouldn't I be okay, Emrys?"

"Well, for one, you're staring daggers at Avery."

Emrys was perceptive. Too perceptive in this instance. The reason I wasn't okay at that moment had nothing to do with Emrys and Joslin, Mom and Dad, Mordred, Excalibur, or the Lust Borne Prophecy. I wasn't okay because Benz had just walked into the American Martyr gymnasium with Avery on his arm.

They'd been voted Fall Fling king and queen the night before, at halftime of the last football game of the season, a nail-biter that knocked American Martyr out of the playoffs. Benz missed a wide-open receiver in the endzone for the go-ahead score in the closing minutes. After the game, all anyone was talking about was that bad pass. But all I could think about were Benz in his dirty football uniform and Avery in her pretty little cheerleading skirt walking across the football field at halftime.

And here they were for the encore.

Avery and Benz crossed the gymnasium floor through a tunnel of applause and painted-on smiles. Avery did her best parade wave, squeezing every last ounce of affirmation from her social sphere of wannabes and bootlickers.

"Let's talk about something else," I insisted.

Emrys shrugged. "Like what?"

I reached up and brushed back a few loose strands of Emrys's hair from his eyes. "I dig the new haircut."

"You do?" The strands fell back over his eyes immediately. He threw his head back hoping to arrest what my fingers and gravity could not.

Emrys went with what I liked to call the Euro soccer player cut—shaved on the sides, long and slicked back on the top transitioning into a mini-mullet in the back. It wasn't an easy haircut to pull off, but he managed to do it. "If I didn't know any better, I might almost mistake you for being hip," I joked.

"Really?"

He tightened his necktie, which was paired with a button-down short-sleeved shirt. His pale white arms stuck out like chicken wings. "Like I said, almost."

Apparently, our location wasn't inconspicuous enough. Avery saw us and steered her date in our direction, wanting to show him off.

Benz was the first to say something. He smiled politely in his tailored skinny suit. "Hey there, Emrys...Rosemary."

"Benz," we said in tandem.

"Hello, Rosemary," Avery said. She was wearing a two-piece dress with a lace applique overlay that exposed her bare midriff. On anyone else, the dress would have looked trashy, but on Avery, it was perfect.

"Avery," I replied.

She nodded her head with a knowing smile at the refreshments table laden with fruit punch and finger foods. "Have you tried the brownies?"

"No, Avery," I replied, tight-lipped with clenched fists. "I have not tried the brownies. No telling what kind of chemicals and preservatives are in those things."

"I had heard you were more of an *organic* person."

She attacked, I counter-attacked. "Tried a batch of homemade brownies awhile back. They were pretty terrible. They tasted like someone was trying too hard."

Avery dodged my blow, mustering a counter of her own. "Is that a new dress?" she asked, even though she already knew the answer. "Cream is such a brave color for your skin tone."

"I borrowed it from my mother."

"Oh, that's sweet. Either way, you look *wonderful tonight*."

I smiled.

Okay, I hated her.

Benz dragged Avery away. After a couple rounds of fruit punch at the refreshment table, Emrys escorted me to the bleachers. Per usual, he read the look on my face.

"Come on, 'you look wonderful tonight'? You have to admit, that was clever."

"I don't have to admit anything," I said. Father Jules stood on the other side of the gym, arms folded, staring at me.

Emrys followed my eyes, nodded at Father Jules. "What's the Monsignor doing?"

"Lurking," I answered. "It's kind of his specialty."

"You don't like him?"

"He doesn't like me."

"Maybe he just needs to get to know you."

"Since when are you on his side?"

"*His* side?" Emrys smirked. "I'm not on anyone's side, Rosemary. I'm merely suggesting the possibility that your overbearing, micromanaging principal is just an overbearing, micromanaging principal. Is it too much to imagine that his life doesn't revolve around yours? That he gets up every day just wanting to make a difference in the lives of his students?"

"Yes," I answered. "It's too much to imagine."

"If you ask me, I think you're just taking your frustration with Benz out on Father Jules."

Emrys was right of course, and I had only myself to blame. My ambivalence outside the locker room last month was why this had happened. Avery landed Benz because I couldn't move past *maybe*. My hang-ups were justified; Benz hurt me. But seeing him here with Avery tonight hurt worse.

"My turn yet?" Joslin approached us. With her multiple necklaces and long, layered dress, she looked a little bit like a gypsy. She'd never even mentioned me standing her up again because, well, she was Joslin. Of course, it didn't hurt when I swore up and down that Emrys was more like a brother to me and insisted that we go as a threesome to the dance.

Emrys shook his head while waving Joslin off. "I don't think I should."

I pushed him off his chair. "Go, have some fun."

"You sure?" he said.

"Two of us should at least try to salvage this night."

"I don't know, Rosemary. I feel really bad about—"

"Come on already!" Joslin said, yanking him on to the dance floor.

The DJ transitioned from a surprisingly good boy band medley into a predictably bad prep school synchronized line dance. Emrys and Joslin had been dancing for a while now. In another world, one in which they weren't separated in age by a couple millennia, they might have made a cute couple—even while doing the "Cha-Cha Slide." After the "Cha-Cha Slide," the DJ introduced Benz and Avery onto the floor for the king and queen dance. They danced to Eric Clapton's "Wonderful Tonight." Avery had her head on Benz's shoulder the whole song. If I hadn't been so pissed off, I might have stopped to appreciate the poetic irony of me being the one who gift-wrapped the moment for Avery with my student council coup.

After their dance ended, Avery and Benz split up to work the room. Avery did her best to avoid me. Benz did not.

"Is this seat taken?" Benz offered me a cup of fruit punch. He thought he was being cool. Per usual, he was overestimating both his charm and grace.

I took the cup in my hand. "It's a free country."

Benz sat down next to me without waiting for an invitation.

"Well, technically, it's a representative republic."

"Well, technically, you're a jerk."

He jumped up. "Maybe I'll just stand for now."

We were both tense. He was trying really hard to be cordial. I was trying really hard not to be. "That's probably best."

"Having fun tonight?" he asked.

"Not as much fun as you, gas-pipes."

"Gas-pipes?"

"It's a term my mom uses to describe ridiculously tight pants."

Benz stepped toward me, his gas-pipes leaning against my exposed leg just below the hem of my dress. "You think I'm enjoying this, not getting to be with you?"

I pointed up at him with one hand while swatting his leg away with my other hand. "I *think* that skinny suit makes you look like you dressed yourself out of your fourteen-year-old brother's closet. I *know* you're enjoying this."

"I don't have a fourteen-year-old brother."

"It was a joke, at the expense of your personal appearance."

"Glad I could be of service."

"Me too."

"There's nothing going on between Avery and me," Benz said. "We're just friends, barely even that."

"Avery's behavior would seem to contradict this."

"She has some big college boyfriend. Everybody knows that. Everybody also knows she's a shameless flirt."

"Takes one to know one."

"H-hey," Benz stammered.

I tried to stay composed between sips of punch. "I saw you two out on the dance floor. That looked more like something than nothing to me."

"Don't let Avery get to you, Rosemary."

"I could say the same to you."

"Come on, I was just into the moment. "Wonderful Tonight" is a great tune."

"I know it is!"

I stood, tripping almost immediately in my heels. The remaining fruit punch in my cup splashed in a puddle at my feet. I slipped and fell in the punch.

Benz reached to help me.

"Don't touch me!" I barked. People turned to us, reacting to the commotion. Still on the ground, I reached down and removed my heels. Shaking them off, I paused for a moment to compose myself. I stood and straightened my dress, chin up. It was as graceful of a recovery as I could've hoped for before my barefoot exit from the gymnasium.

St. John Neumann was the K-8 feeder school for American Martyr Prep. The schools stood side-by-side on the western edge of Severna Park, along the banks of the Severn River. The campus occupied a hundred-acre peninsula that on a map looked like a giant loon craning its neck across the river. The focal point of the campus was St. John Neumann Basilica, a Gothic church made of the same Maryland marble that wrapped the Washington Monument. It towered in judgment over everything.

A children's playground acted as a buffer between the high school and the grade school, boxed in by streetlights and a half-dozen holly trees. I sat in one of the playground swings, rocking back and forth while playing in the mulch with my toes. Closing my eyes, I inhaled the air around me. The school replenished the mulch once a year with cocoa bean hulls, so the playground smelled perpetually of chocolate. The smell of my childhood, of a time when everything didn't have to be…well, everything.

"Forget something?" Benz stepped into the streetlight holding a pair of open-toed high heels.

I waved off his offer. "Keep 'em."

"No thanks." He gently placed my shoes upright in the mulch and sat in the swing next to me. "They're not my color."

Benz laughed.

I wanted to laugh too, but his humor came across to me as forced, awkward. That moment encapsulated what was so frustrating about my relationship with Benz Cooke. He was forever that boyfriend who struggled to be my friend. It wasn't even his fault really. He'd been there for so many of the big moments in my life that I rarely knew how to navigate the small ones with him. I was more comfortable with him being my obsession than my boyfriend. But tonight, that frustration felt, I don't know. Different. With all that had happened in these last few weeks with Emrys, maybe my big moments with Benz weren't so big. Maybe everything with my boyfriend didn't have to be...well, everything.

"Tough game last night," I said, trying half-heartedly to make small talk.

"Yeah," Benz mumbled.

"Where's Avery?"

"Still inside being totally awesome for her vast entourage."

"The queen and her loyal subjects," I observed.

"Rosemary, can we maybe not talk about Avery?"

My stomach clenched. I stopped swinging, my heels digging into the mulch as I tried to resist looking into his hazel eyes. But why resist? He wasn't my boyfriend anymore. They were just eyes. I had the blood of Guinevere and Lancelot coursing through my veins. What could Benz possibly do to me?

Switch on.

Oh crap. I was looking into his eyes. This was just how it worked with Benz. Just like that, I was back to being obsessed. I could never explain it—to Joslin, to Mom, to myself. It was an internal switch that only Benz could switch on and off.

His hazel eyes picked up the green in his boutonniere—the boutonniere Avery had most likely bought him. I could picture her pinning it to his chest, her fingers lingering a little too long. Her parents snapping a photo. Avery asking for more photos. Benz pretending he didn't love the attention.

Switch off.

"We're not doing this, Benz. Not tonight."

"I think I'm at least entitled to—"

"*Entitled?*" I said, exasperated. "What are you entitled to? What do I owe you exactly? Less than nothing!"

"I-I'm sorry, Rosemary. That came out wrong. I know you're still angry and hurt, and..." Benz trailed off, shaking his head while striking his fists together. He scrunched his nose, a nervous tick he exhibited when he was frustrated. "It's just that you and me, we're like, you know. And I freak out, and I do stupid stuff. And then you come into school always looking so pretty, always smelling so good. And then there's Avery, and you're all mad at me and Emrys Balin is asking you to Fall Fling. And I tell you that I still love you, tell you to keep my class ring, I drop hints all over the place, and it doesn't even faze you. And I'm like, *really?* I don't know, I'm not saying this right."

"We've had this fight already, Benz. I was scared, you were scared. We had sex, and then you left. Do I need to remind you that *you* were the one who dumped *me?* On top of which, you haven't been particularly kind since we broke up. You're dating Avery."

"We *hang out*," Benz argued. "Avery and I don't date."

"You took her to Fall Fling! You have to know that kills me inside. You can't be this oblivious. Why Avery, of all people? The least you could've done, and I mean the very least, is ask some rando to Fall Fling."

"What can I do to win you back, Rosemary? I said I was sorry."

"Go above and beyond proving to me you're sorry. Stop being so wishy washy and trying to flirt your way out of everything. Don't say it, mean it."

"How much more could I mean it, Rosemary? You were my first."

"Yeah, we need to stop making that a thing in our relationship."

"It's not just a thing," Benz countered. "It's everything."

"It doesn't have to be."

If I said it enough times, maybe I would start believing it. We were both virgins the night we slept together, and it was a thing. It was a big thing. There was no real mystery why I was a virgin. An underclassman with a know-it-all attitude whose only real friend was a purple-haired gypsy. But Benz's virginal status? Yeah, that was quite the bomb he dropped on me.

Benz shared his inexperience with me right before we slept together. He told me he hadn't even kissed a girl with tongue until the summer before his freshman year. He confessed he taught himself using Whole Foods' cupcakes. I wish I could say there had been a poetic profession of love between us or some euphoric moment when we both realized it was going to happen, but it was those damn cupcakes. We ended up having sex because Benz made me laugh. The mental image of my boyfriend French-kissing a pastry totally disarmed the moment. I barely even noticed him slipping his hand up the back of my shirt and unhooking my bra.

My swing squeaked in the humid Chesapeake air. Benz shuffled cautiously toward me. Extending his arms, he grabbed hold of the swing's chains and hovered over me. "I want us to be together again, Rosemary Banson."

Switch on.

I pulled myself up by the swing's chains, rising until we were face to face. Standing on my tip-toes in the mulch, I stared at Benz's lips as I leaned in to kiss him. He reached around my waist, pressing his hand into the small of my back. My left leg was wedged between his legs. He pulled me toward him, leaned in and kissed me on that small soft spot on my neck just below my earlobe. I exhaled. It felt like I'd been holding my breath for weeks.

CHAPTER

16

Emrys walked outside, a mug of black coffee in his hand. "Where are your parents?"

"Sleeping off their Friday night mead binge," I answered.

It was the Saturday of Thanksgiving weekend. Fog blanketed the early morning landscape. I sat on the back porch in an Adirondack chair, knees pulled to my chest. The chair was painted white, save for a few spots on the armrests, the seat and the back where human contact had peeled the paint down to bare cedar. I sipped on my heavily creamed and honeyed tea, squinting my eyes as the early morning sun rose over the Chesapeake Bay.

"You talk to Benz this morning?" Emrys asked.

I sipped my tea, swallowed and cleared my throat. "That is none of your damn business."

Emrys was asking a question to which he knew the answer. Of course, I talked to Benz that morning. It had been a week since our kiss on the playground. While not officially boyfriend and girlfriend again, we were doing everything couples do: holding hands, making out, getting in stupid fights.

The fights had occurred mostly over these last few days, and mostly over text. I hadn't seen Benz since Wednesday night, so sometimes we argued just because we missed one another and were cranky. Other times, I was knee-deep in the white noise of my parents and a certain wizard who shall remain nameless. They seemed to not even care why I was trying to repair my relationship with Benz. If they ever bothered to ask, I'd tell them it was because a broken heart was the only thing that felt real in my life.

"Sorry, I'll butt out," Emrys assured me.

I extended my legs until my feet touched the deck. Rolling my eyes, I stood from the chair with an exasperated sigh. "No, you won't."

When Emrys invited us down to his place for the holiday weekend, I didn't know what to expect. My parents and I still hovered in an odd limbo, somewhere between total silent treatment and casual pleasantries. When I pressed them for a reaction—*any* reaction— to their daughter almost getting killed by two fencing faeries, they dismissed it as a joke.

"They weren't there to kill you, Rosemary," Mom said, as if that made it all better.

We were all clearly avoiding any talk of the prophecy or Mordred. Was their dismissiveness just a defense mechanism, honed by years of accepting the unbelievable as commonplace? And were they planning on casually murdering any more of the American Martyr faculty?

On Thursday we did the traditional Thanksgiving Day meal of turkey, green beans, stuffing, and mashed potatoes. Emrys surprised us the morning after Thanksgiving with a breakfast of pan-fried crab cakes and scrambled eggs. He followed that up with a day of hiking his property and a Friday night of watching Mom and Dad inebriated on his homemade mead. They were really drunk. Dad dared Mom to jump in the Bay, boasting, "It's a scientific fact, Jennifer, that the Chesapeake is warmer on Thanksgiving Day than it is on Memorial Day." Mom believed him before she jumped in the water, but not after. Not to point out the obvious, but for people reluctant to live on this farm, we really liked to "live" on this farm.

They still called each other "Jennifer" and "Alan" instead of "Guinevere" and "Lancelot," which I found strangely comforting. They were going to counseling once a week. Dad had replaced late nights in his office with surprise dinners and flowers for no reason whatsoever. If one good thing had come from all this, it was Mom and Dad rediscovering one another.

"You're welcome," Emrys said.

"What am I thanking you for exactly?"

"For getting your parents hammered."

"How is that doing me a favor?"

"While they're passed out, we don't have to constantly entertain them. I'd like to have some one-on-one training this weekend."

"I thought this was supposed to be a vacation."

Emrys grabbed my cup of tea, placing it on the porch railing. "Let's go."

The fog lifted as the sun leaked through the clouds. We approached the red barn.

Emrys waved his hand. "*Aper—*"

"Allow me," I said, sliding open the massive doors with little effort. "Wizards first."

Emrys stepped into the barn. "Did I hear that your restitution ended at Laurel Park?"

"Several weeks ago," I answered, following close behind. "They offered me a part-time job, but I turned it down."

"Why?"

"Turns out balancing my school work with my love life and saving the world can be quite the time suck."

"Then you might not be ready for this."

I eyed him suspiciously. "How about we just assume 'not ready' as my default position from now on?"

Emrys smiled, his fingers in his mouth. He whistled sharply. I heard a snorting sound, followed by the stomping of hooves. A familiar gray horse trotted out of one of the stalls.

"Gatecrasher!" I shouted.

"He's missed you," Emrys said.

"The last day I was at Laurel Park, they told me they were shipping him out because he was untrainable."

"Crash *was* shipped out," Emrys confirmed. "Turns out there were some clerical errors in the shipping department. They sent Crash to the wrong address and seem to have misplaced the paper trail. A most unfortunate set of circumstances. Who knows how long it will take for them to track him down, or his buddy."

"His buddy?" I asked.

Emrys whistled again. A black stallion rambled out of the next stall down from Crash, similarly laden with riding tackle.

"Raven!"

"In the flesh." Emrys raised his hand as Raven approached, reaching for the saddle. His motion was deft and effortless as he swung his legs around and mounted the big horse.

"Well?" Emrys said.

"Well what?" I asked.

"You going to hop up on Crash or just stand there with that stupid grin on your face?"

Emrys took me on a tour of his 200 acres. We raced one another back and forth along Parker's Creek for about twenty minutes. I use the word "race" loosely when it comes to these two horses; Crash is a lot faster than Raven.

Emrys pulled back on the reins, slowing Raven as he approached the creek's edge. Crash and I had beaten them to the creek by a good minute or so, but neither horse seemed winded.

"Been fishing for trout lately?" I asked.

"No," Emrys answered. "How's your fishing going these days?"

A phantom pain in my right shoulder reminded me of my daily fishing sessions, casting a pole until I couldn't feel my arm from my fingers to my neck. I placed my left hand on that shoulder while rotating my right arm counter-clockwise. "I'm officially retired."

"We'll see about that," Emrys said. He leaned down and stroked Raven's shimmering black neck.

"Beautiful animals," I observed.

"Special animals," Emrys added.

"Let's not get carried away." My left hand holding on to the reins, I reached down and stroked Crash's sinewy shoulder. "I'm not so far removed from scooping this guy's poop that I'd want to keep him in my backyard any time soon."

"Close your eyes," Emrys said.

"What?"

"Close your eyes."

"Why?"

"This is one of those times when I can't slowly work my magic into your everyday life. I'm going to need you to trust me."

Against my better judgment, I did as he said. "Now what?"

"Rest your head against Crash, and relax."

I tentatively leaned forward, nestling my head in his pillowy mane. "Okay."

"*Pegasoi aithiopes, revelare!*" Emrys commanded.

Crash reared up, letting out a deep-throated neigh. A burst of air blew my hair back, like when you're running down a country road and the trailing wind from a passing truck hits you full in the face. I opened my eyes to a gray curtain of feathers. Crash's feathers.

My horse had wings.

My horse...had wings?

"I thought it was time you saw the real Crash," Emrys said.

Only then did I notice Raven had sprouted similar appendages. "Raven too?" I asked, stunned.

"Raven and Crash are brothers."

"Their wings are *huge*!"

"In many ways, winged horses are more avian than equine, more bird than horse," Emrys observed.

"They look a solid eighty-percent horse to me," I countered. "Like you just said, they're horses with wings."

"Or are they birds with four legs?" Emrys pondered. "They have a deep, solid breastbone to anchor their wing muscles, parts of their skeletal structure have been fused or eliminated, and many of their bones are practically hollow. Even their respiratory systems are completely different from a land-based horse, having evolved specifically for the rigors of flight."

"Flight?" I said, not even trying to conceal my huge gigglemug. I eased Crash from a trot into a cantor. Standing up in my stirrups, I raised my torso into a light seat position while shortening the reins.

"Rosemary, wait up," Emrys said.

I couldn't believe this was happening. Aside from a few casual walks inside the barn back at Laurel Park when no one was looking, and of course the night I instinctively rode him bareback before decapitating Rolo, I had barely ridden Crash. And now I was going to *fly* him?

Emrys and I both leaned into a forward position, our horses

accelerating into full gallop. Emrys came up along aside me. "How's he feeling underneath you?"

"Solid," I answered.

"Okay, now let go of the reins."

"What?"

"Drop the reins and take Crash's mane in your hands. He'll do the rest."

I released the reins, grabbing a fistful of Crash's mane. Crash bowed, then raised his head. He neighed again, this one a little more high-pitched than the first. The clip-clop of his hooves accelerating faster and then faster again. I closed my eyes until there were no sounds but Crash's breathing and the *whoosh-whoosh* of wings beating the air.

When I opened my eyes, Emrys and Raven were next to me. We were flying, ascending fast into the air. Too fast. My stomach rose in my throat. I felt like I was going to puke.

"You might have some motion sickness at first, but you'll adjust," Emrys shouted above the wind. "And Crash's personality isn't any different than it was back in the stables."

"You mean he's still part jackass?"

"He has a tendency to turn over on his back sometimes and tumble out of the air, just to be ridiculous, or else because he's forgotten that he's flying. Trust yourself and your horse."

I tried to disguise the panic in my voice. "Trust a flying horse that has a tendency to forget he's flying?"

Emrys winked. With a nudge of his knee and a tug on Raven's mane, he peeled away from us, heading out across the Chesapeake. I lost them in the morning sun. I should have brought some sunglasses, but in all fairness, I didn't expect to be on top of a horse 10,000 feet in the air.

Without Crash's hooves hitting the ground, I found I could manage a lazier seat. I eased back into the saddle. Heels down, thighs rolled in. Crash dipped for a second. Emrys was right about the motion sickness: I felt a twinge of nausea, but the sensation wasn't as intense as last time.

We caught a warm updraft just before the sun hid behind the clouds. Ascending another thousand feet or so, I saw Emrys and

Raven to my right. Emrys gave me a thumbs up. I nodded back.

"It's our turn now," I whispered to my horse, grabbing his mane with both hands and leaning forward.

Emrys knew what we were up to. He shook his head from side to side while waving his arms in the air. Crash and I both dipped our heads in defiance. I squeezed my thighs tighter around Crash as he pulled his legs up. He rolled, flattening his wings against his body and nosing us into a dive.

The wind rushed past my face. At first, it was exhilarating, but as the bay fast approached, I grew concerned. A normal human probably would have passed out by now, but my enhanced physiology could handle the g-forces. It wasn't that. I just didn't want to get wet.

Crash's wings splashed the water as he pulled up at the very last second. As he reared back and started to ascend, I carelessly lost my grip on Crash's mane. I reached for the loose reins fluttering in the wind while my knees instinctively pinched Crash's ribs. Sensing my distress, he leveled off.

Emrys glided up beside me, allowing Raven to nuzzle Crash. "Thought you were going in the drink for sure," he said.

"No worries," I lied. "I had it all under control."

"Was that before or after you almost fell off?"

"After," I said. "Definitely after."

We landed one ridge over from Emrys's farm. As Crash nuzzled Raven, I raised my hand. "Obvious question that I probably should have asked before our joyride," I said.

"Hopefully the answer is as obvious," Emrys replied.

"No telling with you," I said. "How is it no one can see us flying in broad daylight?"

"Could you see Crash's wings before today?"

"Well, no."

"Neither can anyone else. These are magical horses. The wings of a *Pegasoi aithiopes* are never visible to the human eye."

"A pega soy *whati?*"

"That's their Latin name," Emrys clarified. "When it comes to Pegasus, most people see what their minds tell them can be seen. The magic is in the horse, not in me."

133

"But it was your enchantment that made their wings appear. You were the one who said, '*Pegasoi aithiopes, revelare!*'"

"Indeed I did," Emrys affirmed. "But that was a command, not a spell. I was literally saying, 'Reveal yourself, Pegasus!' When a Pegasus is on the ground, most people see a horse. When a Pegasus is in the air, they might see a bird or a cloud or nothing at all."

"And they don't see me awkwardly floating in the air on top of the bird or the cloud?"

"Thanks to the magic of Pegasus, you're both hidden."

"Mom and Dad know about these horses?"

"Do they know Pegasus exist? Yes. That I have two live Pegasus in my barn? I don't think so. Pegasus are actually quite widespread throughout North America. Fortunately for them, we live in a world full of disbelievers."

If there were words that had ceased to have meaning in my vocabulary, "skeptical" and "unbelievable" were near the top of the list.

"Let's let Raven and Crash relax a little bit and cool down." Emrys nodded across the valley toward the farm. Fresh smoke curled out of his house's chimney. "Looks like Jennifer and Alan are awake."

"Speaking of that, Emrys," I said, "I wanted to say thanks. For having us over for Thanksgiving, for inviting us into your home for the weekend. It might not seem like a big deal to you, but with everything that's happened, it was nice to just sit around a table and pretend to be a normal family—you know, before you and I took the flying horses for a spin. And sorry about snapping at you earlier when you brought up Benz. He and I are in a weird place, boyfriend and girlfriend wise, and Mom and Dad's new lovebird routine doesn't help. I just really…"

Emrys wasn't even listening to me, so I stopped talking. He dismounted, walked over to a solitary white oak tree. A tall, polished stone stood near the base.

It was a grave marker.

I jumped off Crash, following Emrys around to the front of the marker. I noted the simple inscription on the stone:

TESS NORTHCUTT BALIN
1922 – 1959

"Who's this?" I asked.

Emrys ignored me. He went to work clearing some weeds and fallen leaves from the base of the stone. He took a knee, whispered something with his hand on the word "TESS." He knelt there for a minute or so, just long enough for the silence to grow uncomfortable. He stood and turned to me, nodding at the headstone.

"Rosemary," he said, "I'd like you to meet my wife."

CHAPTER

17

Emrys and Joslin sat across from me in the cafeteria. The school bought too much food for last Tuesday's Pre-Thanksgiving Party, so today's lunch was debatably safe leftover turkey swimming in brown gravy.

"When did you two get back from the farm?" Joslin asked. A triple helping of mashed potatoes without gravy sat piled on her plate. She didn't trust the turkey.

"Late..." I said.

"Last night," Emrys added.

"I leave you two alone together for a few days, and suddenly you're finishing each other's sentences?" Joslin ate her mashed potatoes like ice cream, sticking her spoon in her mouth and licking it clean. "What's Benz going to say about that?"

Emrys scoffed peculiarly. "It would be nice if we could go one conversation without bringing up Benz Cooke's name. That's all Rosemary talked about on break."

Joslin raised her eyebrows at me. "Oh, really?"

I didn't mind Joslin's meddling. It was harmless and usually well-intentioned. It was Emrys's tone that concerned me. He'd started having more of these peculiar moments—moments when he'd go from being protective to possessive, moments when I'd catch him staring idly at a girl in the hallway or lingering over the pages of

Mom's latest *Athleta* catalog. He and Joslin cooled off almost as quickly as they'd heated up. Joslin told me the Monday after Fall Fling, "Emrys is nice and all, but there's something just a little, I don't know, *off* about him. He has these moments, like he suddenly isn't present. Like he's playing a part."

Playing a part. What did I really know about how this aging in reverse worked with Emrys? I pictured him staring in the mirror every morning with a little less facial hair. His voice getting higher instead of lower. Minus the revelation—*hello*—that he had a wife in the 1950s, Emrys was discarding his maturity. He was descending into puberty instead of growing out of it—a hellacious hormone yo-yo of emotions and impulses I wouldn't have wished on anyone.

The yo-yo continued. "Benz doesn't own Rosemary," Emrys said. "What's he have to complain about, anyway? He went to the beach with his family. I assume there were plenty of pretty girls around."

"The beach" was an overstatement on Emrys's part. Benz's parents dragged him to their Bethany Beach condo every Thanksgiving for a Cooke family reunion. The condo overlooked the tiny stretch of Delaware-Maryland sand that kissed the Atlantic Ocean. Benz hated it. "Delaware and Maryland beaches in November suck," he'd say. "Why live on the ocean if you can't swim in it all year round?"

"So what do you think of Andrew Sparks?" Joslin asked, oblivious to Emrys's hormones.

"Benz's best friend?" Emrys rolled his eyes.

Joslin leered at him. "I'm not talking to you, Emrys."

I shrugged. "Good guy, great hair."

"Any religious hang-ups or sexually transmitted diseases I should know about?"

"Joslin!" I said.

She grinned. "You're not giving me a whole lot to work with."

"Hello," Emrys said. "Am I not here?"

"Girl talk, Emrys," Joslin replied.

"As far as I know," I said, "Andrew is a healthy, casually Catholic, nearly eighteen-year-old dude. Just be careful. I don't want to see you get hurt."

"You just said he's a good guy," Emrys countered, apparently not understanding what we meant by *girl* talk. "Is he or isn't he?"

"He's friendly enough and has been Benz's best friend forever," I said. "Andrew just has a reputation for, you know, getting around. But then again, that's what they said about Benz, and he turned out to be a…"

I stopped short, barely catching myself as I looked around the cafeteria.

"A *what?*" Emrys asked.

"Nothing," I said, my ex-boyfriend's terrible reputation still reasonably intact.

"Sounds like a bad guy to me," Emrys added.

"Where was this overly protective, macho routine when I was clearly hitting on you at the Fall Fling dance, Emrys?" Joslin asked. "There's nothing Andrew Sparks can do to hurt me. He's just a dumb boy. And speaking of dumb boys…" Joslin looked over my shoulder.

Benz stood behind me wearing his red and grey American Martyr Prep letter jacket. An interlocking gold "AM" covered his beating heart. I missed that jacket. I used to wear it to bed and pretend Benz was spending the night with me.

"This seat taken?" he asked.

"Yes!" Emrys decreed.

Joslin smiled. "Oh, hello, Benz. Actually, Emrys and I were just leaving."

"No, we weren't," Emrys said.

"Yes, we were." Joslin grabbed him by the arm. "We'll talk later," she said to me, standing up from the table.

Emrys was slow to leave. He glared at Benz. To make matters worse, Benz picked up on this aggression and threw it right back at him. "You have a problem with me, buddy?"

Emrys eyed him back. "Should I?"

"Boys, boys, boys," Joslin jumped in. "Save the pissing contests for the urinals."

Joslin somehow managed to corral Emrys. Thankfully, they exited the lunchroom to minimal fanfare. Benz walked around the head of the table.

"What's up with that guy?" Benz asked.

"Who, Emrys?"

Don't play dumb, Rosemary. "He's awfully possessive of you."

I'd peddled the same lie to Benz that I did to Joslin: Emrys's host father had invited us to his farm just outside Prince Frederick for Thanksgiving dinner. In the context of this fabrication, Benz probably had a right to be suspicious. If he had a platonic relationship with an attractive female foreign exchange student, I'd certainly be a lot less understanding than he was being. (For the record, I was *not* implying Emrys was attractive.) But Benz and I also still sucked at being boring, at finding a reasonable equilibrium between the passion and the pause button.

"Put yourself in Emrys's shoes," I said. "A foreign exchange student, you're in a new country without any friends. I'm guessing the friends you do make when you get here are probably pretty special, pretty unique. They're friends you want to keep, friends you'd fight for."

"I guess," Benz affirmed weakly.

Little did Benz know the fighting was much more than metaphorical. I could tell this conversation needed to be redirected. "Ready for rugby season?"

He nodded. "Can't start soon enough."

"I can't wait to see you in those tight rugby shorts." My compliment was purposeful. I could already sense his suspicion.

"How was your Welsh Thanksgiving?" he asked.

"Probably not as fun as your Bethany Beach one."

"Yeah," Benz said, my reply deflating his hostility. "Stared at the ball-shrinking-cold ocean for hours at a time thinking about you."

"Am I supposed to take it as a compliment that thinking about me made your balls shrink?"

Despite his best effort not to, Benz laughed. "You know what I mean."

"You've told me watching football with your dad on Thanksgiving is your favorite Cooke family tradition. Stuffing your face with your mom's homemade banana cream pie. Eben sneaking you beers."

"I guess I just didn't have the heart to watch much football after we lost our playoff game."

Thinking about the playoff game made me think about the night after the playoff game. Fall Fling. The playground. Stolen kisses smelling of chocolate and the wet Chesapeake air. Despite my best effort not to, I winked. "If I recall, you seemed to recover pretty quickly from that loss."

Benz reached across the table and squeezed my hand. "I just want to put all of that behind me and focus on—"

"Yes, I agree," I said. It was about time he asked me to be his girlfriend again.

"And focus on rugby."

"Oh," I said. "Yeah, rugby."

Like a lot of the American Martyr jocks, Benz played football in the fall, rugby in the spring. I knew very little about the game of rugby, and whenever I described it as "football without pads," Benz would give me a ten-minute speech about how that wasn't true.

"Rosemary?" Benz said. "You okay?"

I nodded, pulling my hand away from his. "Boys and their games."

"Those games are going to earn me a football scholarship."

Benz played rugby for fun. With football, it was all business. "What use do you have for a scholarship?" I asked. "Your parents are loaded."

"I want to make my own way in the world, not depend on Mommy and Daddy for everything."

"Can we talk about something else besides college? I barely kept it together going five days without seeing you. The thought of saying goodbye to you forever gives me panic attacks."

"Forever, huh?" Benz reached out once more to grab my hand. This time he came at me with both hands, and I returned the gesture. "I've been thinking a lot about us. These last five days were freaking torture. I don't want to put a label on whatever this is between us, but…"

"But *what?*"

"I…it's just…I don't know."

"I could go for a label right about now, Benz Cooke." I raised our clasped hands, nodding. "What is this between us?"

Benz inhaled, held the breath for a second, then exhaled, as if he was working up the courage for what he was about to say to me. "So, I keep thinking about our night together."

"On the playground?" I asked.

"No," Benz refuted. "Our night together. When we, you know..."

"Had sex?"

Most of our conversations ultimately came back to the sex part: the shame, the regrets, how bad it was the first time, how good it might be the next time, if there would even be a next time. If only it was just about Benz and me. Everything was now informed by the Lust Borne Tide. Benz's virginity, my virginity. Mordred's fertility, my fertility. Sex as power. The idea that Benz's virginity was a secret worth keeping, as if he was more or less of a man based on his virginal status.

Although, let's be honest here. I didn't need an Arthurian prophecy to tell me sex could mess things up, and neither did Benz.

"I was just, well, such a creep the next day, in the morning, the morning after. I messed up. I messed up real bad. But the thing is, it's not the sex part that's freaking me out right now."

Benz was hilarious, and not in a good way. I tried not to crease my brow, but it had its own ideas. "Could've fooled me."

"Be serious, Rosemary," Benz said. "You're the one sitting here telling me that the thought of us saying goodbye to one another gives you panic attacks. You're the one casually throwing out words like 'forever.'"

"Will the jury note for the record that this word didn't scare you off?"

"See, Rosemary. Right there! What am I supposed to think when you say crap like that? You drive me crazy."

"Crazy, huh?"

"In a good way," Benz clarified. "Where to even begin? Your gigglemug that makes my day..."

I smiled. "You used 'gigglemug' in a sentence, correctly."

Benz continued right on talking, ignoring me. "The sound of your voice on the phone because you'd always rather talk than text, the way you listen to me and no one else when we're in a crowded room. And the smell of you. Oh my God, Rosemary, when you walk by and I catch a whiff of—"

"The smell of me?" I pondered, halfway flattered and halfway not. "I use unscented antiperspirant, and I don't wear perfume."

"It's not antiperspirant or perfume. It's just your, whatever. Your...*you*. I love you, Rosemary Banson. Always have, always will. I want to be your boyfriend again. There's nothing else I want more in this world."

I ran through my internal checklist why Benz professing his undying love shouldn't mean that much to me: my training with Emrys, the looming threat of the Lust Borne Prophecy, my distrust of love given the origins of my parents' relationship. And now, here was the boy of my dreams asking me to trust in something that would almost certainly lead to another broken heart. Yes, Benz and I had just used the word "forever," and it felt like both of us meant it. But when the only love you know is each other's love, forever is all you know.

As we sat there in the middle of the school cafeteria, our hands clasped, I knew for sure that I loved Benz with all my heart.

But I couldn't take him back. I refused to be that selfish, to put him in potential harm's way.

Then again, what reason did I have to think Benz would be in any real danger? If I had to choose between the threat of a potential prophecy and the love of an actual boyfriend, that's no freaking contest. Benz wins every time. Worst case, he'd be my sidepiece. I doubted Mordred would care.

Sidepiece? Get ahold of yourself, Rosemary!

"Well?" Benz said. He leaned in with pursed lips and kissed my hands. As he closed his eyes, I could feel the suction from his nose as he smelled my fingers. What a weirdo. Only one choice made sense.

CHAPTER

18

"I love you, Benz Cooke, and I want to be your girlfriend again."

It felt like the words were coming out of my mouth in slow motion, as if with every syllable I had yet another opportunity to take everything back and didn't. I was being selfish. It just felt good to do something that felt good. Benz gave me back his class ring. I wore his letter jacket to bed.

"Over here, Rosemary!" Emrys waved me down right before I drove past. He was standing on his front porch, looking quite dapper in a throwback three-piece suit.

Finals were over, and winter break had started. Save for Honors Pre-calculus, a class in which I scraped and clawed just to earn a C-, I aced everything. Benz invited Joslin, Emrys, and me to the Christmas party at the Annapolis Yacht Club, his parents' club. Joslin and I had planned to stop by Emrys's house for a pre-party, but Joslin said she was running late and that she'd meet us at the yacht club instead. The truth was Benz had invited Andrew Sparks to the party, and she was nervous.

This was my first time visiting Emrys's actual house. He told me to look for the narrow house with stained cedar shake, white trim, and a front porch. In Eastport, that narrowed things down to about half the town.

Connected to downtown Annapolis by the Spa Creek Bridge and

surrounded on three sides by water, the peninsula town of Eastport was an odd mix of people: professors and officers from the Naval Academy, Annapolis residents wanting a little separation from the overly commercialized downtown, direct descendants of former slaves, and a nine hundred-going-on-sixteen-year-old boy who insisted on making my life interesting.

I parked the Subaru along the curb across from his house. "Nice place," I said.

Emrys gave me a once over. "Nice dress. Trying to impress someone?"

Emrys took the news that Benz and I were back together better than I thought he would. When I told him about my internal checklist, and how I ended up doing the exact opposite of what I should have done, he shrugged his shoulders and said, "Screw the checklist."

"Are you sure I look okay?" I grabbed the hem of my black chiffon dress, a half-sleeve, lace and beaded number Mom picked out. "You don't think it's too much?"

"Rosemary, I'm wearing a vintage three-piece suit. I'm the last person to ask about being overdressed. Trust me, Benz will love it."

I slid my hand up one of the porch columns. "You and your host father live in this house together?"

"Not exactly," Emrys answered. "Atli has been in on my secret for a very long time. He comes over for the occasional meal and watches the place when I'm not here. Otherwise, he lives on his boat."

"Atli Saevarsson lives on a boat? So he looks, sounds, *and* lives like a Viking?"

"You should mention that to Atli the next time you see him. Let me know what he says."

Emrys's suggestion came across as a challenge. Holy crap, did Atli have secrets too? "How do you pull it off?" I asked.

"Faking it has become old hat for me." Emrys leaned against the porch rail. "Fake social security numbers, fake driver's license, fake bio, fake everything. I figure I have maybe a thirty-year window left to pull off late teens, early twenties. After that is when it's going to be a challenge."

Entering the house, the warped and weathered oak floors protested our every step. No space was wasted in the narrow home, and so the rooms were stacked one in front of the other. The front door opened directly into the shiplap-wrapped parlor, which transitioned into the kitchen, which transitioned into the dining room at the back of the house. A staircase rose on my left to the second floor. A couple logs burned in the fireplace to my right, the hearth framed by a wall of old leather-bound books.

"Nice library," I said.

Emrys nodded. "Thanks."

I ran my fingers along the embossed spines of books whose pronunciations I didn't feel like mangling: *Il principe difeso, Paradiso Perduto, Festa Christianorum.* "This library must be worth a small fortune."

"More like a large fortune," Emrys countered. "Some of these texts are over 400 years old."

"What's the newest book you own?"

Emrys pointed to the bottom shelf. "Fourteenth edition of the Encyclopedia Britannica, copyright 1957."

"Mid twenty-first century? That's practically brand new."

"I didn't invite you over to talk about my library. Where's Joslin?"

"She's running late. Said she'd meet us there."

"Any problems I need to know about?"

"Problems, yes. Problems you need to know about? No."

"What's that supposed to mean?"

"Joslin has a crush on Andrew Sparks."

"She's still on that Andrew Sparks kick?" Emrys jeered. "What does Joslin see in *that* guy?"

There it was again. That tone Emrys adopted whenever the teenage boy fought to assert himself over the old wizard. He wasn't being judgmental of Andrew—he was being jealous. "You sound disappointed," I said.

"What if I am?"

"You're not allowed to be disappointed."

"I'm not allowed to feel *things*?"

"Not for her, you're not."

"I may have the mind of a 2000 year-old wizard, Rosemary..."

"Nine hundred," I amended.

"Whatever. My point is still that I have the physical body and the hormones of a sixteen-year-old boy. This may seem hard to believe, but there are moments when my urges and impulsiveness simply overwhelm everything else. Maybe I'm like you—someone who's just ready to be in love again."

"Emrys, that's probably the most honest thing you've said to me since we met."

"It is?"

"Kind of icky, but honest."

"*In love again*," Emrys repeated, not laughing. Not doing much of anything really.

"Emrys?"

He was still physically here with me, but mentally he was somewhere else. I tried not to notice the smell of alcohol on his breath when I first came inside the house, but he had definitely been drinking.

Emrys took several slow steps across the room until he was standing at a writing desk in the corner. He stared at the wall calendar pegged to the shiplap just above the desk. Today's date was circled twice with bright red marker.

CHAPTER

19

The annual Cooke Christmas party was being held on a 150-foot three-masted, white-hulled schooner named *Arabella*. Emrys, Joslin, and I stood topside on *Arabella's* upper deck with Mrs. Cooke, a glass of champagne in her right hand, a bottle of champagne in her left. She leaned in and gave me a faux kiss on the cheek. "So glad you and your friends could come, Rosemary."

Benz's mother had a love-hate relationship with me. And by that I meant Mrs. Cooke loved when Benz and I were broken up, and she hated that we were back together.

I faux-kissed her right back. "Thanks for having us, Mrs. Cooke."

Claudia Cooke, "Cookie" to her friends, owns Severna Elite Academy. "S.E.A." was where I spent much of the first fourteen years of my life, from Mommy and Me classes at eighteen months to when they disbanded the gymnastics club my freshman year in high school. S.E.A used to have one of the more competitive gymnastics clubs on the East Coast, but Mrs. Cooke dismantled the program shortly after buying S.E.A. to concentrate on competitive cheer. She was actually my gymnastics coach when I was little, back when she was fresh out of college, desperate for a paycheck and not as mean. I vaguely remember Benz back then, when he'd bounce around in tumbling class with his smile and pre-teen baby fat.

I was loath to admit where Benz got his good looks, but it was obvious: the same hazel eyes, the same upturned nose they scrunched up when they were frustrated. Mrs. Cooke's brown hair, tonight streaked with blonde highlights and ending in a 1960s go-go flip, offset a fair and expressive face that was more natural than the spray-tanned, tight-skinned faces I saw on most older Severna Park moms. Unlike those other moms, Mrs. Cooke's top lip actually moves when she talks.

Mrs. Cooke didn't even bother to acknowledge my gratitude. She ignored me, like always, and it pissed me off. I wanted to be on her good side, really I did. The last thing I needed was to be stuck in a weird power dynamic with my boyfriend's mother. That was a contest the girlfriend rarely ended up winning. But to not even get a "You're welcome" from her? It wasn't easy to like someone who worked so hard to despise me.

Emrys stepped in between us, perhaps sensing my disdain. "I love your club's boat, Mrs. Cooke."

"Me too," Joslin said, grabbing my arm and pulling me behind Emrys.

Mrs. Cooke held her glass of champagne in the air, toasting no one. "She is beautiful, isn't she?" She finished her glass, handed the champagne bottle to Emrys. "Pour a lady a drink, young man?"

"Of course, Mrs. Cooke."

"Please," she said. "Call me Cookie."

Eyes rolling, I was about to say something I knew I'd regret just as Benz stepped up top.

"Where's Andrew?" Joslin asked.

A brief word about Andrew Sparks, Benz's best friend since kindergarten. Andrew had been reduced to cameo appearances in his life lately. Andrew was too cute for his own good, quick-witted, and forever the life of the party. I liked Andrew, and I trusted him more than his intentions probably merited—intentions that kept him on the periphery of our social circle. Yes, I had specifically told Joslin that Andrew was a "good guy," but I had also never been in his crosshairs. There were several girls at American Martyr—*several*—who might dispute my assertion.

"No, really, Joslin," Benz joked. "I'm fine, thanks. And you?"

"Sorry," she said, acknowledging her rudeness. She was going to have to improvise some small talk. And Joslin hated small talk. "How's football?"

"Uh, over," Benz said.

"Yeah," Joslin nodded. "I knew that."

She didn't know that. But to his credit, Benz played along. "I feel you, Joslin. Not a day goes by that I don't wish I could go back in time and get another shot in the playoffs."

"If only we could all go back in time," Emrys barked. "Not merely to perhaps save a life or right a wrong, but to watch the great Benz Cooke throw a melon-shaped leather ball through the air and bask in his greatness."

Joslin blushed, and Joslin Kelly never blushed. She was embarrassed. All she wanted was for this night to go well, to impress Andrew and his friends. She didn't know Emrys was acting out. She just thought he was a jealous teenage boy trying to ruin her night.

"On that note," I said, "how about we all go down and mingle?"

"You three go ahead." Emrys waved the champagne bottle at us. "Cookie and I will catch up."

Andrew finally showed up only to immediately disappear with Joslin. *Good for Joslin,* I thought. She was due for a win.

I sat at the bar near the stern of the boat between Emrys and Benz, my stomach filled with ginger beer. If Mrs. Cooke giving Emrys champagne wasn't bad enough, Benz's father had been sneaking Emrys tumblers of scotch.

Alcohol or no alcohol, something was definitely *off* with Emrys tonight.

"What's gotten into you?" I asked.

"Wouldn't you like to know," Emrys said dismissively. He shook his tumbler of half-melted ice cubes, nodding discretely at Eben Cooke for a refill.

Benz's father has one of the more colorful backgrounds in Severna Park. A direct descendant of seventeenth-century Maryland tobacco farmers, he converted a small inheritance into a large career as an award-winning music producer. Mr. Cooke has a lot of money, but he's uncomfortable with his wealth and status. He doesn't even like being called "Mr. Cooke," answering only to "Eben" or even just "Eb." He's a good father and a nice man. Mrs. Cooke doesn't deserve him.

"Sure thing, kid," Eben said. He grabbed a new bottle from under the bar. "How about some of my good scotch?"

Benz shook his head, waving his father off. "I think Emrys is plenty hydrated, Dad."

Eben nodded, setting the bottle on the bar. "I would agree with you, son."

"I'll say when I've had enough, thank you." Emrys reached clumsily across the bar for the bottle, spilling a half-dozen glasses in the process. His discretion was apparently exceeded by the sheer volume of alcohol he'd consumed.

Benz steadied Emrys in his chair. "It's probably time for you to go home, buddy."

"*Buddy?*" Emrys said. "Who are you calling, buddy? Do you know who you're talking to? I am—"

"*Really* drunk," I interrupted. "How about we take you home?"

Emrys tried to stand, but his legs were uncooperative. He stumbled. Benz made a move to help steady him, but did more harm than good. Emrys's elbow accidentally caught him square in the mouth, busting open Benz's lip. Flinching from the blow, Benz failed to catch Emrys. Momentum did the rest, as Emrys face-planted on to the deck.

Both of them were bleeding now. The amount of blood, especially against *Arabella*'s gleaming white side decks, made it look worse than it really was.

"You dropped me on purpose," Emrys said to Benz.

Benz nodded apologetically, his hand on his mouth. "My bad, Emrys. If it makes you feel any better, you got me good."

I could see the recognition in Emrys's eyes—the anger, or whatever he had boiling inside him tonight, starting to dissipate.

"My apologies to you and your family," Emrys said humbly. "You have been most gracious hosts."

"Most gracious?" Eben replied. "Let's not get carried away."

Emrys tried to stand up, but the blood rushing to his head and the booze had other ideas. He stumbled again, reaching for one of the barstools but missed. Emrys kissed *Arabella*'s teak decks for the second time in the last thirty seconds.

Suddenly, the whole world froze in place. Everyone on the boat was unnaturally immobilized, still and silent, except me.

"Well..." A woman's voice pierced the stillness. "That was quite the scene."

The woman glided around the impassive party guests. Draped in a long cloak of brown and white feathers, she seemed to hover more than walk. Beneath her cloak, she wore a suit of armor that looked like white fish scales, accented by a sheer silk cover-up. Straight, silver-streaked black hair hung down to her waist. She was perfect in every way, but to call her "beautiful" would have been an insult. It hurt to stare at her. She took a knee beside Emrys. His head faced her, his eyes wide open although he was frozen like everyone else.

"Can he see you?" I asked.

The feathered woman shook her head. "No one can see me except you, Lady Banson. A veil has been cast over them. They are as devoid of sight as they are still in form." She rested her arm on her knee. With her opposite hand, the woman leaned down to Emrys and brushed his hair out of his face. It was then I noticed her forearm guards, metal gauntlets extending from the elbow to the knuckle with two talon-like blades curving out from each wrist. Those talons looked like they could do some damage.

"Oh, my dearest Merlin," she said.

I pointed at Emrys, then at the bird lady. "You know each other?"

"Indeed we do."

"How are you freezing him? He's too—"

"Powerful?"

"Isn't he?"

"Merlin has not possessed that level of power in ages, my dear girl. Taking into consideration the alcohol and his eternal heartbreak, he was easily bested tonight."

Her tone was intense, familiar. "Eternal heartbreak? What are you talking about? *Who* are you?"

"My name is Vivian, sister to Morgause and Morgan le Fay. Most people know me better by my more formal title." She bowed. "I am the Lady of the Lake, and I was once Merlin's lover."

"Excuse me?" I replied.

"I suppose that is not information he would have occasion to divulge. We were amorous for only a short time. I did it only to make my sister Morgan jealous. She was the one who loved him, not me."

"Sisters like you make me thankful I'm an only child."

"I was doing her a favor. She had to see Merlin's true nature. Men cannot be trusted."

"Did he even know Morgan loved him?"

"Does Merlin know you love him?"

Full stop. "*What*? He's like a brother to me."

Vivian pointed at Emrys, then at me. "You mean you two have not…"

I shook my head. "Freaking gross, lady!"

Vivian stood, surveyed the boat. She was looking for something. "Ahh, there we are." She walked to the bar, took the glass of scotch out of Eben's frozen hand. She sipped the scotch, licking her lips. "Mmmm…" she said. "Lagavulin 1991. Only 522 bottles were made. One of the things the twenty-first century does exceedingly better than the late fifth century is alcohol. If I never drink another cup of stale, warm mead, it will be too soon. 'Tis a shame, really, about you and Merlin. You would make a cute couple. It's him, isn't it?"

"What are you talking about?"

Vivian nodded at Benz. "The handsome young man standing over Emrys with the green-brown eyes. He is your boyfriend, is he not?"

"My boyfriend?" The simple question didn't call for an awkward answer, but I was giving her one. "I mean, yeah, h-h-he's my boyfriend."

Vivian shook her head. "You surprise me, Arlynn Banson."

"It's Rosemary," I said. "Rosemary Banson. And how so?"

"I thought you would be less of a…"

"Less of a teenager?"

"Less of a girl, more of a woman."

"You don't know anything about me."

"Dear girl, I know everything about you." Vivian fluttered over to me, spreading her arms like she was going to lead me in a waltz. She framed my torso with her hands, squeezing and turning me from side to side. But Vivian wasn't dancing; she was sizing me up. "You certainly look the part. Such a waste of good birthing hips."

"I'm about tired of you." I swatted her hands off my hips, breaking her hold. I had meant to push her away. Instead, I stepped back, bringing my right hand up, palm out, and drove the heel of my palm into her sternum.

Vivian didn't even flinch. It was like I'd punched a brick wall—the difference being I was capable of punching a hole in a brick wall. Vivian had established she was strong, stronger than me maybe. But was she as fast as me?

My right hand behind my back, I summoned Excalibur. "*Gladio!*"

Spoiler alert: She was as fast as me.

In the time it took me to spin my right arm around, Vivian knocked Excalibur out of my hand with one forearm guard while raising her right taloned fist to my face. She pinned me against the boat's guardrail, the tips of her talons pressing into my throat. Excalibur lay at my feet, useless.

"I see you have my sword," Vivian remarked. "Now where is she?"

"Who?" I asked.

"Do not play games with me, child. Where is my sister, Morgan? 'Twas not but three months ago I ventured here during the equinox to find her."

"So your sister summoned you here?" I asked. "Then that means Mordred knows I'm here too?"

Mordred. The two syllables tasted bitter in my mouth. For the very first time, the hypothetical threat to my existence was no longer hypothetical.

Vivian shook her head. "My sister was not the one who summoned me, and Mordred does not know I am here. At least not yet. It is I who sent the incubus and faeries to visit you. I was skeptical of your prowess in combat, but seeing you here with Excalibur removes all doubt. I know Morgan hid you from us for all these years. Sister always loved a good cloaking spell. And Merlin has been here this whole time, preparing you."

"Preparing me?" My brain raced. Sarcasm came easy to me, but sarcasm at knifepoint, not so much. "I don't mean to rain on your Lust Borne parade, but do you really think he's capable of preparing me for anything? I mean, look at the boy. If you hadn't immobilized him, the whiskey sure would've. I can take care of myself just fine."

"Your overconfidence will be your undoing, Lust Borne. My elder sister and nephew will certainly think little of your boastfulness and even less of your skill."

"Oh, you mean Morgause and Mordred?" I nodded over her shoulder as if they were there.

Vivian bit on the old bait and switch, following my eyes. It gave me my opening. I reached up and knocked her right arm to the side. One of her talons cut me, but the wound wasn't deep. While grabbing both of her arms, I head-butted her in the face. The move was a bit of a miscalculation; her face was almost as hard as her sternum. We both staggered backward, but she seemed to have received the worst of it. In the time it took for her to recover, I grabbed her taloned hand at the wrist while raising my right hand. The right hand that now held Excalibur.

"My turn," I said, my blade at Vivian's throat.

She struggled, but smiled. "My sword fancies you."

"What?" I asked, pressing the edge of the blade against her windpipe.

"Excalibur," Vivian said. "It likes you. That makes sense. Men are such cruel masters. Emrys has prepared you for Mordred, better than you think he has. I suppose we will finish this another time."

She closed her eyes. A light flashed. My vision blurred, but I could see enough. My imagination took care of the rest. Vivian's cloak of feathers wrapped around her as she slumped to the ground. A white haze hovered just above the mound of feathers, retaining the vague shape of Vivian's slumped form. The mound glowed for a few seconds, then a few seconds more. A bird's head poked out of the mound, and then two massive wings. Vivian, now in the form of a giant osprey, let out a series of high-pitched chirps, either scolding me or warning me, I couldn't tell. With a flap of her wings, Vivian took to the air.

The Lady of the Lake turned osprey screeched one last time at me as she disappeared into the night.

I didn't know how long Vivian had been gone when her spell wore off, but it was as if someone had pressed the play button on the remote control.

Mrs. Cooke turned the corner to see the aftermath of Emrys's tantrum. She screamed. "There's so much blood! Somebody call a doctor!"

Emrys struggled to his feet. Next to him, Benz held a napkin to his face. Meanwhile, Eben offered a measured dose of reassurance. "A doctor? Come on now, Cookie, we just need rags and some ice."

Well, he was briefly measured.

"Hey! Who the hell drank my good scotch?"

I could almost make out Emrys's reflection in Eben's empty glass of Lagavulin 1991. I turned to face them both, staring down the length of the bar. He and Benz sat side-by-side on barstools, an unspoken but palpable truce hanging in the air between them. "How are you doing?" I asked.

"*I'm fine,*" they said in unison. Each boy assumed I was talking to him and him alone, each assuming he possessed a monopoly on my sympathy.

Vivian was only half right. The things the twenty-first century did exceedingly better than the late fifth century were Scotch and presumptuous teenage boys.

CHAPTER

20

Atli opened the door in between my second and third knock. "That was quick," I said. "You expecting me?"

"Emrys told me zat you'd be coming." Atli rarely spoke. He kept a pack of Parliament cigarettes in his front shirt pocket and had the voice of a smoker, low and raspy. The burnt-ash smell clung to his beard and long hair. "*Bitte, eingeben.*"

"Excuse me?"

"Please, enter," Atli translated.

I had once referred to Atli Saevarsson as "the record store guy with the beard and slicked-back ponytail who looks like a cross between a Nordic god and a librarian and always smells like cigarettes." That description did him a disservice. He was somebody before he became Emrys's collaborator. I knew that much from the pictures and books Emrys kept around the house. He'd been a runway model, the live-in boyfriend of a famous fashion designer, a glider pilot, an author who penned a memoir in German about a year he spent in Cuba. "Smelly bookish Viking" just got to the point a little faster.

I stepped inside. "You meet everybody at the hospital?"

"Just Eben and zeh two boys," Atli clarified.

"How much do you know?"

"Enough."

It was a loaded answer. How much did Atli know, not just about tonight but about everything? Was he content to live in a world of "enough," or did Emrys trust him in a way he didn't trust anyone else?

Atli held open the front door. "I'll show myself out. *Auf wiedersehen.*"

"Goodbye to you too, Atli," I said. "And thanks."

"*Für das?*"

"For what? For watching out for Emrys. Being the parent for that hot mess, real or fake, can't be easy."

Atli grinned, punctuating the gesture with a subtle nod. "*Danke schön.*"

"You're welcome," I replied.

I walked toward the rear of the house. Emrys sat at his kitchen table, holding a bag of ice to his face.

"Vivian?" I said, "Talk."

"What?"

"Crazy blonde wrapped in osprey feathers, has these cool talons that came out of her hands, froze everyone in time, talked about you two being lovers. Who is she, what is she? How does she fit in to all this?"

Emrys lowered the ice from his head, dropping his hand to waist-level. "The Lady of the Lake is here, in Maryland? That cannot be. I would have sensed her approach."

"I'm guessing the falling-down drunkenness had something to do with that."

"Maybe it was a lesser creature. Another faerie perhaps masquerading as Vivian?"

"Yeah, I'm pretty sure it was her. Said she was Morgan le Fay's and Morgause's sister, which makes her Mordred's aunt, right?"

Emrys nodded. "What happened?"

"Nothing much," I answered. "She asked me where Morgan was. I played dumb. That's when she threatened to cut me, so I head-butted her in the face, pulled Excalibur on her, and then she escaped by turning into a bird. Good times."

Emrys pointed into the great room at one of the chairs fronting the hearth. "Have a seat, Rosemary. Let me tidy up, then we'll talk."

Emrys disappeared into the kitchen. He returned the peas to the freezer, ran some water, and banged some dishes around. He went outside for more firewood, returned to the hearth, and restacked the pile. He fiddled with the wood in the fireplace and put on a pot of coffee. He had a nice fire going. The coffee simmered in an old iron kettle hanging over the fire by a hook. That made two of us. I sat there simmering, waiting, aching for answers. We settled into matching high-backed leather chairs parallel to the hearth, facing each other, Emrys's full mug steaming on the small round table between us. He grabbed his cup, took a cautious sip.

"Coffee?" he asked.

"No," I said. "And stop stalling."

Emrys stood again and re-approached the fireplace. He grabbed the fire iron from its stand, giving the glowing embers a few half-hearted pokes. "Sure you don't want any coffee?" he said.

"*Emrys*," I scolded.

"My relationship with Vivian is *complicated*, Rosemary. As is yours."

"Explain," I said, expecting little in the way of real information.

"I cannot deny that Vivian and I were once lovers."

Emrys starting off with a clear admission? Nothing cryptic or paradoxical? Maybe I'd get something out of the old boy today.

"I shared a bond with all three sisters," Emrys confessed. "It was the oldest, Morgause, to whom I taught magic. Vivian, my lover, was the middle sister. And then there was the youngest, Morgan le Fay, my dearest Fay. When I say 'sisters,' they're half-sisters actually, all of them sharing Igraine as a mother but none of them sharing the same father."

"They're all half-sisters to Arthur then?"

Emrys nodded. "Correct."

"And that makes Arthur both Mordred's dad *and* uncle?"

"I assumed you'd already done that math in your head."

"Disgusting," I said. "But go on."

"Morgause generally kept to herself. Her meddling came later. Vivian was always the troublemaker, adopting that whole Lady of the Lake disguise, teasing men with Excalibur. Teasing me with her affections."

"Vivian said you were together for only a short time."

"I thought I loved Vivian, and that she loved me. I didn't know she was seducing me just to hurt Fay until it was too late. Fay walked in on us consummating our relationship. She'd come to my quarters to profess her love to me."

"But wasn't Fay the one who showed up to the hospital the day I was born?"

"Indeed she was." Emrys leaned back into his chair. He rubbed his knees, as if the words needed to be massaged out of him. "Even though I broke Fay's heart, she never held it against me. When she came to your delivery room, I almost expected her to be there. It was her spell that protected you all these years, Rosemary. That's just who Fay is. Her love is selfless and unconditional. But it's because of Fay, because of what I did to her, that I almost never loved again."

"Is it really such a big betrayal if you didn't know she had feelings for you?"

"Well, I didn't know, but I sort of had an idea."

"Ahh..." I pondered. "The old conveniently oblivious routine."

"The what?" Emrys asked.

"Never mind," I said, not caring to unpack the obvious, that he was a guy doing guy things. "You said you almost never loved again. Who was she?"

"Obviously, I need to explain my actions last night," Emrys said.

"Obviously," I echoed.

The wood in the fireplace was still a little green. I could hear the sizzling of the maple sap in between the crack and pop of the wood. Emrys stared at the fire. I felt like I should say something, but I was coming up empty. He was drunk last night—really drunk. He was acting so, so *young* lately. What was I supposed to say to an ancient wizard who seemed to be, for whatever reason, willingly surrendering to his teenage identity?

"She was a beautiful young woman with her whole life in front of her when we met," Emrys said.

"An explanation or even a small attempt at a transition would be nice here," I said. "Who are you talking about?"

"My wife, Tess." He took another sip of his coffee.

"I wondered if you were ever going to tell me about her."

"She was twenty-one years old. She had graduated college, but her parents had her whole life planned out for her—the handpicked house, the handpicked husband—and she turned her back on all of it to enlist in the Navy during World War II."

"Young, smart, ambitious."

Emrys nodded. "She was a Naval Reserve Sergeant, one of the first commissioned officers in WAVES."

"Waves?"

"*Women Accepted for Volunteer Emergency Service.* She worked communications and intelligence ops at NRL, the Naval Research Laboratory south of Chesapeake Beach. They hired me in the summer of '43 to teach the WAVES how to sail."

"You've had jobs over the years, like real adult jobs?"

"I had to do something besides just waiting around for your parents to show up. I've been a fireman, a logger, a fisherman of course, an elementary school teacher, and a dozen other things."

"I'd love to see your full resume some time," I joked. "They never asked questions about your youthful appearance?"

"I could pass for my twenties back then. My facial hair grew a lot faster than it does now. I thought it would be a great diversion for me. Three months of getting paid just to hang out with beautiful and intelligent women on sailboats."

"What's not to like?" I mused.

"Precisely," Emrys affirmed. "But Tess was my very first student, and over that summer I never so much as looked at anyone else. She was perfect. I still remember how the corners of her mouth would go higher than the dimple on her top lip when she smiled. On anyone else, the facial expression might have looked clownish, but Tess's smile just drew you in, especially when she talked. She had this slight British accent from spending summers at her family's ancestral home in Devonshire, England—like so many beautiful English maidens' voices I'd known over the centuries and yet not like any of them at all. Her hair was long and cherry-brown. Her skin was soft to the touch, and the color of fresh milk. She smelled like pine trees. She was the most compassionate creature I have ever known, in this realm or any other. We were married by the winter."

I leaned against the side of the high back chair, inhaling the caramelized smell of the syrupy firewood. I loved Emrys's story. It made me think of Benz in a way I hadn't before. I didn't want a high school boyfriend like everyone else had. I wanted a fairy tale.

"Yesterday was our wedding anniversary," Emrys added. "I'm sorry for last night. I have a bad habit of getting out of hand on that day."

The date circled twice with bright red marker on his wall calendar.

"Oh, Emrys." I didn't know why I did it, but I grabbed his hand. Affection between us didn't come naturally, our physical interactions being more of the punching and kicking variety. I squeezed Emrys's hand a couple times. He squeezed back.

Back to the grave marker. I didn't want to be nosy, but I couldn't help myself. "Why is Tess buried beneath that tree?"

Emrys's eyes were red, but he resisted crying. "That was her favorite spot. We would go out there and watch the sun rise over the Bay almost every morning."

"What happened in 1959? How did she die?"

"I'd rather not talk about it."

"You can't just end the story there."

"Why not?"

"You can tell me. I'm a big girl. Not all fairy tales have happy endings, even when gods are involved. I get that."

Emrys smiled, squeezing my hand right back. "There's no story left to tell, Rosemary. Tess simply did what all mortals do at some point. She said goodbye."

We didn't hold hands for much longer after that, our uncomfortable intimacy surrendering to the more familiar confines of teenage awkwardness.

"So, I guess back to Vivian, the Lady of the Lake. Why is she so keen on tracking down Morgan le Fay? And what would motivate Vivian to seek me out and nearly gut me?"

"I doubt very much Vivian would gut you, Rosemary."

"You weren't there, Emrys."

"I didn't have to be there. I just know Vivian wouldn't do that."

"How do you know?"

"Because Vivian is Lancelot's mother and your grandmother."

CHAPTER
21

The Subaru coasted home on fumes. It was just before dawn, so my parents were likely still asleep. I tried to tip-toe into the house through the front door, but the hinges welcomed me home with a loud squeak.

"I keep telling myself I'll fix that door one of these days," Dad said. He sat at the kitchen table with a package of Pop-Tarts and a glass of milk, still wearing the clothes he had on the night before. "Mom and I pulled in about ten minutes ago. We went for a moonlight sail at the Academy that ended up being an overnight."

I grabbed an empty glass from the cupboard, sat down across from him. "You're quite the couple lately."

"We're trying our best," he affirmed.

"I don't mean to be such a pain sometimes. I really am glad you two have figured out the magic again."

"Love doesn't come down to magic, Rosemary," Dad said. "It comes down to hard work."

"I don't know about that," I said. "It seems to me that the moment you put that sword back in your hand, things changed for the better."

"Your mother is way beyond being impressed by Arondight."

"Aron*what?*"

"That's the name of my sword. Some people also call it the Sword of Charlemagne."

"I prefer Arondight."

"Me too. But as I was saying, a fancy sword might encourage someone to look at you, but it won't convince them to stick around, let alone deal with your mommy issues."

"So, counseling is going well I see."

"It's painful but necessary, Rosemary."

"Mommy issues?"

"Long story."

Come on, Rosemary. Poker face. "I bet it is, Dad. But speaking of Mommy issues, where is she?"

"*My* mother?"

Keep it together. He's being sarcastic. He doesn't have a clue. "No, silly. Jennifer."

Dad nodded up at the ceiling. "Your mother is up in the shower, which gives us a chance to talk. Merlin called me. He told me you met Vivian."

Okay, so he wasn't being sarcastic.

"I almost killed your mother. Did Emrys tell you that?" I said.

"I doubt you could have killed Vivian, and she's most certainly not my mother," Dad replied.

"But Emrys said—"

"It's part of his job description, Rosemary. While I think Emrys is really and truly trying to be straight with you, Merlin always enjoyed the double talk and riddles. I think sometimes Emrys does that just to see if he can still be the world's cleverest pain in the ass. Vivian was never my mother. She kidnapped me as an infant and raised me as her own. My mother was Elaine of Benwick, the wife of King Ban."

"He said that Vivian was my grandmother."

"Barely," Dad said. "My father had been mortally wounded in battle by his arch-enemy Claudas de la Deserte, and Mother was attending to him when Vivian snuck into my tent and stole me away."

"So you were kidnapped as an infant. Classic Arthurian family tale. Weird-ass family connections aren't a guarantee of anything except more weirdness."

"I think that's an exact quote from Sir Thomas Malory."

"Monty Python would be my guess," I said. "Did you ever see her again, your birth mother?"

"Yes, once. I went to see her long after I'd grown into a man, right before she died. Seeing me put *her* heart at peace, but it did the exact opposite to me. My heartbreak was like an open wound. Pop-Tart?" Dad held out the opened foil package, the frosted pastry peeking out the top.

"Thanks," I said. I pulled the Pop-Tart out of the foil, bit off a corner. Frosted strawberry, my favorite.

"I should have never gone to Camelot when I did," Dad said, pouring milk in my glass.

"What makes you say that?" I grabbed my milk from the table.

Dad did the same, eyeing the inside of his milk glass like an oracle looking into a crystal ball. "I was vulnerable," he confided. "My mother had just died when I answered my king's call to the Round Table. At first, my friendship with Arthur more than compensated. He was everything to me, I loved him as a brother. But a fraternity of men could only fulfill me for so long. I yearned for the love of a woman. I yearned for Guinevere. It was wrong, but I didn't care. Being with her took the pain away. It filled me up inside with something good, something pure, something…"

"Noble?" I pondered.

Dad nodded. "Yes, noble."

"Mommy issues, huh?"

"Big time," Dad said.

I raised my glass of milk. Stripped of all its pretense and fantasy, Dad's world wasn't so different than mine. We both looked for love to fill the void, and neither of us did it right on the first try. But he was still a knight, and so I stood, toasting him with a slight bow of my head. "To heartbreak, m'lord?"

Sir Lancelot du Lac stood and raised his glass of milk high. "To heart…"

"Dad," I said, acknowledging his pause. "You okay?"

"No, I'm not. You and your mother need to know the truth about my job."

CHAPTER
22

Dad convened the meeting at Cantler's Riverside Inn, his and Mom's favorite crab shack on the north side of Annapolis. We sat at a long table on the deck overlooking Mill Creek. The table was covered in brown craft paper. There were no utensils or plates between us, just a pile of steamed blue crabs, a roll of paper towels, a mason jar stuffed with wooden hammers and metal lobster crackers, a couple small bowls of melted butter, and a shaker of Old Bay seasoning.

Once she confirmed the blue crabs were local and not shipped in from the Gulf of Mexico, Mom ordered two pounds for the table, which she proceeded to bludgeon with a hammer. She picked the claw meat out with her fingers, raising a piece of crab meat to her mouth as she eyed Dad's duffel bag curiously. "Going on a trip, honey?"

Mom sat directly across the table from Dad, while I sat opposite Dad's bag. It was Dad's favorite bag, something he bought from a second-hand store when I was a little kid. It smelled of musty books and pipe smoke.

"Alan?" Mom pressed.

"What if we offered Mordred a trade?" Dad asked.

"A trade?" I asked. "Like another girl?"

"Of course not," Dad said, shaking his head. "The whole purpose of Mordred traveling through time is to have you bear his children."

I nodded. "Yeah, we've covered that."

"But think about it, Rosemary. Does Mordred really want kids, or does he just want to preserve his legacy? Does he want to make sure the Pendragon line endures? If we could offer him immortality instead of your hand in marriage, would he take that trade and just leave us alone?"

Dad reached into his duffel bag. He extracted from the bag an object that looked vaguely like a grapefruit. This grapefruit was in fact a liquid-filled glass orb—translucent and wrapped in multiple intersecting strips of oxidized copper. One end of the ball had a slightly recessed cap on it, the diameter of a milk jug lid.

"I give you the Triton Orb," Dad said, looking around cautiously. "A replica of the Orb rests within the Triton Light, the navigational beacon on the northeast seawall of the Naval Academy. This is the original."

Mom pointed her crab hammer at Dad. "Why do you have the original, Alan?"

"Because I swapped it for the replica," he answered.

Mom continued the interrogation, as if she was looking for an answer she already knew. "What's so special about the Triton Orb that my husband would pursue a life of crime?"

"Well, I have been living a double life of sorts," Dad said.

And there it was.

"Yes, my long nights in the office have been partly about getting a promotion, and I'm still in line for one. But I'd have likely been promoted up the chain much faster if my research wasn't monopolized by the Triton Light. It's become a private obsession of mine that until now I thought I was going to just keep private."

"How fast would you have been promoted?" Mom asked, exasperated.

"Bear with me for a second, Jennifer."

"I'll give you exactly sixty," she said.

"I guess I'll have to talk fast. In 1960, the *U.S.S. Triton*, a Navy submarine, completed a submerged circumnavigation of the world. The submarine collected water from the twenty-two seas through which it passed, which were used to fill the orb built into the light's base. But the thing is, nobody ever knew for sure exactly which twenty-two seas the *Triton* visited. I know this because I've spent the better part of the last decade trying to discover them. There are more than twenty-two bodies of water listed in the ship's log. A lot more. Sometimes, the captain even recorded multiple bodies of water simultaneously."

Mom was fuming, and Dad noticed. "Please bear with me, Jennifer. Both you and Rosemary will want to hear this." He wiped the last remnants of crab off his mouth, yanked his bib off his neck. "There was this one day in which the captain logged the English Channel, the Celtic Sea, and the Loe Pool all at once."

Mom's eyes perked up. Mine did not. "And that should mean something to me?" I asked.

"The Loe is where the Lady of the Lake, where Vivian was said to reside. There's an actual sample of my stepmother's home waters within the Triton Orb."

"This can't be just a random coincidence," I said.

"It's not," Dad said, holding Mom's free hand while reaching across the table for mine. "Did you think I wanted to be away from you and your mother?"

"Well, we can be kind of annoying," I remarked.

"Rosemary, please. You're not making this any easier."

Mom yanked her hand away. "What's she not making any easier, Alan?"

"You and Emrys have kept things from me, Jennifer," Dad said. "I think I've earned the right to have my own secrets."

"Earned the right?" Mom asked. "I didn't realize we were keeping score."

Dad wiped his mouth, placed his hammer meticulously on the table. "In early May 1960, shortly before the *Triton* ended her circumnavigation, she visited Bimini Island in the Caribbean. There's a freshwater tidal pool on Bimini Island said to be the location of the Fountain of Youth. When you combine two mystical places like the Loe Pool and the Fountain of Youth, plus throw in twenty or more other bodies of water, that's basically a magic cocktail. Nearly every immortality spell I've ever heard of has some sort of co-mingling of earthly waters. The waters of William Wordsworth's favorite lake, Grasmere, when combined with the one and only Loch Ness, reportedly allowed him to live with lung disease for twenty years."

"So your plan is what exactly?" I grabbed the orb, casually juggling it in my hand. "Mordred gets the Triton Orb in exchange for just leaving us alone?"

"I know that your father is trying to protect you, Rosemary. And that he thinks he's trying to protect us." Mom grabbed the orb from me in midair, as if only the person holding it had the right to talk. "But I'm still trying to wrap my brain around him being an obsessive-compulsive workaholic for half our marriage just because of a goddamn glass ball."

"Bullocks," I said, trying and failing to hold in a laugh.

"Umm, ladies?" Dad said.

"Yes, dear," Mom said.

"Yep," I added.

"You didn't let me finish."

"There's more?" Mom asked.

"It's my stepmother."

"What does Vivian have to do with this, Alan?"

Dad fidgeted in his chair. Whatever secret he was holding on to was going to be a doozy. "Because of her connection with the Loe Pool, I've been able to communicate with Vivian through the Triton Orb for a while."

"Define a while," Mom insisted.

Dad looked at the ceiling while counting on his fingers. "Oh, about seventeen years."

"So pretty much ever since you and Mom got here?" I asked.

Dad nodded. "Vivian knew we were here all along, but I asked the mother I once knew to protect the son she once loved. I asked her to protect us. She agreed to help—right up until she didn't."

Mom stood, leering at my father. "What do you mean by that, Alan? Right up until she didn't?"

"It was just Vivian being Vivian, and I realize that now. In hindsight, I never should have trusted her. I said to you a minute ago, 'I think I've earned the right to have my own secrets.' I didn't mean that. What did I gain from keeping this secret from you? Why would I put you through those years of me being so distant and not present in our relationship, not present as a husband or a father?"

"Because you didn't know you were keeping a secret," I said.

Dad pointed at me with his right index finger, then tapped the same finger on his nose. Tears puddled beneath his eyes. "Because I didn't know I was keeping a secret. Vivian told me to be silent, and I obeyed without questioning her. She said she would be there for me, that she would always be my connection to the Old World, and that I could come to her when things got too complicated at home and just talk."

I could see it on Mom's face. That admission stung a little. The idea that Dad felt more comfortable, enchantment or no enchantment, talking to an invisible evil stepmother than his own wife.

Dad continued. "But that connection was never real. She'd put a spell on me. I was in this *fog* for years. Vivian told me she was just waiting until you turned sixteen to give you a sporting chance, Rosemary. I believed her, unquestioningly. Waiting seemed like the right thing to do. But in the end, the Triton Light wasn't a naval beacon. It was a Mordred beacon. And now our only hope is offering up this orb's immortality to protect my daughter's honor."

"Yeah…" I rocked back in my chair. "About that."

CHAPTER
23

"Let's do this!" I exclaimed.

We paid our tab and exited the restaurant, but not before an ex-Notre Dame football player hit on me outside the restrooms. He introduced himself as Braden—McCormick or McClintock, I didn't quite get the last part because of his beer-induced slurring. He was tall, obviously impressed with himself, and in town with some buddies for the Navy-Notre Dame game. Dad informed him I was sixteen, Braden made a quick exit, and I told Dad he didn't need to fight my battles.

The real battle was in the parking lot of Cantler's Riverside Inn.

Mom and Dad stood to either side of me, their arms folded in judgment. I caught myself starting to assume a boxer's stance—right foot planted, fists raised—but I willed myself to relax. Hands open, resting on my thighs.

"What have you done?" Mom asked pointedly.

"I thought that was obvious, *Jennifer*. I had sex with Benz Cooke. I'm no longer a virgin." My use of her first name was purposely disrespectful. I was setting the rules of engagement and choosing to go low.

Dad would have none of it. "She may have made some mistakes, but Jennifer is your mother, young lady, and you will address her as such."

A quick eye roll from Mom. She barely acknowledged Dad's support. This was a two-front war for her, and she didn't like either of us that much right now. "Rosemary, do you have any idea what the ramifications of your actions might be?"

"No," I said, "and neither do you."

"You could conceivably be pregnant this very moment with the next heir to the Lust Borne Tide."

My index finger in her face preempted my words. "You know that's not true, Mom. You were the one who put me on the freaking pill when I was fourteen years old. Plus, Benz wore protection."

"That's still not one-hundred percent guaranteed effective."

"Then thank God for Plan B."

"You didn't," Mom said, half questioning and half denouncing me.

"I did."

"Ladies, please." Dad raised his hand, surveying the parking lot for any innocent bystanders. "Keep it down. Show a little restraint."

"Uh-uh, Dad." I wagged my still-extended index finger at a new target. "You of all people do not have the right to play the prude card. Neither of you do."

Mom jumped back in. "We're not being prudish, we're being parents."

I raised both hands, palms up, and shrugged. "What's the difference?"

Dad's turn. "The difference is we know that these kinds of desires, these kinds of decisions have real-life consequences."

"So that's it, huh? I'm a mistake?"

Mom's demeanor changed instantly from dogmatic to placating. She shook her head, waving her arms. "That's not what your father and I are say—"

"Fuck you both!"

Three words I thought I'd never say to my parents as I stormed away from the Cantler's Riverside Inn parking lot.

Fuck you both. It hurt when I said the words. It hurt when I replayed saying the words in my head, over and over again.

Benz's virginity, my virginity. Mordred's fertility, my fertility. Sex as power. The idea that Benz's virginity was a secret worth keeping, as if he was more or less of a man based on his virginal status. The idea that my virginity was a secret worth keeping, as if I was more or less of a woman.

Fuck you both. Did their reaction to my news deserve anything less profane? Mom and Dad were perfectly willing, eager even, to leave my sexual agency to a prophecy laced in innuendo and double-speak, written no doubt by some horny fifth- century dude who thought "Maybe another time when I'm a little less drunk" constituted a "Yes." My identity as a young woman, as a future mother (if I chose to be one), and as a sexual being defined by a handful of implausibly rhyming couplets. And once they found out that it was my body, my choice, the world's most famous adulterers labeled me a mistake.

Thank God for Plan B, indeed.

CHAPTER

24

Benz leaned back on the weight bench with me as his spotter. "Are you sure you can do this?" he asked.

"Are *you* sure you can do this?" I countered.

"You got some stones on you, Rosemary."

"I've spotted you before."

"Not talking about that," Benz said. "Telling your parents we slept together? How does that even come up in conversation?"

I never told Benz about taking the morning-after pill, and I certainly wasn't going to tell him about the fight I just had with my mom and dad. "You wouldn't believe me if I told you. Let's just drop it, okay?"

I didn't need to come to Benz's workouts to stay in shape. Emrys made sure of that. When he wasn't drowning his sorrows in expensive scotch or making the honor roll at American Martyr, he spent much of his time upgrading Mom's obstacle course in the woods behind our house. He added a few more rope exercises, made the climbing wall twice as high, the moat twice as deep. Being here with Benz served two purposes: One, I got to hang out with my boyfriend while he wore tight-fitting shirts; and two, I got a lot of practice turning my power off.

When I was a kid, hiding my aptitude was a lot easier because there wasn't such a pronounced gap between me and the other kids.

Pretending to be normal when I was extraordinarily talented was tough but manageable. Pretending to be normal when I might be the strongest and fastest human on Earth? Not nearly as easy. Turning off my powers—or more accurately just hiding my abilities— was the hardest part about the Lust Borne Prophecy. It required extraordinary mental and physical discipline. Being here with Benz—as his girlfriend, as his cheerleader, as his spotter—honed that discipline in a way few other arenas afforded. Imagine competing against your boyfriend knowing you could beat him every time, and having the mental and physical restraint to never win. Considering the fact I could literally bite his tongue off by accident in the heat of passion, it was a lot like kissing him. The thought both scared me and empowered me.

Lying on the bench, Benz lifted the bar loaded up with 275 pounds off the rack. So far, so good. He blew air out through puffed cheeks, psyching himself up. He dropped the bar, dug his feet into the rubber floor while trying not to arch his back, and pushed.

275 pounds was over one-and-a-half times Benz's body weight, and I had never seen him bench more than 225. At first, the bar sat suspended just above his chest.

"Come on, Benz," I said. "Don't arch your back. Lift with your chest."

The bar started to rise, slowly. *Come on, boyfriend!* I thought. Benz groaned from the effort. *Over halfway there!*

I caught Coach Lou Joe out of the corner of my eye, just as he walked into the weight room. "Benz!" he shouted.

If only the coach had waited ten more seconds to enter the room. But the damage was done. I could see Benz's hands slip as he reacted to the sound of his name being called. He was about to drop 275 pounds on his throat.

Benz closed his eyes, bracing himself.

"W-what happened?" Benz stammered, opening his eyes. The bar hovered just above his face, nestled in the little safety nubs halfway up each side of the rack.

"I saw you lose your grip and just guided the bar back to the spotter catches. You totally had it."

"Yeah, no. Appreciate the pep talk, but I'm not quite ready for that weight. We'll get it next time." Benz exhaled. "Thanks for the assist."

He bought it. Thank God he did, as I wasn't ready to explain to Benz or Coach Lou Joe how a sixteen-year-old girl could deadlift 275 pounds with one hand.

Coach Lou Joe walked over to us. "Lou Joe" was short for Luigi Giovanni. He was American Martyr's head football and rugby coach.

Benz swung his feet a quarter turn and stood up. "Hey Coach," he said.

"275, huh?" Lou Joe eyed the bench skeptically. "Biting off a little more than you can chew there, Captain?"

"Maybe don't run me so hard at practice, and I'll have a little more energy."

Lou Joe patted Benz on the back. "Fat chance that's happening."

"What's up, Coach?" I interjected.

"Livin' the dream, Rosemary. Can I borrow your guy for the next twenty minutes or so?"

"Sure thing," I said.

Lou Joe thumbed in the direction of the glass doors on the opposite wall. "Let's go in my office. I'm on a Zoom call with Towson in five."

"Be right there, Coach," Benz replied. "Just give me a sec to catch my breath and get some water."

For weeks Benz had been waiting on a football scholarship offer from Towson University. Staying close to home was a big thing to Benz. It was a big thing to me too, and Towson was a whopping thirty-four miles door-to-door from my house to the football team's dorm. Benz's parents had offered to pay his tuition bill, but he still refused their help.

Benz turned to me. "What do you think Towson's going to say?"

"Is there any doubt, boyfriend?"

I reached up to comb his hair with my fingers. Benz had these two cowlicks on the left side that simply never cooperated. "You should really wear a hat or something,"

"Can you maybe, like, not be my mother right now?" Benz pleaded.

I grabbed him by the collar. "Don't ever compare me to Cookie."

Benz pulled my hands off his shirt. "Relax, girlfriend." With a wink, a nod, and an "I love you," he turned on his heel to Coach Lou Joe's office.

After folding and refolding it for ten minutes, I finally stuffed the black and gold Towson hoodie in Benz's gym bag at the foot of the weight bench. I bought it for him last night on the way back from my family dinner at Cantler's. More to the point, Dad bought it. He offered to spend some guilt money on his wife and daughter, and we happily obliged. The sweatshirt fit snugly in between a change of clothes and a green folder embossed with an eagle's head and the words "LIFE U" in big block letters.

"I did it, Rosemary!" Benz shouted, pumping his fists as he came running out of Lou Joe's office. "Almost a full ride."

I sat on the weight bench. Benz's gym bag sat open next to me. "Almost?"

"Partial athletic scholarship plus a partial academic scholarship will pay about ninety percent of my way. Figure I'll throw Mom and Dad a bone and let them pick up the remaining ten percent."

"Congrats," I said, managing a muted smile.

"Have to admit, I expected a little more enthusiasm."

I reached into his gym bag and pulled out the green LIFE U folder.

"What are you doing going through my stuff?"

"I accidentally came across it when I was sneaking a brand-new Towson sweatshirt into your gym bag. It was going to be a surprise. I guess you wanted to surprise me too. Life University?"

"What's the big deal?" Benz said. "I'm just keeping my options open."

"And your options include a chiropractic school in Georgia?"

"Life has a great rugby program. One of the best in the country."

"But what about all that talk of earning a football scholarship?"

"I'm a solid small-college football player, Rosemary, but I'm a great rugby player. I know you don't understand the sport, but—"

"My opinion of rugby is not the issue."

"Look, Life hasn't even offered me anything yet, but Towson has. Let's celebrate that."

I reached out and placed my hand on his chest, as if I could somehow hold him there forever. If I wanted to, I could certainly pin him down on that weight bench for an undetermined amount of time. "But what about you wanting to stay close to home?"

"I do want to stay close to home, to you."

I could feel his heart beating faster. He was lying.

"When are you going?"

"Going where?"

"To Life U, for a campus visit."

"Rosemary, I—"

"Just tell me."

"First week of April," Benz conceded.

"For how many days?"

"I'm going for the whole week."

"You're skipping senior spring break in Fort Myers?" I asked. "What's Andrew think about that? Haven't you two been planning this trip since you were like twelve years old?"

Benz shrugged. "He's not speaking to me right now."

I opened the folder, reading from the pamphlet stuffed inside. "*Life University is at the forefront of the vitalistic health revolution by offering studies within the fields of Chiropractic, Functional Kinesiology, Vitalistic Nutrition, Positive Psychology, Functional Neurology and Positive Business, using entrepreneurship for social change.*"

"A lot of big words," Benz said. "Do you really see me going to a place like that, Rosemary?"

"The question is, do you see yourself going to a place like that?"

"I don't know," he answered, almost too quickly.

I should have been thankful, really. The senior spring break entourage would have no doubt included Avery, as well as most of the cheerleading squad. If I had to choose between Benz being surrounded for a week by bikinis in Fort Myers or rugby players in the middle of Georgia, that's a no-brainer.

But I wasn't thankful. Not at all. I was shattered by the notion that my boyfriend was seriously thinking about a life without me in it.

CHAPTER

25

Now Emrys was the one standing on my front porch. I opened the door. "Seven o'clock on a Tuesday night, and I have homework up to my ears. This better be good."

"Where are your parents?" he asked.

"Off communicating with the Lady of the Lake via magical orb."

"What?"

"Long story."

"We have the time." Emrys nodded over his shoulder to the Subaru in the driveway. "You got the keys?"

"Yeah, but how did you get here?"

"I walked. Road trip?"

"You realize I can't just drop everything on a school night when you snap your fingers, right? I have a life, you know."

"Two hours is all I'm asking for. Three, tops."

"I'm driving, not you."

"Fine by me," Emrys said.

I fiddled with the hem of my American Martyr plaid skirt. I didn't have any homework, and Emrys was a welcome distraction from Benz, especially after the Georgia news. The alternative was inviting Joslin over, putting on Level 42's *World Machine* album, and telling her things she wasn't ready to hear. "I'll need to change."

"Why? You look fine."

"My Catholic school uniform tends to invite trouble, or at the very least clumsy flirting. I want neither."

"I think you can handle yourself, Rosemary."

"I'm not in the mood to handle myself." I said this as a Level 42 song played inside my head. The one I was stuck on was "Lessons in Love." Peaking in 1987 at #12 on the Billboard Hot 100, it's about being confident of your love for someone only to have that love blow up in your face.

"I just want to introduce you to an old friend," Emrys assured me.

I sighed. "*How old?*"

"One of my oldest," Emrys confirmed. "Been putting off introducing you two. She owns a bar and grill down in North Beach, just north of my farm. Popular local hangout called Mabel's."

"Is that your friend's name, Mabel?"

"Some of the time."

"Some of the time she's your friend or some of the time that's her name?"

"A little of both," Emrys said, approaching the passenger side door of the Subaru. "A word of warning. Try not to look directly into her eyes when you talk to her. She has a way with people."

"Understood," I said. "A word of warning for you as well."

Emrys opened the car door. "What's that?"

"Dad has had Vivian on speed dial for the last seventeen years."

Halfway seated, one leg in and one leg out, Emrys jumped out of the car. He stood with his back turned me to me as he tapped his fingers on the hood of the Subaru. "Go change, Rosemary," he said over his shoulder.

Emrys was still processing my father's revelation about the Orb when we pulled into North Beach.

"Are you mad at my dad?" I asked, finally.

"No," Emrys answered. "I'm mad at myself. Alan has been homesick for Camelot since the moment he left. Probably didn't take much of a nudge at all from Vivian to enchant him. This is all my fault. I should have been more vigilant."

I tried to reassure him. "None of us saw this coming. Not me, not Mom. There are a lot of reasons I could've come up with for Dad being an absentee husband and father. Engaging in a clandestine relationship across space and time with his evil stepmom was not on my shortlist. It wasn't even on my longlist."

Mabel's stood on the main drag, about halfway between an ice cream parlor and an Italian bistro. A two-story sandstone building with pin-striped black awnings, Mabel's was known for (according to Emrys) their tuna bites, mussels by the pound, and the jalapeno broccoli slaw they made fresh daily.

A large group of smokers stood outside Mabel's, spilling on to the sidewalk. One of them stood nearer to the entrance, his hand on the door. He wasn't smoking, and he wore an apron. The cook, I guessed. He was burly, with the type of build you'd call "big" more than "fat." A necklace of large brown shark teeth hung around the man's neck. He nodded at Emrys. "Junior."

"Evening, Chef," Emrys said to the man, conveniently confirming his job.

"*Spes messis in semine*," Chef said as he opened the door for us. "This who I think it is?"

I offered my hand while eyeing his necklace. "Name's Rosemary. Cool shark teeth."

The cook half-ignored me, shaking my hand while his gaze remained firmly on Emrys. "All-you-can-eat mussels tonight, Junior," he said. "But I'm guessing that's not why you're here."

"*Spes messis in semine*," Emrys repeated. "Where is she?"

Chef nodded into the bar. "In the back, taking inventory."

The inside of Mabel's was cramped. A row of tables and chairs ran the length of the room on the left, the bar on the opposite wall. The place was filled to capacity and bustling with opinions about Washington Capitals hockey and D.C. politics. Between that and Waylon Jennings on the jukebox, it was loud enough that you could carry on a conversation without anyone outside your table hearing you. Emrys and I sat down at the one empty booth near the restrooms.

Mussels gross me out, so I ordered a basket of chicken wings dusted with Old Bay. Emrys was halfway into a lap around the bar saying hello to people I'd never met. I was halfway into my basket of wings. Mabel was taking her own sweet time.

"Hey, Emrys," I mumbled through a bite of chicken wing. "What was that all about?"

Emrys sat across from me. "Sit up straight, Rosemary. And don't talk with your mouth full."

I chased the bite with a sip of ginger beer, wiped my mouth with the back of my hand. "What's the story with Chef?"

"Been cooking for Mabel since she bought the place. He's her Mr. Fix It. Does jobs for me down on the farm too."

"What's up with the shark teeth?"

"He collects them. They're Megaladon teeth."

"Bracing myself for the useless trivia," I said.

Emrys obliged. "Megalodon was a sixty-feet-long prehistoric shark that lived in the Miocene period, anywhere from five to twenty-three million years ago. The western shore of Maryland is one of the largest sources of Micoene fossils in the world."

"Twenty-three million years? That's even older than you."

"He probably found those teeth all within a mile of his back porch."

"Which is where exactly?"

"Chef lives in a private bayside community close to my farm called Scientists' Cliffs."

"Why did Chef call you 'Junior'?"

Emrys rotated his head around the room, eyeing his surroundings warily "It's a nickname I've picked up around these parts."

"I assume there's a backstory there too."

"Contrary to what you might think, it's not that easy to just walk around a small town for a couple hundred years without people noticing that you aren't aging. Every now and again, I disappear from rural southern Maryland for a while and come back as my own son."

I ripped another piece of meat off a chicken bone, swallowed. "And they buy that?"

"When the truth is unbelievable, you'd be amazed at how the human psyche seeks the path of least resistance. For sure, there's the occasional tinfoil hat sitting in his parents' basement who figures me out, but it doesn't take too long to run those types out of town."

"That's real neighborly of you, Emrys."

"I don't have anything to do with it. Given the choice, people here are more comfortable with a person who has secrets than a person who can't keep his mouth shut. Plus, I have friends, allies. They call themselves the Knights of Leo. They're a secret society dedicated to protecting me and now to protecting you."

"That a nod to your old boss, Leonard Calvert?"

"It is," Emrys said. "I started the Knights as a small club in the 1920s. That community I just mentioned, Scientists' Cliffs? The official story is that it was founded by scientists in the 1930s, but it's really just one big cover operation for the Knights. We didn't have a name for the club back then, it was all pretty informal, and I lived a relatively quiet life. But with the proliferation of mass media in the 1960s, I needed more help."

"So Chef is a Knight?" I asked.

"You think I make a habit of talking to random people in Latin?"

"You act like that question deserves a definitive 'no.'"

"Well, *hello there*, stranger."

Her long red hair ran down her back and past her waist, sprouting restlessly from a beat-up straw cowboy hat. She wore a green sequin tank top with jeans and cowboy boots.

Emrys stood, bowing. "Mabel," he said.

"I've missed you, *Junior*." She cooed his name more than she spoke it; her arms open wide, strangely inviting. I could tell immediately that Mabel liked Emrys, a lot.

Emrys hugged her. Initially, it was one of those courtesy in-and-out hugs, but I noticed as he started to let go, they locked eyes, and Mabel brushed her cheek against his. In response, Emrys moved in again, hugging her tighter. That's when Mabel pushed him down, back into his chair.

"Try not to look directly into Mabel's eyes when you talk to her. She has a way with people."

Apparently, Emrys decided to ignore his own advice. As if reacting to my observation, he shook his head, recomposing himself. "Damn you, Mabel."

"Oh, Junior. If only you looked a little less *illegal* these days. The things I'd do to you." She looked at me. "Who's your friend?"

Emrys put his hand on my shoulder. "This is my *classmate,*

Rosemary."

"Classmate, huh? That's the story you're going with?"

"Yep," Emrys replied.

"It's not a story," I said. "Emrys is actually quite good at being a terribly awkward teenager. He's got all of American Martyr fooled."

"But we're not fooling you, are we Lady Banson?" Mabel cupped my cheek with her long fingers. "Rosemary is a pretty name. A pretty name for a pretty girl."

I tried not to look into her eyes. But her touch was so warm, so comforting. I had to look.

Emrys stepped in between us. "Okay, Mabel, you've had your fun."

She smacked him playfully in the chest. "You might be a teenager, but you still act bloody old."

Their banter mitigated Mabel's spell on me. "Nice place you have here. I imagine the tips can't be beat."

"How'd you guess?" Mabel winked.

I could feel her hold on me ramping back up. My cheeks were warm. Was I blushing? I tried to reassert myself. "Emrys tells me you're the oldest of friends."

"The oldest and the best." Mabel handed Emrys a fresh iced tea as she slid into the booth next to him.

"*Ahem.*" Emrys cleared his throat. "Mabel is, uh, she's from… where I'm from."

"Yeah, Emrys," I said. "I picked up what you were throwing down about an hour ago. Sometimes you're clever, sometimes you're not."

"She met you as a baby, on the day you were born in fact," he told me.

"Whoa, whoa, woah!" I said, waving him off. "Mabel is Morgan le Fay?"

Merlin had downsized from World's Greatest Wizard to a hormonally awkward teenage boy. Mom and Dad had traded Camelot for the suburbs. As far as reveals go, Morgan le Fay as a bartending cowgirl was definitely the coolest.

Mabel smiled at me. "I wish the story behind the story was exciting, but it isn't. After I met up with Emrys and helped hide you, I was planning to head down to Mexico. The cab driver couldn't understand my accent, took several wrong turns, and we got lost on the way to the airport. I eventually stopped into this place for a drink, struck up a conversation with the owner, and it turned out he was selling the place. It allowed me to keep an eye on your friend here. Anyway, that was seventeen years ago. Emrys loaned me the down payment."

"A loan she repaid within a year," Emrys chimed in.

"…and I've been behind this bar ever since. For obvious reasons, I didn't name the place 'Morgan le Fay's.'"

"What's the significance of 'Mabel'?" I asked. "Why pick that name as your alias?"

"It's a tongue-in-cheek reference. If either of my sisters showed up in the twenty-first century and bothered to crack open a book, they'd find me." Mabel pointed to the large placard hanging above the bar:

> *Immediately there was a loud blowing of seashells, conches and so forth, and a stout, jolly-looking gentleman appeared seated on a well-blown-up cloud above the battlements. He had an anchor tattooed on his stomach and a handsome mermaid with Mabel written under her on his chest. He ejected a quid of tobacco, nodded affably to Merlyn, and pointed his trident at the Wart.*
>
> —"The Once and Future King," T.H. White

"Speaking of your sisters showing up…" Emrys said.

"I figured you didn't come in here with the Lust Borne on your arm looking to make introductions," Mabel acknowledged. "Wait, did I say something wrong?"

Mabel was observant. Too observant. She'd noticed me bristling at the words "Lust Borne."

"I've decided I don't like that term, *Lust Borne*," I said. "It diminishes the love my parents have for one another, and it diminishes me."

Mabel smacked her knee as she looked at Emrys. "Oh, I like this one. I like her a lot." Turning her gaze back to me, she added, "That makes two of us. I've always felt 'Lust Borne' to be too melodramatic, too medieval. What would you prefer?"

"How about just Rosemary?" I said.

"Okay, Just Rosemary..." Mabel smiled. "That's what I will call you."

Emrys sipped on his tea intently, looking but not looking at Mabel. He sat his tea down on the table, licked his lips. "Vivian's in town, and she's looking for you."

"In town?" Mabel asked. "You mean here, in North Beach?"

"Not necessarily," I replied. "Turns out Vivian and my father have been Snapchatting for the better part of the last two decades. And a few weeks back, Vivian crashed a Christmas party up in Annapolis that I was at. She's kind of rude, and she smells like a wet bird."

"She gets that from her father," Mabel said. "Morgause, Vivian, and I are half—"

"Yeah," I interrupted, "Emrys walked me through that. You're like the Deadbeat Dad Triad, which would be a great band name, by the way. How did you all come to be witches? Is it genetic?"

"Most of the time," Mabel confirmed. "What we do with those gifts can ultimately take us on very different paths, as it did with my sisters and me."

"Mabel is a sea witch," Emrys said.

Mabel shook her head. "'Witch' is such a loaded term. I prefer 'sorceress' or 'enchantress.'"

"Or 'Siren?'" he added.

Mabel sighed. "*Retired* Siren, Emrys."

"Wait, *what?*" That explained why Emrys said not to look directly into her eyes. That explained the mermaid reference in the T.H. White quote. I tossed a picked-clean chicken bone on my plate, wiped my mouth. "By 'Siren,' do you mean those half-naked girls who sit on the shoreline singing to sailors, causing their ships to crash into the rocks?"

Mabel wagged her finger at me. "You are wildly misinformed about Sirens."

"Am I?"

"Yes," Mabel replied. "In addition to singing, we also play lyres and flutes."

Silence. But then, laughter. All three of us joined in. It was a needed tonic.

Composing myself, I wasn't quite ready to end Mabel's interrogation. "You said you and your sisters chose different paths. What paths were those?"

Mabel nodded sideways at Emrys. "Morgause studied under this guy of course. And then after Merlin broke my heart, I took an extended sabbatical to the Italian island of Capri and honed my craft with the Sirens."

"That's what I call a revenge tour," I joked.

Emrys puffed out his chest, noticeably perturbed. "I didn't even know you liked me like that!"

"Settle down," Mabel said, stroking Emrys's arm. "All is forgiven."

I picked up another chicken wing. In lieu of eating the wing, I pointed it at Mabel, punctuating my words. "Morgause studied with Merlin, you studied with the Sirens, and Vivian?"

"Vivian was the only one of us who was empowered from the womb. It was just a matter of her learning how to control that power. Forging Excalibur in the fires of an active volcano, shape-shifting, the ability to time travel nearly at will, an almost limitless supply of mystical energies: Vivian used to be the apex predator of wizards."

"How'd she become so powerful?" I pressed.

"Vivian was granted the power of a god because she *is* a god. Goibniu, the Druidic god of the forge and chief smith of the Tuatha De Danann, is her father. The sword you carry with you, Excalibur, was smelted from his enchanted ore."

"Wait a second. I got in a sword fight with a freaking god?"

Mabel shook her head. "I said, Vivian *used to be* an apex predator. They don't call her 'Lady of the Lake' for nothing. Her power comes with a price: omnipotence in return for eternal imprisonment in her home waters."

"Not the Chesapeake Bay, I take it."

"Nowhere near," Mabel replied.

"Maybe the Loe Pool in Cornwall, England?" I countered.

"You know of it?"

"Let's just say there's a sample of the Loe Pool located in Maryland, and my father has it."

"Then that's it," Mabel affirmed. "That sample gives her remote access. Still, knowing Vivian's father, my sister no doubt had to negotiate some sort of trade with him. Less power in return for more mobility. That at least gives all of us a chance."

"All of us?" I looked around the bar. "I take it you mean the Knights of Leo."

Emrys nodded. "*Spes messis in semine.*"

"The hope of the harvest is in the seed," I translated. "What you and Chef said to one another outside. Is that like your motto or something?"

"Well, well..." Mabel said. "Aren't you the educated Catholic school girl?"

"How do you know I'm a Catholic school girl?"

"I'm an immigrant from the late fifth century, not an alien, Rosemary. Emrys and I text."

"He texts you?" I cast my judgmental brow at Emrys. "So I suppose I'm the seed, and that's why Chef looked at me like I had a nasty case of impetigo?"

"You're the seed, obviously," Mabel confirmed. "But why so hard on Chef?"

"He's got that standoffish, shut up and do your job vibe."

"We're all on your team here, Rosemary. If we're going to keep you out of Mordred's clutches—"

"...and his bed," I amended.

"Yes." Mabel nodded. "And out of his bed. If we're going to do that, it'll take all of us working together."

"You know I've never cared for Chef either," Emrys added.

"Are we having this fight again?" Mabel was talking to Emrys but still keeping one eye on me. "Chef is opinionated, but he's tough and loyal to the Knights of Leo above all else."

"He's loyal to his vision of the Knights," Emrys said.

I only now noticed that I'd been staring at Mabel for the entire conversation. "And what vision is that, Emrys?"

"He thinks the Knights' job is to protect the sword and the wizard, Excalibur and Merlin. *Protegat gladium, protegat magum.*"

"Well, that technically was the Knights' original motto until you changed it in the sixties," Mabel clarified.

Emrys tapped his thumb to his chest. "And instead of taking the new motto to heart, Chef thinks I'm the seed and that Rosemary is expendable."

Mabel winced. "'Expendable' is a pretty strong word."

"I came here to introduce you to Rosemary, and to tell you to be on the lookout for Vivian. I think I've completed that task." Emrys stood up from the table and tapped me on the shoulder. "Time to go."

It was weird. I'd gotten into a rhythm talking to Mabel, and I couldn't stop staring at her or wanting to hear her voice.

"Rosemary?" Emrys said.

She was like a beacon of light. So inviting. I could feel myself opening up to her.

"Rosemary!" Emrys pulled me up by the arm, yanking me out of my chair. Mabel and I stood face to face.

I still couldn't find the words.

"Mabel," Emrys cautioned, "stay out of Rosemary's head."

"But I'm not in her head," she assured Emrys, caressing my face with her right hand. She rubbed my chin softly between her thumb and index finger. I could feel her looking at me—no, looking *into* me. "In fact, someone else is in Rosemary's head, and in her heart."

She was talking about Benz.

"Am I talking about Benz?" Mabel asked, reading my thoughts.

I brushed her hand off my face. "What are you doing?"

"Okay," she confessed. "Maybe I was in your head a little."

"Enough!" Emrys said as I broke eye contact finally. He held my hand, ushering me out of the restaurant. Chef gave me a noticeable side-eye on the way out.

"I have to say, I think that went really well," I joked, extracting the car keys from my coat pocket. "You want to drive? I'm just a bit *off* after that meet and greet."

"Sure," Emrys answered, picking up on my distracted state. "Hey, don't let Mabel screw with your head. She's a sweet soul, but it's hard for her to turn the Siren off."

I pretended to listen to Emrys in earnest, but I couldn't stop replaying Mabel's parting words to me. *Someone else is in Rosemary's head, and in her heart.* Who in the world was she talking about? She had to be talking about Benz. He was my guy, my person. There was no one else.

CHAPTER

26

Andrew slammed his wallet on the glass-top counter of the concessions stand. "You have to let me pay for something, Joslin."

Avery tapped Emrys playfully on his chin. "Okay, how do you say 'Hello' in Welsh?"

"*Su'mae,*" Emrys replied.

Benz leaned over and whispered in my ear. "You okay?"

"Don't talk to me right now," I said.

We all needed a break. Emrys gave me some needed time off from training. Joslin and Andrew seemed to be ready for pretty much anything. It was Benz's idea to go out on the group date. Avery's college boyfriend had just broken up with her, so Benz suggested we set her up with Emrys. I knew he'd agree to it, not because he liked Avery, but because he wanted to ease the tension with Benz. Emrys wasn't going out on a date with Avery DeVincent as a favor to anyone but me.

This was officially the worst idea ever.

I could see this wasn't going well for Emrys, but I didn't know how to react. Thankful that Benz was making an effort to be nice to him? Sad that Emrys didn't have anyone special in his life? Or just mad at Avery? I was leaning toward the latter. She wanted to treat Emrys more like an exotic pet than a date. I pulled him aside when I got the chance and asked him what his safe word was when he needed to bail.

Emrys said, "You be you, Rosemary, and let me be me." What the hell was that supposed to mean?

"How do you say 'What time is it?' in Welsh?" Avery asked.

"*Faint o'r gloch ydy hi*," Emrys replied.

I doubt this would merit even a passage in the mythical scrolls a thousand years from now. No one would ever know of the boy who spent three hours reciting Welsh phrases like a trained monkey. But I would remember the singular sacrifice made by a wizard for his chosen one. Assuming of course Mordred didn't, you know, kill us at some point.

Benz and I were spending a lot of time together. Shockingly, Joslin followed suit and started getting serious with Andrew. This was new territory for us. Joslin and I had never been into guys at the same time. One was always the other's voice of reason.

Much to everyone's surprise but hers, Joslin had changed Andrew's womanizing ways. In a heartbeat, Andrew went from the type of guy she avoided to her greatest challenge. Andrew never saw her coming. He was immediately smitten. Although she had yet to admit it, Joslin was right there with him.

We decided to go to the newest Pixar flick. Andrew wanted to buy Joslin her ticket, but she'd pre-purchased it online.

"I just want to take my girlfriend on a normal date like a normal boyfriend," Andrew bemoaned.

Joslin wouldn't let him get away with that. "So you're saying a girl who pays for her own movie ticket is abnormal?"

"Can I at least buy you popcorn?"

"Maybe," she said.

"Butter or no butter?" Andrew asked.

"Butter, and how about we make a deal?" Joslin teased.

"What kind of deal?"

"I'll let you pay for everything from now on, if you can resist locking your eyes on my breasts when we talk. I didn't pay for my movie, *you did*. I fleeced your pocket in the back seat of Benz's car, when you were staring at my boobs."

Andrew held out his hand. "Well, seeing as you were so principled about paying, can I have my ten dollars back?"

"Consider it a security deposit." Joslin grabbed the bucket of popcorn, pulling Andrew by the hand toward the theater entrance.

"A security deposit for what?"

"You figure it out," Joslin said.

Joslin and Andrew continued to argue well past the guy taking tickets. They insisted on going inside early. "Previews are the best part of the movie," Joslin argued. Avery and Emrys trailed close behind.

Benz and I lingered near the concession stand. He reached around my waist. "They're like a married couple."

"Who?" I said. "Emrys and Avery?"

"That was a bad idea, wasn't it?"

"You think?"

"I'm talking Joslin and Andrew."

"I know you are."

Whoever thought those two would be so perfect together?"

I squeezed Benz's hand. "I thought *we* were the perfect couple."

"One of us is certainly perfect," Benz said. He reached up to my chin, turning me toward him with his index finger and thumb. "I just have some catching up to do."

Benz kissed me. As we separated, I ran the tip of my tongue across his cinnamon lips.

I motioned to the concession stand. "You want some popcorn?"

"Get whatever you want." Benz handed me a twenty dollar bill. "But you're never paying for a movie while I'm your boyfriend."

To me, this meant free movies forever. Such was the unbridled recklessness of young love. I kissed him on the cheek.

Coke and Raisinets purchased, we handed the hulking, acne-faced usher our tickets. He looked at the tickets, ripped them in half, and handed us our stubs. "Second theater on the right," he said. "And can you tell your friends to pipe down?"

"Our friends?" Benz said.

"Yeah," the usher said. "The boy getting yelled at by the girl with the purple hair and the other two talking some kind of foreign crap."

"Foreign crap, huh?" I chimed in, flashing the usher the peace sign. "Make America great—"

"We'll make sure they behave, buddy," Benz said, diplomatically pushing my hand down.

"Hey," I said as we walked arm-in-arm down the hallway. "I can fight my own battles."

Benz smiled at me. "I'm sure you can."

If only he knew just how accurate my statement was. "Thanks, by the way."

"For what?"

"For at least trying with Emrys. For trying to, you know, include him. I know it's weird, the friendship he and I have. I wish I could explain it. Your matchmaking skills leave a lot to be desired, but I just wanted to let you know that I love and appreciate you."

"I got accepted to Life University."

"And maybe, I don't know, sometime soon we can think about… wait, what did you just say?"

We stopped walking only a few feet away from the theater doors. Benz turned to me with a deep breath. "I got accepted to Life University."

"Scholarship and everything?"

Benz nodded, exhaling. "Not as much as Towson. A partial that could eventually become a little more if I meet or exceed certain academic thresholds my freshman year."

"What are you going to do?"

"I don't know. I could possibly start for Towson as a true freshman, but playing rugby for Life U is like playing basketball for Duke. I might get my shot in two, maybe three years. But I'd be playing against the absolute best."

The knock on Benz from football recruiters was that he was athletic enough but not tall enough to play football at the next level. I didn't know the first thing about rugby, but Benz told me he "had the prototype body for it," whatever that meant. As much I'd been lying to him this whole school year, I owed him a little honesty. "Benz, as long as I've known you, you've never been one to pick the easy way."

Benz let go of my arm to open the theater door for me. "You really mean that, Rosemary?"

"Of course I do."

"But what about all that stuff you were saying back at the gym, when you found the Life U folder in my bag?"

"Benz." I said his name reluctantly, just as I was about to encourage him with equal reluctance. "I would never stand in the way of an opportunity for you."

My boyfriend's pouty smile confirmed to me his appreciation of the cheesy cliché. "What did I ever do to deserve you?"

"That's a good question," I said. Mimicking when he'd pulled my hand down in front of the usher, I pulled his hand off the theater door handle. I kissed him full on the lips this time, my last words barely out of my mouth. Our kisses had become comfortable again. So comfortable I was about to do something stupid. "Benz?" I asked, our lips still pressed together.

"Yes?" he mumbled out the side of his mouth.

I wrested my face from his, committed to my stupidity. "You interrupted me with your Life University news. I've been thinking about things."

"Things? What things?"

"Us, together."

"It's great, isn't it?"

"Yes, but I'm talking a different kind of together." I stepped back and clasped my hands, shaking them as I spoke. "I feel like maybe sometime soon we can think about being *together* together again."

"Wait, you mean..."

I nodded.

"Oh," Benz said. "*Ohhhh...*"

"Yeah," I acknowledged.

"W-when, when, when will we?" Benz stuttered.

"Cool your jets, mister," I said. "What are you doing Friday night after your rugby game?"

The American Martyr rugby team was kicking off their season with the annual rivalry game against Saybrook Prep. The teams had played every year since 2000, with Saybrook winning the last three. Benz had never beaten them. It was the only thing he could think about it. Well, maybe not now.

"I love you, Rosemary," Benz said.

"I love you too."

He hugged me, resting his head on my shoulder. "No. I mean I really love you."

I felt a vague moist sensation where Benz had buried his face. "Are you crying on my shoulder at the prospect of having sex with me?"

"No." Benz raised his head. "Okay, maybe."

"Can you *maybe* dry your tear ducts and rein in your hormones before we spend the next two hours watching a cartoon surrounded by children?"

"The tears I can deal with, meh lady." Benz opened the theater door for me, bowing. "No promises about the hormones."

It was a cheap, throwaway line that I appreciated almost as much as Benz opening the door. While I generally hated playing the role of damsel in distress, I was cool with the king of Fall Fling being both chivalrous and obsessed with me.

Benz tripped as we entered the dimly lit auditorium. My eyes adjusted quicker than his to the darkness, so I took his hand. Halfway up the aisle, their voices called out to us in a volume more than a whisper.

"How do you say 'cuddle' in Welsh?"

"*Cwtch*," Emrys replied.

Ancient gods, please watch over my friend tonight.

CHAPTER

27

After our big fight, Mom and Dad did what all good parents do: They forgave and forgot. I had done neither, but chose the next best thing.

Mom ducked under my right cross, tagged me in the ribs with a right jab and then under the jaw with a left uppercut. She wore a neon coral tank top paired with black capri pants with neon coral accents, both of which were soaked through with sweat. Her mop of hair was braided into a side pony that hung over her left shoulder.

"Emrys gives you some time off, and you get soft," she scolded. "What do you think Mordred will do to you?"

"He was like three years old when you and Dad last saw him," I noted through clenched teeth. "*You* don't even know what he'll do to me."

"Oh, I have plenty of educated guesses, Rosemary. And none of them are pretty."

I usually left my hand-to-hand training to Emrys—well, Emrys and the occasional professional mixed martial arts fighter he'd bribe to come down to the farm and fight me in the ring. What Mom termed "soft" I'd probably call "overconfident." My last fight down at the farm put a Golden Gloves boxer in the hospital. Atli and Emrys were visiting right now with the guy's attorneys, trying to avoid a lawsuit. The attorneys were pressing for a court date, the fighter was pressing to settle and not advertise to the professional boxing world that he'd been hospitalized by a sixteen-year-old girl.

Emrys wasn't one to leave my side for more than a day, but he trusted my mom in the ring with me. He knew what she was and wasn't capable of, and he knew she could keep up with me. He suggested these mother and daughter sparring matches after he found an old boxing gym for lease in downtown Baltimore.

My next right cross found its mark. Like those ridiculous slow-motion fight scenes in the movies, Mom's jaw seemed to peel off my fist one frame at a time. Spit and blood circled her reeling head like a red halo.

We both wore full pads—headgear, girdles, the works. It was more for Mom's protection than mine, obviously. But what Mom lacked in strength and speed, she made up for in experience.

I should have seen this coming. While the sparring was new for us, Mom and I had started racing a couple times a week through her obstacle course. She kept up, even managed to beat me once. Not being conceived in lust apparently, she had no concealed Guinevere superpowers she could turn on or off.

Like the difference between most mothers and their daughters, she had me when it came to simple focus and maturity. Even in the ring, I had all these fighting disciplines hard-coded into my brain, but Mom possessed an improvisational caginess that would take me years to master.

Decking my own mother was not as satisfying as I thought it would be. I had said what I said in that parking lot to her and Dad, and I had no plans to apologize for it. My words hurt her more than my fists ever could. But in my ambivalence, I left my arm lazily extended, frozen in the punch, off balance with my left hand dropping to my waist. All rookie mistakes. In a flash, Mom unleashed a combination of punches and kicks that landed me on my back.

Mom offered me her hand, helping me to stand. "That's good for today," she garbled through her mouthpiece.

"Got you good, didn't I?" I garbled back.

"Yeah," Mom said, removing her mouthpiece. She slinked under the top rope and stepped down from the boxing ring. "You got me good, right before you left yourself wide open. I let you have that punch, just to get your blood flowing. You seem a little distracted today. What's up?"

My exit from the boxing ring was decidedly less graceful. I plopped down, grabbed the bottom rope with both hands, and slid on my butt to a standing position. As my adrenaline ebbed, the exhaustion from chasing my mother around the ring caught up with me. I was tired and vulnerable, maybe a tad guilty for the vicious right cross to my mother's face. Removing my mouthpiece, I paused to catch my breath one last time.

Mom interpreted my fatigue as reticence. "Never mind. It's okay if you don't want to tell me what's bother—"

"Benz and I are talking about resuming our relationship," I blurted out. "Intimately."

Mom reached for my hands, a scene rendered somewhat ridiculous by the fact we were both still wearing boxing gloves. Come to think of it, two people talking about love while wearing boxing gloves was pretty much the perfect metaphor for my life at that moment.

"Rosemary, as your mother, I'm officially required to say, 'No sex is the best sex' and 'Wait until you're married.' But as a woman speaking to another woman, I will tell you that making love to the right person is the greatest feeling in the world."

I could feel my cheeks growing flush. "*Mom...*"

"What? I'm just being straight with you."

"But you're talking about Dad, as a sexual object."

"I'm not talking about your father as an object. I said 'making love,' not 'having sex.' It's about trust, about giving yourself to someone completely. Anyone can have sex. Ninety-nine percent of multicellular creatures reproduce sexually. But not a whole lot of us ever learn how to make love. Towel?"

Mom offered me a fresh towel, which I accepted, if only to hide my face from this conversation. I ran the towel down my throat, then threw it over my shoulder. "I shouldn't be surprised by your reaction. As your daughter, I'm officially required to be horrified at the prospect of you and Dad knocking boots, but I'm not surprised."

"What are you talking about, Rosemary?"

"You've found love with Dad again after a really long time of being lonely. You know when love works and when it doesn't. While it likely won't last forever, it's working right now; nothing feels, smells, or tastes the same as it did a few months ago."

Mom sipped on her water bottle.

"I nailed it, didn't I?"

Still sipping.

"Mom?"

"Give me a second," she replied, punctuating her request with a few more sips and a considered exhale. "Sometimes you're such a serious and intuitive thinker."

"I am my mother's daughter."

"Thanks for the compliment, but you didn't get that from me. If I had your self-awareness when I was your age, it would've saved me from a lot of problems."

"So I've been upgraded from a mistake to a problem?" I mocked, crossing my fingers. "With any luck, I'll be an unintended consequence the next time we talk, and, fingers crossed, a welcome surprise after that."

My sarcasm didn't go unnoticed. But really, who in the hell would want their sarcasm to go unnoticed? Unnoticed sarcasm is just a bad joke. And the thing is, you don't even have to be funny. Sometimes, it's all about the timing.

Mom's jaw tightened. "You good now? Get it all out of your system?"

I shook my head. "Not even close."

"If you have love all figured out," Mom pushed back, "then why are we having this conversation?"

"Because I'm facing the same questions with Benz that you are with Dad."

"Questions?"

"Did we learn our lesson the first time around? Can we reignite our passion without extinguishing the flames of everyone else around us? Can I lie as well as my parents?"

Mom placed her hand on my shoulder. "You're my daughter, and I love you, but that's not fair, to me or your father."

"If life was fair, you'd still be with Arthur and Dad would still be his best friend. Or at the very least, I would be living the life of a normal teenage girl, not stuck in this weird limbo between loving my boyfriend and fearing my baby daddy."

"Limbo?" Mom asked. "Baby daddy?"

"I'm talking about Mordred, obviously. Thanks to Dad's secret convos with Vivian, he's been kept out of the picture, been more of an idea than a real threat. So Merlin is left to be little more than my glorified personal trainer. Guinevere and Lancelot are fluttering about, acting like oblivious newlyweds. And here I am, going from one day feeling guilty about keeping secrets from Joslin to the next day freaking out about having sex with my boyfriend. The notion of fulfilling a Druidic god's fertility prophecy is almost an afterthought."

"That's a lot to handle," Mom acknowledged. "I never stopped to think about it like that or put myself in your shoes."

"That's because no one has, Mom! No one ever just asks me how I'm doing. No one ever asks me if I have any ideas how to fix this. I think that's partly the reason I went nuclear on you and Dad the other day."

"We're all just trying to protect you, Rosemary."

"I don't want protection." I could feel my right hand humming inside my glove. "I want agency."

"I'm your mother. Why wouldn't I want to protect my daughter from—"

"*Gladio!*" My boxing glove exploded as Excalibur materialized in my right hand. "I think I have my protection covered."

"Was that really necessary?" Mom asked.

"Sorry," I said. "I didn't quite think that one through."

"When did you learn that trick?"

"It's Emrys's spell of portability. I have to be touching Excalibur with my bare skin for it to appear or disappear, and it defaults to appearing in my sword hand. The boxing glove got in the way."

"Can you please send it back to where it came from? What if someone walked in on us right now?"

"I'll just say you're my fencing instructor, and that I put you on retainer after you killed the last two."

My sarcasm notwithstanding, Mom was right to be concerned. The space was more a room than a full-sized gym, sharing the building with some artist lofts. In that moment, I didn't really care much for discretion.

"You're not a mistake, Rosemary. You know your father didn't mean it like that, right?"

"Yes, no, maybe, I don't know."

"I get that you're frustrated."

"Do you? I countered. "It's just that you, Dad, and Emrys keep expecting me to swallow what you're feeding me, you point me and my sword in the direction of the bad guys, and you just assume I'll survive, all the while saying you're the ones protecting me. Never mind the mixed messages, doesn't that seem a little, I don't know, reckless to you?"

"Social services would probably throw your father and me in jail."

"This isn't a joke, Mom."

"I'm only a few days removed from my daughter telling me to fuck off. I know you're not joking." Mom sniffled, wiped her nose with her boxing glove. She took a breath. I hadn't noticed until now because of all the sweat running down her face. She was crying.

"Evanescet." I commanded. Excalibur disappeared. I offered Mom a spare dry towel, but she shooed me away. I had no plans to apologize to her, to anyone at this point. And yet there I was, opening my mouth. "Mom, I'm sor—"

"You don't think this is tearing me apart? That not a day goes by that I don't picture Arthur's son putting his hands on you? And you have to know that argument in the parking lot just gutted your father and me. Your words were so hurtful, and we deserved every last syllable. What can we do, other than wait and hope for the best?"

"Are you asking me how we can fix this?"

"Yes, Rosemary. I'm asking you how we can fix this."

"Simple," I said. "I stop being the bait—and start being the shark. "Can you let me do that?"

Mom nodded. "I think so."

"That means letting me stand on my own two feet—with or without a sword, with or without a boyfriend. That means allowing me to not be sorry for our fight, and making sure Dad is on the same page. Can you do that?

More tears. Mom had never stopped crying. She reached for my face, stroked my cheek in that gentle way only a mother knew how to do. "Daughter, I love you more than anything on this earth. You have my word that your father and I will never again question your motives, your strength, your integrity, and your love. You are the best of us."

CHAPTER

28

After our sparring match, I dropped Mom off at her massage therapist's office. The office was less than a mile from our house, and Mom said she'd just walk home. "I might fight like a twenty-year-old," she bragged, "but I recover like a thirty-six-year-old."

We left our conversation about Benz decidedly open-ended. Mom said to trust my feelings and trust myself.

What? I mean, yeah, I guess technically I had just lectured her about letting me stand on my own two feet, but come on. *Trust myself?* That's terrible advice. In fairness to Mom, she thought my plan to speak with Headmaster Benedict was an equally terrible idea.

"Why do you see your principal as the shark?" she asked me. My metaphor was probably a bit off. Father Jules wasn't the shark. He was more like the crazy scuba diver who throws on a chainmail suit and is unrealistically confident in his ability to swim with the sharks.

In the mile drive from the massage therapist to home, the Subaru died on me twice. I didn't trust it as my chariot for the night, so Joslin's parents offered to drive us to the rugby game. I sat on my front porch waiting for the Kellys' arrival, while Dad, just home from work, busied himself with his usual ritual of walking around the house and turning on all the lights in preparation for Mom's return.

Even at his most disconnected, turning the lights on for his family was Dad's thing. He made a big show of it on vacations. He would insist on always entering the house first before allowing Mom and me inside. He'd poke his head into every room of the lake cabin or beach house, flip on all the lights, then walk outside and declare our abode, *"Monster free!"*

My father always told me his job was to chase away the monsters. I never thought he was speaking literally.

Dad stepped outside. Already out of his work clothes, he wore an Atomic Books graphic tee and blue jeans. He reached down and tousled my hair like I was a child.

"Dad," I said, annoyed. "I just brushed it."

"Big game tonight?" he asked.

I nodded, not wanting to continue the conversation I'd started with Mom. My plan could wait, at least for the night. "The biggest," I said. "American Martyr versus Saybrook Prep, under the lights."

"Saybrook? Where's that?"

"Connecticut, I think."

"As in Old Saybrook, Connecticut? That's way up there on Long Island Sound. They come all the way down here to play American Martyr?"

"It has something to do with our rugby coach helping their rugby coach get Saybrook's team off the ground ten years ago. They had a handshake deal to rotate games between Connecticut and Maryland, but Coach Lou Joe says that was the old coach's handshake, not his, and refuses to play Saybrook anymore unless they come down here. Needless to say, it's a fierce rivalry now, and the two teams basically hate each other's guts."

"Sounds like we're kind of the bad guys in all this."

"It does, doesn't it?"

"And Benz, he plays rugby just to stay in shape for football?"

"He used to," I said. "Now, I don't know."

"You don't know?"

Something about Dad's weirdly forced pleasantries bugged the crap out of me. Thinking about Benz lying to himself about Towson and Life U, and me lying about everything to everybody, I was done with small talk. "How long can we keep this up, Dad?"

"Keep what up?"

"All the deception. It's exhausting."

"It takes some getting used to, but you'll find your groove. Your own personal truth. Something that's true enough to keep you going."

"But how do you and Mom make it look so easy?"

"You forget that between our lives in Camelot and our lives here, we have about twenty years of practice."

"So I'll be cool with all this sometime around my thirty-sixth birthday?"

"You're too young to start counting the days of your life, Rosemary."

I stood abruptly and hugged my father.

"Thanks," I said.

"For what?" Dad asked.

"Chasing away the monsters," I said.

"Monsters, huh?" Dad said, apparently incapable of listening to my internal monologue.

The Kellys' ragged old Honda Odyssey minivan pulled into our drive. A Georgetown University employee parking tag hung from the front mirror. His window rolled down, Mr. Kelly yelled to my father, "What's up, Banson?"

Dad nodded with a smile and a wave. "Hey, Patrick." He gave a second wave to the woman sitting in the front passenger seat. "How are you today, Mindy?"

"Come on, Al." Mrs. Kelly leaned across her husband's lap. "Since when does anyone call us 'Patrick' and 'Mindy'?"

Dad actually loved the Kellys: their sincerity, their irreverence, their humor. How Patrick could have the most fun of anyone at a party even though he had been clean and sober for fifteen years. How Mindy prayed like a nun and cussed like a trucker.

"Sorry," Dad demurred. "Hey there, Pat and Dee."

Mrs. Kelly grinned warmly. "Now that's more like it, Al."

"Do me a favor tonight, Al?" I joked to my father.

Dad smiled again. "Anything, daughter."

"Mom will be home real soon, and she's probably going to be pretty upset. I have a plan."

"A plan?" Dad asked. "For what?"

"I need you to listen to Mom respectfully and then, no matter what she says, I need you to be on my side."

A perfectly timed car horn from the Kelly minivan punctuated our exchange. I headed for the minivan, but not before Dad stopped me.

"Why so cryptic?" he asked, his hand gently tugging on my elbow. "What's this plan you're talking about?"

I nodded at the minivan. "The Kellys are waiting for me, Dad. And if I told you anything more, you'd probably get mad."

Dad let go of my elbow. "Sounds like *you're* kind of the bad guy in all this."

CHAPTER

29

The rugby pitch ran along the Severn River. A spectator mound ran the length of the pitch opposite the river, which is where Pat and Dee Kelly had staked their claim with three blankets, four camping chairs, and a cooler full of food and beverages.

"Don't look now," Joslin said, nudging me with her elbow, "but evil approaches."

The procession of doom began with the Headmaster in his familiar black cassock. He looked and pointed at just me. "No trouble tonight, Ms. Banson. Got me?"

"I got you," I said. "We still on for Monday?"

"Looking forward to it," the monsignor said as he rushed past me. "Sorry. Don't want to miss kickoff."

"What was that about?" Joslin asked.

"I have a meeting with Father Jules on Monday. Long overdue. Time to clear the air."

Joslin felt my forehead. "You feeling alright? Who kidnapped my best friend and replaced her with this alien?"

"If I'm going to stay out of trouble and tolerate two more years with that celibate misogynist, we need to at least be on speaking terms."

"And there's my girl," Joslin said.

Mrs. Cooke was next in line as she marched her American Martyr cheer squad past us. As captain of the cheer squad, Avery walked directly behind Mrs. Cooke.

"Rosemary," Mrs. Cooke said, nodding through terse lips.

"Cookie," I replied.

Mrs. Cooke flashed me a predictable scowl at my presumptive use of her nickname. It was Avery's reaction that surprised me.

Did she just *smile*?

Her date with Emrys was a predictable one and done, but not for lack of effort. Emrys and Avery had accepted another invitation from Benz for a group date, right before Avery and her college boyfriend got back together. I caught Emrys in a rare text exchange with someone, and that someone was Avery. There was a sweetness to her apology. She texted him, *"Maybe when we've all stopped pretending to be who people want us to be, you can show me around Wales for a few days."* I could almost believe her intentions went beyond having him teach her Welsh phrases.

Holy crap. Was I beginning to like her?

Joslin leaned her head on my shoulder as my nemeses walked away. "Sucks, don't it?"

"What?" I replied. Did she see Avery's smile too? Did my reaction tip her off that my defenses were weakening against our arch-nemesis?

"How Mrs. Cooke basically gets to openly hate you and you have to kiss her ass for Benz."

Joslin knew me better than I knew myself. I owed her so much. I owed her the truth. But not tonight. I had other obligations tonight. Maybe that was the wrong word, *obligations*. Or maybe it was telling that this was the first word that popped into my head.

American Martyr defeated Saybrook Prep 40-29. From what little I knew about rugby, it appeared to be a good game. There was some running around, and then everybody ran into each other all at once, then some more running around, then they lifted a couple guys in the air, and even kicked the ball a few times like soccer. Both Benz and Andrew scored, I knew that much.

The American Martyr student section stormed the pitch with the team to reclaim The Sound and the Bay Trophy. Representing Saybrook Prep's home waters of Long Island Sound and American

Martyr's Chesapeake Bay, the silver trophy was a rolling sea wave crowning a square pedestal with the names of each year's winner engraved on the sides of the pedestal.

Joslin and I were buried in an avalanche of people. "Okay," Joslin screamed, "I know I'm not into organized sports, but this is kinda cool!"

The crowd parted like the Red Sea for the man of the hour and his girlfriend. He was sweaty, dirty, and sour smelling. Before I got to him, Avery jumped in between us and gave him a hug. It was more of a brother-sister hug, and I noticed.

"Rosemary, I have no idea where Avery came from. I—"

"Relax, Benz," I said, leaning in to kiss him on the cheek. He tasted salty. "She is no longer the enemy."

Benz stepped back abruptly, reacting to a tap over his shoulder.

"Uh, sorry to interrupt."

"Tyrell!" Benz shouted in greeting, bringing his adversary in for a manly handclap and chest bump, trying way too hard to be cool.

Tyrell backed away from the embrace. "Hell of a game, Coker. Hell of a game."

Benz slipped more comfortably into the conversation, as he tended to do when talking about sports, and especially when another rugby player called him 'Coker.' "You almost beat us by yourself. How many points you score?"

"Most of them," Tyrell answered.

"I rest my case." Benz turned to me. "Have you met my girlfriend? Rosemary Banson, Tyrell St. John. Tyrell, this is Rosemary."

Tyrell shook my hand. "Hello, Rosemary. You can call me 'Ty.'"

His handshake was firm in a reassuring way. He seemed like a nice guy, not particularly hard on the eyes, taller than Benz by at least a couple inches, maybe more. But I was not to be distracted. Not tonight. This was Benz's moment. This was *our* moment. I forced a courtesy smile. "Nice to meet you, Ty."

Benz smacked Ty on the back. "Tyrell and I have been playing on the East Coast All Stars the last couple summers. He's the best. I'm making it his job next year to look after you."

"Excuse me?" I said.

"Tyrell is transferring to American Martyr for his junior year."

"Why?" I asked.

If I was uncomfortable, Ty appeared even more so. This clearly seemed like something Benz had not discussed with him. "My dad got a job with a publisher based in Prince Frederick."

I thought of Emrys's farm. "In Calvert County?"

"Yeah." Ty nodded. "We have some relatives down there, but Mom refused to move to the middle of nowhere. She wanted to live in D.C. or Baltimore. Dad's compromise was Annapolis."

This was what high school was supposed to be about. Not needing Arthurian superpowers to feel absolutely invincible and in love. Your boyfriend winning the big game, giving your rival for his affections the cold shoulder, and kissing you midfield with pickled lips. Boy loves girl, girl loves boy, boy rejects other girl, boy kisses girl. Cue the closing credits.

Villainous rival for boyfriend's affections reinvents herself in act three as likable and sympathetic? Boyfriend handpicks uncomfortably attractive rugby player from Connecticut to be your indefinite chaperone? These were not the plot twists I anticipated.

CHAPTER
30

"What's wrong, Rosemary?"

"Nothing," I said.

Eben and Cookie left straight from the game to sneak in one last skiing weekend in West Virginia before spring. They'd packed Benz a bag, assuming he would go with them. They assumed wrong.

The Cooke family yacht was docked behind their home. It was a forty-two-foot Chris Craft, navy blue with white trim and a red boot stripe just above the waterline. The boat's name ran the width of the stern: *Docked Paycheck*. Benz told me his dad thought of it. I could picture Eben with his polished bald head and broad gigglemug when the idea came to him.

"Did I say or do something to make you feel uncomfortable?"

"No, not at all. I just didn't expect to be, I don't know, this nervous."

Benz had set out strawberries and sparkling grape juice on the boat. A dozen or so white candles flickered on the boat's back deck. Although his parents were gone, I appreciated Benz's gesture of having our date at the boat instead of the house. The memory of that house—the drinking, the dancing, his parent's bed, the morning after—was still too distracting. For both of us.

I felt a little underdressed in jeans and an American Martyr Rugby Club t-shirt, especially with Benz wearing a white oxford and khakis, but he kept reassuring me that I looked fantastic, that I was wearing exactly what he'd hoped I'd wear. Granted, at that point Benz would have said I looked fantastic if I was wearing a garbage bag and Crocs.

"What do you need from me?" Benz asked.

"It's not a question of what you need to do," I said. "It's a question of whether or not I'm ready to do it."

One of Benz's personal playlists played on the boat's speakers. The songs were obviously meant to set a mood. And when I say "obviously," Benz literally named the playlist "Gettin' Bizzay Beats" on Spotify. We'd been making out on the sundeck of the boat for a solid half hour, nearing that point of no return again, like so many times before. Somewhere between first and second base, I lost my nerve and pushed his hands off me.

I could tell Benz was plotting his next move, and that it was going to be clumsy, and that I'd hate him for saying whatever was about to come out of his mouth.

"We could always do, you know, *other things*."

Benz did not disappoint, but I figured I might as well let him wither on the vine. "What *other things* would you be talking about?"

"You know," Benz said.

"No, I don't."

"There are other ways to fool around, to take care of…"

"You?"

"Well, if you insist."

The cutest boy I had ever known was getting uglier by the second. "Benz, you might need to stop talking."

"What did I say?"

"Too much."

"You want me to give you a back rub?"

Dear God in Heaven, *not* the back rub line. And yet I found myself nodding compliantly. Walking to the back deck of the boat to the well-padded L-shaped couch. Lying face down, my chin resting on my hands. "Knock yourself out," I said, not even a little bit hesitant.

Benz was already transitioning into obvious but acceptable foreplay, switching back and forth between a massage and kissing me between the back of my ears and my neck. His move was to kiss the back of my neck with his chin stubble, and then finish the kiss by gently blowing down the back of my shirt.

And cue the goosebumps. His hands were stronger than I expected. I'd spent so many months toughening myself up that I had started to believe touch was a fleeting sensation—something my extraordinary resistance to injury would eventually just numb away. I was wrong. I was *really* wrong. Benz worked on my shoulders, rubbing his thumbs in opposite circular patterns while squeezing my skin with his other eight fingers. He framed my spine with his hands, rubbing and squeezing, moving slowly down the small of my back.

"Easy, boyfriend," I said, reaching with both hands behind my back and grabbing him by his wrists. I surprised Benz with my reaction. I surprised myself. "Let's keep it above the equator, shall we? Strictly Northern Hemisphere tonight."

Benz sighed. "My bad."

I straightened my shirt, pulling it self-consciously past the waistline of my jeans. "I could go home, you know."

Benz rolled off me. He sat back on the couch. "You were the one who wanted this, Rosemary."

My throat was dry from all the making out. I grabbed my glass of sparkling grape juice, raised it to my lips and finished it in three swallows. "Can't a girl change her mind?"

"I had it all planned out, and you're messing it up."

"Messing up your sex?"

"No, my plan."

"Your plan for sex?"

"No, Rosemary. I mean, yes, eventually. But not right away. I had a surprise for you."

"The plot thickens," I remarked as I slid next to him on the couch. "Are we talking a surprise as in, 'Whoa, put that thing away before you hurt somebody,' or a surprise like, 'A puppy? For me?'"

"Something in between, I guess, kind of?" Benz stood up from the couch. He started unbuttoning his shirt.

"I thought I said—"

"Strictly Northern Hemisphere, I promise." He unbuttoned his shirt all the way. "You ready for this?"

"I've seen you shirtless before."

Benz peeled off his shirt, like a curtain revealing the third act of a play to an anxious audience. I'd forgotten just how indescribably hot he was. He was muscular, but not in a gross, body-builder way. I had a weird fetish for his chest muscles. He insisted I call them "pecs" and got annoyed when I called them "boobies." Pecs or boobies, I didn't care. The tattoo looked great either way.

Hold up. The tattoo?

The American Martyr logo, the letters "A" and "M" intertwined, covered most of my boyfriend's left pectoral muscle. The tattoo was fresh, the black ink still raised and swollen.

"Where did you get that?" I asked.

"Surprise!" Benz said. "Mom and Dad let me do it. I went to the same guy that did your rose."

"I can't believe Mrs. Cooke agreed to this."

"Agreed to it? Mom went with me to the tattoo shop. Signed off on it and everything. She fainted when I started bleeding. Dropped like a sack of potatoes."

"The lettering is cool," I said, running my hand over his chest. "I guess I could see why Eben and Mrs. Cooke let you do it, being true to your school and all. But an American Martyr tattoo? Really?"

Benz grabbed my hand, tracing the letters with me. "That's exactly what I told my parents it was, otherwise there's no way they'd have signed off on it. But what they don't know is that the initials 'AM' on the American Martyr crest actually stand for 'Auspice Maria,' not American Martyr. In Latin, the phrase literally means 'under the protection of Mary.' It's an old Catholic symbol—the monogram of the Virgin Mary."

"Okay, so it's a Catholic thing. Even more reason for Mrs. Cooke to like it."

"Not a Catholic thing either."

"You just said it was Mary's symbol."

"I know I said that." Benz pulled my right forearm to his chest, holding it above his heart and lining up our two tattoos.

A rose vine and the monogram of Mary.

Rosemary.

CHAPTER

31

"Say what you want to say, Joslin. I know you need to get it out of your system." I looked at the clock on my iPhone. "Benz and Andrew will be here any minute to pick us up."

"Did you at least scold that ass bag for being so pushy?" Joslin asked. "Pressuring you to have sex is *not* cool."

The plan tonight was for the four of us to not have a plan. This was assuming I could keep Joslin quiet about mine and Benz's sex life.

"He didn't pressure me," I replied. "He made his move, I shut him down, he acted all mopey, and then he busted out the tattoo. It was almost...sweet."

"I didn't take you for the sentimental type."

"Up until last night I had never seen someone carve half my name in their chest for me."

"Well, there's that I guess," Joslin mused. "But can I punch him in the balls when I see him. Just once?"

"No!"

"What if it's like, just an accidental knee graze? Painful but not crippling."

"Joslin!"

She meant well. Joslin always meant well. She was more than just my best friend. More than my chuckaboo. She was my normal. She was probably the only person in my life who could still picture me non-ironically as that pig-tailed third grader running wild on Field Day. To my parents and Emrys, I was preternatural. To Joslin, I was still, as Mabel would say, "Just Rosemary." I kept telling myself I was keeping Joslin in the dark for her welfare, but I was really doing it for mine.

As for Benz, in a way his tattoo was predictable. Disguising the simple truth with a grand gesture to make himself feel better. Don't just tell a girl you love her, get a tattoo that reminds you about that love forever, when she's sixty years in the rearview mirror and your hard pecs are replaced by saggy old man boobs.

I tried Joslin's approach of playing hard to get, to make Benz feel uncomfortable and see how he reacted. He didn't react that well initially, but after he showed me the tattoo, he turned sweet and gentle. Saying "yes" felt less like an obligation, and I guess that was enough.

The good news was something just clicked into place for us the second time around. We'd both figured out a way to either cure or ignore our emotional hangovers from that first night together. I was feeling more secure with Benz and myself. Having sex made him happy, obviously, but it made me happy too.

Joslin nodded at Benz's black Acura RLX pulling into the driveway.

"Here comes the sex machine," she said.

I talked Benz, Joslin, and Andrew into a dinner date at Harry Browne's in Annapolis. The main floor was booked, so they sat us at a large six-top corner table in the upstairs room. In retrospect, I wish they hadn't.

"Rosemary!" Mabel shouted the moment I came upstairs. She sat alone at the bar, sipping on a glass of whiskey. She stood and approached our table, looking as naturally beautiful as ever with her long, red hair held back from her face by a knit beanie. A denim jacket, black jeans, and her usual cowboy boots completed the ensemble. "To what do I owe the pleasure, Lady Banson?"

Even though I was the only one in the room besides Mabel who knew the title to be literal and not figurative, I still winced. "Date night."

"I see you brought friends. You mind?" Mabel helped herself to one of the extra chairs. She offered her hand to Joslin first. "This must be Joslin."

She shook Mabel's hand, not knowing how to react. I could feel the pheromones rising in the room as Joslin blushed noticeably. "How do you know Rosemary?"

"Old family friend," she answered. "You can call me 'Mabel,' Miss Joslin. And who are these two handsome gentlemen?"

"Mabel," I said, "this is Benz and Andrew."

Mabel reached across the table, grabbing the boys' chins in each of her hands. Their initial reaction was shock, but that of course soon wore off. "Benz and Andrew, huh? Must be pretty special to land such special ladies." She released Benz but continued to firmly hold on to Andrew's face. "I like this one."

Mabel reached behind Andrew's head and started stroking his long, flowing locks. "I know women who would kill for this kind of hair."

"Ahem," Benz said.

"Yes?" Mabel gave me a quick sideways glance, so quick that I was the only one who probably caught it. "Something you want to say, young man?"

Mabel knew Benz was my boyfriend. That's why she was toying with him. He offered her an awkward handshake. "I'm Benz."

"Yes," Mabel replied, "when Rosemary said, 'This is Benz and Andrew,' I took her word for it. You don't like me complimenting your friend, do you Benz?"

"You can compliment Andrew all you want," Benz said. "Doesn't bother me."

"*Anyway*, Mabel," I said. "Now that we've dispensed with introductions, can we get on with our date night?"

Mabel diplomatically slinked back to the bar, starting up a conversation with a random business man. One of those guys in love with the sound of his own voice, with rolled-up shirt sleeves and an expensive watch too big for his wrist. Easy prey for Mabel. Three more couples walked into the room, creating an even larger buffer between us. Thank God for the buffer, as my boyfriend wasn't taking

Mabel's teasing very well.

"Seriously, what's that woman's problem?" Benz whispered.

"Relax, Casanova," I said. "You still got game. Mabel is just having a little fun with you. Trust me. If she really wanted to push your buttons, you would know it. And you would like it, probably even love it at first, but not later. Some friendly advice, if you want to get on her good side."

"What's that?"

"Don't refer to her in the third person as 'that woman.'"

"We have more pressing matters to discuss than the fact I'm more attractive to older women than Benz is," Andrew joked. "Spring break!"

Joslin rolled her eyes. "We've had this conversation a million times. You know I can't be your plus one, Andrew," Joslin said. "Pat and Dee are cool, but they're not send-your-sixteen-year-old-daughter-to-Florida-unchaperoned cool."

Mabel approached our table again. "Did I hear someone mention spring break?"

Andrew assumed ownership of their exchange. "You did indeed."

Mabel titled her head, pondering. "Give me one second." She walked back to the bar. Expensive watch guy's eyes lit up. She ignored him, reaching into her purse, which was hanging off the back of her bar stool.

"What's that crazy woman up to?" Benz chimed in.

"Jealous much?" I said.

Mabel was about halfway back to our table when she shouted, "Rosemary, catch!"

Still looking at Benz, I caught the keys without even looking.

"Whoa!" Benz jumped. "Nice reflexes."

"Lucky catch." I opened my hand to a keychain with a rubberized lime, a miniature plastic salt shaker, and a few keys attached. "What are these?"

"Keys to my place in Mexico," Mabel answered.

"To where?" Joslin asked.

"I own a condo down in Cancun. Very relaxing. Jennifer was asking me about going there with Alan. Why not make a family trip out of it? Invite Joslin and Emrys along."

"Why Emrys?" Benz wondered.

"Why Life University?" I countered. That shut him down quickly. I turned to Mabel. "So you made it down to Mexico after all?"

"Of course I did," Mabel said. "I love Maryland, but I'm not an idiot. I go at least three times a year."

"Great." Andrew shrugged his shoulders, looking at Benz. "Our girlfriends are going to Mexico without us, and I'm flying solo in Fort Myers while you're picking out wallpaper for your dorm."

"Dorm?" I asked. "Why would Benz be thinking about decorating a dorm?'

Andrew looked at Benz, then at me, then at Benz again. "You haven't told her?"

"Told me what?"

"I wanted to tell you sooner, or at least before I told Andrew. He saw the orientation packet this afternoon at my house, and I had no choice. Life offered me a scholarship, and…" Benz paused. "And I accepted their offer."

The distance from Towson University to Severna Park is thirty-four miles. The distance from Life University to Severna Park is 681 miles. I'd memorized the difference—647 miles—in the thirty seconds it took for me to see that stupid folder in Benz's gym bag and type "Life University" in Google Maps. That was the moment I knew Towson was off the table. Before Benz made the effort to include Emrys. Before we made love.

"Rosemary, you okay?" Joslin asked. "You look a little pale."

The lump in the back of my throat and the shortness of breath were not what I expected to feel in this moment. I was crushed and panicked, all at once. I had taken Benz for granted, and I wasn't ready to let him go.

CHAPTER
32

I didn't wait for Atli or Emrys to answer the door this time.

Emrys sat on the couch, his feet propped up on a coffee table.

"How'd the meeting with the lawyers go?" I asked.

Emrys sat up. "Looks like you're not going to get sued for almost punching that guy into a coma. How'd your dinner date go last night?"

"Benz wants to play rugby instead of football in college and has decided he's on going to a chiropractic school in Georgia."

"Back up," Emrys said. "A chiropractic school? Since when does Benz want to be a chiropractor?"

"Who knows? Since yesterday? The school is called Life University."

"What happened to Towson?"

"Too close to home, I guess. Too close to me."

"Don't be so hard on yourself. Benz still loves you."

"Not enough to stay."

"He's not going anywhere for what, another five months? How about you just get busy loving him and stop worrying about losing him?"

"So that's your sage advice? A country music song? Love him like tomorrow will never come?"

"Get up," Emrys said, helping me to my feet. "What you need is an ice-cold bottle of Barritts and a rocking chair."

We sat on Emrys's front porch in dueling rocking chairs, each of us rocking at our own pace, a rickety old bar stool between us acting as a makeshift table. Emrys had set out two bottles of Barritts on the table. We sipped quietly for a few minutes, listening to the Chesapeake frogs and crickets harmonizing.

"Love is special, but fickle. Especially young love," Emrys said. "Not all fairy tales have happy endings, even when the gods are involved."

"Are you really throwing my own words back in my face right now? I'll be fine, Emrys."

"I'm not throwing anything in your face." My friend stood suddenly. "Sit and listen."

"Here cometh the lesson," I announced mockingly.

Emrys held his ginger beer in front of his face like a microphone, talking to himself. "I wandered this world alone for centuries. It was my penance. For whisking away your mother and father only to lose them 400 years in the future, for the way I toyed with Arthur all those years. I was broken. I was dispassionate. I was hopeless. And then I met Tess. She was my do-over for everything I'd done wrong. There was no moment wasted, no token of affection taken for granted. I was giddy and nervous, not just for our first kiss, but for every kiss. I loved everything about her, even her imperfections. *Especially* her imperfections. I came to love this world again and believe in the all-encompassing power of the human heart because of Tess.

"We decided to have a family later than most, at least back in those days. Tess was in her late thirties. Although I was 'independently wealthy,' Tess's military career had us traveling around the world. We always knew we were going to have kids, but not until we settled down. Tess took a desk job back in D.C. in '58. When we went to the doctor's office for her physical results and the all-clear to start trying to get pregnant, the doctor told us she had advanced ovarian cancer."

"Oh my God, Emrys. I'm so very sorry." I covered my mouth with my hand, afraid to say what was on my mind. "And your powers. You couldn't...y-you couldn't help her?"

Emrys shook his head. "I tried, Rosemary. Believe me, I tried.

Healers are a dime a dozen, but it takes a special kind of healer to kill cancer. It takes a god."

"How'd she go?" I pried. "Was it…"

"Peaceful?" he said.

I nodded. "Please say it was."

"Tess refused to spend her last days in a hospital, and she loved our farm. I think Tess loved it even more than I did. She died in my arms in our bedroom. I kissed her goodbye as Bing Crosby's 'Sunday, Monday, or Always' played on the record player. I gave her that forty-five on our one-month anniversary, the day I told a woman I had known for four weeks that we were going to spend the rest of our lives together. It was our song."

I don't know when I started hugging Emrys exactly. We stood on the front porch together, as if we were dancing. My head rested on his shoulder. I started crying again, but I didn't cry for me. I didn't cry for Benz. I cried for Emrys. The wizard was working his magic without even trying, transforming my tears of sorrow into tears of compassion.

"Screw Guinevere and Lancelot," I said. "*That* was the greatest love story ever told."

Emrys handed me his handkerchief, the mere fact he owned a handkerchief reminding me how old he is. "I don't think your mother and father would necessarily agree with that assessment. But yes, Tess was my one and only."

"And she never knew about where you came from? She never knew Merlin?"

"No," Emrys said. "Tess fell in love with Emrys, who was a better man than Merlin could ever hope to be."

"I'd have to agree with Tess that the wizard has nothing on the man." I grabbed his collar, pulling him toward me. I kissed him on the cheek.

"Rosemary, I—"

"Need to learn how to take a compliment?"

"Yes," Emrys sighed. "I suppose I do."

"And so, that stint in a Catholic seminary in the early sixties you told me about? That was you trying to get your head on straight after

Tess died?"

Emrys nodded. "When did you put those two things together?"

I had put more than two things together since Emrys told me he was once a Catholic seminarian. But he didn't know that yet. I'd leave that surprise for later. "It was when we were on the farm for Thanksgiving, and you and I went horseback riding. You said you were in the seminary in the early 1960s, and then two hours later I saw that Tess died in 1959. It doesn't take Sherlock Holmes to figure that one out."

"Indubitably, my dear Banson," Emrys aped.

I didn't bother to acknowledge his compliment, let alone laugh. It was hard to shake the image of Tess dying in Emrys's arms. Hard to stop crying. "What's that reading from the Bible they always use at weddings, the one from the Book of Corinthians?"

"'Love is patient, love is kind. It does not envy, it does not boast, it is not proud.' That the one you're talking about?"

"Yeah, that's it. I think they forgot to add, 'Love is not tidy or convenient.'"

Emrys grabbed his handkerchief from my hand, gently dabbing under my eyes. "When I finally pass from this world, there's no place I'd rather be than on my farm, lying next to my wife, underneath that old oak tree."

"As beautiful and heartbreaking as that story is, where does that leave me with Benz?"

"It leaves *you* nowhere. Benz is going to college in Georgia, so what? Maybe you two will be that high school couple that makes it. And if not, he's simply doing what all teenage boys, what all mortals do in the end. He's saying goodbye. And ultimately, the best heart is the one that's been broken a couple times. Like a fractured bone, it's stronger after it heals."

"You're living proof of that, Emrys."

"When it's impossible to die, all there is to do is live."

Blowing my nose into his collar on purpose, I patted his chest. "I hate it when you're suddenly all wise and acting your age. Have I ever told you that?"

"Now that you mention it, Rosemary, I don't think you have. And that's saying something, because you talk a lot."

"Shut up!" I said. Emrys's wisecrack deflated the intimacy of the moment, but I couldn't decide if I was thankful or disappointed.

"No," Emrys retorted, "you shut up."

"Hey, you want to go to spring break in Mexico with me?"

Emrys coughed, choking on a swig of Barritts. "I doubt your parents would sign off on us going to Mexico alone right now."

"Oh, they're going too. We'll remain firmly on Mordred watch. It'll be Mom, Dad, me, Joslin, and, pending your answer, our resident teenage wizard."

Emrys accepted the invitation to spring break. I was much more grateful for his company than I led him to believe. Watching his sixteen-year-old hormones confronted by a sea of Mexican girls was the perfect distraction from thinking about Benz dumping me for the first Georgia co-ed he met during orientation.

We cracked open two more bottles of Barritts. With the amount of sugar pumping through our veins, we'd probably stay up half the night. The Chesapeake Bay's volume had gone from serene to restless as we settled back down into our rocking chairs. Under the light of a full moon, the frogs and crickets battled for the microphone with the owls. Croaks, clicks, *hoot hoots,* and something else. Emrys held his index finger to his ear. "Hear that?"

"The owls?"

"No."

"The crickets?"

"Try again."

"The frogs?"

Emrys nodded. "Northern Spring Creepers. The first frogs of spring."

"Hey, Emrys."

"Yes?"

"I know you think being an endless source of random trivia is endearing, but I don't need to know *everything* you know."

"I thought in this instance I was providing some information relevant to our situation."

"Relevant and interesting aren't necessarily the same thing."

"You really are an uncurious creature, Rosemary."

"Hello..." A bottle of Barritts in my left hand, I pointed to myself with my right. "Teenage girl in the house. If I ain't talkin', I ain't listenin'."

I was listening, though. I'd heard exactly what Emrys heard. It wasn't owls, crickets, or Spring Creepers. It was the "something else" out there in the night, rustling amongst the trees. It was hard to pin down where exactly the sound was coming from. Somewhere on that block, for sure. What kind of animal was it? The usual culprit would be a fox or a raccoon, maybe even a muskrat. But the footfall sounded heavier, bipedal.

It was definitely a person.

"What is it?" I asked, exchanging raised eyebrows with Emrys, as if we both had the same question on our minds. "Is Mordred here, now?"

Emrys looked down at his iPhone. He used technology so little that it was always shocking to see. "Security cam spotted our Peeping Tom. Nothing to be alarmed about."

"How can you be so sure?"

Emrys shoved his phone in his pocket. "When Mordred shows his face, I doubt he'll be hiding behind the bushes wearing an American Martyr letter jacket."

"Letter jacket?" I didn't even need to see the video footage. "It was Benz."

Emrys nodded. "The fact he's going to college out of state doesn't mean anything. He loves you enough. Make no mistake, at first, I hated him. You had a larger destiny. Benz seemed so beneath you. It was easy to dismiss him as a dumb jock just trying to get in your—"

"I appreciate you coming around," I said, not wanting Emrys to give me *that* lecture, in any context.

"What I'm trying to say is that Benz is a keeper," Emrys redirected. "When we get on the other side of this, he's worth chasing down."

"Let's face it, Emrys. A part of me will always want to chase Benz down. He's my kryptonite. You know this, maybe more than anyone except Joslin."

"Then let him be your kryptonite."

"But Tess," I said, my voice cracking.

"What does Tess have to do with this?"

"When I know how broken your heart is, really and truly broken, it seems unfair to think mine is anything more than bruised. You said so yourself, 'Not all fairy tales have happy endings.' Benz is going to do what all mortal teenage boys do and say goodbye."

"Oh shut up, Rosemary."

"Shut up?"

"That's the kind of bullshit adults say."

"That's the kind of bullshit *you* just said."

"Did you really take away from all this that you shouldn't let your heart get broken?"

"Well…" I pondered. "Yeah."

Emrys placed his hand on my shoulder. "Take it from someone who used to be an adult, for a very, very long time. Don't let your parents, your teachers, don't let anyone diminish your feelings."

"You mean you're not going to give me the 'someday you'll look back on this and laugh' speech?"

"I freaking *hate* that speech, Rosemary. Your first kiss, your first love, your first heartbreak, the smell of your boyfriend, a song that instantly transports you back to a time and place: These moments will be with you for the rest of your life. Someday you'll likely turn the page, as I suggested earlier, but you'll always keep this page earmarked. Always."

The smell of my boyfriend. What's with all these teenage boys obsessed with smelling things?

The wizard dropped to his chair. He sat in silence, allowing the moment to stand on its own, his shaken apprentice at a loss for words.

No, seriously. How long had Emrys been keeping all *that* in his bag of magic tricks?

I couldn't think about all this. Not right now. Looking at my watch, I segued to my exit.

"A lot to unpack in that monologue, Emrys."

"There's nothing to unpack. I spoke only the truth."

I peeked once more at my watch, this time a little more obviously. "Let's put a pin in this emotional epiphany. I have to make sure I get a good night's sleep tonight. Early day for me tomorrow."

Emrys sat back in his chair. Extending his arms out, he grabbed his knees with knowing conviction. "Meeting with the Headmaster in the morning?"

"Who told you?"

"Does it matter?" Emrys asked. "What are you going to talk about?"

"Does it matter?" I echoed.

Emrys eyed me cautiously beneath his furrowed, youthfully thinning brows. "Be careful, Rosemary. The truth might seem obvious to you, but it's never obvious. You should've learned that by now."

CHAPTER
33

Ms. Vandergriff showed up to her office in heels and a tailored pantsuit that flared at the ankles. She took a seat behind her desk. I followed her lead, occupying the chair on the opposing side.

I signed the word for *love*, crossing both hands over my chest. "Love the outfit, Ms. Vandergriff." I eased back into my chair. "Very *Charlie's Angels*."

Ms. Vandergirff signed *thank you* back to me, touching her fingers to your chin and bringing her fingers forward, as if she was blowing me a kiss. "Like you've ever seen that show."

"I've seen the movies, and my mom purchased the entire five-year run of the original series on Apple TV. She has a thing for women who kick ass."

"I bet she does, Rosemary."

"Why you looking so fancy?"

Ms. Vandergriff blushed. "Oh, it's nothing. I have this lunch thing today."

"A lunch thing? As in a date? Who's the lucky guy?"

"I don't know if I'd call it a date. Just a light lunch in Annapolis. You know him, I think. It's Mr. Schuetz."

"Daniel? My dad's attorney?"

She nodded.

"You go, Ms. Vandergriff!"

"Really?"

"The most eligible bachelor in Severna Park? Please, that's a no-brainer."

"Enough about my love life." Ms. Vandergriff said. "Thanks for coming to see me before your meeting with Headmaster Benedict. Anything you want to share?"

"Not really," I replied. "I mean, I know that you always tell me your office is a safe space, and that everything I tell you is in confidence. But Father Jul—I mean, Headmaster Benedict and I have to sort some things out, just between us."

"Are you hearing yourself right now?"

"Crap. Am I being disrespectful?"

"Just the opposite. When did you get to be such a grownup? Is this the same girl who handed me a weed brownie in this very office? You've changed quite a bit in six months."

"If you only knew the half of it."

"I take it you're not sharing that with me either?"

"You have your personal life, I have mine."

In my many hours spent in Ms. Vandergriff's office, I knew she wouldn't give up so easily. She stood up from her chair and circled around the desk to her favorite spot for a face-to-face chat—right next to her student, leaning against the edge of her desk, with her elbows slightly bent and bracing herself with her hands. "Mind if I impart one last nugget of priceless guidance counselor wisdom?"

"Is it baking tips?" I joked.

Ms. Vandergriff giggled at the reference. "You can still be a grownup and accept someone's help. Changing is part of becoming better and stronger, but you still need to surround yourself with good people for those times you fall and can't get back up—whether that be your mom, your dad, your best friend, or sometimes, yes, even your boyfriend. Independence can be both a strength and a flaw."

"Dang, Ms. V." I had never called her that in my life. "Look at you dropping the knowledge. Smoking hot *and* smart!"

Ms. Vandergriff eyed the clock on her wall, reluctantly realizing that was all she going to get out of me. "How about we get you to the Headmaster's office?"

Father Jules's office occupied the entire eastern side of St. John Neumann Basilica. His office walls were lined with dark-stained wood paneling, giving it the feel of a giant confessional booth.

Father Jules nodded from behind his desk. "Please, have a seat, Ms. Banson. Just put your bag there on the floor next to you."

Per his instructions, I dropped my ruddy old JanSport backpack at my feet. Crossing myself, I began with the standard Catholic recitation: "In the name of the Father, the Son, the Holy Spirit, Amen. Forgive me Father, for I have sinned. My last confession was, oh, probably—"

"There will be none of that," Father Jules interrupted curtly.

"Sorry, Headmaster," I said. "Force of habit."

"*Headmaster*? Not your usual sobriquet? And habit? Clever turn of phrase there."

Oh, habit. As in a nun's habit. I was so funny I made a joke without even realizing it. "So bruh *what*?"

"It's another word for nickname. Never mind. Thank you for calling me by my proper title."

"Hey, I'm trying. Can we be straight with each other, Headmaster?"

Father Jules nodded. "I expect nothing less."

"You don't like me," I replied. "You've never liked me."

"That's not true. Not true at all."

"You've had it out for me since grade school. Remember third grade Field Day? When you tried to make sure the boys got trophies after I kicked all their butts?"

"You remember that?"

"Of course I remember," I said. "I was awesome, and you tried to take that day away from me. Did you really feel threatened by a nine-year-old girl?"

Father Jules bowed, tapping his folded hands to his nose with just his index fingers. "As both the pastor of St. John Neumann and the headmaster of American Martyr, I am tasked with both the spiritual and scholastic well-being of literally hundreds of souls. I possess neither the time nor the capacity for personal vendettas."

"Now you sound like Emrys."

"Emrys Balin?" Father Jules pondered. "Are you talking about the foreign exchange student from Wales?"

So this was how he was going to play it. I hadn't known the whole truth about Father Jules until I walked into his office today. I'd never even entertained the idea. Some of the clues were obvious, others not so much. He was like a puzzle that only made sense after the very last piece was put in its place.

"Yes," I affirmed. "I am talking about the Welsh foreign exchange student."

"Rosemary, we are all sinners, and we are all offered the gift of atoning for our sins through God's grace, and His grace alone."

"Did they make you memorize that on the first or second day of seminary?"

"Seminary?" Father Jules pondered. "What do you know of seminary?"

"Oh, you'd be surprised," I said.

Father Jules unclasped his hands. Was he going to take the bait? "Enlighten me."

Yes, he was.

"You've made a point of sticking your nose in my business these last ten or eleven years of my life, so I've recently made a point of discovering more about you. Like a lot of priests growing up, you were Catholic-educated kindergarten through college. After that, you attended St. John's Seminary in the village of Wonersh in the Waverley district of Surrey, England. Five years later, you were ordained and moved back to the States, where you gradually worked your way up the clerical ladder to where you are now."

"So you actually do homework on occasion," Father Jules responded. "I'm impressed, Rosemary. Very thorough."

"I even know the answer to the extra credit question."

"Lay it on me," Father Jules said.

"Your idea of a perfect day is watching Notre Dame football with some schnitzel and a tall German pilsner."

"How did you know that?"

I nodded at the two pictures featured prominently on his desk. One was of Father Jules posing with a distinguished-looking gentleman in matching Notre Dame visors at a golf outing, the other a picture of Father Jules pounding a giant stein of beer at Oktoberfest in Munich. "An educated guess."

Father Jules bowed his head. "My compliments again. It would seem you have me all figured out."

"Maybe," I said.

"Maybe?" Father Jules straightened his black cassock as he rose to his feet. He turned his back to me, like he knew what was coming. "What else do you want to know?"

"You befriended someone in seminary."

"I befriended a lot of people in seminary."

"This friend was special," I said. "He challenged everything you were ever led to believe. Over the course of your first two years in seminary together, this young man revealed things to you, and in doing so nearly chased you away from the Church. But instead you became stronger in your faith, and you and this classmate developed a mutual fondness and respect for another. But he left after his second year and went back to America, where he pulled some strings to eventually get you a job."

"Did that classmate have a name?" Father Jules asked, turning back to face the conversation. He was patronizing me now.

"He's had plenty of names over the years," I answered. "Ambrose, Emory, Merlin. Today you and I know him as Emrys Balin, the foreign exchange student from Wales. Emrys got into American Martyr because of you. If I pulled his file, I'm guessing there would be no background check on his host father Atli Saevarsson, no forwarding address to his parents in Wales, no school transcripts, pretty much no file."

Father Jules folded his arms, saying nothing. He looked at me, gritted his teeth and inhaled as if he was about to speak, then shook his head. "Hmm," was all he could muster.

"That's all you have to say," I replied. "'Hmm?'"

"It's a lot to process, Rosemary," Father Jules spoke up, finally. "I could stand here and accuse you of having an overly active teenage imagination, but why insult your intelligence like that?"

"That never stopped you before."

"How did you put the pieces together?"

"*Spes messis in semine.*"

"The hope of the harvest is in the seed," Father Jules translated. "Where did you hear that?"

"Emrys said it once."

"I'm assuming he said it to Chef."

"So, what? You're a member of the Knights of—"

"The Knights of Leo?" he interrupted. "Supreme Knight, actually."

"Well, for a Supreme Knight, you're pretty terrible at covering your tracks."

"Why do you say that?"

"Took me five minutes on Google after I read your bio in the school directory. Turns out '*Spes messis in semine*' is not just the secret motto of the Knights of Leo, it's the very public motto of St. John's Seminary in Surrey, England." I stood up from my chair, turning and pointing to a spot high on the wall. "And the motto you have stenciled in giant letters over the doorway to your office."

Father Jules walked to his doorway and looked up, shaking his head. "Well, this is embarrassing."

"What do you know? Specifics please."

"I know that I've had to reconcile my deeply Catholic spirituality with a world in which mythical kingdoms, godlike wizards, magical swords, and dragons are real."

"Hold up," I said. "Dragons are real? I didn't get that memo."

"Are dragons any more contrived or fanciful than a mystical prophecy linking and empowering royal-blooded children conceived in lust?"

I pointed at Father Jules, my eyebrows raised. "I guess you do know enough."

Father Jules spun his chair until his back was to me. He stood facing the exposed confessional booths. "It's not that I have disliked you, Rosemary. I hope you realize that now."

"Then what would you call it?"

"Testing you."

"*Testing* me?" I asked in disbelief. "By harassing me for over a decade? By getting me arrested? Was this all one big setup just to make sure Emrys and I had detention together? Was the whole Dungeons & Dragons story just a story?"

Father Jules held up his right index finger with a muted sigh. "Unfortunately, the gambling ring was a very real thing. You might not be aware of this, but Emrys tends to sometimes act like a—"

"Sixteen-year-old boy?"

Father Jules nodded.

"Well aware," I said.

"Please understand, Rosemary, none of this has been personal. I just needed to make sure you were worthy."

"Worthy of what? My third grade Field Day trophies? Getting arrested for pot brownies that weren't even mine? The prophecy?"

"I'm sure you're plenty worthy of the prophecy."

"I feel like that's an insult, but I'll let it slide. If I'm worthy of the prophecy, then what's the problem?"

"*Protegat gladium, protegat magum,*" Father Jules recited.

"Protect the sword, protect the wizard. Yeah, I got it."

"*Do* you get it, Rosemary?"

I smirked. "No, but I have a feeling I'm about to."

"You may be worthy enough to fight the occasional evil minion, but can you defeat Mordred? Are you worthy of Excalibur? Are you worthy of Merlin? Does it make sense for us to invest so much in a teenage girl?"

"Okay," I replied. "Now I know *that* is an insult."

CHAPTER

34

"Found it," Joslin said, brandishing in her right hand the spare boat key that Pat Kelly wrongly assumed he kept sufficiently hidden.

"Where was it?" I asked

"Tucked into the lining of his sheath," she answered.

"A sheath for what?"

Joslin raised her left hand to reveal a finely sharpened blade about a foot long with a varnished wooden handle. "His fish fillet knife."

I saw the leather sheath on the floor of the boat by Joslin's feet. I crouched down and picked up the sheath, offering it to Joslin. "Put that thing away before you hurt someone."

Joslin's Manhattan Beach neighborhood occupied the entire peninsula between Dividing Creek, Cypress Creek, and the Magothy River. The Kelly house was one of the oldest on the peninsula, a 1930s cottage Pat and Dee had repainted green to hide the moss on the north face of the house. A rickety old pier extended out from the Kelly backyard into the Bay. Halfway down the pier, Joslin and I sat in her family's sixteen-foot Boston Whaler, an old motorboat that had earned the nickname *Stoned Whale* after a creative (and funny) vandal peeled off the first two letters and last letter in "Boston Whaler" and spray-painted an "ed" in the middle of the two words. The wind was coming out of the southwest at a mild two or three knots. It was a perfect night for a ride.

I checked my phone. It was a text from Emrys. *There in 20*, it read. A curiously hip text in its brevity, especially for Emrys. My guess was Father Jules hadn't told him about my visit yet. "She gassed up?"

Joslin inserted the boat key into the ignition. "I assume so."

"How fast can you get us out to Dobbins Island?"

"Fast enough," Joslin replied, turning the key a quarter clockwise. The black Mercury outboard roared to life. "Why?"

"I'm going to ask you, as my chuckaboo, to trust me tonight, Joslin. There's a lot you're going to need to take in. Just let it happen."

"Sure…" My best friend shrugged her shoulders. "Whatevs."

Joslin backed down the throttle as *Stoned Whale* approached Dobbins Island. By day, the seven-acre island in the middle of the Magothy River was a popular raft-up destination for power boaters and power drinkers. By night, it was a place you went to not be bothered. Joslin coasted on to the beach. We stepped off the boat.

"Rosemary, what are we doing?"

"I came clean with Father Jules, and now I have to come clean with you."

"What did you need to come clean with Father Jules about?"

"I'm just wanting to make amends, get my house in order before…well, I'm wanting to make amends."

"Amends for what?" Joslin asked.

I scanned the boat intently. "Please, have a seat."

"What are you looking for?"

"Something I can use for a demonstration. There!" I pointed toward the bow of the boat. "The anchor. How much does it weigh?"

"Fairly standard galvanized steel plow anchor. I'd say probably about forty pounds, over fifty if you throw in the weight of the chain."

"That'll have to do." I walked to the front of the ship. Joslin sat on the beach, looking confused.

"You ready for this?"

Rosemary shrugged her shoulders again. "I guess?"

Reaching down, I grabbed the chain firmly and raised it over my head. "As far back as elementary school, you saw in me what no one else saw. You've always known I was fast, you've always known I was strong. Now it's time for your own personal demonstration."

I stepped a few feet back toward the middle of the boat, finding my center of gravity. My luck, I'd lose my balance and fall in the water, outing myself only as a clumsy idiot.

No. Not tonight.

The anchor and chain were light in my hand, my feet secured. I began to swing the forty-pound anchor and chain over my head in large, concentric circles, the boat barely rippling the water. My pace was purposeful, accelerating with every revolution.

Joslin stood there with a befuddled look on her face. I let go of the anchor, impaling the beach only a few feet away from where Joslin stood. I secured the end of the anchor line to a cleat on the boat and stepped onto the beach. "Pretty cool, huh?"

"But...how did you do *that?*" Joslin approached me. She reached for my hand that had been holding on to the anchor chain, caressing it like it was a magical talisman that she needed to remind her she was real. "Put that thing away before you hurt someone."

I squeezed her hand, smiling. "I am what I've always been, Joslin. I'm your chuckaboo. If I've learned anything my sophomore year at American Martyr, it's that hiding things from the people closest to us only brings heartache. I want you to know all of me."

"Up until about thirty seconds ago, I thought I did."

"Come on, you had to have suspected that I was hiding something, maybe didn't know something about myself. What about third grade Field Day?"

"That's why you kicked all the fourth grade boys' asses?"

"Yes and no."

"Yes and no?"

"I wasn't really super-powered yet back then, but I had no idea that I wasn't *really* super-powered, and by the time I found out I wasn't really super-powered, I became really super-powered."

"I think I follow you," Joslin said. "And when did that happen? The really super-powered part?"

"In October."

"Of this year?"

"Yep," I affirmed.

"How?"

"How? Like how did I get my powers?"

Joslin nodded. "Yeah."

Deep breath, Rosemary.

"A jockey at the Laurel Park horse stables tried to rape me, or at least I think he was trying to rape me, right before Emrys struck me with a bolt of energy that activated my latent superpowers, affirming my place in a line of mystically enhanced ancient warriors conceived in lust destined to fight the evil hordes of Arthurian myth until only one of us is left standing."

"Oh, is that all?" Joslin joked.

"There's more."

Joslin raised her hands, pressing them out in a slow-down motion. "Let's take this one step at a time, Rosemary. What happened to the jockey?"

"He lost his head."

"I can imagine. Seeing you shot up with a bolt of energy by Emrys. He's going to think twice the next time a woman says 'no' to him."

"He's not going to think anything. I literally cut his head off."

"You physically separated his head from his neck?"

"Well, not completely separated. I stabbed him in the neck and then his head sort of rolled off to the side and just hung there by some loose strands of neck skin."

"Thanks for that image," Joslin said sarcastically. "I didn't really need to have a restful night's sleep any time in the next calendar year. Forgive me for my ignorance, but how does one sever another person's head these days? With an axe or something? And what's this about evil hordes?"

"*Gladio!*" I shouted. The familiar arc of light flashed in my hand, giving way to the shimmering silver Sword of Power. "Joslin, I'd like you to meet Excalibur."

"Excalibur?" Joslin shook her head. "As in, *the* Excalibur?"

"I realize I'm dumping a lot on you."

"Ancient warriors and magic swords set against the backdrop of an East Coast prep school? I feel like I'm in a bad movie."

"I'd like to think you're in a good one actually. Snappy dialogue, extraordinary but believable plot twists. And now, finally, the resolution of the secret identity fallacy."

"The secret identity fallacy?"

"Like in the comic books," I clarified. "The suspension of disbelief that allows superheroes to maintain their secret identities against all odds and in the face of supremely intelligent and intuitive peers. Lois Lane, Pulitzer Prize-winning investigative journalist, doesn't recognize Superman when he puts on a pair of glasses. Joslin Kelly, the smartest girl I know, discounts and rationalizes away countless feats of physical prowess by her best friend."

"And I'm Lois Lane in this analogy?" Joslin asked.

"Well, you're not Superman. And did I mention I have super pets?"

"You finally got that Bernese Mountain Dog you've been wanting your whole life?"

I raised my eyebrows. "Something like that."

"*Pegasoi aithiopes!*" Emrys's voice echoed across the Bay.

They started out as two indistinct specks approaching from the west over Gibson Island. Joslin couldn't see them, obviously. I was trying to time our conversation just right so that when Emrys swooped down he could cast the reveal spell. And I totally nailed it.

Joslin ducked. "What in the..."

Emrys led the way on Raven, a riderless Crash trailing behind. Flying close to the water like pelicans, they were a sight to behold. Emrys circled the island once, then guided both horses to a soft landing on to the island's northwest beach.

His timing was perfect. I didn't want to give Joslin a smug smile, but how could I not?

"Emrys?" Joslin said.

"So they tell me." Emrys dismounted, handing Raven's reins to Joslin.

Joslin was no longer hiding anything. She was white as a sheet now. "W-what...what's happening here?" she mumbled.

"Uh-uh-uh, Joslin," I said, shaking my head while waving my right index finger back and forth. "We had a deal. Just let it happen."

I flirted with the notion that my double life was falling away. All the things I could never say to Joslin, all the experiences I could never share were finally out in the open. She was here—seeing me, all of me, for the very first time. But it wasn't the catharsis I'd hoped for. It didn't explain my capacity to so effortlessly compartmentalize my life over these last five or six months. It didn't explain my continued reluctance to include Benz, the love of my life, in on my secret.

Maybe that was it, the fact that I'd only been a fully amped-up Lust Borne for a short time. There was this weird layer of hyper-reality to my life. It didn't feel as cathartic to be real with Joslin about my life because my life no longer seemed real.

Emrys handed me the reins for Crash. "Why?" he asked.

"Why?" I echoed. "You know I've been wanting to tell Joslin for months."

"I'm not talking about Joslin. I'm talking about bringing Benny into this."

"Benny?" I asked.

"Monsignor Benedict."

"Oh, Father Jules is 'Benny' now? Do you know he's the Supreme Knight of the Knights of Leo? When you met him in seminary, was that by accident or all just an elaborate setup to stack the deck with some extra babysitters for me along the way?"

"In answer to your first question, yes." Emrys said. "In answer to your second question, initially by accident, but definitely a babysitter later on."

"How can I bring someone into this who's apparently already in it?"

Joslin jumped in. "Why do you keep talking about Father Jules?"

Emrys shook his head, starting down the beach toward the boat. He waved as he walked away. "You two kids have fun."

"Fun?" Joslin pointed at my gray horse. "I'm not getting up on that thing."

"You're right." I nodded at the much more imposing Raven. "You're on the big, black one."

"Rosemary, I can't."

"You can't ride a horse?"

"Well, sure I can ride a horse. You know Mom and Dad used to have an old Quarter Horse at the house."

"Then what's the problem?"

"I can ride a horse. I can't *fly* a horse."

"Same basic concept. Just use his mane instead of the reins to guide him when you're in the air."

"Are you crazy?"

"Remember what I said? You're just going to have to trust me tonight. No more questions."

"But as your best friend, I think I'm entitled to at least some—"

"Answers?"

"*Patience*, Rosemary. Patience! Remember what I said? One step at a time. My life-long best friend has just gone from being an unusually athletic girl who drives around in her mom's old Subaru to being a mystical warrior princess who flies around on a winged horse. You've given me a lot to, you know, untangle."

"Speaking of my old mom," I deflected nicely, "wait until you hear her life story."

"Jennifer too?"

"Not technically super-powered like me, but she has her moments."

Joslin shook his head. "I-I don't know, Rosemary. This is all just, just too—"

"Here's how I see it, Joslin," I interrupted. With a step, leap, and swing of my legs, I mounted Crash. "You have a choice. You can either be stuck sitting in uncomfortable silence with Emrys on a boat ride back to your house, or you can be flying above the clouds with your chuckaboo. I trust you'll make the right decision. *Evanescet!*"

My sword stashed away, I encouraged Crash forward with my heels. Crash reared up, flapping his wings, and started down the beach. Increasing his speed, generating lift, slowly, we rose off the ground. I looked back. Joslin was still just standing there. Emrys waited offshore in the Boston Whaler with the engine running.

I lightened my seat, grabbed a fistful of Crash's mane and steered him back toward the island. He reacted quickly, acting like you'd expect a flying horse that had been cooped up in his barn to act. "Are you coming or not?" I shouted as we buzzed the beach.

Emrys had been kind enough to help Joslin onto Raven. She still looked out of sorts. Flying horses had a way of doing that to a person.

"Give me a second!" Joslin shouted back, showing signs of life. "I need some time to get acquainted with my *flying horse*."

"Ha!" I laughed. "You got this, Emrys?"

Emrys nodded with a wave. "Leave it to me, Rosemary."

"Hold on to something, Joslin," I cautioned.

A three-note whistle from Emrys, a smack on Raven's rear, and Joslin was airborne.

Dobbins Island was already a quarter mile behind me as I headed out the mouth of the Magothy River over the Chesapeake Bay. Crash flew close to the Bay's foamy chop, so close that it looked as if he was running on the water's surface. A little too close for my liking. I encouraged him upward again with a slight click of my heels. Crash responded, settling a few thousand feet above the Bay.

A long, exuberant neigh broke the silence of the early night sky. It was growing darker by the minute, but I didn't have to see what was coming my way. I recognized Raven's full-throated exclamation anywhere.

"Look out below!" Joslin shouted.

Raven leveled off next to us. "Welcome," I said.

"This is the best day of my life, Rosemary."

"What did I tell you? Nothing to it. Easier than driving a car."

Just then, Crash eyeballed me.

"I don't think he liked that," Joslin said.

"What did I say?"

"I think Crash can sense you getting cocky."

"Nonsense," I said, thinking about the last time I took Crash for a spin. Emrys's voice rang in my head: *He has a tendency to forget he's flying*. "Hey, chill out, you big dummy." Crash exchanged a series of snorts and neighs with Raven, then eyeballed me again. I squeezed his mane tight, drawing my heels under his ribs. "Don't even think about it."

With a dip of his head, Crash pulled his wings against his body, and turned over on his back into a roll. He plummeted headfirst toward the water like a satellite falling out of orbit.

Raven dove parallel to us. "What do I do?" Joslin yelled.

My smile belied my fear. "Pray."

Joslin avoided the water, pulling Raven up at the last second. I wasn't so lucky. Crash spread his wings like a parachute, which at least softened the landing. He landed upright in the water, his wings still churning. He was submerged all the way to the middle of his neck, which meant I was submerged all the way to my chest.

"Okay poophead, you've had your fun," I said. A quick smack on Crash's butt, and we were free of the Bay's grip. "Now take us up… *please.*"

We ascended quickly, Crash's speed picking up as the water weight wicked off. I was still soaked though, thank you very much.

Raven tucked in next to us. "You okay?" Joslin asked. Raven neighed at Crash. A reprimand maybe?

"I've been drier," I said. "Now try to keep up."

Joslin rested her head against the horse's massive black neck and closed her eyes. After a few seconds, she opened her eyes, sitting upright. Raven began to accelerate. "I have a better idea," she shouted over her shoulder. "How about *you* try to keep up?"

CHAPTER
36

Spending spring break in Mexico was never my idea. When Mabel offered up her condo in Cancun, I accepted her invitation just to make Benz jealous. The saving grace of our vacation was that I got to bring Joslin along. Emrys still wasn't particularly happy with my Father Jules stunt, but to be fair he hadn't exactly been transparent about the old monsignor. Joslin was my buffer. She knew everything about everybody now, but neither my parents nor Emrys were comfortable talking about it around her.

I guess that's why Emrys waited to pull me aside.

"What are you doing?" I asked as Emrys dragged me into the poolside cabana. "Let go of me."

Emrys drew the curtain shut. "We need to talk."

"I'd prefer not to. Oh good, food. I'm starving!"

With Mabel loaning us her condo free of charge, Mom and Dad could afford to rent a cabana for the week. They even splurged on the optional catering. This morning's cabana spread was comprised of a continental breakfast of pastries and fruit. I grabbed a bunch of grapes and popped an inappropriate number of them in my mouth.

"Rosemary," Emrys cautioned, "Alan's revelation about the Triton Orb and Vivian means we need to be more careful, not less. You bringing Benny and now Joslin into this complicates everything."

I pointed at Emrys, my mouth still full of grapes. The conversation stalled awkwardly. I swallowed the last bite of fruit. "I owed Joslin the truth, something that's been in short supply in my life. And I didn't bring Father Jules into this, *you* did. Sixty years ago. When you went on a broken-hearted walkabout and confided in a total stranger."

"What are you two yapping about?" Joslin barged in on us. Her speech sounded a little slurred, no doubt courtesy of the half-dozen Alabama frat boys who kept buying her watered-down cocktails at the poolside bar.

"The usual," I said.

"Oh," Joslin said. For the moment at least, she didn't yet share my parents' and Emrys's discomfort in talking about the mythical-turned-everyday world. Maybe it was just easier for her to disconnect because she was still the normal one in the group.

The thought of Joslin being the normal one in the group, in *any* group, made me laugh a little. I tossed her an orange. "Think fast!"

The orange flew by Joslin through the slit in the cabana curtain. "You going to get that?" she asked me, a frozen margarita in her left hand, a cocktail napkin embossed with the resort's name—*Summer Winds*—in her right hand.

"Let the lizards have it," I said, in reference to the spiny-tailed iguanas that freely roamed the resort grounds. I nodded at her tall frosted glass of yellow liquid. "Starting a little early, aren't we?"

Joslin smiled. At sixteen, she was still two years under the legal drinking age in Mexico, but neither the frat boys nor the bartenders seemed to care, and Mom and Dad had gone for a day sail. "When in Rome, Rosemary."

I hadn't gone full bathing beauty like Joslin just yet, and my two-piece wasn't nearly as cute as hers. She wore a wrap, I wore a mid-thigh length black cover-up. My iPhone vibrated in my pocket with a text alert.

It was Benz. We hadn't spoken in two days, other than to let each other know we'd arrived safely at our destinations. Why was he texting and not calling me? I missed his voice.

Through no fault but our own, the cabana had turned into party central. I'd have felt guilty about the frat boys buying Joslin and me alcohol, if they hadn't picked the breakfast buffet clean. Emrys had already ditched us. When I asked him where he was going, he said, "For a walk," which I took to mean stewing in a dark corner of the resort about my life choices.

I left the cabana about an hour after Emrys. I couldn't decide what was more annoying—how every other song the boys played was by Luke Bryan or how Joslin pretended to be stupid just so they'd keep flirting with her. Joslin was drunk. I didn't even know if I could *get* drunk with my Lust Borne metabolism. I'd been tipsy enough at the random house or boat party to know alcohol could affect me, but the last time I touched anything besides church wine was the previous summer, before everything. What about now?

After my last text exchange with Benz, I was prepared to test-drive my new Lust Borne alcohol tolerance. Sitting alone at the poolside bar, I raised my right index finger. "One Dark 'n' Stormy, please."

"Miss, I'm going to need to see some identification."

One of the poolside waiters, or possibly the manager, had snuck up on me while I wasn't looking. The only ID I had on me was my driver's license, which clearly stated I was underage. My chest seized up in a panic, the lump in my throat restricting my speech. "There seems to be some confusion, sir," I said, not looking at him. "I-I'm just getting this for my mother."

"For your mother, huh?" His voice reeked of skepticism. "What about the other six Dark 'n' Stormies those Alabama meatheads bought you?"

Alabama meatheads? I was still trying to be respectful, not hazarding so much as a peek at my accuser. But what kind of resort manager uses the word "meatheads"? Slowly, I cast my eyes upward. Flip-flops? Odd. Chubbies-brand swim trunks? Wait a second. *Shirtless?*

The man was no cop. He was no man either. He was a boy, a boy I knew. And I'd recognize that penny bronze skin and woolly black head of hair anywhere. "Tyrell St. John?"

Tyrell shook his head in astonishment. "What are the odds?"

"*Senorita,*" the bartender said, sliding my freshly mixed Dark 'n' Stormy down the bar.

I caught the glass, nodding. "*Gracias.*"

"Never figured you for a Dark 'n' Stormy girl," Tyrell said. The bartender used an off-brand of ginger beer, not as sweet as my Barritts, but I managed.

"Couple things," I said. "One, I drink my ginger beer with rum instead of vodka because Moscow Mules are for day-drinking Severna Park housewives who don't like the taste of alcohol. And two, what in the hell are you doing here?"

"My mom and dad have been dragging me down to Cancun for as long as I can remember," Tyrell answered. "Usually we do one of those all-inclusive places. Thought we'd check out *Summer Winds* this year. You?"

I tried to mouth the straw without looking down at my drink, nearly stabbing myself in the eye. "Friend of the family owns a condo."

"Quite the hookup," Tyrell said. "And like I told you before, call me Ty."

Ty was trying to make small talk. The last thing I wanted was to make small talk. "Ty, I'm sure you mean well, But I'm going through some…some stuff."

"I've been told I'm a good listener." Ty sat in the bar stool next to me. "And besides, I got nowhere else to be."

I could usually guess early on in a conversation with someone whether their interest in me was genuine or driven by their own personal agenda. Watching my parents hiding so much from each other, I now saw where that skill came from. Ty was being persistent, but I knew he could be trusted. Why? Based on what? Just a feeling I guess. Benz trusted him, so there was that.

"You want to know what's bugging me? See for yourself." I handed Ty my iPhone.

He scanned the screen. "What am I looking at here exactly?"

"A conversation between me and my boyfriend."

Ty set my phone face down on the bar. "I don't think a private text exchange between you and Coker is any of my business, Rosemary."

His respect for my privacy almost caused me to overlook the drink Ty was holding in his opposite hand. I nodded at the Moscow Mule.

"You got me," he said. "I'm secretly a day-drinking Severna Park housewife who doesn't like the taste of alcohol."

"We all have our faults." I picked up my phone, shoved it in his face. "Just look at the one message at the top."

"*Prom?*" Ty squinted. "That's all Coker texted you was the word 'prom' and a question mark?"

"So you get it?"

"I think so. Maybe?"

"Heather Loheide!"

Ty looked perplexed by my random name vomit. "Who?"

"She's a senior at American Martyr. Her girlfriend changed out the morning announcements one day last week, knowing our headmaster reads the script without even paying attention to what it says."

"Her *girlfriend?*" Ty mused. "How progressive."

"It was quite the scandal," I said. "Father Jules said over the PA, 'Today is Fajita Friday, boys and girls. Your last chance to eat meat on Friday until after Easter. Make sure to ask Heather Loheide when you see her if she'll go to prom with Denise Govan.'"

"I get it. You want the grand gesture."

"Yes!" I affirmed. "Or, maybe. I don't know. Benz has got a lot on his mind—graduation, college, adulthood. I'm a reasonable girlfriend, at least when I'm not inventing worst-case scenarios in which he dumps me. I can cut him some slack. But he hasn't seen me for close to four days, and his grand gesture was to text me, *'Prom'?*"

"Pretty lame," Ty affirmed.

"I don't know if lame is the right word." I finished off Dark 'n' Stormy number seven. "More like confusing. Got any insight?"

"On Benz?

"On relationships from a guy's perspective. Benz tells me he loves me, that he never wants to be away from me. Then he decides out of the blue to go to college in Georgia."

Ty couldn't contain his enthusiasm. "Benz got into Life U?"

"Not helping," I said. "Then Benz gets my name tattooed on his chest, only to ask me to prom as an afterthought."

"He tattooed his name on your chest?"

"Still not helping," I repeated. "I realize my parents' relationship is so dysfunctional that I wouldn't know a normal relationship if it fell on my head. But does any of this sound normal to you?"

"You're the least normal person I know, Rosemary." Ty winked, nodding. "And I mean that as a compliment."

"Thanks," I said. What was happening? Was Tyrell St. John flirting with me?

"Have you answered him yet?"

Okay, good. Back to small talk. He was just being nice. "No."

"What do you want to tell him?"

"Yes, of course."

"Or maybe?"

Ty was a smooth talker. Too smooth. But his wordplay deserved at least an acknowledgment. "I see what you did there."

"I was hoping you would," Ty said, standing. He threw a handful of bills on the bar, flagging down the bartender then pointing his index and pinkie fingers at the two glasses, indicating he was buying another round. "How about we make a deal, you and me? Let's agree to make this week a drama-free zone. You don't talk about Benz and his tattoos, I don't talk about my parents making me spend my last two years of high school surrounded by a bunch of strangers. You want your boyfriend to give a shit, and I want to stay in Connecticut, the only home I've ever known, surrounded by the only friends I've ever known."

"Hey, you'll know me when you move to Maryland," I said, gently backhanding his forearm. It was the smallest of consolations, and I could see it in Ty's eyes. A boy as nice as Ty had too many friends to count. A boy as good looking as Ty had to have a girl back home he was saying goodbye to. And in typical Rosemary fashion, I had made this conversation all about me.

A boy as good looking as Ty. The Dark 'n' Stormies were doing all the talking now. Newsflash: I can get drunk!

I noticed Ty's looks when we first met after the rugby game, when Benz introduced us. I'm in love but I'm not blind. Ty is hot, but in a different way than Benz. He's more striking than hot— unapproachably attractive, if that's a thing. If you saw me and Benz together, you'd probably think something like, *there goes a cute high school couple.* If I walked into a room on Ty's arm, you'd ask, *how'd she snag him?*

I extended my hand as a peace offering. "No more talk of Benz and his tattoos or moving to Maryland. Deal."

"Excellent," Ty said, shaking my hand. "In celebration of our agreement, what are you doing tomorrow morning?"

His touch was…a surprise. Warm and strong. Strong enough for even me to feel. Exciting. I prayed my sunburn hid the blushing.

"I don't know," I pondered. "What am I doing tomorrow morning?"

"Watching the Six Nations Rugby final *with me* over breakfast."

His emphasis on "with me" was practically smoldering. He moved quickly from a handshake to a breakfast date. Too quickly.

"Not my first choice," I said. "What is Six Nations Rugby?"

"An annual rugby tournament played by England, France, Ireland, Italy, Scotland, and Wales. Kind of a big deal."

"If you say so," I said. "Where are we watching this tournament?"

Ty pointed over my shoulder. "The Swinger's Bar, between the two main pools, by the bridge."

"Excuse me?" I asked.

"You know," Ty said. "The bar with the wooden benches hanging by ropes instead of bar stools."

"You mean the *Swing* Bar?"

"Oh." Ty blushed. "That name makes more sense, now that I hear it out loud."

"Who are we rooting for?"

"England of course," Ty said.

"Why?"

"I'm English, at least on my father's side. St. John is an English surname. My mother's side of the family is admittedly a lot more Technicolor. That is where my family down in Maryland comes from—slaves, Piscataway Indians—although most people just see a Black kid when they look at me." His face darkened, eyes downcast in a glare at no one. "Most people annoy me."

"Whoa," I said. "Is that something we need to unpack right now?"

"Maybe later," Ty said. "But you don't have anything to worry about. Like I said, you're the least normal person I know. You're not most people."

I waved him off. "Please. You've met me twice. I'm not the person you think I am. I don't even like rugby. Benz has tried to explain the rules to me, but I just don't have the patience to learn."

Ty smiled. He reached for my hand with his comparatively massive mitt and gave me an encouraging squeeze. "Maybe Coker is the one who needs a little more patience."

I jerked my hand away. "Stop it, Ty."

"Stop what?" he asked.

"Flirting with me."

"Is that what I'm doing?" he asked, his hand to his chest, as if he was offended by the accusation. "Flirting?"

"Oh, Ty." Elbow on the bar, my chin resting on my palm, I shook my head in judgement.

"What?" he asked.

"I fear for the girls of American Martyr next year," I said.

"Why?" Ty shrugged. He appeared to be legitimately unaware of his magnetism. But maybe that was part of the act.

I poked Ty in the chest, hard enough for him to notice. "If this is you flirting by accident, I'd hate to see how charming you are when you actually try to be."

Ty rubbed his chest. The look on his face was somewhere between shock and amusement, like he was saying to me, "*Ouch, that hurt... can you do it again, please?*"

"I have a better idea than watching men play kids' games on television," I said.

"What's that?" Ty asked.

"How about you join us on a sightseeing trip to the Mayan ruins at Tulum?"

"I love Tulum," Ty said. "But who's the 'us' I'm joining on this trip?"

"My parents and my two chuckaboos."

"Chuckaboos?" Ty asked, eyebrows raised.

"My two best friends, Joslin and Emrys."

"The couple hanging out with you by the pool before the meatheads showed up?"

"The couple?" I asked. "Hardly. Emrys is sort of our perpetual third wheel. Joslin's got a boy back at American Martyr, and I have, well, Benz of course."

"*Well*, Benz?" Ty pondered, eyes widening below arched eyebrows.

"You're doing it again," I warned.

The bartender handed us two fresh ginger beer cocktails as Ty smirked. "Doing what?"

"Flirting."

What the hell was my deal? Ten minutes ago, my stomach was in knots thinking about Benz. Then this new boy waltzed into my field of view looking beautiful and saying nice things, and I was back to being what exactly?

A teenage girl. That's what.

"Hey Siri..." I instructed, maintaining eye contact with Ty. "Text Benz Cooke."

"*I'm on it*," Siri said to me her familiar robotic voice. "*What do you want to say?*"

"Maybe," I replied.

CHAPTER

37

It was raining.

In hindsight, I should have seen this coming. The guilt began to creep in the moment Ty accepted my invitation. When the skies opened up the following morning and drenched the Yucatan peninsula in its first measurable rainfall in nearly six months, it felt like I was being punished.

"You're not being punished, Rosemary," Mom said.

"Sure I am," I countered.

Mom and Dad rented a Land Rover and insisted on driving us. I agreed only after they promised to stay far away from us when we got to the ruins. The trip from Cancun to Tulum would take us a little over eighty minutes. Mom and Dad sat in the front, Joslin and I in the middle seat, while Ty and Emrys squeezed into the third row.

Just outside Tulum, Ty and Joslin spotted a taco truck, which was where they stood at the moment, just beyond earshot. They couldn't hear what Emrys and I were arguing about, just as we couldn't hear them haggling with the food truck vendor.

Something about Mexico had flipped the script again with Emrys and Joslin—the booze, the walking around all day in glorified underwear. In Emrys's defense, Joslin wasn't trying particularly hard to dissuade him. It was almost like the more she knew, the more intrigued she was. Emrys had gone from being the weird kid, to the fascinating foreign exchange student with passable line-dancing skills, back to the weird kid, and finally to the mysterious teenage wizard. The fact that he was 900 years old didn't seem to matter to Joslin; if anything, it was a turn on.

"She's kind of amazing," Emrys said. "You know that, right?"

"She's also kind of jail bait."

He shook his head. "What if I want to be jail bait too?"

"Excuse me, *Merlin?*" Mom chimed in, purposely calling him by his older name.

Emrys gave it right back. "What part didn't you get, *Guinevere?*"

"The part where you said you wanted to be sixteen," I replied, noticing Dad staring at me in the rearview mirror. "Dad, tell Mom to stay out of this."

"Noted." Dad nodded, turning to Mom. "Jennifer, stay out of this."

"You don't think Joslin is hot?" Emrys continued. "Because everything in me says that she is."

"*Hot?*" I asked. "Are you hearing yourself talk, Emrys? Joslin is your friend, not your girlfriend. And she has a boyfriend."

Emrys spread his arms, palms upturned as he looked at his hands. "What else am I supposed to do?"

"I don't know, but not *this*. Sixteen sucks. Why would you want a do-over?"

"I don't want a do-over, Rosemary. But can't I just be someone else for a few days?"

And so, the yo-yo continued. I thought he'd gotten it under control lately, not bouncing around so much between man and boy, between mourning widower and hormonal teenager. How could I be his babysitter when I wasn't ready for him to stop being mine? If Emrys was insistent on being a teenager, maybe I needed to treat him like one.

"Andrew's a decent guy, you know," I said. "He loves Joslin and doesn't deserve any of this."

"You're one to talk," he shot back.

"Meaning?"

"Meaning I've spent the last six months respecting your feelings, giving you your space and letting you be boy crazy when you should've been training. And all it takes is some guy buying you a drink for you to forget Benz even exists?"

"Um, tacos anyone?" Joslin stood next to the Land Rover, a grease-stained brown paper bag in each hand. Ty trailed a little behind. "And maybe ix-nay the aining-tray talk," she said under her breath.

The rain eased up to a light drizzle. Ty stood behind Joslin holding four ice-cold bottles of mandarin-flavored Jarritos. He nodded at Emrys and me. "Sounds like you two need a timeout."

"I have an idea," Joslin said. "Rosemary, you and Ty both ordered carnitas, while Emrys and I both got the chicken. Why don't we switch seats? You split the bag of carnitas tacos with Ty in the middle, and Emrys and I sit in back with our bag of chicken tacos."

Dammit, Joslin, I thought. The whole point of the Land Rover seating chart was to keep me away from Ty St. John.

By the time we arrived at Tulum, the rain had started back up. The upside to the bad weather was that we had the place all to ourselves.

Mom and Dad picked up everyone's entry fee, and, as promised, made themselves scarce. A couple reenactors lingered around for some tips: a man in full Mayan tribal garb, including an elaborate peacock-feathered headdress and a cape made from a jaguar's pelt; a barely clothed woman tattooed from head to toe and draped in an albino Burmese python. The woman invited us to hold the python. Ty and I posed for a picture, the snake wrapping around both of us. Our smiles masked our terror, but we still paid her twenty-five dollars for the photo.

As ruins go, Tulum was hardly awe-inspiring. Not the massive Pyramid of the Sun in Teotihuacan, over by Mexico City. Certainly not the Gizan pyramids of Egypt or the Parthenon in Athens. But what it lacked in size it made up for in preservation. Surrounded on three sides by limestone walls—Tulum is literally Mayan for "wall"—and on the fourth side by the Caribbean, you could still almost imagine it as a working fortress. The *Castillo*, or castle, perched on the edge of a four-story cliff overlooking the Caribbean coast was like an ancient middle finger, taunting the Spanish conquistadors to do their worst. Unfortunately, that's exactly what they did.

We made our way down to the beach. This was the real visual attraction of Tulum—the contrast between the ruins, the limestone cliffs capped by the green vegetation, the sandy beach, and rolling waves. The sand looked too white and the water too blue to be real. Fortunately, we'd all worn our swimsuits.

I sat in the shallows, the water just above my waist. A flock of seagulls flew overhead.

Ty sat down next to me in the water. He nodded at Emrys and Joslin running down the beach. Emrys was chasing Joslin with a baby iguana in his hand while Joslin giggled and screamed playfully. "Those two."

"Don't say it," I begged.

"They're really terrible at not being a couple."

"Or, you know, say it."

"How about you?" Ty asked.

I threw his question back in his lap. "How about me?"

"You figure things out with Coker?"

"What happened to the guy who wouldn't read my texts for fear of invading my privacy?"

"He's sitting at the Swinger's Bar watching rugby and wondering why a pretty girl stood him up."

"The *Swing* Bar, Ty!"

"Sorry!" Ty said, grinning. The air between us, tense with our inconvenient but plainly obvious chemistry, seemed to dissipate. "Rosemary, I—"

"Me first," I jumped in. "Just in case you decide to make a fool of yourself and say something you can't take back and I can't unhear."

Ty bowed. "By all means."

"You're a sweet guy, a *really* sweet guy. And I can relate to what you're going through back home, to seeing your world taken away from you and feeling like you don't have much of a say in it. But I love Benz. I'm *in love* with Benz. Crazy, insane, dumb love. We've been through a lot together. For me to sit here and lead you on while Benz is stuck in a dorm with a bunch of smelly rugby players is not fair to him and not fair to you. I'm calling him tonight, I'm apologizing for being petty and mean, and I'm saying to him, "Yes, Benz, I will go to prom with you. And I love you.""

"You know…" Ty sat there for a few seconds, not finding the words. He dropped his chin and leaned a little too much into my personal space. "Coker is one lucky dude."

I looked away.

"Fresh coconut water for the *señor* and *señorita?*"

We both jumped, startled by the voice behind us. Tattooed python lady stood without her snake, holding a green coconut in each hand instead. With their pulp-white caps and straws poking out from the centers, they looked like little green monks wearing skullcaps and hairpins.

Ty patted his swim trunks. "Those look delicious, but I spent my last twenty-five dollars on the snake picture."

"No, no, no." Tattooed python lady said, shaking her head. "Free. On the house."

"*Gracias,*" we replied, both of us standing to accept her generous refreshments.

Tattooed python lady made her exit. "What do we toast to?" I asked.

"To saying goodbye to old friends and making new ones," Ty answered.

"Well said, Mr. St. John. Well said." We each sipped on our coconuts. It was warm but soothing on my parched throat. It felt weird going down though, tingly. I knew something was wrong when it hit my stomach, which was also when Ty fell to the beach unconscious.

My knees felt rubbery, my vision blurring with each passing second. "*Gladio!*" I shouted, summoning Excalibur with what would likely be my last coherent syllables. Someone had poisoned the coconut water. But who? Who knew we were here?

I had my answer right before I passed out. Out of the corner of my eye, I saw it.

A giant osprey swooping down from the sky and ripping a seagull in half.

I woke up in a strange bed on a dirty old mattress. I was still dressed, but my hands and feet were shackled and chained to the four bedposts. My prison was an abandoned beach house—vines creeping through glassless windows, door frames without doors, air conditioning units and anything of value looted, every inch of wood or plaster in some stage of decay.

"Good afternoon, Lady Banson." A man's voice surrounded me, like it was coming from inside the walls. To suggest the voice was bellowing imparted a menace that wasn't quite there, if only because of the pronounced lisp.

Ladies and gentlemen, the Big Bad has just entered the room.

I'd presumed a lot about what Mordred would look like, and I wasn't too far off. Young, only three or four years older than me, he had a slightly androgynous look. He was tall, lean, with long hair and mischievous eyes. His distinctive feature was a crooked-toothed overbite that protruded jarringly from his face.

"Give that back," I said, eyeing the scabbard held fast to his waist.

Mordred tapped the pommel of his sword. "This is not your sword, Lust Borne. This is Excalibur's brother."

"His brother?"

"You can call him 'Clarent.' People often confuse the two swords. This is what you probably know as the 'Sword in the Stone,' the Sword of Kings. Excalibur is the Sword of Power. It's right there on the bed next to you."

Excalibur ran parallel to the left side of my body, well out of reach. I flailed, jerking my fists and feet in vain.

"Arlynn, what would you even do with Excalibur? All it seems you and Merlin have done thus far is waste its potential."

"Let me out of these things and I'll show you what I would do with it. And my name is Rosemary!"

His cloak was long and broad, a shimmering dark blue clasped on one shoulder with a circular brooch bearing the three crowns of the Pendragon crest. He was shirtless, wearing gas-pipes ending in boots. "You can stop wasting your precious energy," he cautioned. "In your current state, you aren't getting out of those chains."

"My current state?" I remembered the coconut water and then the osprey. The back of my throat was dry. I lunged forward in vain, the chains pulled tight but very secure. "What did you do to me?"

"I dispensed into your bloodstream a generous dose of snake venom. A magical potion made with snake venom, that is. There's something about snake venom that the Lust Borne can't handle. It weakens us, makes us more mortal than mortals. The preferred venom is that of an Adder, the only poisonous snake indigenous to England. But Maryland's native Copperheads and Timber Rattlesnakes work almost as well. In Mexico, I made due with the venom of the Fer-De-Lance, which I have to say really knocked you out."

"Did you say Copperheads and Timber Rattlers?"

"I did indeed. Why?"

"No reason," I said.

"Those were the ones your mother taught you to kill, weren't they? How is Guinevere these days? Still as beautiful as father describes?"

"You should know." I lunged again. "Where is Emrys? What have you done with my friends?"

"I assume you noticed the osprey?"

"Yes," I affirmed. "Barely."

"I let Vivian handle them of course."

"But how did you know I was in Mexico in the first place? The only one outside my family and friends who knew were we were going was..."

No, I thought suddenly. *It couldn't be. She didn't.*

"I wouldn't be too hard on Morgan le Fay," Mordred cautioned. "I left her little choice but to tell us where you were after I enlisted a giant to hold her stepmother as collateral."

"Her stepmother?"

"I abducted Terpsichore, the Mother of Sirens. I will owe those ladies quite a few favors for this."

"Where are my friends? Where are my parents? Why am I tied up? What are you going to do—"

"So many questions, Lust Borne," Mordred mocked. "Maybe this will offer you some insight." He reached beneath his cloak, producing a familiar glass globe.

"Where did you get that?"

Mordred twisted the Triton Orb around to show me that it was uncapped, then turned it upside down to reveal it had been emptied of its contents. He licked his lips. "Very refreshing, and an exceedingly generous gesture from your father. He's granted me immortality, and in return I will not be taking you back with me to Camelot."

It was over. Dad's gamble had paid off.

Mordred paced the room. "Something on your mind, Lady Banson?"

"If the Orb worked, then why are you still here?"

"I wasn't going to let you go just so you could turn around and kill me. You're young, inexperienced, and completely overmatched, but you're still Lust Borne."

"What if I promised not to lay a hand on you?"

"Tempting, but how gullible do you think I am?"

"Dead serious," I implored. "Say goodbye to your stepsister, jump in your time machine, and leave me to live my life."

"Stepsister?" Mordred asked, tilting his head.

"Whatever it is you want to call me. You're the son of Arthur and Morgause, I'm the daughter of Lancelot and Guinevere, and since Guinevere was married to Arthur that makes us sort of step-siblings."

"I think someone has been misleading you, Lust Borne."

"Hate to break it you, but that really doesn't narrow things down. You basically just described my entire life."

"I need to sit down for this." Mordred surveyed the room for a chair. "Do not get up. I'll come to you."

"Is there any chance you're going to come right out and tell me whatever it is you're going to tell me, or am I going to have to endure another tedious monologue?"

Mordred seemed entertained by my bravado, or at least intrigued enough by my questions to humor me with answers. Dragging a wooden chair from the corner of the room to my bedside, Mordred sat down in the chair backward. His legs spread, he rested his forearms atop the back of the chair.

"I must say, Lust Borne, you are keenly smart for a girl. I can see why Merlin is so taken with you"

I let the "for a girl" comment slide, but not the other comment. "Taken with me? We're just good friends."

"That's not what Vivian and Morgan le Fay tell me. No matter.

I am trying to compliment you and especially Lancelot on your intuitiveness. In giving me the Orb, he correctly assessed my motivations. I do covet immortality. I do covet power. And I want absolutely nothing to do with fatherhood."

"Then what are we doing here?" I asked. "Why confront me?"

"If it had been up to me, I would have approached you years ago and dispensed with all these histrionics."

"Exactly my point."

"We did not know precisely where you were until a few weeks ago."

"Who's this 'we' you're talking about?"

"Morgause and Vivian, my mother and aunt of course. Thankfully, Aunt Vivian tired of her games and finally told us about her continuing association with your father. You also have a lot of associations of your own that precluded an earlier public engagement."

"You mean the Knights of Leo?"

Mordred nodded. "And Emrys's friend, Atli Saevarsson."

"You're afraid of a one-star chef, an eighty-year-old priest, and an Icelandic record store owner?"

"If only that is what they were," Mordred cautioned.

More secrets. Terrific.

"Then I ask again, why go through all this trouble? Go forge your own path. Be the king of your kingdom, and let me just be the queen of my prom."

"You really do not know?" Mordred asked. "They never told you?"

"Know what?"

"It was not my idea to marry you or to make you the mother of my child. It was the wish of my king."

"Arthur?"

Mordred nodded. "I was originally supposed to come here, under my father's orders, to bring you back to Camelot and put you on the throne as my queen."

"And now you don't have to." I raised my hands, offering Mordred my upturned wrists. "Take these chains off of me, walk away, and we can forget this ever happened."

"You are missing the whole point, Rosemary. It was my king's intention that I serve at your *side*, not above you. It is your birthright as the sole heir to the throne. You are *not* my stepsister, you are my half-sister. You are the only child of Guinevere and Arthur. Lancelot is not your father."

CHAPTER
38

"Welcome back."

"How long have I been out?" I asked, my eyes opening slowly to the light. I was hoping everything had been a dream. That I was in my bed being told by my mother I was late for school. Or better yet, that I was lying on Benz's bed, talking about what I was wearing to prom.

Well, I was lying on a bed at least.

"I thought you would never awaken from your induced slumber," Mordred said.

"You're telling me I fainted?"

"I assumed you at least had a notion of your heritage. How is it you think that you came by your powers?"

"Emrys told me that for whatever reason, my mother, as Arthur's wife, fulfilled the Lust Borne Prophecy. Guilt by association, so to speak."

"And you just accepted that explanation and moved on?"

"Well, no. I said to Emrys, 'So technically, I'm not a Pendragon. I'm more Lust Borne Adjacent.' And he just blew me off."

"The Lust Borne Prophecy is a blood curse, a curse bound by direct bloodlines and bad—"

"Intentions," I interrupted. "Yeah, I got that part."

My clearheaded engagement with Mordred belied my horror.

Blacking out was long overdue, and the revelation of my royal lineage was the tipping point. My shock at being told the only father I've ever known was not my father converged with my fear of Mordred. My body was shutting down, but I knew I had to keep him talking.

"I have to say, I'm a little disappointed in the honeymoon suite."

"You're the only full-blooded child of King Arthur and Queen Guinevere, and all you care to do is comment on the décor?" Mordred was oblivious to my banter. "The current state of this domicile is due to a violent storm that wiped the place out years ago. I believe people in this century name their acts of God, yes? Hurricane Wilma was this storm's designation. There are dozens of destitute bungalows just like this one, and we are the only ones here for miles around."

His message to me was clear: *No one is coming for you, Rosemary.* My message to him was, "So, no room service then?"

"Oh, Rosemary." Mordred stood up, spinning the chair off to the side as he draped his blue cloak over the back of it. He removed his sword belt, carefully placing his scabbard on the seat. He crawled into the bed and straddled me, reaching down and gripping Excalibur with his right hand. "*The moon shall be from whence the sea consumes the fallen son. The lust borne tide, thy will subside, the course of Avalon run. Her fertile song naught overlong shall play then play no more. By the blade, the bed is made. The kingdom at your door.*"

"By the blade, the bed is made." I recited the words aloud, as if that could somehow make it less horrific.

"It is almost like a song. Do you not agree? Perhaps, it could be our love song."

Now Mordred was the one engaging in idle small talk, but his intentions were different than mine. He wasn't stalling. He was drawing things out. He was psychologically torturing me. All that was left for me to do was beg.

"Please, Mordred. You don't have to do this."

"Oh, I am afraid that I do. In hindsight, I was a fool to trust your retrieval to mere underlings. The incubus and faerie Vivian sent on my behalf—they all could have easily killed you. But thankfully, you exceeded our expectations. In the end, I found the immortality I have so desperately craved, which means I can outlive Arthur and ascend to the throne. For that, you have my eternal gratitude. But why let this sudden turn of events deny us our destiny, our one moment of passion? My gift to you is the privilege of sharing my bed and then a quick and painless death. All Arthur will ever know is that I tried to retrieve you, but unfortunately you resisted and were accidentally killed in the ensuing battle."

Easing the tip of Excalibur between my bikini strap and clavicle bone, Mordred flicked his wrist ever so slightly, cutting my shoulder strap. The blade nicked my clavicle in the process. Blood ran down my bare shoulder, staining the bed sheet. My lips parted to speak, but no words came out. I felt like a ghost, hovering in a far corner of the bedroom as I watched a strange young man crawl into the bed of a fearful young woman. I was a spectator, not a participant. None of this was happening to me. It was happening to her.

Mordred tossed Excalibur playfully over my head, like a toy, transferring it from his right hand to his left. He placed Excalibur to my right, on the side of the bed. The Sword of Power ran not quite parallel to my body this time, still out of reach of my hand but tapering toward my feet. He stroked Excalibur's blade. "We shall let the sword watch."

Mordred leaned down, licked the blood off my bare shoulder. I could smell him, a sour stench of sweat and body odor. He reached down with his right hand, toward my waistline, his fingers brushing the elastic of my bikini bottoms. My abs tensed up, my back curving downward into the bed, as if I could still somehow magically leave this place.

This was happening. Mordred was about to rape me.

I was on the verge of blacking out again, my body disconnecting from reality. I'd lost all hope. The only thing I could feel was the cold steel of Excalibur touching my bare right foot.

Hold on. My foot was touching Excalibur?

"You must remain in contact with the sword," Emrys had told me. *"You need to be touching it with some body part, any body part, to make it disappear."* It was the asterisk to Excalibur. The goddamn asterisk!

I made sure my foot was firmly touching the blade. And then I closed my eyes.

"Evanescet!" I screamed through my tears. *"Gladio!"*

Right before Mordred slipped his hands down my bikini

bottoms, the bright white light flashed twice. As the light dimmed and Mordred opened his eyes, his smile changed…to something else.

"*Aaaarrrrrggghhhh!*"

His shriek soothed me, snapped me back to reality. I'd carefully positioned my wrist when I summoned Excalibur so that it would materialize not only in my hand but also inside Mordred.

The sword went through his side and clean out the back.

Mordred rolled off the bed in agony, his shrieks turning to long groans. Judging by his cries, the wound might not have been as clean as I first suspected. God willing, I nicked an internal organ or two. He somehow managed to drag himself to his knees while grabbing the grip of Excalibur with both hands. Blood pouring from the wound, his face tensed up as he breathed in and out, preparing himself. And then, with a violent tug and a shriek even louder than the first one, he pulled Excalibur out of his body, dropping it on the ground.

I knew how the Lust Borne healing factor worked. I only had minutes until Mordred's delirium subsided and the anger took over.

Or seconds.

Mordred stood, holding his hand to his side. "You should not have done that."

"Didn't anyone tell you?" I asked. "I don't give it up on the first date."

Mordred reached for his sword on the chair. He removed Clarent from its scabbard. "I really do not care for you, least of all if you live or die. All I care about is our father. I have spent my whole life trying to honor him. This was to be my crowning gift, the moment I proved my worth as his son and Camelot's future sovereign."

"First off, he's *your* father, not *our* father. And your *gift* to Arthur was raping his daughter?"

"Like I said, I really do not care for you." Mordred raised Clarent above his head, steadying his feet. He leapt at me. I followed the white arc of Mordred's sword stroke.

And then it stopped. No, it was blocked. By a narwhal tusk.

"Hello, Emrys," I said.

"Working up a sweat?" he asked, trying to lighten the mood.

I appreciated the gesture. "Kind of wish I wasn't."

Emrys closed his eyes. He didn't quite look the part of a wizard in his button-down shirt, swim trunks, and Vans, but I always thought his narwhal tusk was cool. The yellow gemstone in his staff started to glow. He raised his hand at Mordred. "*Incendiarius extitisti*!" he commanded.

I thought I smelled something burning, but it was fleeting.

The Latin told me it was a fire-summoning spell. At least it tried to be one. But Emrys wasn't Merlin anymore. And Mordred laughed at him.

"That all you have for me?" Mordred giggled more than laughed, a reminder that at only nineteen or twenty years of age he was still more of a boy than a man.

"No," Emrys said, not missing a beat. He swung his staff around like a baseball bat, tagging Mordred across the face. Turning to me, Emrys crouched down and retrieved Excalibur off the ground. "Rosemary, care to join us?"

With four quick swipes of Excalibur, Emrys struck the shackles on my wrists and ankles, cutting me from my chains. As I stood up from the bed, Emrys handed me my sword and my cover-up. He was sometimes a weirdo, but he was always a gentleman.

"Hey, Mordred," Emrys said. "I brought you something." He tossed one of Vivian's taloned gauntlets at his feet.

"What did you do to Aunt Vivian?" Mordred asked.

"Kicked her ass," Emrys wheezed.

I heard the blood in his lungs. Seeing my friend up close, I could tell his fight with Vivian hadn't been an easy one. He was in bad shape. There were too many entry and exit wounds to count. I wanted to be mad at him—for Arthur, for everything—but that was a fight for another day. "Emrys, I—"

I caught him in mid-sentence as he dropped to one knee. Kneeling in a pool of his own blood, he wouldn't be much help to me from here on out. His breathing was labored, his face swollen and dirty, his eyes bloodshot.

"You were right," Emrys wheezed.

"I'm right about most things," I said.

"I mean about Mordred." Emrys spit out half-dollar globs of blood between sentences. "He does have terrible teeth."

As Emrys winked, a strange calm descended over me. This was

more than just an offhand, juvenile wisecrack. He wanted me to know that he was fighting alongside me as my dearest friend, not my wizard.

"Now why don't you do us all favor," Emrys added.

"What's that?" I said.

"Go knock those terrible teeth out of Mordred's ugly, weasel face, and then let's go home."

My opening offensive was obvious, too obvious. Mordred blocked me cleanly. Stepping to the side, he grabbed my sword arm in an attempt to disarm me, distracting me just enough that I didn't see the pommel of his sword in his other hand before he smashed me in the face.

I stumbled backward. Mordred pressed the advantage with a series of attacks. Not surprisingly, he was a near-perfect fencer. My deflection of his initial lunge was about the only positive move I could muster. He avoided my parry, then cut me once, twice, three times—across my sword arm, my chest, and then my opposite arm. Mordred was stronger than his svelte appearance indicated—he was Lust Borne, after all—but he didn't need it. His fencing technique was balletic. He knew how to transfer his body weight to give force to his attack as opposed to relying too much on arm strength. He never retreated backwards, only sideways.

My technique wasn't nearly as graceful. I had the training, but unlike Mordred it could be measured in months, not years, so I still leaned heavily on instinct. I was nauseated, seeing stars, and most likely concussed.

Mordred took another swipe at me, which I managed to block and counterattack with a left jab to his midsection. I wasn't the technician Mordred was, especially with a concussion, but I was still fast. Finally, Excalibur found its mark. Just a small cut though. I wasted too much time admiring my handiwork and not enough time anticipating the next move. Mordred stabbed me in the abdomen, burying Clarent in me, almost to the hilt.

I fell to the floor. The pain was excruciating. All my discipline and training fell away. The metallic taste of my own blood flooded my mouth.

Mordred was butchering me.

From a fetal position, I somehow managed to deflect the killing blow and knock Mordred off his feet with a sidekick. It was a desperate move—buying me some time, delaying the inevitable. I didn't know how much longer I could stay conscious, let alone fight.

"Hey Mordred, how about picking on someone your own age for a change?"

Emrys taunted Mordred, his narwhal staff in hand, illuminating the room with gold light. His shirt and trunks were gone. In their place he wore a long, flowing indigo robe covered in shiny bright yellow stars and moons, which matched the color and pattern on his pointy hat. He looked completely ridiculous…and amazing.

Emrys raised his staff, illuminating the room with the glowing yellow gemstone embedded in its tip. "*Combustum!*" He pointed the staff at Mordred, letting loose a torrent of radiant gold energy. The smell of burnt flesh was real this time. Emrys was trying to burn Mordred alive.

"Enough!" Mordred said, deflecting Emrys's blast back at him with Clarent. Mordred's shimmering blue cloak was reduced to a few burnt remnants hanging around his neck. His tight pants fried all the way up to his upper thighs, rendering them short shorts. Nearly naked, his body singed from head to toe, the Lust Borne Prince looked more like someone who'd just been dragged out of an exploding meth lab. He stalked over to Emrys, yanking him up to his feet. How any of us were standing, I didn't know. Emrys looked the worst of us, having summoned every remaining ounce of magic he possessed to perform that light show.

I drew Excalibur back, preparing to end this. Mordred could see the ill intent in my eyes, and he was no dummy. Throwing Emrys in front of him like a human shield, he held Clarent to Emrys's throat. Emrys's arms hung limply at his side, like two wet noodles. He was too weak to fight, too weak to even resist.

I stood only inches from the pair, Excalibur raised. "What are you doing, Mordred?"

"He owes you an apology, don't you think? For lying to you about Arthur."

"I'll get over it," I said.

I could see the tears in Emrys's eyes as he quietly and ever so subtly raised his free right hand to his chest, balling it up to a fist. He rotated his fist in two clockwise motions.

"*I'm sorry,*" he signed to me.

I had never told Emrys that I knew sign language.

I touched my right hand that was holding Excalibur with my left hand, dragging the tip of my free index finger downward on my sword-palm. I signed to him, "*What,*" as in, "*What are you sorry for?*"

Emrys made a flurry of hand motions, replying, "*Everything.*" He switched his hand position, extending his pinkie, index finger, and thumb: "*I love you.*"

He swiped his hand back and forth: "*Sword.*"

Then he extended two fingers, his palm facing in: "*Two.*"

Then he tapped his chest with his middle finger: "*Heart.*"

Emrys repeated the last three signs: "*Sword...two...heart.*"

"If Emrys doesn't intend to give you an explanation for his actions, then we appear to have a standoff," Mordred said. "Come any closer, and I will kill him. Then maybe you kill me, maybe I kill you. But if you let me go, we all live to fight another day."

"Which means you live just to hunt me down at a later date," I countered.

"Perhaps, Lust Borne. Or perhaps I take your advice and forge my own path."

"Yeah, I don't know about that," I said. "My money is on hunting me down at a later date."

Emrys signed again. "*Sword...two...heart.*"

Sword two heart. What was he trying to say? It didn't make any sense. Think, Rosemary. What would Emrys have you do? Assess the situation. I have the attacker at a total disadvantage, but the victim is equally disadvantaged. What are my scenarios? Scenario #1: Mordred cuts Emrys's throat and he bleeds out, and then either Mordred kills me or I kill Mordred. Scenario #2: I throw down Excalibur, and best-case, Mordred kills none of us, or worst-case he kills all of us. What was I missing?

I was missing the third scenario.

Sword two heart. Sword. Two hearts.

Emrys stood directly in front of Mordred. It was the one attack move Mordred would never see coming.

I shook my head at Emrys. I wouldn't do it. There had to be another way.

Emrys signed again, this time tapping his thumb on his chest with his fingers extended. "*I'll be fine.*"

I almost couldn't see through my tears. I balled my left hand into a fist on my chest and rotated it in two clockwise motions. "*I'm sorry.*"

Emrys nodded again.

I gripped Excalibur tightly, and Mordred noticed.

"Rosemary," he said. "What are you doing? You know I will—"

Emrys and Mordred fell to the ground, pinned together. I'd pierced almost simultaneously through both of their hearts with Excalibur, killing them instantly.

CHAPTER
39

I woke up highly sedated in a Mexican hospital. Whether the sedation was for my own protection or my mother's was debatable.

Mom sat in a chair near the foot of my bed. "You gave us quite a scare. It was touch and go there for a—"

I silenced her with a raised hand. "Stop. Just, stop."

"Stop what, sweetie?"

"Mordred told me."

"Told you what?"

"The truth about Arthur," I said. "About my real dad."

Mom folded her hands in front of her mouth, as if in prayer. A prayer for the secrets to end or a prayer for the secrets to go back to being secrets, who's to say? "This isn't how we wanted you to find out."

"We? So, Dad—I mean Alan, Lancelot, whatever the hell his name is—he's in on it too?"

Mom nodded. "We held out hope. But it was pretty obvious when you were born. You have Arthur's eyes."

If she was trying to compliment me, I didn't care. "But why did you sleep with Arthur if you were in love with Lancelot?"

"It was one night, Rosemary. The night I left Arthur for good. We had too much to drink, and I guess I just saw it as some sort of send-off, a fond farewell to what we had once meant to one another.

The mere fact that you inherited the Lust Borne curse tells you all you need to know. If I had been in love with Arthur the night you were conceived, you would not have been the heir to the prophecy. A married couple who are mutually in love with one another cannot conceive a Lust Borne child."

"I'm sure Alan appreciates the fact you had meaningless sex with Arthur just for old time's sake."

"I regret the pain my one reckless night with Arthur brought your father," Mom said. "But I can never regret that night completely. It gave me the gift of you."

"I was wondering how long it would take you to play that card."

"Card? What card?"

"Your do-over card for calling me a mistake. Just once I'd like for you, Dad, or Emrys to acknowledge when you screw up, take your lumps, and move on."

Emrys. Between the drugs in my system and waking up to Mom's latest mythically- proportioned mistake, I'd pushed the battle with Mordred deep into the recesses of my mind. But saying Emrys's name brought it all back.

"I'm no longer the heir to the prophecy," I said. "We were wrong about the curse. But Emrys, he knew the truth. I think he may have always known it."

"What do you mean?" Mom asked.

"The Lust Borne Prophecy was even more literal than we thought. As Mordred was about to rape me, Emrys literally came to the door to save me. Camelot was not the kingdom at my door—Emrys was."

"But why didn't he summon your father and me?" Mom asked. "We could've helped you both! We could have saved him. We could have saved you from being…from being…"

"Mordred didn't rape me, Mom."

Now that the smoke was clearing on the ruins of our lives, I had wondered how long she could kick that can down the road. As far as plot holes go, a mother not obsessing on every goddamn page over the possibility of her daughter being raped was a doozy. Jennifer's lies of convenience and benign obliviousness had caught up with her. She was desperate to be a mother, to be a hero, to bear my burden.

"Look, Mom, as much as I'd love for you to feel guilty right now about something, anything, you couldn't have done much. Everything happened so suddenly. My guess is Emrys's plan was to distract Vivian, draw her away from you, Dad, Joslin, and Ty. Everything after that was kind of a blur. Can you do me a favor right now, though?"

Mom nodded. "Sure, honey. Anything."

"Stop interrupting me."

"Oh, sorry."

"A wise old wizard once said to me, 'The truth might seem obvious to you, but it's never obvious. You should've learned that by now.' Emrys was the kingdom at my door. It wasn't yours or Dad's destiny to save me from Mordred's bed because that's not the bed in the Lust Borne Prophecy. The prophecy wasn't referring to a bridal bed or to Mordred *bedding* me. It was referring to a death bed. Killing Mordred fulfilled the prophecy and ended the curse."

My mother remained skeptical. "How can you be so certain?"

"Because I felt whatever was inside me turn off. I'm still strong and fast. My senses are still sharper than normal. But I'm back to where I was at the beginning of the school year, before Emrys flipped my switch."

"So, you can have a normal life?" Mom could barely temper her joy. "You can go to college, marry someone you love, have a ton of kids, grow up and grow old?"

"Don't start picking out baby names just yet, Mom. But yes, I think I can do all of that. I think Emrys's final gift to me was the normal life he never had. I used to think I owed him nothing, and now I owe him everything. Oh, Emrys..."

She could see the emotion bubbling up. "Joslin and Tyrell are fine, by the way."

"Where is he?" I asked. "Where is Emrys?"

Mom danced around the question. "Whatever was in their coconuts wasn't nearly as strong as your snake venom cocktail. They're already back at the resort with your father."

"Take me to him," I ordered.

"We had to get creative with our story with Tyrell, but I think he bought it."

She wasn't getting the hint. "Take me to him, *now.*"

As Mom wheeled me into the room, I was still in denial. I wanted to speak to the nurse about bringing some more color in the room. Maybe some flowers, or a couple pictures from the farm. I thought they could at least have turned on some more lights. And where was the television? It was just Emrys, lying quietly on a gurney in the corner, with his eyes closed.

And that's when it really hit me.

"It's okay, baby." Mom grabbed me, refusing to let go. Right now, she was stronger than I could ever be. "Let it out. Just let it out."

After I'd reasonably composed myself, I asked Mom to bring me my iPhone and a cold, wet towel. I needed both, to say goodbye.

I stood next to Emrys's bed. "They did a good job of cleaning him up."

Mom nodded. "They sure did."

I reached down and brushed back the few strands of long hair that had refused to cooperate with his haircut. "If I didn't know any better. I might almost mistake you for being hip." I leaned in, kissed him on the forehead. My tears soaked his cold face.

Oh, Emrys. Sweet, sweet Emrys. What did you make me do, you dumb old wizard?

As if I had even pictured him that way in months. Emrys wasn't dumb, and he certainly wasn't old. He was a boy. And he was my friend.

Benz broke my heart, but to suggest losing Emrys was any less heartbreaking would be a lie. If anything, it hurt worse. Emrys could claim the one thing Benz could not: a selfless and unconditional love for me.

"Does Merlin know you love him?" Vivian was the first one who put the thought in my head, though she'd said it by accident and I barely recognized it at the time. Mabel was the one who knew before even I realized it. *"Someone else is in her head, and in her heart."* Even Mordred had something to say about it, but I tried not to think about Mordred. I had an inkling of the depth of our connection that night on Emrys's front porch—when I danced with a wizard, and couldn't make up my mind whether I was thankful or disappointed he wasn't a boy.

I pulled up Spotify on my phone and typed in, "Sunday, Monday, or Always." Scrolling through several covers, I finally found the Bing Crosby original.

I wiped Emrys's face with the cold, wet towel. I leaned in and kissed him one last time, this time on the lips. A goodbye kiss. "Say hello to Tess for me," I whispered, my lips hovering just over his. "And I love you, too."

CHAPTER

40

We buried Emrys yesterday morning. I don't have a will, but if I did, I would insist on being cremated. Burials are morbid, scarring. Burials freaking suck.

Prior to the funeral, I managed to stand at Emrys's grave for a whole thirty seconds before collapsing. As I dropped to my knees crying, images and memories of Emrys overwhelmed me. I remembered our first few encounters in the halls of American Martyr. His stutter. His awkward mannerisms. His terrible sense of fashion. How I was such an idiot and didn't know the difference between Scotland and Wales. His weird-ass crush on Joslin. But then I remembered his sweetness, his loyalty, his curiosity, his affection. He taught me a lesson all high school girls would do well to learn: Sometimes the greatest love affairs aren't packaged inside letter jackets and perfect smiles.

Joslin sat there next to me, not caring that she was staining her dress with the Maryland mud, holding on to me with a quiet desperation only she could give. She spoke, finally. "Are we supposed to just go back to our school and our lives and pretend like none of this ever happened?"

"Welcome to my life," I replied. In truth, nobody was pretending right now. Not anymore. I thought I'd run out of tears somewhere over the Gulf of Mexico on the flight back to Baltimore. Not even close.

The private funeral service was attended by me, my parents, Joslin, Chef, Atli, and Father Jules. Chef, Atli, and Father Jules were the ones tasked with the dirty work in the aftermath of Cancun. Chef was in charge of disposing of Mordred's body and bribing the Mexican authorities. Atli's job was to cover up Emrys's death. Father Jules quietly transferred Emrys out of American Martyr. I was hoping to see Mabel at the funeral, but Chef told me she was off searching for her stepmother. Her betrayal, justified or not, would still need to be dealt with.

We laid Emrys to rest next to Tess under the white oak tree. Father Jules gave a beautiful eulogy. Mom and Dad offered to help with the burial, but I insisted on digging Emrys's grave alone. Chef and Atli took the shovel away from me when my hands started bleeding.

Ty was back in Connecticut, at least for now. He'd wanted to come to the funeral, but I told him not to. As much as I appreciated the gesture, my life wasn't ready for Tyrell St. John. Filling the void of Emrys with the magnetism and charm of Ty was not fair, to anyone. I'd see Ty next semester at American Martyr, and that was soon enough.

Following Emrys's funeral, Joslin and I decided to hang at the farm for the remainder of the weekend. It felt like the only place where I could still feel Emrys, like he was still alive.

Dad came down early Sunday morning to surprise us with breakfast. He found us standing by Emrys's grave. I was crying again.

"Rosemary?"

I turned to my father and said nothing, burying my face in his chest.

"You can tag in for a little bit, Mr. Banson." Joslin nodded over to the house. "I think I'll go inside, catch up on some homework."

He held me tight, allowing me to steady my breath, ebbing the endless tide of grief inside me.

"How's my girl doing?" he asked, handing me his handkerchief.

I blew my nose. "Not great, Dad. Not great."

The fact I'd never really stopped calling Alan "Dad" wasn't a surprise. It wasn't as if Arthur was the one who changed my diapers, woke up for midnight feedings, taught me to how to ride a bike, or convinced Mom to put on some Level 42 when she'd get on a Duran Duran kick and listen to nothing else. If anything, it made Dad's distance these last ten years seem more understandable, or at least more believable than "an orb made me do it."

"I owe you an apology, Rosemary," Dad said.

"For what?" I asked. "Raising me as your own and never treating me as anything less than your flesh-and-blood daughter?"

"As much as I appreciate the revisionist history, I haven't been a good father to you lately, and you deserved to know the truth a long time ago, or at least when you turned sixteen. You were mature enough to handle it. Your mother and I just weren't mature enough to trust you."

"If it makes you feel any better, I guarantee you I wouldn't have handled the news maturely."

Dad eked out a half-smile. "I tried, in small ways, to tell you the truth over the years. But I think I was being more clever than honest."

"Small ways?"

"Your first name," Dad said. "It was my idea to name you 'Arlynn.' I told your mother that it was a combination of 'Arthur' and 'Alan,' but in truth I did it to honor Arthur's memory alone. He was a good king to his subjects, a good husband to your mother, and a good friend to me. Under different circumstances, I believe he would've made an excellent father to you."

"And by 'different circumstances,' you mean circumstances that don't involve a father forcing his daughter to marry his son?"

"We lived in different times, Rosemary. Rather than being stigmatized, incestuous marriage was seen as a way to preserve the purity of the royal blood line. Your mother and I left Camelot when Mordred was only three years old, so I can't speak to Arthur's motivations or what turned Mordred into such a lecherous young man. It's all speculation at this point, but my guess is Mordred was envious of Arthur's affection for you. I wouldn't be surprised if Arthur wanted to bring you back to Camelot and install you on the throne as the lone monarch."

"That's highly speculative, Dad. Some might even say 'bullocks.'"

"You know that doesn't mean bull—"

"Yeah, yeah," I said. "Emrys told me."

"Speculative maybe, but I believe in my heart that Arthur loved you. 'Arlynn Rosemary' is a name to be proud of, not a heritage to ignore or hide from. But your mother has always insisted we only call you 'Rosemary,' and I will continue to respect her wishes."

"You ever get tired of respecting people's wishes, Lancelot?"

"That's a loaded question, daughter."

"So give me a loaded answer, father. Quick, the first thing that pops into your head."

"Rosemary," he said, taking a deep breath.

"Come on, Dad. Just say it!"

"Arthur didn't deserve your mom!" he blurted out. "He was a wet blanket to her fiery heart, and the fact the fates decided to also gift him a perfect daughter pisses me off."

"Boom!" I said. "That's what I'm talking about. Unvarnished honesty. Feels good, doesn't it?"

Dad smirked. "A little."

"This whole chivalry thing you got going on. Mom says I have Arthur's eyes. That's a load of bullshit."

"Rosemary, language."

"I'm serious. At some point you must have grown tired of looking at me and seeing him. All these people around you trying to be heroes and make sacrifices—your wife, your daughter, and worst of all, Emrys—and you might be the biggest hero of them all."

"I will never tire of you, Arlynn Rosemary Banson." Dad's bottom lip was trembling. He raised his hand to my cheek. "I look at you, and all I see is my daughter."

"And I look at you, and all I see is my father. Call me 'Rosemary,' call me 'Arlynn,' I don't care. But the name I will always be most proud of is 'Banson.'"

As we closed our eyes and leaned in to touch foreheads, I noticed I hadn't run out of tears.

"You might want to press the pause button on my medal ceremony," Dad said, looking up.

I wiped tears from my cheeks with the heel of my hand. "Why is that?"

Dad pointed to the black Acura RLX parked up by the house. "I hitched a ride here from Severna Park with your boyfriend."

CHAPTER
41

"What happened to your hands?" Benz asked, nodding at my white gauze mittens.

"I cut them up burying one of my chuckaboos," I said very matter-of-factly.

It was late afternoon. Benz and I walked arm-in-arm along the mouth of Parker's Creek, at its widest point where it dumped into the Chesapeake Bay. Benz wore a green and white Life University Rugby sweat suit. I had finally changed out of my black dress I wore to the funeral, replacing it with a pair of athletic shorts and one of Emrys's oldest flannel shirts—one I liked to pretend that Tess bought him for an anniversary or birthday.

"Rosemary, I can't even begin to imagine."

"Then don't," I countered. "How was Life University?"

"I don't want to talk about it."

"What *do* you want to talk about?"

"What do you think I want to talk about?"

"How much do you know, about me?"

"Enough," Benz said. "But I had my suspicions for quite some time."

"Like hell you did."

"I realize I do stupid things on occasion, but I'm not a stupid person, Rosemary."

"I didn't say you were stupid."

"You don't think I notice you always half-assing your workouts with me? Or your crazy reflexes? Or when you stopped the barbell from crushing my windpipe on the bench press and just casually dead-lifted 275 pounds with one hand?"

"Or when you were hiding in the bushes in front of Emrys's house spying on us?"

Benz stopped dead in his tracks, stammering. "W-wait. You saw me?"

I nodded. "Emrys's security cameras did. What were you doing there?"

"I felt terrible after telling you I accepted the offer from Life U. I went to your house, all ready to say I'd changed my mind and was going to Towson. Your parents told me I could find you at Emrys's house."

"Thanks for that, Mom and Dad," I said to no one. "Why didn't you say anything?"

"What was I supposed to say? It was a lot easier to pretend I didn't hear what I heard. I thought either I was crazy or you were, but at least we'd be crazy together."

"That's stupid, Benz."

"People in love do stupid things. I figured you would tell me when you were ready."

People in love. Benz's words made it hard to do what I was about to do. "Benz, I—"

"He called me, you know," Benz interrupted.

"Who?"

"Emrys." Benz encouraged me forward as we both resumed walking. "He called me, from Cancun."

"What for?"

"I believe his exact quote was, 'You need to get your shit together, stop taking Rosemary for granted, and ask her to the prom properly.'"

"And how did you react to that?"

"How do think I reacted?" Benz asked. "I was doing my part before then, being the supportive boyfriend, inviting him to stuff."

"Setting him up with Avery?"

"Hey, those two made the best of it."

"Yes, they did," I conceded. "So, Emrys presumed to tell you how to be my boyfriend. I assume that went over well. You told him *what* exactly?"

"I told him to quit sticking his nose where it didn't belong."

"You said that? Those were your exact words?"

"Y-yeah," Benz stuttered, trying to avoid eye contact.

"What did you say, *really?*"

"It was a heat of the moment thing, Rosemary."

"What. Did. You. Say?"

"I told Emrys to stick to what he knows best: Dungeons & Dragons and masturbation."

"Benz!"

"Hey, cut me some slack. You were heading to spring break with Merlin the magician."

"But Emrys didn't know you knew that."

"Exactly," Benz affirmed. "So I could afford to be the asshole. I didn't know any better."

"Nice, Benz." I shrugged my shoulders. "Well?"

"Well, what?" Benz shrugged back.

"Are you going to take his advice?"

He rolled his eyes, his brow furrowed. "Look up."

I craned my neck backwards, like a giant loon.

"Not straight up, goofball," Benz admonished. "Look out, over the water.

Benz grabbed me by the shoulders and spun me around. "That!"

I stood facing the Chesapeake Bay, my eyes cast out over the horizon. A small single-prop airplane buzzed low over the water. Behind the plane trailed a sign that said in big block letters, PLEASE SAY YES, ROSEMARY.

CHAPTER

42

Emrys had plans in place in the event of his untimely death, such that in the weeks since his passing nearly every loose end had been knotted and packed away. An anonymous million-dollar lump sum was donated to Laurel Park's Companion Pony Rescue Organization. Emrys's lease on the boxing gym reverted to my parents, with the understanding, I'm sure, that they continue to kick my butt as much as he'd like to.

Mom and Dad inherited the Eastport house, too. They were planning to move there and put our Severna Park home on the market as soon as possible. I would miss Cypress Creek—the canoeing and the sunbathing, the apple trees and the blue crabs, the skating and the ice fishing, Hector drunk on moonshine and taking his annual plunge. Not to mention, the commute up to Severna Park from Eastport was a total pain. But our new place was a convenient walk to work for Dad, Mom didn't have to worry about snakes, and sipping ginger beers on that front porch comforted me in a way no other place could.

Emrys left me a college fund, the farm, two flying horses, and a hole in my life I didn't know if I'd ever fill.

Father Jules said a brief opening prayer to begin the prom, then quickly exited the school gym. He'd taken to walking the other way in the hallway when he saw me coming. Earlier in the week, he'd announced his retirement. If Emrys's death had blown a hole in me, it had shattered Father Jules.

"What's wrong with the song 'First Kiss'?" Avery asked me.

Avery, Joslin, Benz, and I gathered around the punch bowl. We were debating the relative merits of the Kid Rock medley that the DJ was spinning.

"Oh, I don't know," I said. "Probably the fact that it's an overplayed redneck rip-off of The Outfield's 'Your Love,' or that Kid Rock is a transphobic turd."

"The Outfield?" Avery said.

"They're a band from the eighties."

"Never heard of them."

"Your loss," I said.

Predictably, Benz and Avery were crowned prom king and queen. Less predictably, Avery ceded the official dance with the king to me. Continuing in her path to redemption, Avery was making a play for full-on BFF with me. Either that or she was putting up a good front because her college boyfriend dumped her again. That was the big rumor of the night.

Joslin adjusted her satin cream babydoll dress. I picked it out for her, said she needed to show off her legs. Talking her into the ruffled lace anklets and leopard-print heels took a little more convincing. She motioned to Avery. "That was a pretty cool thing you did up there, giving the dance to Rosemary."

"He's her king, not mine." Avery sipped on her cup of fruit punch while switching between staring at Joslin and the pile of unused paper straws sitting next to the punch bowl. Was she really going to bring up Strawgate now? "You look beautiful in that dress, Joslin. You should wear dresses more often."

Thank God.

Joslin continued to fidget. "Thanks. I generally don't wear dresses because they objectify women and reinforce the patriarchy."

Hard habits died slowly. Our "Little Goth," as Emrys once called her, wasn't quite there yet with Avery.

Andrew came up behind Joslin, sliding his hand around her waist. "What Joslin meant to say was, 'Thank you for the compliment, Avery.'"

As Andrew and Joslin sashayed on to the dance floor, Avery smiled at me, tilting her head and staring at me with her suddenly likable face. "You look beautiful too."

That was easy for Avery to say, in her perfect emerald green V-neck sequin dress with a slit down the side showing off her perfect olive skin. Although, Avery was right: I didn't look half-bad tonight. My hair was perfect. I couldn't remember the last time I wore this much makeup. And my dress—a wine-colored, corset-style evening gown—had turned more than a few heads.

Mom deserved most of the credit. Between the new dress, the new shoes, and the appointment with her hair stylist, she blew a ton of money on me. I was convinced she was overcompensating, but on my way out the door, she told me the makeover was actually Dad's idea.

Of course it was Dad's idea. He was my hero, now and forever.

Benz stood at my side, holding my hand. I was thankful when he showed up to my front door wearing a more classically lined black tux as opposed to that comically skinny suit he wore to Fall Fling. No gas-pipes tonight. The white spats were a nice touch too.

Avery pointed at us. "You two look ridiculously cute together. You know that right?"

"No date for you, Avery?" I asked. Benz gave me his sincerest *don't poke the bear* look.

"I'm sure you heard," she responded without missing a beat.

I poked one last time. "College boy dumped you again, huh?"

"What are you talking about?" Avery flashed me that touch-of-menace smile that haunted me throughout my first two years of high school. "I dumped *him* this time. I was just using him for his frat parties. He was actually starting to bore me."

I reached for Avery's hand. If this was an act, I was totally falling for it. "You want to hang with me and Benz tonight?"

"On one condition," Avery said.

"What's that?" Benz asked, caught noticeably off-guard by Avery's earnestness and vulnerability. I admit it took some getting used to, but dammit, she wore it almost as well as she wore that emerald green V-neck sequin dress.

"Let me come clean with you two," Avery said.

"This I've got to hear," I replied.

"I used to be in love with Benz. I'm talking head-over-heels, swooning in love."

"I knew it!"

Benz tried not to bask in the idol worship, and failed terribly. "Can you let her speak, Rosemary?"

Avery raised the hem of her dress, revealing a stainless steel hip flask fastened to her thigh with a white lace garter. She extracted the flask and unscrewed the flask, looking around the room.

"Coast is clear," I said. "Cheap whiskey?"

Avery shook her head. "Expensive vodka."

"Well this explains your sudden brutal honesty and generosity of spirit," I said.

"What?" Avery asked, not hearing me over the music.

"Never mind," I replied. "So, tell me more about your head-over-heels, swooning love for my boyfriend."

Avery swatted at me. "Oh, he never loved me back. I mean, we were always friends, and we even tried dating a couple summers ago, but he just never felt the same way for me that I felt for him. When we came back to school junior year, and he saw you walk down that hallway for the first time, it was all about Rosemary Banson from then on. He told me on that very day that you were going to be the love of his life."

"You told Avery *what?*" I said.

"I don't know if that's exactly the way it happened." Benz replied.

Avery nodded, mouthing the words to me, *yes it did.*

I swatted Benz hard in the chest. Probably too hard. Definitely too hard. "You know that's the same day I fell in love with you, asshole. And you've never felt compelled to tell me that you felt it too?"

"Cut him some slack," Avery said. "Sometimes I feel like Benz wouldn't know where his nose was if it wasn't attached to his face. It's bad enough I had to coach my own Fall Fling date on how to get back together with his ex-girlfriend."

There was absolutely no chance that I heard that correctly. "Uh, come again?"

She smiled. It was a devilish gigglemug, but she'd earned it. "The night of the Fall Fling, when you two locked lips on the playground."

"Wait, you know about that?"

Of course Avery knew about that. She was on a roll. "Let me guess. Benz acknowledged your feelings and admitted to being an asshole."

Hands on my hips, I could feel the profanity swelling inside me. "Mother—"

"Hey now," Benz said, "don't knock a boy in love for pulling out all the stops. No one ever said love was predictable."

No one ever said love was predictable. Oh, my dearest Benz. Why did you have to say that?

If there's one thing I'd proven to be this school year, it was a glutton for punishment. That's why I requested the DJ play the José González ballad, "Heartbeats." This wasn't supposed to be my final dance with my boyfriend.

But I had a feeling it might be.

Benz and I swayed to the opening chords. I arched my head up and kissed the sensitive spot on his throat, just under his jawline. He sighed. I didn't want this moment to end.

"What's your favorite color?" I asked him for the very first time.

"Orange," Benz answered.

"What's your grandmother's name?"

"Which one?"

"Both."

"Freda on my dad's side, Hazel on my mom's side."

Benz leaned down, resting his head on my shoulder. I whispered the lyrics of the song softly into his ear.

"What's happening here, Rosemary?" Benz jerked back suddenly. "Is this about me not telling you I loved you when we first met or getting pickup lines from Avery? I think you and I are well past getting tripped up by the little things."

"I know we are, Benz."

"Then why are you crying and humming Lucas and Peyton's love song from *One Tree Hill* in my ear? Don't get me wrong, tonight has been great. You've been your old self again. But since Emrys passed, you've been distant. I know you're hurting and that you and Emrys shared a connection that I still can't quite wrap my head around. Just let me in, Rosemary. Please."

My heart ached at the thought of what I was about to do. I'd already chickened out once, down at the farm after Emrys's funeral. The timing would have been so much better. It would have saved us from this night.

More tears. Dear God, when would I stop crying? "I can't, Benz."

"Then I guess I'll just wait it out."

"Wait it out?"

"It's what boyfriends do."

Benz's fearless belief in us came to him like reflex. He was in love with me. I was in love with him too, which is why I had to be just as fearless. "You don't understand. I can't do this anymore. I can't do *us* anymore."

"W-what?" Benz stuttered. "Where's this coming from?"

I pointed at my heart. "Here."

"Bullshit, Rosemary. That's not fair."

"Nope, it's not," I said. "But I'm tired, and you deserve better than me."

"That's my decision to make!"

"Apparently not."

"I don't deserve this, any of this," Benz said. "These last few weeks you've asked me to believe the unbelievable, and I've done that."

"It's not you, Benz. It's me. A part of me always saw this coming. When my world changed, I knew your world would change too. I never wanted to tell you."

"Well, technically you didn't."

"Exactly! It would've been so much simpler if you didn't know. We could've spent the rest of the summer together going out on dates, making love, you in blissful ignorance. And then summer would end, and I'd make up some lame excuse about us breaking up because you were leaving for college and that's just what people do."

"You would break up with me because that's just what people do?"

Benz's voice cracked. I wasn't just breaking up with him; I was breaking *him*. I had to offer something in this moment to make him feel better, to make me feel better. But what? "After you knew our secret, I thought that maybe our shared world would change for the better. A part of me held on to this naïve idea that as crowded as my life had become, there would always be room for Benz Cooke."

"So you're just giving up?" Benz lamented.

There was a time when I was on the other end of this fight, when all I wanted to do was make him pay for what he did to me. Did he feel this awful back then? Those same impulses that brought Benz back to me were now urging me to hold on. But the more I thought about losing Benz, the more I thought about losing Emrys. And I just didn't have any love left to give. My boyfriend and I had come full-circle: He couldn't change the past, and I couldn't get over it.

"I'm not giving up," I argued. "I'm giving you a chance to live a normal life. You're going to school far away. I have two years of high school left, and you'll be in college surrounded by women, real grown-up women. This was going to happen one way or the—"

"Because that's just what people do," Benz said.

"Benz, please know I'll never stop lov—"

"Don't, Rosemary," he interrupted, eyes reddening. "Just... don't."

He stormed away, his back to me. He wasn't going to let me see him cry. His pride gave me hope. Just as he opened the gymnasium door, he paused. He stood there, staring me down. Unyielding. Did he still want to fight for me? Did he still want to fight for us? *Please don't come back, Benz,* I thought. *Please walk out that door.*

As Benz turned and left, a part of me was relieved. I wasn't afraid that I'd say no to him and break his heart all over again. I was afraid that I'd say yes. But Emrys had given me one last parting gift: the courage to say goodbye.

CHAPTER

43

The prom began to lose its momentum and was in serious need of a second wind. After crying on Joslin's shoulder in the girl's restroom for an hour, I returned to the dance floor.

"Are you sure you're okay?" Joslin asked.

"Well, obviously I'm not okay," I replied. "But I'm not going to monopolize your freaking prom night. Go grab Andrew and do something spontaneous and stupid. I'll be fine."

"I don't know, Rosemary. I feel like I should—"

"Get out of here!" I shouted, pointing her out of the gym. Reluctantly, Joslin obeyed my command.

Before I'd had a moment to myself, Avery bounced over to me. "Where have you been? Smooching under the bleachers with Benz?"

"I wish," I said unenthusiastically. I didn't feel like rehashing our breakup, so I made something up. "Benz wasn't feeling great, so he went home for the night."

"Too bad for him," Avery said, holding my hand. "I guess that makes us officially prom dates then!"

Damn this girl. Her enthusiasm was infectious. "I guess it does."

"I wish I'd gotten to know him a little better," Avery said.

"You and Benz have known each other since you were toddlers."

"Not Benz, silly. Emrys. Our date was kind of fun, in its own way. I know you hated me going out with him."

"Avery, I didn't hate—"

Her eyes cut me off.

"Okay, I hated it."

"I know Emrys's move back to Wales was totally out of the blue."

"Yeah, it took us all by surprise."

"I can see how close you two had become just by how hard Emrys leaving hit you. I tried to call him."

"You did?" I asked.

"Yes," Avery replied. "To tell him goodbye, to thank him for teaching me a little Welsh. Some guy with a German accent answered his phone."

"That was Emrys's host father, Atli."

"So he told me. He also told me Emrys's number had changed and that he didn't have his new number or a forwarding address. Have you talked to him?"

"We communicate in our own way."

"You planning on visiting Emrys someday?"

"Not unless you have a magical orb handy."

"What?"

"Nothing. Just, you know, thanks for being nice to Emrys and especially for being nice to me lately. I might have to even give you some credit for tonight. You didn't even mention the paper straws."

"You *might* have to give me credit?" Avery said, ignoring the straw comment. "Better watch it. You could pull a muscle trying so hard to almost compliment me."

"I'm serious. For putting on an Angels of Maybe-themed prom, you've shown remarkable restraint."

"You haven't been to student council in quite some time. I got Benz's dad to pull some strings with his music friends. Here, hold this." Avery handed me her cup of vodka-spiked fruit punch. She ascended the stage, taking the microphone from the DJ.

What was she doing?

"I'd like to take a few seconds to thank everyone for coming," Avery said. She drew her mouth closer to the microphone as she spoke, which punctuated the ends of sentences with a tinge of feedback. "A special thanks to the students, administrators, teachers, and parents who volunteered their time to help make this event possible."

There was a courtesy clap as Avery looked out across the gymnasium. I followed her gaze to Joslin, who stood near the rear doors. Joslin nodded to Avery, gave her a thumbs up. Avery nodded back. What were they up to?

"I have a confession to make," Avery said into the microphone.

Really? Another confession? How much vodka did she drink tonight?

"Earlier this year," she continued, "I tried to steamroll my fellow student council members into having an Angels of Maybe-themed Fall Fling..."

A discernible groan rolled over the crowd.

"I know, I know. I was stupid, I was immature, and I was spiteful. But my fellow student council members, including one person in particular, put me in my place. I want to make up for that day. I want to make up for every day I was mean to someone. Granted, that's a lot of days."

The applause was much more than courteous now, the laughter sincere.

"Tonight is dedicated to the repentant bullies among us, to the heroes who keep them in their place, and to our well-intentioned friends who insist on using paper straws instead of plastic ones even though they're awful."

The crowd didn't get the joke. Avery smiled at me and winked. Sometimes, it's all about the timing. I bowed properly as she continued.

"Ladies and gentlemen, teachers, staff, and students of American Martyr Preparatory School, please welcome to the stage...Level 42!"

What in the...

Avery's gigglemug was devilish.

She had vowed to have an Angels of Maybe-themed prom, and instead booked my favorite eighties band, a band that probably no one in the gymnasium but me had ever heard of. She barely had time to step aside as the curtain opened behind her and Level 42 lead singer Mark King stepped to the front of the stage, a red bass guitar hanging off his neck. "Hello, American Martyr!" he shouted.

"Rosemary Banson..." Mark said into his microphone. Grabbing the microphone stand with one hand, he found me and pointed to me with the other. "We're here tonight because Eben Cooke, a dear old friend of ours, called us up and said you are our biggest fan. This one's for you, darling."

I smiled through my tears. Level 42 wasn't here because of Avery. Benz had asked this favor of his dad, as the greatest surprise ever for his girlfriend, and he didn't even stay to watch.

If you'd told me back in August that my sophomore year at American Martyr would end with me riding the rail with Avery DeVincent while Level 42 sang "Running in the Family"—a woefully under appreciated Top Ten hit in the UK and New Zealand that barely charted in the U.S. at #86 on the Billboard Hot 100—I'd have told you to ease up on Avery's chocolate chip brownies. It seemed like forever since she and Benz walked into this gymnasium the night of Fall Fling to the adoration I mocked but secretly craved. Even longer since Mom and Dad shish-kabobbed a couple faeries only a few feet from where I stood. We were all different. Changed. Joslin was in on my secret. Benz was gone—for now. And Emrys was gone for good.

After the dust settled that summer, the reality would set in that Joslin and I were going to be juniors, upperclassmen. Next year was our turn to rule American Martyr. And if sophomore year was just prologue, who was to say what kind of trouble we'd find from here on out? Maybe next year I'd be the one crossing this gymnasium floor at Fall Fling or prom through tunnels of applause and painted-on smiles, doing my best parade wave. But for now, for tonight at least, I was content to be a sophomore for a few more days. Pretending to not be curious about my birth father. Pretending to not be attracted to Ty St. John. Pretending I was on the mend from a perpetually broken heart.

My name is Arlynn Rosemary Banson, but people just call me Rosemary. I have a cool sword and cool friends. As measured by blood, I am the daughter of King Arthur and Queen Guinevere Pendragon. As measured by love, I am the daughter of Alan and Jennifer Banson.

Love wins. Benz would probably dispute that right now, but love has to win, eventually. Doesn't it?

It was a question Level 42 seemed inclined to answer:

B.P. Sweany

We only see so far,
And we all have our daddy's eyes.
Looking back it's so bizarre.

THE END